C000182874

SUNSHINE OVER BLUEBELL CLIFF

DELLA GALTON

Boldwood

First published in Great Britain in 2020 by Boldwood Books Ltd.

Copyright © Della Galton, 2020

Cover Design by Debbie Clement Design

Cover Photography: Shutterstock

The moral right of Della Galton to be identified as the author of this work has been asserted in accordance with the Copyright, Designs and Patents Act 1988.

All rights reserved. No part of this book may be reproduced in any form or by any electronic or mechanical means, including information storage and retrieval systems, without written permission from the author, except for the use of brief quotations in a book review.

This book is a work of fiction and, except in the case of historical fact, any resemblance to actual persons, living or dead, is purely coincidental.

Every effort has been made to obtain the necessary permissions with reference to copyright material, both illustrative and quoted. We apologise for any omissions in this respect and will be pleased to make the appropriate acknowledgements in any future edition.

A CIP catalogue record for this book is available from the British Library.

Paperback ISBN 978-1-83889-001-8

Ebook ISBN 978-1-83889-003-2

Kindle ISBN 978-1-83889-002-5

Audio CD ISBN 978-1-83889-252-4

MP3 CD ISBN 978-1-83889-737-6

Digital audio download ISBN 978-1-83889-000-1

Boldwood Books Ltd
23 Bowerdean Street
London SW6 3TN
www.boldwoodbooks.com

For Gord, AKA 'Mr one letter out'.

1

Clara King was driving through the Isle of Purbeck on a gorgeous June morning on her way to work when her phone on the passenger seat beside her beeped with a message. The bluetooth in her car didn't allow texts through when she was driving and so she didn't take much notice.

Ahead of her, the ruins of Corfe Castle, perched high on one of the surrounding hills, had just come suddenly into view, rising up above the little town of Corfe that nestled below it.

Even though Clara passed it every single morning, it was a sight that never failed to take her breath away. Today, the jutting pillars of grey Purbeck stone were silhouetted starkly against the clear blue summer sky. The eleventh-century castle, built by William The Conqueror, was impressive, even in ruins. It was a huge tourist attraction, now owned by the National Trust, and its more intrepid visitors climbed up the gravel path to the summit to wander around and imagine old ghosts inside its ancient walls.

Clara had once taken a more unorthodox route to the top, straight up one of the castle's almost vertical grassy sides. It had been dark and she'd been wearing three-inch heels, having just spent the evening at the pub with a group of catering-college friends. She couldn't remember which of them had suggested a night-time visit to the castle, but it had seemed like a good idea after several glasses of wine. She was amazed she hadn't broken her neck, or at least a heel. But that was the kind of mad thing you did when you were young and trying to prove to your new 'into anything' boyfriend that you were up for an adventure.

She was thirty-four now and newly single – although not from him, no, that particular relationship had fizzled out faster than a summer firework over the sea – and much more responsible. She had just landed her dream job as Manager of the Bluebell Cliff, a fabulous hotel, perched on Dorset's stunning coastline, which was where she was heading right now.

Ten minutes later, she drew up in its gravel car park, turned off the ignition and picked up her phone.

The message was from her boss, Kate Rawlinson. It said:

Morning C, I need to talk to you urgently. Come straight into my office when you arrive.

Kate was the most laid-back of bosses. What on earth had she done to warrant being summoned? Suddenly all of the sunshine flew from the day and Clara's palms felt sweaty as she clicked the remote control to lock up her poppy-red Mini Cooper.

As she reached the low wall that separated the parking from the lawns that enclosed three sides of the hotel, she gulped in a lungful of fresh sea air mixed with the scent of roses and lavender that grew in the hotel gardens. Above her head, a lone seagull soared on the breeze.

But despite the beauty of her surroundings, Clara's stomach crunched with nerves. She racked her brains. Had she done something wrong? She walked apprehensively towards the staff entrance.

The Bluebell Cliff, affectionately called The Bluebell by its staff, had been named after the locally renowned bluebell woods, alongside which it stood. It perched on a headland overlooking the English Channel with Studland Bay on one side and Anvil Point on the other.

The hotel itself was a long, low, white painted art deco-style building with a flat roof, which had stood there since the thirties. It had gone through various transformations, but the most recent had been a huge refurbishment the previous year, headed up by Kate, who also owned it. It had opened for business at Christmas.

Kate had been acting manager ever since but had employed Clara to take over the role three months ago. She was just coming up to the end of her probationary period. Clara loved the job and she had worked her socks off, which was why she was so nervous now.

She walked through the foyer, which smelled sweetly of vanilla air freshener. Zoe Wilkins, the bubbly young blonde receptionist, was dealing with a guest, so she couldn't sound her out. Breakfast noise and the smell of bacon and coffee filtered through from the restaurant. All seemed normal.

The door of the manager's office was closed. Should she knock?

Yes, perhaps today she should. Just the one knock to show respect. She did this, and then stepped inside. Kate was on the phone, but she gestured Clara towards a chair with her hand.

Kate's dog, Foxy, so named because she looked like a fox, with her pointy ears and sharp snout and smooth reddish brown fur, was curled up in her basket. She gave Clara a sleepy wag but didn't get up. Clara bent to pet one of her soft ears before sitting down.

This room was big enough for two modern desks and two office chairs on wheels and some filing cabinets and a cupboard where they kept brochures and other paperwork. It was a mixture of old and new with the beautiful decorative cornice running around its high ceilings and a big bay window that overlooked the lawns. Usually this room buzzed with Kate's energy. She was a workaholic, which was something she and Clara had in common. But at the moment all Clara could feel was tension.

She tried to read Kate's body language. She was talking to a guest by the sound of it. She looked tired. There were shadows beneath her eyes. Kate was thirty-three and her usual demeanour was one of organised calm. Nothing ever seemed to faze her, but today she was definitely stressed.

'Don't worry, sir. That will all be in place before you arrive. Leave it to us. It's our job. Thanks. You too, sir.' She finally put down the phone. 'Good grief, some people are pedantic. Clara, hi. Thanks for coming in so promptly. You got my message?'

'I did.' Clara waited.

'Don't look so worried. It's not bad news. Well, it kind of is, but for me, not for you. I'm not explaining myself very well. Sorry.' She rested her elbows on the desk in front of her. 'I'll start at the beginning. Last night, I had a traumatic phone call from my mother. She lives with my stepfather and – well, to cut a long story short – they're getting divorced. It's messy. He's a lawyer. Mum is in bits and there's no one to help her but me.'

Clara nodded, feeling slightly bemused that her employer was sharing such a confidence.

'I expect you're wondering what any of this has to do with you?' Kate's worried eyes met hers. 'The thing is, they live in Australia. Adelaide in Southern Australia to be precise and I need to go out there. I can't be any help at all from here. I realised that last night. Mum's desperate. And I know you've only been here three months and your feet have barely touched the ground, but I need someone I can trust to look after this place.'

Clara felt a thump of shock. 'You mean the hotel?'

'Yes. I know it's a huge ask.' Kate rubbed her eyes distractedly. 'But I can't help Mum from England. I need to be out there by her side. And I'm totally torn. It's the worst possible timing. We're barely established and, as you know, this place is my baby. It was my Aunt Carrie's dream.'

Her eyes flicked towards the portrait of an elegant, rather beautiful woman sitting at a grand piano, that had pride of place on the wall of the office. Caroline Rawlinson had been a world-renowned concert pianist and had made her fortune composing and doing recitals in England and the US. She had been both the brains and the financier behind the Bluebell. The hotel had been her retirement project. Her swansong.

Kate had told Clara the story the first time they had met. Tragically, Caroline had died in a car accident on her last ever tour and Kate, who was a builder cum project manager and already involved in the refurbishment, had inherited the hotel and had made it her mission to complete her Aunt Carrie's dream.

'This place was what she worked for all her life,' Kate was saying. 'She entrusted it to me for safekeeping because she knew I felt as passionately about it as she did.' She stopped talking as abruptly as she had begun. 'Hell, I'm not sure I'm making any sense. I've been up half the night worrying about it.'

No wonder she looked tired. Clara felt a tug of empathy. Family break-ups stirred up all sorts of horrible emotions. Helplessness and frustration to name but two. She'd had enough personal experience of family break-ups of her own in the last few months.

'It would mean that you'd be in sole charge of running the

place. You don't have to decide straight away,' Kate offered. 'I'll get Zoe to bring us some coffee.' She half rose from the chair.

'When are you thinking of flying and how long do you think you'll be away?' Clara asked.

'As soon as I can get a flight and, I'm not sure yet, but, realistically, I'd need to be away for at least three weeks. I don't know how long it's all going to take.'

'It's fine,' Clara heard herself saying in a voice that was a great deal calmer than she felt. 'I'd be happy to help.' What was she doing? It was one of her life rules never to make split-second decisions.

But it was too late. Kate was already looking at her hopefully.

'Really? Are you sure?' She sat back down again. 'I'll need to get someone to look after Foxy too. I was about to phone the kennels when Zoe put that customer through.'

'She'll hate kennels,' Clara said, wishing she'd edited the words before they'd come out of her mouth because Kate looked worried again.

'I know. She'll think I've abandoned her.'

Foxy was an ex-street dog and had been living from bin to bin – she'd been adept at avoiding the dog catcher – before she'd been hit by a car and ended up with three legs. It was Clara who had rescued her and taken her to a vet's because the driver who'd hit her had failed to stop.

Clara would have kept her if she'd had a garden, which she didn't, but Kate had stepped in and offered. She had known about it all because Clara had been on her way to interview for this job at the time and the rescue operation had made her late. Clara still felt slightly guilty that Kate had ended up with Foxy, but it had seemed a good solution. That was another thing they had in common. They loved dogs and couldn't bear to see one in trouble.

'I can look after her,' Clara said, breaking her life rule not to make split-second decisions for the second time in as many minutes.

'But you haven't got a garden... unless...' Kate broke off, thoughtfully. 'This may be a bit "out there" – but how would you feel about house-sitting my bungalow too? You'd be really close to work, which might be easier than driving in from Wareham, especially with the summer traffic. That road can get gridlocked. It's only an eight-minute commute from mine. Foxy would be happier too. Oh my God, listen to me... that's a mad idea.'

'It sounds pretty sensible to me.' Clara's head was starting to spin, but in a good way. This was so not what she'd been expecting when she had walked in this morning, but every instinct she had was telling her it was a good idea, if a little crazy.

'There's a heck of a lot to organise,' Kate said. 'I'll have to brief the rest of the staff. I'll call a team meeting to let everyone know what's going on. I'm not expecting you to be here all the hours that I am. I haven't asked him yet, but I'm sure Phil would step up to the plate and help. I'd want you to be in overall charge though.'

Phil Grimshaw was the maître d'. He was a darkly handsome, forty-year-old RADA-trained actor who had never quite made the big time but acted between catering jobs. He could be unpredictable – Kate said it was his artistic temperament – but Clara had liked him from the moment they'd been introduced.

Kate was on her feet again. 'I'll be back in a second. But, Clara, are you absolutely sure you don't need some more time to think about this? I feel as though I've sprung it all on you. I could call our agency and get in a temporary manager, but I'd much rather have you.' She stood with one hand on the doorknob. 'And Foxy could go to kennels. It wouldn't kill her. House-sitting as well as doing my job is completely above and beyond...'

'I'm absolutely sure,' Clara said, and Kate smiled for the first time since she'd arrived before disappearing into the foyer.

When she'd gone, Clara let out a breath. Looking after a three-legged dog and living at her boss's bungalow were actually small fry when compared to being in sole charge of the Bluebell.

The Bluebell was not your average kind of hotel. Its seven-acre plot incorporated a decommissioned lighthouse which had been refurbished to a very high spec and was listed as one of the top ten most luxurious and unique places to stay in the United Kingdom. As well as the lighthouse, there was a small amphitheatre, where it was rumoured Richard Burton had once performed. At least that's what it said in the hotel brochure.

The hotel itself boasted twenty individual gorgeous boutique bedrooms. There was a selection of other specialist rooms too – they included writing rooms, a yoga studio, which converted to an art room with the addition of and/or removal of some furniture, and a dedicated music room that housed a vintage Steinway grand piano because of Aunt Carrie's musical background. There was even an in-house recording studio.

Kate had been right. It was a big ask. The Bluebell was unique. And not just because it had specialist accommodation and facilities. The guests who came to stay didn't just come for the sea air and the beautiful Dorset location and the chef's fabulous cooking. Although, of course, all of that was part of the package. They came for another reason entirely.

The Bluebell was a hotel where people came to live out their dreams.

Its mission statement was, 'We're here to help you make your dreams come true.'

As Kate had said, the whole concept had been her much-loved, late aunt's idea and the hotel had only been open six months. They were at the beginning of their first all-important summer. Kate had told her when she started that they were also licensed to hold weddings and their first 'no expense spared' dream wedding was taking place on the second Saturday in October. Kate would be back by then by the sound of it.

Clara squared her shoulders as she sat at the desk and doodled circles around the distinctive bluebell logo on a notepad in front of her. She wasn't new to the hotel trade – she'd worked in kitchens as soon as she'd been old enough to get a Saturday job. She had a degree in Hotel and Hospitality Management. She'd managed a hotel with double the amount of bedrooms. Even so, The Bluebell was one hell of a responsibility. She hoped she hadn't bitten off a great deal more than she could chew.

2

This was not how Clara had expected to be spending her Friday evening, she thought, teetering slightly on her heels, as she shielded her eyes against the sun and watched the man climbing like a giant spider up the side of the hotel's lighthouse. She must be mad. Although not quite as mad as him!

The things people did for love.

It was a beautiful evening, with the merest wisp of a sea breeze just beginning to disperse the heat of what had been another fabulous summer day. Beyond the squat vanilla-coloured lighthouse, the sky was pink, turning the ocean far below the cliffs into a mirror of strawberry glass.

'Did we need extra insurance for this?' asked Zoe, who was standing by her side. This was her first job on a hotel reception and she was keen to learn every aspect of the hospitality business.

'Yes.' Clara patted her Radley bag, which was strung over her shoulder. 'I printed out the email just in case.' Years of experience in the hotel trade and a natural caution had taught her to dot every i and cross every t. If something could go wrong, it invariably did and she was keen to make sure it couldn't.

Kate had only left for Australia three days ago, leaving her in charge of all her worldly assets. She was still reeling from the upheaval of moving from her tiny house into Kate's spacious bungalow – she was putting her house on Airbnb as soon as she got a few hours to spare – but she was also hugely excited and proud at the amount of trust Kate had invested in her and she was determined not to let her down.

'The insurance company were a bit surprised,' she went on, 'but abseiling down high buildings and indeed climbing up them isn't that unheard of these days. There are a few height restrictions and the health and safety precautions are endless. We had to get a professional climber in to set up the ropes, which is why Matt's here, but we're covered.'

'I hope she says yes,' Zoe said. 'I've been trying to imagine how I'd feel if a guy proposed to me after climbing up to my window with a box of chocolates. It's all a bit Rapunzel, isn't it!'

'I suppose it would depend on who he was.' Clara thought of her ex, Will Lightfoot, who'd been a techie on a help desk for Apple. Which was still recent enough to twinge a bit.

'It might also depend on how good the chocolates were,' Zoe added thoughtfully.

A couple of feet away, Foxy, who'd been sniffing at a patch of grass – pricked up her ears at the sound of the word chocolate – she was a total foodie, Clara had discovered – and looked hopefully in their direction. Not seeing any evidence of any of her favourite doggie chocolate on offer, she didn't bother coming over but resumed her sniffing.

Arnold Fairweather, the man currently climbing up the lighthouse, had an enormous purple box strapped to his back, which was hampering his progress slightly as it had just slipped round a little and one corner was now wedged under his armpit.

'The Milk Tray advert has a lot to answer for,' Clara mused.

'The guy in the 2003 one was quite hot. You weren't even born then, were you?'

'I was five,' Zoe said.

'Blimey, that makes me feel old. I was eighteen.'

'But I've seen them all on YouTube. I checked them out when you said this was happening.' Zoe blushed, her English rose skin going pink. 'Is that overkeen? It probably is, isn't it? Anyway, I wasn't so struck on the shark-infested sea one. I guess we should be relieved he didn't want to set that up!'

'It would have made a great video,' Clara said, glancing at the cameraman a few feet away. He and Matt Davies, the professional climber, who was currently looking bored but on standby in case he was needed, were the only other spectators – or at least the only other invited ones. A couple of dog walkers on the coast path were pointing at the unfolding drama – or perhaps spectacle would have been a more accurate description.

'Although we may have had trouble finding any co-operative sharks on the Dorset coast.'

'I think the insurance company might have quibbled a bit more too,' Clara said.

'What was that stroppy message from the Manor House about?' Zoe asked.

Clara sighed. 'Just a misunderstanding about a booking.' This wasn't quite true – Adam Greenwood, the manager of the Manor House Hotel, had been very rude. He'd had some bee in his bonnet about them stealing a booking, which was ridiculous, not to mention petty. It had taken all of her self-restraint not to hang up on him and all of her tact to calm him down, which she'd done, eventually.

But she didn't want to get involved in hotel politics with Zoe right now. It was too lovely an evening.

Arnold Fairweather had just reached the halfway point – fortunately their lighthouse was on the squat side and only twelve metres high – and he had paused for breath. Like the original hero, he was dressed all in black. Wasn't black supposed to be a slimming colour! But this was where the similarity to heroes ended. He was bigger than the average climber and carrying an extra couple of stone around your middle could only hamper you, Clara thought, feeling a twinge of trepidation. His age was against him too. He was fifty-one – not that she hadn't met plenty of fit fifty-one-year-olds in her time, but Arnold Fairweather wasn't one of them.

'He looks like he's doing OK, doesn't he,' Zoe said. 'And he's right, it'll make a great video for posterity. They can show it to their grandkids...' She broke off, because it was at that very moment that things started to go wrong.

One moment Arnold had been making slow, if a little laborious, progress up the lighthouse and the next he was dangling. No longer a spider but a frantically struggling fly on a thin rope strand of web.

'Oh my God, what's happening?' Zoe clutched Clara's arm.

'It's OK. He's just lost his footing that's all. He has the safety rope on. He's perfectly fine.'

Arnold didn't look fine. His arms and legs were thrashing about and he was clawing at his chest.

Clara was struck by a dreadful realisation. 'Good grief, I think he might be having a heart attack.'

Both women were suddenly galvanised into action. Matt had woken up too. He darted in to steady the ropes, calling up to Arnold as he did so. The cameraman was still filming. Couldn't he see something was wrong?

Then, to make matters worse, the window, which was only a few feet above Arnold's head, was flung open and a tousled blonde head popped out. 'Arnold Fairweather, what the bloody hell do you think you're playing at?'

* * *

At least everything had turned out OK in the end, Clara thought as she finally put the key into the front door of Kate's bungalow at midnight on that same Friday evening. Although it had been touch-and-go for a while.

She had spent the entire evening in Poole Accident and Emergency department, where she had followed the ambulance, along with Arnold's prospective fiancée, Maureen Grey. Maureen had not been impressed with what she called 'Arnold's shenanigans'. She had not been impressed that the last evening of their holiday had been wasted in A&E. She had not been impressed when it turned out that Arnold wasn't having a heart attack at all, nor even an angina attack, but a common-or-garden panic attack, brought on by his fear of heights.

'What on earth did you think you were doing?' she had yelled at Arnold, once it was clear there was nothing at all wrong with him. 'You know you hate heights.'

'I was trying to do something romantic.' He had visibly shrunk under her gaze.

'Well, you failed, you great wassock.' Her voice had got shriller and shriller. 'I don't even like Milk Tray.'

Poor Arnold. Clara had begun to feel sorry for him under this rather unfair, in her opinion, onslaught. The contrast of his white face against his black clothes wasn't as marked as it had been earlier, but he was still quaking in his Nike trainers.

She had just been wondering whether she should perhaps intervene before he really did have a heart attack, when, to her horror, she had noticed that a scraggy-looking teenager, also in

A&E, had started to film the exchange on his mobile. That was all they needed.

She had marched across and demanded he stop, and the teenager, who'd towered over her, even with her heels, had scowled but reluctantly obeyed. Maureen Grey had stopped shouting after that, but the whole thing had been a complete nightmare.

Finally, in her boss's gorgeous, stainless-steel kitchen, Clara kicked off her three-inch heels, made herself a hot chocolate and tried to calm down. Foxy was overjoyed to see her – she wasn't used to being left alone for long, but fortunately Zoe had offered to feed her and let her out while Clara had been at A&E. Now the dog pushed her cold wet nose into Clara's hand and wagged her skinny red tail. Clara fondled her ears.

'I don't know what Kate is going to say about all this,' Clara told her. 'We don't need any unnecessary publicity.'

Foxy wagged her tail some more and Clara gave her a treat. Was she really discussing her evening with a dog? She must be more exhausted than she thought. Thank heavens no real harm had been done.

She would tell Kate in her Monday report. Fingers crossed, she would understand that none of today's events could have been foreseen. Just as Arnold Fairweather hadn't foreseen that his big romantic gesture was going to backfire on him.

Did men ever think things through? Clara wondered later, when the adrenaline spike of the evening finally subsided enough to make sleep an option and she climbed into the king-size bed.

She might not have approved of Maureen Grey's outburst in A&E, but she did have a smidgeon of sympathy for the woman, having only recently been on the other end of a big, but misguided, romantic gesture herself.

That too had been an unfortunate series of events. Will, her partner of almost a year, had decided to surprise her a couple of weeks before their first anniversary with an equally unexpected proposition.

It hadn't been of the 'let's get married' variety, thank heavens. Will must have spotted the element of coolness in their relationship lately. Clara had been thinking of telling him they should call it a day. They'd been drifting apart for a few weeks. Will, however, had put it all down to the fact that they didn't see enough of each other, due to their conflicting work patterns. They didn't live together – although their houses were only a few miles apart – but he worked nine till five and she worked shifts.

His answer to this had been to take her out for a spontaneous slap-up meal at her favourite Italian. Clara wasn't a fan of surprises, although she'd been touched by the gesture and had insisted on contributing her half. But then, just after they'd paid the bill, he had presented her with a small white envelope.

'It's an investment in our future,' he'd said, his eyes gleaming in the candlelight. 'It's got a long date on it, so I think it could work.'

Feeling only a slight sense of foreboding, Clara had opened the envelope and discovered it had contained a round-the-world plane ticket.

For a whole ten seconds, she'd been speechless. Had she ever in their entire relationship given Will the idea that she might like to go travelling? She didn't think so. She was a home bird, through and through. Dorset was the county where she'd grown up. She loved living and working by the sea. She was also terrified of flying.

'What do you think?' Will had said. 'I'm coming too. They were doing a "buy one get one free".'

She'd put up a hand before he got too carried away. 'Will, you really should have asked me.'

'I am asking you.'

'I mean, before you bought it.' Although technically she supposed he hadn't bought it if it was a 'buy one get one free'.

'Don't you want to go?' He was clearly puzzled by her reaction.

She should have just said no there and then, but she hadn't wanted to throw his grand gesture completely back in his face. His heart had clearly been in the right place.

'Have you forgotten I've just taken on a new job?'

'Well, no, but they can get someone else and you'll easily get another fab job when you get back. You're brilliant at what you do.'

'Thanks, but I want this job.'

'More than you want to go round the world with me?'

That was a toughie too, but she had bitten the bullet. 'Er – right at the moment – yes.'

He'd looked so crestfallen, but this would have been bad timing even if she had wanted to go round the world with Will, which she had known in that moment with a terrible clarity that she didn't.

In fact, his out-of-the-blue proposition had clarified everything for her, just as it must have done for Maureen when she'd seen Arnold's upturned red, panting face, inching up towards the window of her boudoir in the lighthouse.

Not only did Clara not want to go round the world with Will, she had also known for sure then that she didn't want to carry on seeing him.

Will had taken it badly. Since their split at the end of April, just over two months ago, she hadn't heard a murmur from him, despite the fact that, at the time, once he'd calmed down sufficiently, he had elicited from her a promise that they could still be friends.

She had agreed that she would like that. Will was a nice enough guy. But 'nice enough' just wasn't what she'd had in mind for a life partner. Both her mum and her older sister, Rosanna, had told her she was being too picky.

'There is no knight in shining armour,' Rosanna had said, prodding her husband, Ed, in his ample middle – he drove artic trucks for a living – and smiling so he knew she was teasing.

'Compromise is the key,' her mother had said. 'I compromised when I met your father and I still do!'

As her parents had been married for thirty-nine years, Rosanna had just sneaked in under the radar, Clara didn't take this too seriously either.

Anyway, she didn't want to compromise on love. She had decided she would far rather be on the shelf than in the wrong cupboard.

Even so, splitting up with Will had been the only dark spot this year. Everything else had been rosy. She had a fabulous new job, a gorgeous free bungalow on the cliffs, which meant she could put her own house in Wareham up on Airbnb – Rosanna had agreed to help out with the changeovers – she needed the cash. And she had an overfriendly three-legged dog to take care of – what could be better?

As Clara yawned and stretched across to switch off the rather twee Cath Kidston bedside light, she found herself praying that Arnold Fairweather and his shenanigans hadn't wrecked the whole thing before she'd really had the chance to get started.

3

Clara was at her desk in the manager's office on Monday morning, she had just written up her manager's report, when Kate Rawlinson's name flashed up on her mobile.

Oh heck. She shouldn't have waited. She should have phoned her about Arnold first. But it was too late now.

Stiff with tension, she answered it. To her immense relief, Kate sounded relaxed.

'Just a routine call, Clara. How are things?'

Clara felt as though she'd been given a second chance. Keeping her voice as matter-of-fact as possible, she told her what had happened on Friday.

Kate took the news a lot better than she'd expected.

'I really don't see how you could have foreseen what would happen. Why did he want to climb up our lighthouse anyway?'

'He said something about Maureen being a fan of *Mission Impossible*.'

Kate snorted. 'And did they say anything else when they checked out?'

'Not much,' Clara replied. 'Although they didn't look like they were very happy. I don't think Maureen had forgiven him for being what she called "a proper show-up". She turned him down apparently.'

'Oh dear. Mmmm. We'll just put that one down to experience, but maybe no more lighthouse climbs.'

'Definitely not,' Clara said, feeling as though a great weight had been lifted from her shoulders.

'So, how's it going otherwise? Do we have any other guests coming who have crazy OTT dreams I should know about?'

'Not many are as crazy as that one,' Clara said, scrolling through the online bookings' diary on her laptop. 'We've got a troupe of actors here this week. They're rehearsing for an open-air production of *Romeo and Juliet* in Regent's Park and they've booked every room for a fortnight, plus the amphitheatre and a full catering staff.'

'Ah yes. I remember.'

'Then, on the eighteenth of July, we've got a dog display team who are hoping to perform at Crufts next year. I'm really looking forward to meeting them.'

'Maybe they'll be able to teach Foxy a thing or two. How is my gorgeous girl?'

'She's asleep in her basket, under my desk.' Clara nudged Foxy with her toe and she opened one sleepy brown eye and wagged her skinny tail. 'She's been chasing seagulls on the coast path. She's tired out.'

'Bless her.'

'How's Australia?'

'Hot – even though technically it's winter over here.'

'Sounds lovely. It's still hot here too. By the way, the dog handlers are sharing the place with some young musicians who plan to record their debut single.'

'Ooh, how exciting. We might be responsible for a Number One. Wouldn't that be something?'

'You never know.' Clara could hear raised voices in reception. She hoped Kate couldn't. 'I'd better get on,' she told her boss. 'Don't worry. Everything's under control.' She hoped that were true too. The voices were getting louder, or at least one of them was. Clara put her hand over the phone. 'I'll be in touch again very soon.'

'No rush,' Kate said and Clara hung up hurriedly and shot out into reception.

To her immense relief, there wasn't a row going on. Zoe was just mid discussion with a woman who had an incredibly loud voice.

'They won't be able to hear a thing – we'll be as quiet as little mice,' she screeched, seemingly unaware that the entire hotel, including the postman, who'd just got out of his van outside, were listening to her now.

'I'm sure that's true,' Zoe said, looking slightly strained as she glanced up at Clara.

'Is everything OK?'

The woman turned and beamed at Clara. She didn't look cross. She was just ultra-loud.

'This is Mrs Jones, Chair of the WI,' Zoe introduced them. 'As you know, we're hosting an event for them in December.'

'Very pleased to meet you, Mrs Jones.'

'Call me, Dora,' she yelled at the top of her voice.

Clara resisted the temptation to wince. It was painful at close quarters.

'The WI would like to come in and set up the room the day before if that's possible?' Zoe was pointing at the bookings screen with a frantic 'help me please' expression in her eyes.

Clara leaned over her shoulder and saw that they had a

convention of Quakers doing a silent retreat booked in for the day before. She turned back to the Chair of the WI. 'Dora,' she began, 'I couldn't possibly put you to the trouble of sending an advance party. We will organise everything for you. Maybe, as you're here now, you could show me what you would like?'

* * *

At around eleven thirty, Zoe appeared in the doorway with two lattes and a packet of ginger nuts, Clara's favourite.

Oh to be effortlessly slim like the twenty-two-year-old and not have to worry about how many biscuits you ate, Clara thought, unconsciously holding her stomach in. Unlike most of the hotel staff, Clara didn't wear the Bluebell Cliff uniform, which was a smart navy suit with a distinctive curving bluebell logo on the pocket of the jacket. She did wear a suit to work, but she had her own personal collection, all of which were especially cut to flatter her petite – OK, make that short – figure and she had them in an array of gorgeous colours. Today's was lemon and she had a co-ordinating designer bag to go with it.

Not because Kate paid her too much, she had taken pains to point out once, but because she never bought anything new. She was an experienced eBayer and great at getting bargains. She had recently introduced Zoe, an eBay virgin, to the benefits of auctions and had given her a crash course in getting a good deal.

'Thanks for sorting out Mrs Jones?' Zoe said, sitting at the other desk opposite her.

'No problem.' Clara picked up her latte and tried, unsuccessfully, to resist the biscuits.

'Did you say something to her? When she said goodbye, she was speaking normally.'

'I noticed she was wearing hearing aids and I thought that her batteries might be low – which, it turned out, they were. Luckily, she had some replacements with her.'

'Wow. Respect.' Zoe's eyes widened. 'I'd never have thought of that.'

'My gran has the same problem sometimes.' Well, actually Gran deliberately switched hers off when she'd had enough of a conversation, but it would have felt disloyal to say that to Zoe.

'Have you heard any more from Arnold Fairweather?' Zoe asked.

'Yes.' Clara sighed. 'As it happens, I had an email from him just now. When you get a moment, could you please send a small bouquet of flowers with a card from us all, wishing him a speedy recovery. It's probably best if you don't include our usual feedback form. You win some, you lose him.'

'I'm on it. Good point. He was OK though, wasn't he? He seemed all right on Saturday. I thought they'd ruled out anything physical?'

'He had groin strain apparently. And a touch of rope burn on his hands, poor chap. Probably just as well his lady friend didn't accept his proposal.'

Zoe's lips twitched.

Clara remained straight-faced. She did not want to tempt fate. People were far too unpredictable. No matter that Arnold had signed a disclaimer saying he was taking full responsibility for his antics, and in his email he'd also grudgingly accepted that the hotel wasn't to blame, you couldn't be too careful these days.

'No dramas with the thespians?' she added.

'Only the ones they're rehearsing, which are going well, I've heard.

'Excellent. By the way,' Clara said, pushing the plate of biscuits away resolutely, although not so resolutely that she hadn't already wolfed down two! 'regarding the dog handlers, I did tell you that there would be four actual dogs coming, didn't I? They're using the amphitheatre for their practice sessions. The weather is supposed to be good, but we do have a contingency plan in the form of a marquee that we can erect if needed.'

'No problem,' Zoe said, glancing at her phone, which had just pinged with an email.

So had Clara's. It was eBay, informing her that she'd just been outbid on a beautiful vintage bag. How annoying.

With a couple of swift clicks, she upped her bid.

Zoe was doing something on her phone too.

An email pinged back almost immediately to tell her she needed to go higher.

Zoe's phone pinged too and she looked smug.

Clara cleared her throat. 'Are we by any chance bidding against each other for the same bag? Purple vintage with a touch of rose. Really pretty?'

Zoe's face dropped. 'That's the one. What's your max?'

'I've exceeded it already,' Clara lied because she knew Zoe was probably over her budget by now. 'How many other people are bidding?'

'I don't think there is anyone else, but there are still eleven minutes left.'

'Well, I'm done. I wanted it to go with a rather nice lilac jacket I've just bought. I've got another one.'

'If I get it, you can borrow it,' Zoe promised.

'You've got yourself a deal.'

Zoe disappeared and Clara filed Arnold Fairweather's email for future reference and hoped that was the last they would hear from him.

She looked back at her to-do list. Doing the rotas was the next thing on it. Zoe did daytime reception and Keith Armstrong, who was the spit of Jack Nicholson, and had been a night porter his entire life, did the nights. He was close to retirement age and ponderous, but meticulous.

Mr B was the head chef and oversaw the kitchen. He was brilliant, if a little eccentric – he had once told her that his two ambitions in life were to find a cure for insomnia and to keep kunekune pigs. Clara had never seen a kunekune but she was pretty sure that any kind of pig wouldn't be a suitable pet for a flat, which was what Mr B had. He was also a conspiracy theorist, which Kate had said could sometimes cause problems.

Jakob Novak, who hailed from the Czech Republic and had a tendency to be ultra-serious for a man in his mid-twenties, was head waiter. He reported to Mr B.

In addition, they had two regular kitchen staff, a waitress and a couple of chambermaids and two part-time gardeners. They also used a catering agency for backup.

A knock on the office door interrupted her thoughts and Mr B popped his head round it. His chef's hat was slightly askew and he was frowning.

'Have you got a minute, boss?'

'Of course. Come in.' Other than Kate, she was the only one who knew his full name, but actually it had become quite fun to play along and call him Mr B like he insisted everyone else did.

A quote popped into her mind. *You don't have to be nuts to work here, but it helps.* You probably weren't allowed to put up notices like that any more. But it certainly applied to the staff here. They were all a bit quirky. Maybe you had to be to work somewhere like this. They were all hugely loyal too, which was one of Clara's favourite traits in a person. Loyalty and kindness. They were hugely underrated qualities, in her opinion.

'What's the problem?' she asked as Mr B sat down in Zoe's recently vacated swivel chair., It was on wheels and the kind you could twirl around, which he did now, his long, checked-trouser-clad legs sticking out in front of him. He was very tall and thin and he reminded her a little of a young Rowan Atkinson with his mobile face, black hair and slightly bulbous nose.

When the chair was facing in her direction again, Mr B folded his arms and sighed heavily, his thick dark eyebrows almost meeting.

'I'm having problems with One Stop Watercress. They're sending us an inferior product. I've had to decline this morning's delivery. It was rank.'

'Oh dear.' She paused, waiting for him to elaborate, which she knew he would in a nanosecond or two. Mr B always had plenty to say for himself.

'I know what's happening and I know why it's happening. All the best stuff is going to the Manor House. The manager of One Stop is in cahoots with their chef, who also happens to co-own the place. They've had it in for us since we opened. We're direct competition for them, you see. That's what it's all about. They think that if they sabotage our food chain by sending us inferior ingredients they'll get more business. I've seen it before.'

Of course he had. Mr B had seen every conspiracy under the sun. Barely a week went by without him going head to head with someone or another over real or imagined plots to get at him. They usually blew over fairly quickly and, on the plus side, Mr B was an absolutely brilliant chef. He was one hundred per cent reliable, one hundred per cent loyal, and one hundred per cent respected in the industry. People fell over themselves to work with him.

Clara made soothing noises as he twirled around in his chair and added, 'I might have to change suppliers. Would you sanction that?'

'Is there a better one?' she asked.

'Not really.'

'And we can't grow it here?' She knew they couldn't. It was too specialist. Although they did grow a lot of other stuff in the organic vegetable gardens that were located at the rear of the kitchens. Being as self-sufficient as possible and sourcing the best local ingredients when they couldn't be was part of the ethos of the hotel and something else that she loved about this place.

It was Clara's dream to have her own smallholding and grow her own food, preferably with a hunky bloke by her side who'd have big biceps from felling trees and putting up fences, not to mention an all-over tan. Neither would he want to go travelling. He'd also get on well with her parents and her grandparents and Rosanna, her sister, and Ed, her long-haul brother-in-law.

It was somewhere around here that the bubble burst. Partly because Clara had never met a man like this. He was clearly even rarer than a knight in shining armour. And she could never have afforded a smallholding either – not in Dorset anyway, where a beach hut could set you back over a hundred grand – but it was a nice dream and something to work towards.

'It needs to grow in running water,' Mr B said.

'What does?' Did Mr B know something she didn't about getting the perfect man?

'Watercress.' He looked at her suspiciously. 'Are you even listening to me?'

'Of course I am. Change suppliers if you can find a better one within budget. But maybe give One Stop one more chance. I can talk to them if you like?'

'Thanks, but I can handle them,' he said, just as there was a loud squeal from reception.

Oh my goodness, what on earth was happening now!

Almost immediately Zoe reappeared in the doorway. 'Oooh,' she said, shutting up swiftly when she saw Mr B, but it was hard to miss that fact that her English rose prettiness was all flushed with excitement.

She'd got the bag then!

* * *

At lunchtime, Clara took Foxy for her usual walk. This wasn't strictly necessary. There was more than enough outside space in the hotel grounds for her to run around in, but Clara had a horror of a guest stepping in dog poo accidentally (not a great start to living your dream). Dogs were welcome at the Bluebell and although the gardeners would pick up mess if they spotted it, Clara didn't want to add to their burden, so Foxy got walked outside the premises, where Clara could clear up after her personally.

Today's walk took her past the Manor House Hotel, known locally as the Manor House. Like the Bluebell, their gardens came down to the footpath along the cliffs, but unlike the Bluebell, which had a low fence, they had hedges. There were plenty of gaps and Clara peered through, curious to see what their nearest neighbour and competitor was up to.

The gardens, which weren't as extensive as the Bluebell's, but which were a lot more mature, as theirs had only recently been planted out, were well kept. They clearly had a conscientious gardener. Flower beds full of bright delphiniums bloomed and the lawns were bowling-green smooth and, from her vantage point, she could see the giant chess set, which had four-foot-high marble pieces, reputedly carved by a local sculptor, up near an open-plan terrace.

The Manor House itself, which looked great from the front, was a touch on the shabby side at the back. Salt air played havoc with paintwork and the Manor, which was white, but currently looked grey, was definitely in need of a paint job.

It had Gothic-like turrets at either end of the building and on one of these there were tiles missing. Below this turret, Clara spied a patch of damp. That was interesting. So maybe the Manor House wasn't doing as well as usual. It certainly didn't look like it. Maybe Mr B did have a point about the competition aspects of things.

'Can I help you?'

She was so deep in thought that the disembodied voice made her jump. Clara couldn't see anyone. Then she spotted a man standing just on the other side of the hedge. He was tall and dark-haired and very tanned. Muscled legs protruded from khaki shorts and he wore an olive vest top over bronzed shoulders. He blended nicely with the background. No wonder she hadn't seen him. He was carrying a pair of secateurs. As her gaze travelled back up to his face, she realised with a jolt that he was not smiling.

'Um. No. I was just curious.'

'We have a front entrance. If you wish to make a booking, you should come to that.'

'I don't wish to make a booking.' She was wrong-footed and, to make matters worse, Foxy had just slipped through the hedge into the hotel gardens and was dancing around, wriggling her sinewy chestnut body and wagging her tail ecstatically at this new prospective titbit giver.

'I'd appreciate it if you would call him back. Dogs are not permitted.' His voice was as stern as his almost black eyes.

Foxy ignored Clara's entreaties to come back and wagged even harder. One of the wags touched the gardener's leg and he stiffened and snipped the secateurs in the air a couple of times as if he'd have liked to have cut off the offending tail and be done with it.

'Foxy,' yelled Clara, but Foxy had clearly heard the secateurs too and she'd got the message. With one last affronted look at the man, she wriggled back through the hedge and sat as close to Clara's legs as she could get with her ears back.

'Sorry,' Clara said, bending to clip on Foxy's lead and thinking privately, what a stroppy character – there had been no need for that secateurs performance at all! Never-the-less, she was embarrassed. If Mr B was to be believed, there was enough discomfort between the two hotels without her causing any more trouble.

But when she looked up again, the gardener had disappeared as swiftly as he'd materialised.

She continued with her walk, but the experience had unsettled her. It wasn't as if they were in direct competition with the Manor House. OK, there might be a little bit of overlap. They both did corporate events and they both did weddings. The Bluebell didn't turn down a booking just because it wasn't of an artistic or creative nature. Even so, there was enough business for both of them. The Bluebell catered for a more eclectic clientele and, it would be fair to say, a more discerning customer, but there was no reason the two hotels couldn't exist harmoniously.

At some point in the future, Clara decided she would call round and introduce herself properly to ensure there'd be no repeat of this afternoon's awkwardness. For now, she resolved to put the incident out of her head.

4

The thespians turned out to be excellent fun. It was still a gorgeously hot July with barely a breath of wind ruffling the lawns of the clifftop site. Who needed to go abroad? The local beaches were packed with day trippers and families – if you stood at certain points of the grounds, you could see the strip of gold beach that was Swanage Bay in the distance thronging with people, although the Bluebell was too far away to hear much of the tourists. Clara was glad she wasn't travelling in from her house in Wareham each day. Kate had been right; the traffic was horrendous.

One afternoon, with a sluggish but reluctant to miss anything Foxy in tow, Clara had wandered down to watch part of a rehearsal in the amphitheatre. It was blissful in the shade of a pop-up blue and white striped gazebo that Clara had organised with one of their suppliers to come in and sell refreshing home-made lemonade.

The stallholder always put out a bowl of water for Foxy. Most people on the site loved the three-legged dog with her bright eyes and wagging tail and she was expert at keeping away from the ones who weren't so keen. Since Kate had gone away and the heat wave had arrived, Foxy spent most of her time flopped out somewhere near Clara. She was clearly not about to let another mistress disappear into the distance.

All the staff had been down to the outdoor theatre to watch rehearsals at various times because the actors were keen to have an audience and had invited them. They raved about the beauty of the setting – it rivalled the Minack Theatre in Cornwall apparently, although it was quite a bit smaller. What an accolade that was – Clara had been to the Minack once and during the interval someone had shouted from the clifftop that they could see dolphins going by in the bay.

Clara had never seen dolphins from Ballard Down, but she lived in hope. It would be utterly fantastic if they could put that in their brochure; she had asked everyone to keep an eye out. In the meantime, she had put the bit about the Minack's similarity to the Bluebell amphitheatre in Kate's weekly report and she'd been thrilled.

Even when the thespians were indoors, they slipped unconsciously into character, enthusing everyone they came into contact with and lapsing into Shakespearian. Everyone, from the chambermaids to Phil Grimshaw, who was in his element, joined in at every opportunity.

Now and then, Clara came across Phil, who could pass for a Byronic hero and had played a few on stage in the past, deep in conversation with one or other of the thespians. She suspected he was offering his services to the merry troupe and hoped he wasn't about to take off and join them – she couldn't afford to lose Phil. It would be a disaster if he left on her watch while Kate was away. She decided to keep an extra special eye on him, they were coming into peak season and his experience was invaluable to the team.

In the meantime, the words, 'Wherefore art thou, Romeo,' echoed regularly over the bannisters of the Bluebell's impressive curved wooden staircase, often followed by 'Good night, good night, parting is such sweet sorrow.' This was usually succeeded by a scuttling of footsteps going off to various rooms. The place echoed with the deep booming voices and raucous laughter of actors, all of whom were clearly having a wonderful time.

'It makes you want to be on the stage, doesn't it?' Zoe had said to Clara wistfully.

'No,' Clara had replied. 'I have quite enough drama with Mr B and Phil.' What with the heat and the testosterone, there was the odd spat in the kitchen, but nothing too serious. Truth be told, she'd enjoyed the theatrical fortnight too.

It sounded as though Kate was definitely going to need the full three weeks in Australia. She hadn't said too much about the details on the phone – she was always bright and breezy and positive – but last time they had spoken, she had dropped into the conversation that her mum had one or two health issues, so it was just as well she was around to help with them.

'I think I'll need to be here until the end of July. If that's all right with you, of course, Clara?'

'It's absolutely fine,' Clara had confirmed. 'I'm enjoying myself.' There was a tiny selfish part of Clara that hoped her boss would stay away for the whole summer. She was loving being in sole charge of such a happy team.

Things were going too well. The hotel was running seamlessly, the atmosphere was happy and the staff were united. Then, on the evening of the thespian's last night, a rather large spanner was dropped unceremoniously into the works.

Clara had just handed over to Phil and was walking across the car park, with Foxy, when she heard a voice shout her name.

She turned, shielding her eyes against the evening sun. A tall figure was hurrying across the gravel and at first, because of the angle of light, and also, she supposed, because he was the last person on earth she was expecting to see, she didn't recognise him.

And then suddenly she did. It was Will, her ex, dressed in jeans and a white T-shirt and canvas trainers, his brown hair streaked a little by the sun and longer than she remembered.

'Clara,' he called again. Not that he needed to. He'd already got her full attention.

Her heartbeat had just sped up – and not for any good reason. Why on earth had Will decided to turn up at her workplace out of the blue when there had been complete silence from him since April?

The split had been relatively painless as they hadn't lived together. In fact, when she'd gathered up her possessions from his, they had barely filled a small bag. A toothbrush and some toiletries from his bathroom and her Kindle and a change of clothes from his bedroom.

He'd had more at hers – she'd given him back two box sets, a coat, a scarf, a pair of boots, several pairs of underpants and his favourite pillow. Sometimes she had wondered if he'd been planning to move in by stealth.

But, right now, she waited for him to draw to a halt beside her.

'Hi,' he said, putting his hands in his pockets and looking up at the side of the building, which overlooked the car park. 'So, this is the place you dumped me for.'

'I didn't dump you, Will.' Oh dear, this wasn't the best start to their reunion.

Even Foxy wasn't her usual effusive self. She had managed a couple of wags, but she didn't leave her mistress's side.

'Is that the mangy mutt, you rescued?'

Foxy put her ears back and Clara bristled.

'She's not mangy. She belongs to my boss. I'm looking after her. Not that it's any of your business.'

She clicked the remote button to open the door of her car and Will's demeanour changed. He put an urgent hand on her arm.

'No, wait. I'm sorry. We've got off on the wrong foot. Have you time for a coffee? I won't keep you long.'

That was the last thing she wanted to do. 'Not if you've come to have a go at me, no.'

'I haven't. I promise. I just want to talk. We could go up to The Anchor if you don't want to talk here. Or we could go into town. Where are you living now?'

She saw no reason not to tell him. He must have discovered she'd rented her house out, which was why he'd turned up here. 'At my boss's bungalow in Ballard Views.'

'Wow – sounds classy.' There was the tiniest edge of bitterness in his voice again. Or maybe she was imagining it.

She decided to give him the benefit of the doubt. 'It's really nice. I'm very lucky.'

'If you haven't got time for coffee – maybe we could have a quick chat here? Please, Clara?'

She struggled with herself. She didn't want an argument with him here in the car park. There were too many people milling about. Some of the thespians were packing cases into cars, ready for an early start in the morning. A couple were already looking across. It wouldn't hurt to give Will twenty minutes, but she didn't want it to be here.

'All right,' she said eventually, 'A very quick coffee.'

They went in convoy to The Anchor, which was one of the

closest pubs to the Bluebell and only a short drive away. They sat outside with Foxy in the patio garden, which had hanging baskets of purple and white petunias and trailing variegated ivy and long terracotta tubs crowded with red geraniums abutting the low fence. The air was full of the mixed scents of salt and flowers and, occasionally, when the pub door opened, a waft of cooked food and stale beer.

'Are you hungry?' Will asked, slotting the plastic menus on the table out of their stand.

'Not really, Will. I've got to get back. I have plans.' She didn't want this quick chat to somehow evolve into a date. 'What is it that you wanted to talk about?'

Over a latte for her and a half a shandy for him he told her.

'I won't beat about the bush.' His eyes were vulnerable and she felt a spike of something, not quite guilt, but maybe regret, about the way that things had ended. 'The truth is, I've really missed you. You look really great by the way. You've lost weight – not that you needed to. You've always looked great.' He bit his lip. 'The thing is... I've missed you more, as time's gone on, not less, and I was wondering – well, I was wondering... how you felt...'

'I won't say I haven't thought about you, Will, but the truths is, I don't—'

He put up a hand before she could finish. 'Can I just run something by you?'

'Yes, you can, but...' She had a feeling she knew what was coming and she was beginning to wish she hadn't agreed to this impromptu drink.

'I can see now that I didn't really think that trip through. I sprung it on you. It was mad. But what if we were just to go back to things like they were before. We were good together, you and me.'

She shook her head. 'I don't see the point, Will. Nothing's changed.'

'Ah, but it has. For one thing, I'm not working at Apple any more. I've got another techie job, but it's from home. I can virtually pick my own shifts, which means I could work around yours. It would be so much better.' He leaned across the table, his eyes not quite pleading but getting that way.

Oh heck, why hadn't she trusted her instincts? She stood up. 'I'm so sorry, Will, but I don't feel the same way about you any more.'

It was like whipping a puppy. He looked so broken.

'Have you met someone else?'

'No,' she said over her shoulder as she walked away with a relieved Foxy. 'No, I haven't.'

Maybe it would have been easier for him if she'd said that she had. This thought circled in her head during the ten-minute drive back to the bungalow. Maybe it would have been better for his ego.

She was probably overthinking it, she decided, as she fed Foxy and let her into the garden. She was tired and it had been a shock to see him.

Her mobile pinged as she was standing at the back door and she saw it was a text from Rosanna.

How's your dream job going? Fancy a chat? What time are you in?

Suddenly she did feel like talking to her sister. She speed-dialled her straight back.

'I'll take that as a yes then.' Rosanna's warm, deep voice sounded pleased to hear from her. All the women in her family had deep voices. Their mother sounded more and more like Rula Lenska the older she'd got and Thelma, their grandmother, occasionally got mistaken for a man on the phone. It was much better than being high or shrill, Clara had often thought, and it tended to make you sound authoritative, even when you weren't really trying. Which came in handy in her job.

They exchanged pleasantries about Clara's niece and nephew, Sophie, eleven, and Tom, nine. Then Clara told her about the thespians and about Arnold Fairweather and then finally she told her about Will turning up.

'I probably shouldn't have gone for a coffee with him, but I really didn't think it would hurt.'

'Hmmm,' Rosanna said. 'He always was a bit intense, wasn't he? Very much an all-or-nothing kind of guy. It goes with the geekery, I guess. There isn't any middle ground with a computer. Still, I suppose at least he's got the message now. How was he when you left?'

'Upset. I think he really expected me to leap back into his arms. I don't know why really. He hasn't so much as texted me since April. Anyway, I thought you liked him. You told me I should compromise when we split up.'

'That was Mum. I told you there was no such thing as a knight in shining armour. And there isn't.' She paused. 'I did like him. But I guess he wasn't the one for you. Stop worrying about him, honey. I'm glad the job's going well.'

'Me too,' Clara said. 'Thanks for listening. I think I might sleep a bit better now.'

'Phone back if you can't. I won't be in bed early. Ed's got a delivery in Glasgow and I'm watching YouTube videos.'

'What kind?'

'Funny ones. Or, more to the point, ones my new phone thinks I'll find funny. It's Ed's fault. He bought me this all-singing, all-dancing phone for our anniversary.'

Clara yawned. 'Wow. He's a sweetie. And thanks again. I really appreciate you listening.'

'That's what big sisters are for. And put Will Lightfoot out of your head. It's not your fault he can't move on. However...' A beat. 'There's no reason you can't...' There was another little pause during which Clara could almost hear the cogs in her sister's brain whirring. 'Maybe you should try some online dating – that'll take your mind off Will.'

'You know I don't do the internet. Unless it's eBay or Wish.-com,' Clara murmured. 'So no... Don't even go there.'

'Spoilsport. OK, honey. Not online dating. Although I do have this friend I was talking to who does—'

'Stop.'

'Really? You wouldn't want to try any kind of—'

'I'll think about it,' Clara said, knowing that semi-agreement would shut Rosanna up quicker than full-on resistance. 'Sweet Dreams, Sis.'

Clara overslept. She woke up from a dream in which she was for sale in a Girlfriend Auction and Will was the highest bidder. It hadn't been online either. She'd been in a cage in the middle of a cattle market that smelled faintly of pigs and she'd been staring out at a sea of men's faces, most of whom she didn't know, although Mr B had been in there, so had that stroppy gardener from the Manor House. They'd both been scowling, while Will had been grinning like an overconfident comedian. You had to point your phone at the cage and press a button to make a bid. To make matters worse, she'd been stark naked.

She sat up, galvanised by panic and sweating, before realising that she was not in a cattle market and she was not stark naked –

she was wearing her Central Perk *Friends* nightshirt – but, shit, she was late. What time was it?

Her phone was beeping, which meant it was later than 7.00 a.m. because it was on silent until then. She grabbed it – 8.15. Bloody hell. She hardly ever overslept. She leapt out of bed, aware of the brightness of the sun streaming through the blinds.

The beeping turned out to be a reminder telling her she had a missed call from Zoe. There was also a text from Rosanna, which said

Phone me when you get this. URGENT.

She had to get to work. Saturday was changeover day. Goodbye to the thespians and hello to the dog trainers and musicians. She hoped Zoe wasn't phoning in sick, but suddenly she was more concerned about Rosanna. She wasn't a drama queen, so URGENT was serious. Was something wrong with one of the kids or Ed?

A small whine at the bedroom door reminded her Foxy must have been patiently crossing her legs – the three she had left. She let her out, then raced around the kitchen. Coffee was essential. She phoned Rosanna while the machine was hissing it into a cup.

'Hi. Is everything OK? Are you all right? Are the kids all right?'

'Yes, we're all fine.' Rosanna went into brusque mode. 'But I was worried. Did you see the link I sent?'

'What link?'

'Check your phone. Then call me back.'

Clara did as she was bid. She hadn't scrolled down enough before to even see the link, which, when she clicked on it, took her to a video on YouTube. She pressed play and frowned as a familiar image filled her screen. It was the Bluebell's lighthouse with the backdrop of a gorgeous pink sunset behind it. It looked idyllic. But, hang on a minute, there was Arnold Fairweather climbing up it, a great black spider of a man. He was nearly at the halfway point.

Clara felt a cold dread start in the pit of her stomach as she remembered what was going to happen next. And here it came: the point at which Arnold had lost his footing, switching in an instant from being a spider to being a struggling fly on a thin rope strand of web.

For a moment, the image freeze-framed on the dangling man, and then it got worse because the camera zoomed in on his face. In this close-up version, you could see that Arnold's eyes were wide with terror, his face was pale and sweaty and he was obviously struggling to breathe. His hands came into view, pawing at his chest in a grotesque parody of someone who could be having a heart attack.

Then the camera zoomed out again and a line of text rolled across the screen: The Bluebell Cliff Hotel – The place where dreams come true. Doesn't look like much of a dream to us!

Clara felt sick. For a few seconds, she thought she might actually be sick. But she wasn't. She was just light-headed with shock. YouTube had started to play the next video on her phone. She stopped it, noticing with another surge of horror that the lighthouse one already had more than 7,000 views and several hundred likes.

She called Rosanna back.

'Oh my God. What do I do? How do I get that taken down?'

'I'm not sure, but I've already flagged it as inappropriate content, which means that YouTube will be alerted. You can do it too. It's got to be libellous, hasn't it? Whoever posted it is having a pop at the hotel. It's definitely defamatory. Can you get hold of your boss? What time is it in Australia?'

'They're ten hours ahead. I'll phone her in a minute. I'm not that familiar with YouTube. Can you tell how long it's been there?'

'Someone put it on last night. About eight p.m.'

There was a beat.

Then Rosanna put into words the same thing that was going through Clara's head. 'Will wouldn't do something like that, would he?'

She thought about his silence over the last two and a half months and then his unexpected arrival last night. It was a coincidence, but she didn't really think he'd be that nasty.

'He'd certainly know how to do it, but how would he get the content?'

'No, you're right. Forget I said that. Try not to worry. I'd better let you go. Keep me posted.'

'Thanks for flagging it. I will.'

Clara put down the phone and called Zoe. She was half expecting Zoe to tell her about YouTube, but she just wanted to mention that one of the chambermaids had phoned in sick and was it OK to phone the agency.

'Of course it is,' Clara told her. 'That's always fine on a big changeover. I'll be in soon.' Then she hung up again and called Kate.

5

When she finally got into work, Clara was feeling slightly better. Kate had been straight on to someone she called her friendly solicitor – they must be on good terms, Clara surmised, as he'd interrupted a round of golf to give her some quite lengthy advice first thing on a Saturday. Kate had emailed a list of things to do and with each action Clara took she felt more in control.

One of the suggestions had been to call an emergency staff meeting. The solicitor's advice on the email reverberated in her head – *It's all about damage limitation. You can't reverse what's happened but you can minimise any possible damage by your reaction to it. You'll need to brief everyone in your organisation as soon as possible. It's important to present a united front.*

Clara had arranged for this briefing to take place at midday and it was just before 11.00 when she pulled into the Bluebell's car park.

It was checkout time and several thespians were milling about, transporting luggage into cars. Several smiled at her. One of them flung out his arms and called, 'Shall I compare thee to a summer's day...'

His mate thumped his arm. 'Stop messing about. We've gotta get a wriggle on. Have you set that bloody satnav?'

Someone was playing the Steinway and the faint strains of a melody were drifting across the summer air. This was usually a sound that would have lifted Clara's heart, but today she was too preoccupied and too focused on damage limitation.

There was a young couple she didn't recognise sitting on the low wall that separated the car park from the gardens. They had their heads bent close together and were tittering at something on a phone.

Were they watching the video? No, of course they weren't. She was going to send herself mad if she thought that about everyone she met.

As Clara reached reception, she passed a man with a German shepherd on a leash. He must be one of the dog trainers who'd asked if they could come early to drop off some equipment. He nodded at her and she thought of Crufts and Number Ones and the hotel's reputation.

There's no such thing as bad publicity, she reminded herself. But it would be handy to figure out who had leaked that video. There weren't that many options. Arnold and Maureen of course – but why would either of them want to put themselves up for weeks of potential humiliation in order to have a pop at the hotel? That didn't make much sense. Matt, the pro climber was a possible, but that didn't strike her as particularly likely either, as it would reflect badly on him. Which left the cameraman. He was the most likely culprit.

These thoughts had been circling in her head since she'd seen that video. She was no closer to addressing any of them. Although Arnold was top of her list to phone. Once she'd spoken to him, she needed to brief Phil and then the staff meeting. It would take place in the first-floor meeting room.

* * *

The room was set up in boardroom style from the last time it had been used and Clara took up her laptop and linked it to the projector.

Including herself and Phil, there were eleven people who worked at the Bluebell, either full- or part-time, and eight were here now. Clara hadn't managed to get hold of the contract gardener, but he'd be in later anyway and one of the chamber-maids had called in sick, as Zoe had said. She had also let Keith go home after his night porter shift, having briefed him sepa-rately on the phone before she had left home.

Once they were all gathered, Clara and Phil stood up at the front of the room and she banged her coffee mug on the table to get their attention and cleared her throat. 'Thank you so much for coming in – those of you who weren't here already – I'm sorry for the inconvenience and you'll be paid for your time, of course. But something has happened that you need to know about.'

She and Phil had decided that the best thing to do would be to play them the video. But first she wanted to remind them why they were all here. She flicked a switch and the Bluebell's Mission Statement popped up onto the screen.

> Our mission is to provide the venue and facilities that will enable every guest to step towards the realisation of their dream.

Clara scrolled down to the text below it. The text was on a brochure that she had blown up to full size.

> The Bluebell Cliff Hotel is a place where a person can come to fulfil their dream. We cater for everyone – the artistic, the quirky, the conventional, and even just the plain daft. If you can

dream it, we can help you turn it into a reality. Call us for a no-obligation chat and take the first step to fulfilling your dream.

She could feel her heart hammering as she pressed play. She scanned their faces as they watched it. There were a variety of reactions.

Mr B looked outraged, no change there.

Zoe looked worried. But then she and Clara had already spoken about it and she knew what was coming.

Ellie May Taylor, the youngest waitress, clapped her hand over her mouth and widened her eyes.

Janet Brown, the remaining chambermaid, looked at her Fitbit and frowned. She was probably wondering how long it would be before she was able to get on with bed changing, which may take longer with agency staff, who weren't as used to the routine.

A couple of other people looked amused.

But by the time the video had reached the end and the damning lines of text were scrolling across the screen not a single one of them was smiling. They were all clued up enough to know that something like this could be a serious threat to the future of the hotel and, in turn, to their jobs.

Clara pressed pause. There was a murmur of reaction, but one voice did carry clearly across the room and, by its vehemence, the message wasn't polite.

'*Kurva*,' said Jakob Novak. 'Is this video hoax?'

There were murmurs of dissent. Clearly some of them had already seen it. News travelled fast.

'No, I'm afraid it's not.' Clara looked at him. 'This did actually happen. It was two weeks ago. A couple booked the lighthouse for a minibreak with the proviso that he would propose to his partner by doing exactly what you saw. We kept it low-key because he wasn't sure whether he'd be able to go through with it and he didn't want her alerted in case it spoiled the surprise.'

'That went well then,' Ellie May said.

There were various mutterings and Clara explained that it wasn't as bad as it looked. 'It was a panic attack, not a heart attack. Everything was absolutely fine in the end. I went to the hospital with them.'

'But then he decided to cash in and sell the video,' someone else said. 'YouTube can be quite profitable if you get enough hits.'

'It's more than that,' Mr B pointed out, straightening up in his chair. 'He's not just uploaded a funny video, has he? He's annotated it. It's a direct attack on us. Chances are he didn't even do it. Would you seriously want to invite public humiliation for ever after? You can see his face. It's almost impossible to remove stuff like that permanently from the internet.'

'You're not helping,' Clara snapped and he shut up swiftly. 'But I do think you're right about the fact that he probably didn't instigate this. I spoke to him just before this meeting. He's as shocked as we are.'

Arnold Fairweather had been furious as well as shocked. She'd had to hold the phone away from her ear while he ranted about his ex for several seconds. It turned out that Maureen Grey had ditched him the second they'd got home and she was now on holiday in Antigua with the cameraman he'd hired to film his big proposal.

Clara told them about Maureen's defection now. 'The phone number he gave me for her no longer works,' she added. She knew she hadn't written it down wrong. She'd got him to repeat it twice.

'Who was the cameraman?' Phil asked. 'Was it someone we know?'

'Yes, it's someone whose link we put on our website. Kate

doesn't do that lightly. So it will be someone who she has already vetted. Someone who should be professional. I've left a message on his voicemail – he's obviously away at the moment – and he hasn't yet got back to me.'

'Did Arnold employ him directly or did we set it up?' Phil asked.

'Arnold spoke to him after I gave him the link. They sorted out the details between themselves.'

'Whoever did it must have got the original recording from the cameraman,' Mr B said. 'Flagitious bastards.'

There were more mutterings. Clara wondered idly if anyone besides Mr B knew what flagitious meant. The more traditional F word was banned in his kitchen, but he wasn't averse to using profanities that no one else understood. Well, not unless they'd studied Latin, which Mr B had done for fun, he had once told her.

But it was the quietest voice in the room that made the most impact on Clara. 'It's got 8,000 views already,' Ellie May said in awe. 'It must have gone viral.'

'No that's not enough. You need more than a million views to go viral, these days,' someone else helpfully pointed out.

There was an angry buzz of conversation as they argued over how many views qualified as viral.

Phil banged the table with the mug and the room hushed again. 'Never mind how many views it's got,' he said in his clear authoritative voice. 'What's important is what we do next. That's why we called you in. We need to have a unified front. Has anyone already been asked about this?'

They shook their heads.

Clara was both relieved and surprised. Surely the fastest way of discrediting them would be to send it straight to the press. Although, she supposed, it was still possible that someone had. The video on YouTube had barely been up for twelve hours.

'Do you want us to say "No Comment"?' asked Janet, widening her eyes. She was a big fan of crime dramas.

'What we would like you to say,' Clara said, glancing at Phil because they'd already discussed it, 'is as little as possible. If anyone asks you anything – however obliquely and that means whether they approach you here, or in the pub, or if you're out and about – you just tell them you have no idea why anyone would post a video like that, you don't know anything about it and you refer them to myself or Phil.'

Phil took over again. 'We don't need to tell you that this could severely damage the good reputation that we've all worked extremely hard to build.'

There were more mutterings, but again one voice rose above the others. 'We vill be silent as squirrels. Do not worry.' It was Jakob again. He was standing up on one side of the room, leaning against the wall, with his hands in his pockets, and the staff around him all nodded.

Jakob was almost as respected as Mr B amongst his peers. He was hard-working but also intensely social and kind and he believed in giving people second chances.

'I have had very many chances for myself. So I must give chance to others,' he had told Clara once after a discussion about his family, who weren't rich but who had subsidised his passage to England, where they believed he would have a better life. He still sent regular money back to his parents in the Czech Republic, even though he was now married to an English girl.

'Thank you,' Clara said, nodding to Jakob and then to the room in general. 'Thank you, everyone. We will do our best to get to the bottom of this as soon as we can, and I will keep you all posted. But, in the meantime, please say as little as possible.'

Mr B stayed behind, filling the doorway with his tall frame.

'I think this might have something to do with the Manor House,' he told Phil and Clara. 'Relations between us have become... strained.' He was obviously picking his words carefully. For a conspiracy theorist, Mr B could also be a master of understatement.

Clara felt a twinge of trepidation. 'What do you mean strained? What's happened exactly?'

'I had an altercation with the Brothers Grim.'

'Sorry. Who?'

'Adam and Nick Greenwood. They're known in the trade as the Brothers Grim.' He tapped his nose. 'They co-own the Manor House. Adam's front of house and Nick's the chef. Although Nick's all right. Adam's the nasty one.'

'You had an altercation with both of them? How?'

Mr B was looking slightly uncomfortable now. 'All I did was mention to Nick that I was on to him. After the watercress fiasco. I told you about that.'

'Yes, I remember. But I thought that had all been resolved. So how did Adam get involved?'

'Nick must have told him.' He waved a hand. 'We were all at the wholesalers. Words were exchanged.'

'Just words.'

'Of course.' Mr B looked shocked. 'I don't do physical violence.'

'When did this happen?'

'The Wednesday before last. I apologise if I've caused any unnecessary disruption. I never expected...' He gestured back to the laptop still set up on the table of the meeting room. 'I never expected they would do anything litigious...'

'They may not have done,' Phil said swiftly. 'This still could be

Arnold. He's obviously pretty pissed off about how things turned out. Maybe he blames us for it.'

Clara nodded, but she added The Manor House to her list of things to check. She couldn't quite believe they would go as far as to try and discredit the Bluebell, but it definitely wouldn't hurt to go and introduce herself. She should have done it before. Talking and diplomacy solved most things, in her experience.

When Clara got back downstairs to the unmanned reception, she bumped into an anxious Zoe. She had clearly only just got back too. There was a ferrety-faced man in jeans and a canvas jacket leaning against the counter, his finger poised, in a staged pose, above the bell.

'Ah, so the place isn't totally deserted,' he said, flashing a snide smile at Zoe. 'I'd like to book your lighthouse for a special occasion. I plan to propose to my girlfriend.'

'I can deal with that for you, sir,' Clara butted in smoothly, which gave Zoe, who looked terrified, the chance to escape.

The snidey man introduced himself as Simon Tomlinson, a reporter from *The Purbeck Gazette*, which was a free paper with a distribution area of several thousand properties.

They were certainly on the ball, Clara thought, taking him into the office. Having established that he had no intention of proposing to his girlfriend, either in a lighthouse or anywhere else, but actually just wanted a human-interest piece for his paper, she set about persuading him to leave the Bluebell's name out of it. This was not easy and involved all of her not inconsiderable charm and diplomacy, not to mention a very large slab of good fruit cake.

She also made it crystal clear that his editor would have a court case on her hands if she printed anything about them that was in any way defamatory.

He went away eventually, grumbling about the gagging of free speech, but Clara was pretty sure he wouldn't be writing anything too controversial. Never mind free speech. Free newspapers relied on advertisers to survive. The Bluebell advertised in *The Purbeck Gazette* regularly. As did all their local suppliers. They weren't likely to want to rock the boat too much. She'd just have to keep her fingers crossed that Simon Tomlinson kept his piece benign.

Over the next few hours, she and Zoe fielded several emails, phone calls and tweets on the Bluebell Cliff hash tag. Phil had stayed and helped for a while, but in the end he'd agreed to go home. They may both have to do more hours over the next few days, but they couldn't both be here permanently.

'It'll blow over quicker than you think,' she kept telling Zoe.

'I know,' Zoe kept agreeing.

Privately, Clara wasn't so sure. The internet was such a vastly anonymous place. YouTube could take the video down, but that didn't mean it wouldn't be out there somewhere else. On twitter, on Facebook, hosted by some anonymous website somewhere.

The only saving grace was that so far it didn't seem to have affected them in a business sense. No one cancelled a booking. If anything, they were getting more enquiries about their services than usual. Maybe it was true about there being no such thing as bad publicity.

By five o'clock, Clara was feeling frazzled with stress and too much coffee. There hadn't been time to eat. There hadn't even been time to take Foxy for more than a cursory walk. And she didn't anticipate a particularly peaceful evening either.

On her way home she planned to pay a visit to the Manor

House and diplomatically check out whether they knew anything, without upsetting or accusing anyone.

She had also decided it would be a good idea to speak to Will, just to rule him out of the equation. After yesterday's meeting, she was not looking forward to doing that one bit.

6

The Manor House didn't look busy for a peak-season Saturday in July. Their car park was half empty.

Clara had checked out their TripAdvisor reviews before she'd come and had discovered that most people were complimentary about their stay, although a few had commented on the fact that the hotel could do with a lick of paint, and one person had said his bedroom needed a makeover.

She had to admit, after giving it a brief appraisal from her car, that the front of the building also looked in need of some TLC. The grounds were nicely kept though.

She remembered the gardener with his secateurs. He'd looked as though he was part of the fixtures and fittings of the place. But then it was a lot cheaper to maintain gardens than big hotels.

She walked up the steps to the main entrance and the glass doors opened automatically to greet her. Her first impressions were of red carpet, good quality, but old, a couple of brown chesterfields, same story, and several framed seascapes on the walls. The foyer smelled of citrus air freshener. Stairs led up to the first floor.

There was no one manning reception. Clara tinged the bell and waited. Behind the wooden counter was a door with a mirrored glass panel, which she guessed would be a one-way window. If there were anyone in the back office, they would know she was there. After a couple more moments, she heard movement and the door opened.

'I do apologise for keeping you waiting.' The man who appeared was familiar. He was tall and tanned, but it still took her a couple of seconds to recognise him as the man she had seen in the gardens: no longer in khaki shorts but an open-necked white shirt and trousers. Not the gardener then. Unless they were doubling up on roles.

Today he was wearing a rectangular brass badge that said Manager and he looked every bit as grumpy as he'd looked the first time she'd seen him.

He must have recognised her at about the same moment, and having established she wasn't a customer, his veneer of friendliness vanished.

'I wondered if it was possible to speak to Nick Greenwood please?' At the same moment, she heard movement behind her and an elderly couple dressed for dinner greeted him.

He smiled at them. The transformation was amazing: from grumpy to gracious in one swift movement. He wasn't bad-looking when he wasn't being angry. A teeny bit Orlando Bloom. Then he turned back to her and the impression was gone.

'Nick isn't available. You'll have to make do with me. I'm Adam.'

'You're Adam Greenwood?' She felt almost as wrong-footed as she had when Foxy had been running around his legs. 'Oh, I didn't realise. I'm Clara King, the manager of The Bluebell Cliff.'

'I know who you are.' The slightest of frowns reached his eyes. 'So you decided to use the front entrance this time, did you? No mutt with you today?'

'She's in the car in the shade with the windows down,' she said, feeling the heat of remembered embarrassment flooding her cheeks. That was below the belt. Unless he was being ironic. She was half expecting him to soften his words with a smile. He didn't.

'I assume you're here to apologise for your lunatic chef?'

At a different time, talking to a different person, she might have laughed and agreed with him that, yes, Mr B was slightly eccentric, if a not a full-on fruit cake, but not today. She was tired and he'd already rubbed her up the wrong way. She stiffened.

'I did hear there was some friction.'

His eyes darkened. 'The man is a conspiracy theorist. He is rude, condescending and arrogant and I'd appreciate it greatly if you could tell him to keep his ridiculous allegations about myself and my staff to himself.'

Actually, his description of Mr B, with the exception of the rude bit, was pretty much spot on, but Clara was not in the mood for this full-on attack and she sprang fiercely to her chef's defence.

'Mr B is a very good chef. One of the best I have ever worked with. He is kind and considerate and he is courteous and he inspires great loyalty.'

This time, Adam's reply was the merest raise of an eyebrow.

Clara went on swiftly, 'I'm sure there has just been a simple misunderstanding that we can sort out if we discuss it like adults.'

'I'm not convinced there has.' He looked bored. He drummed his fingers on the reception desk.

She had an urge to lean across it and slap him. She couldn't remember the last time she'd felt so riled. He wasn't even looking at her now. He was writing something on a notebook on the desk.

Taking a deep breath, she was about to try one more time – giving up was not in her nature – when she heard the swoosh of the automatic doors behind her. Someone else had walked into the foyer. 'Good evening, Adam.'

'Good evening Geraldine.'

Geraldine turned out to be another elderly woman in pearls and a jade jacquard dress. It must be the second shift for dinner.

'Fabulous weather, isn't it?' Geraldine was obviously in the mood for a chat. 'I've just had such a lovely walk along the cliff. Did you see that piece in *The Times* about Jacob Rees-Mogg? After what we were saying yesterday about...' she broke off as if suddenly becoming aware of Clara. 'I'm so sorry, dear. Have I interrupted?'

'No, it's fine,' Clara said. 'I was just going.' She was clearly wasting her time trying to talk to him at the moment.

Adam didn't even look at her, let alone make any attempt to stop her. She could feel the heat still in her face as she walked past Geraldine. Part anger, part humiliation. He could at least have been civil. The Brothers Grim reputation was well earned. At least it was in his case. Nick might be nice, but Adam was clearly unpleasant enough for both of them.

Just before the glass doors swooshed shut behind her, she heard him say, 'No one important, Geraldine, no. Please don't worry.'

* * *

When she finally got back home again, just before eight, there was a car parked outside the bungalow that she didn't recognise. Deciding that the last thing she needed was a run-in with another reporter, Clara drove straight past it, glancing in as she passed and noticing a smartly dressed blonde talking on her phone. She may well have just stopped to answer a call, but Clara decided not to take the chance. If she was a reporter, she was going to have a very long wait.

After a moment of indecision, Clara headed back towards her sister's instead. Rosanna and Ed lived in a three -bedroom detached house in Swanage, not far from the family home where they'd grown up and where their parents still lived. It wasn't far and it would be good to have a catch-up in person.

To her very great relief, Rosanna was in and pleased to see her.

'How's it going, honey? Hmmm, not well, I can see. Come in. Will you be needing a restorative glass of Prosecco or maybe cake? I've got both. Or is it more serious than that?'

'That's the best offer I've had all day,' Clara said, breathing in the scents of the familiar house as she stepped into the hall: Rosanna's Jimmy Choo signature scent, the faint mustiness of outside coats on a row of hooks and coffee wafting through from somewhere.

'Is it all right to bring Foxy in? Where is everyone?'

'Of course it's all right.' Rosanna ushered them into the bright family kitchen. 'Ed's still in Scotland and the kids are both on sleepovers. I was just watching back episodes of *Loose Women* with a very large tub of caramel popcorn. But I'd much rather talk to you.' She paced around her kitchen as she spoke, putting cups in the dishwasher, fiddling around with her all-singing, all-dancing coffee machine. Rosanna could never keep still for long. Which was probably how she managed to stay reed thin, Clara had often thought, despite the amount of junk food she ate. Or maybe it was just that the two sisters were completely different. They both had conkerbrown hair and dark eyes, but that was where the resemblance ended.

Rosanna took after their mother, who was tall and willowy, and Clara took after their father, who wasn't. Dad, bless him, had given up the battle to stay slim and regularly patted his round tummy and told everyone that a little of what you fancied never hurt anyone.

'The Prosecco's in the fridge,' Rosanna said. 'Pour me a glass while you're at it. I'm alternating with coffee. Are you hungry? I've got some olives in the fridge too and some cheese. How about the hound? Does she need a drink?'

'Yes please.' Clara retrieved the Prosecco and the olives, noticing as she did so a new fridge magnet, which said, in black italics, *Did I just roll my eyes out loud?* That summed Rosanna up, she thought, amused, as she sat at the oblong oak table, pleased to be in the comforting ebb and flow of her sister's chatter.

Rosanna made coffee and filled up a bowl of water for Foxy. Then she came across to the table, pulled out a chair and sat down.

'So... did you get any further with tracking down the dipstick who put up that video?'

'No not yet.' Clara looked into her sister's concerned brown eyes and sighed. 'It's been a bit of a day.'

'I can imagine. Oh, sweetheart. What a horrible thing to happen when your boss is away. Life is never simple, is it? Have a piece of Battenberg – Sophie made it in Home Economics. It's surprisingly good.

Clara peeled off a small square of marzipan and popped it in her mouth and felt marginally better as its sweetness melted on her tongue.

Foxy, smelling the sugar, put a paw on her knee.

'I just had a totally unnecessary argument with someone,'

Clara explained.

'Not Will?'

'No – I haven't spoken to him yet.'

She told Rosanna about Adam Greenwood and her sister looked suitably outraged.

'What a pompous prat. Did you say he was the owner too?'

'Yes. He and his brother bought it about five years ago, from what I can gather, and they both live and work there, but neither of them have partners apparently. At least not live-in ones. I only went round to introduce myself. I wish I hadn't. I thought Mr B was overreacting when he said that the Manor House were antagonistic towards the Bluebell, but I'm not so sure now.' She paused. 'Funnily enough I had a phone call from Adam Greenwood once before about some long-term booking he was accusing us of pinching. I didn't think anything much of it at the time. I put it down to him having a bad day, but he did seem unreasonably cross. Maybe they are struggling. From what I saw today, the place could certainly do with some money being spent on it – it's quite shabby – and I don't mean in a shabby-chic kind of way.'

'It doesn't sound as though they have a surplus of staff either if the owners are doing more than one job.'

'Exactly. Maybe Mr B had a point about them being behind the YouTube video.'

Rosanna raised her eyebrows. 'Have you decided to rule out Will?'

'Not entirely, I guess. I am going to speak to him, but I can't believe he's behind this. Like I said this morning. Was it really only this morning? That seems like a million years ago.'

'Yes, I must admit I was surprised to see you, although I'm really glad you're here.'

Clara popped an olive into her mouth and Rosanna steepled her hands.

'So who else has a good reason to want to discredit the hotel? Have you upset anyone lately?' she teased.

'Apart from Arnold – no, I don't think so. We haven't even had any dissatisfied customers, as far as I know. The worst review we've ever had on TripAdvisor was from someone who thought their poached egg was on the hard side.' Clara hesitated. 'Besides, I'm no techie, but it has to be someone who had access to the video, which narrows it down to Arnold – I'm pretty sure it wasn't him – and the cameraman. I haven't managed to get hold of him yet. He's in Antigua with Arnold's ex. She ran off with him after the event apparently. Note to self: big romantic gestures can backfire badly. Poor chap.'

'He's probably better off without her.' Rosanna sipped her wine. 'What happened to the chocolates?'

'I'm assuming they ate them. Arnold certainly didn't have them strapped to his back when we were in A&E.'

'What, all of them?! He should have donated them to you by the sound of it.'

'Well he didn't. Perhaps he donated them to the paramedics in the ambulance. A thank you for wasting their time.'

'So the cameraman could have plastered that video all over YouTube and then legged it abroad.'

'Yes, I suppose he could. It's a bit mean though, isn't it – absconding with a man's girlfriend and publicly humiliating him too. And why drag us into it? Talk about biting the hand that feeds you.'

'Yes, that does sound unlikely.'

Rosanna got up and paced around her kitchen, which didn't take long as, like her, it was long and thin. The table was in an alcove, where an old pantry had once been. The house was ex-council, solidly built in a different era. Ed and Rosanna had done loads to it since they'd bought it and because it was on a corner plot it had a big garden too that was great for the kids and also well used for family gatherings.

'How did you come across that video anyway?' Clara asked her. 'Was it completely random?'

'It was. Yes. Like I said, I'd been watching loads of stuff on YouTube and it popped up, possibly because it's local to here – I don't know how the algorithms work. Have they asked YouTube to take it down yet? That must be a bit of a palaver.'

'The solicitor has it in hand apparently.'

Rosanna waved a bottle of Prosecco at her from the fridge. 'Do you want a top-up? You can stay over if you like? Save driving? We're all at Mum's tomorrow for lunch, aren't we?'

'Thanks. And yes, I know. But I think I'd better go home. I want to nip in to work in the morning just to give Phil a hand until things calm down a bit.'

'Is that a step tracker?' Rosanna asked, gesturing to her wrist. 'I haven't seen that before. Are you on a new fitness regime?'

'When am I not?' She sighed.

'You don't need to be. You always look stunning.'

'That's got more to do with the art of disguise. Heels and flattering jackets. Every pound shows. What I would give for three more inches of height.'

'I'll swap you three inches of my height for three inches of your cleavage,' Rosanna said and they both smiled. It was a familiar conversation.

Clara rolled back her sleeve to reveal the plum-coloured strap. 'And yes it is a step tracker. It's a FunFit. I got it cheap on Wish.com. The reviews said it was as good as the market leader, although I have my doubts.'

'It looks the part. What does it do?'

'It counts steps walked and calories burned. It claims to calculate your average heart rate and tell you how well you've slept.'

'Impressive. Does it actually do all that?'

Clara glanced at the screen. 'Well, yes, but it's not very accurate. Let's say it errs on the side of optimism. It reckons I've walked 283 steps since I've been sitting at this table and burnt twenty-five calories. That sounds unlikely, doesn't it?'

'Sadly it does,' Rosanna agreed. 'So it's pretty rubbish then.'

'It is, but it makes me laugh. The reports are hilarious. It's linked to my phone. I'll show you.' Clara hooked out her mobile. 'This is last week's: I got a score of 31. It says: "Walking is a static activity of which one must do more speed if one hopes to achieve fun, fitness and health wise. Very bad, no good movement. Your static activity fitness improvement has not been health wise. Try must harder.'

When they'd stopped laughing, Rosanna asked for a closer look at the reports and Clara handed over her phone.

'Did you read their privacy statement? "If you leak the password you may lose your personality." Do you think they mean identity?'

Clara snorted again. It felt good to laugh. 'I guess you get what you pay for. It only cost £7.50. I think the market leader's about £120.'

'I might get one for Sophie's birthday. It's got to be worth it just for the entertainment factor.'

'My sentiments exactly,' Clara yawned. 'I'd better get home, darling. Thanks so much for the chat.' As she spoke, Foxy put her sharp snout on her knee and looked up at her reproachfully. Flaming heck, she hadn't fed her either. How had she managed to forget that?

At the front door, they hugged and Clara felt the chill night air creep round her shoulders. She didn't realise it had got so late. Phoning Will would have to wait until tomorrow. At least that reporter should have left by now.

7

To Clara's relief, the reporter had gone and, to her surprise, she slept really well too. This was probably due to sheer emotional exhaustion, she thought, although her FunFit didn't agree. Her sleep report on the front screen of her phone was headed up with the word, *Bad*, which was highlighted in red.

```
Your indicators, this night warning, is less
than ideal. Health wise sleep. No no no. Bad.
```

She had overslept though, even for a Sunday. It was just after half eight. She opened YouTube to check whether they had taken down the video and discovered it was gone. Blimey, that was efficient. She wondered if that had been Kate's solicitor's influence or whether they had simply decided to respond to the 'inappropriate content' flags. Or maybe whoever had put it up there had had second thoughts and decided to remove it themselves.

There was also an email from Kate asking how it was going and saying she would phone later for a catch-up. Poor Kate. She had enough on her plate, sorting out things with her mother.

There had been some more complications with the divorce apparently and her mother's health issues weren't helping. Clara was keen to spare her from work hassle as well.

While she had her phone in her hand, she searched Google using various key words that included: Lighthouse, Milk Tray, and Funny Proposals. To her huge relief, she couldn't find any trace of the video. Which didn't mean it was no longer online, of course, but was definitely a good sign.

A WhatsApp message pinged through from Rosanna which simply said:

Chin up, Sis. Don't let the b******s grind you down. Laters. xx

Clara felt warmed – it was good to have such a supportive family around her – they got together for a roast at least one Sunday a month, Mum, Dad, Rosanna, Ed and the kids and sometimes one or the other of her maternal grandparents, Thelma and Eric Price. Her father's parents had both died within months of each other two years earlier, but Mum's parents had the longevity gene. They also had a very long marriage – fifty-seven years – but this was currently under threat because, to the rest of the family's great distress, they had recently separated from each other.

Five and a half months ago, Grandad Eric had what had once been known as a midlife crisis, but, at seventy-seven, he'd had it quite late. He had run off with his whist partner, Mary, who'd been eleven years Thelma's junior. After barely a fortnight, he'd realised he'd made a huge mistake and had tried to come back, but Gran, who was still smarting from hurt and humiliation, had told him he wasn't welcome.

Rosanna had been firmly in Gran's corner and had egged her on at every turn. Rosanna could be quite unforgiving, but their mother had felt he'd been punished enough. She'd hated the thought of her parents splitting up after fifty-seven years of marriage. The situation was still in limbo. Grandad was living with his brother Jim and his wife, Elsie, in Weymouth. Gran was in the family home in Church Knowle, which was twenty minutes or so to the west of Swanage.

Opinion was divided on whether this separation was temporary or permanent. Mum thought it was temporary. Rosanna thought it might be permanent. Clara was hoping and praying that Mum was right.

Today they were all meeting at Mum and Dad's, but fortunately lunches never began until two, so there was time for her to nip into work first.

She leaped out of bed and tugged on an old T-shirt that was really due for the wash and her dog-walking jeggings. She would give Foxy a good long walk to make up for yesterday. One good thing about having a dog to look after was that she was doing tonnes of exercise. Will had been right. She had lost weight. She'd lost half a stone since she'd seen him, and a few more pounds since she'd had Foxy and this certainly wasn't because she'd reined in on the biscuits.

The FunFit bracelet might be wildly inaccurate as far as step counting was concerned, but at least she could tell whether she was going up or down. That was helpful.

She wasn't slender like Rosanna, but she couldn't be described as chunky either. Ten pounds was a lot when you were only five foot four.

* * *

Clara was on the coast path with a delighted 'full of beans' Foxy by nine. The bungalow, like the Bluebell, had a garden that backed onto it and a gate that gave direct access.

It was a bright sunny morning and a brisk southwesterly breeze skittered along the coast path, sending waves ripping through the long grass on the cliffs that echoed the real ones on the ocean far below. As she walked, Clara breathed in the mixed smells of ozone and the sweet coconut scent of flowering gorse. She didn't think she would ever get tired of this view, the vast sky, the endless sea and the greens and browns and olives and gold of the surrounding countryside. Some of the cultivated fields she could see had strips along the edges scattered with wild flowers. There were the bright splashes of poppies, the blues of cornflowers and the yellow of sunflowers. It was breathtaking and despite the emotional hangover of the previous day it was impossible not to feel uplifted.

She met a handful of other walkers, some of them with dogs, some with backpacks, and she spent a pleasant half an hour walking, exchanging chit-chat with strangers about what a glorious July they were having and wasn't it good that for once the school summer holidays were living up to their name, and how much difference a bit of sunshine made.

She felt relaxed as she approached the back gate of the bungalow once more. She whistled to Foxy, who bounded up, wagging her tail, which wriggled the whole of her red gold body. She hadn't had her breakfast yet, which, Clara had recently discovered, was by far the best way to get her to come back quickly. Foxy loved chasing rabbits and seagulls and having a full belly made her selectively deaf, but if she was walked before she was fed, she became far more obedient.

Clara ushered her in through the back gate and was about to follow her when she glimpsed the movement of a red car pulling up at the front of the bungalow. Now that was a coincidence. That reporter had been in a red car too. Could she possibly be back?

As Clara pondered what to do, she heard the slam of a door and then she glimpsed a blonde head. Definitely not a coincidence then and she was not in the mood to talk to another reporter. For one thing, she didn't have time. For another, she hadn't had coffee, which was essential if she was to have a sensible conversation. Also, she hadn't yet showered or put on any make-up and she was wearing old jeggings with, she suddenly realised in horror, the T-shirt that, in her haste, she must have put on inside out. Why hadn't any of those friendly dog walkers told her she was wearing her top inside out? Flaming heck. It was obvious now she'd spotted it. It was also on back to front. There was a label sticking out under her nose.

Clara could see the reporter through the front window. She had just gone up the front path, now she rang the bell, which could be heard jangling through the house. Hopefully she'd go away when she got no answer.

No such luck. Now she was bending, presumably to look through the letter box. Clearly she was the persistent type, which Clara supposed should be obvious since she'd been here last night too. And now Clara's car was in the drive, which meant someone was definitely in.

It was unlikely that she'd come round the back. But just in case she did, Clara considered her options. She could nip back out onto the coast path and mingle with the other dog walkers. Not her preferred option now she knew about the T-shirt. Or she could hide behind the shed. Making a split-second decision, she chose the shed. It was in a corner of the garden and there wasn't a lot of room between it and the back fence so it was quite a snug fit. But Foxy was less likely to worry if she was still in the garden.

The little dog was currently sniffing around the dahlias,

unaware, as far as Clara could tell, that they even had a visitor. She was a useless guard dog. She hardly ever barked. Thank heaven for small mercies, Clara thought. But then the side gate squeaked as someone pushed it open. Flaming heck, the reporter was coming round the back.

From her vantage point, squashed between shed and fence, Clara heard a voice say, 'Oh hello, cutie pie? You all on your own then?'

Clara didn't have to see Foxy to know what she'd be doing. Wagging her tail frantically and greeting this interesting new person as a long-lost friend. That's what she did with everyone she met.

'Where's your owner then? Is she about? Where's she gone?'

Clara closed her eyes. Suddenly she had an awful sense of premonition. Not because she was under any misconception that Foxy understood English, but she did understand games and Clara and her niece and nephew had played hide-and-seek with her a few times.

Unfortunately, she was right. Ten seconds later, a pleased Foxy was leading the unwanted visitor towards the shed. Her tail wagged joyfully as she spotted Clara jammed into her hiding place and the game was up.

There was nothing else to do, apart from step out from the narrow space, brush an accumulation of mildew and dirt and cobwebs from the front of her inside-out, back to front T-shirt and say the first thing that came into her head, which was, 'Terrible mildew problem I'm having with this shed.'

The woman, who was immaculately turned out – of course she was – looked slightly startled, which wasn't altogether surprising, Clara decided, thinking quickly and concluding that attack was the best form of defence

'Who are you? You do realise you're trespassing. This is private property.'

'I do apologise.'

Clara hadn't been expecting this. She was pretty sure that journalists regularly trespassed and never apologised – they probably weren't averse to hiding behind sheds either.

'What do you want?' she pressed.

'My name's Anastasia Williams. I'm looking for a Clara King. Would that be you?'

'I'm her gardener,' Clara said, deciding that lying was probably in her best interests for now. She had never heard of an Anastasia Williams and certainly didn't know why she was looking for her. 'She's away. I can give her a message if you like. But she won't be back for ten days. She's in Tenerife.' Where had that come from? She'd never even been to Tenerife.

'I see. Of course. Yes, I would be grateful if you could give her a message. Thank you. Maybe I could leave you my card.'

Clara nodded sternly. The woman didn't sound like a reporter. In fact, now the video had gone and there was no story to speak of any more, she was beginning to doubt her own assumption that she even was a reporter. She decided it wasn't worth taking the risk. Besides, now she was in character she was quite enjoying playing the part of a grumpy gardener. It was a pity she didn't have a pair of secateurs she could snip the air with.

Anastasia Williams rummaged in her bag and pulled out a white business card, which contrasted sharply with her scarlet fingernails, and handed it over. Clara caught a waft of her scent: something flowery but also faintly exotic and definitely out of a hotel manager's price range.

Apart from her name and a mobile phone number, the card was blank. Clara turned it over and saw it had the words, Happy

Ever After, printed on the back in gold, alongside a small red heart. It didn't look much like a reporter's card either.

'What shall I tell Miss King it's about?' she said in the haughtiest voice she could muster.

'It's confidential. But thank you.' The woman smiled. She had scarlet lips too and were those eyelash extensions? She looked more like a beauty therapist than a reporter and what was that Happy Ever After line about?

Clara was desperately curious now, but there was no way she was going to backtrack and admit she had been lying through her teeth.

'I'll make sure she gets the card. Is it urgent?'

'Not at all,' Anastasia said. 'I was just passing.'

Well, that was a lie – no way had she just been passing both last night and this morning. But Clara wasn't about to contradict her. Especially as it looked as though she was about to leave.

'I'm actually on holiday for the next fortnight, so there's no rush,' Anastasia added. Then, with a swift goodbye to Foxy – she clearly liked dogs – she was gone.

Clara fled with relief into the house. 'Well, that was a narrow escape,' she said. 'No thanks to you, you little traitor.

An unrepentant Foxy pounced on her breakfast and devoured it. Clara peered out of the window to make sure the car had gone and then she googled Anastasia Williams and found a photograph of a black American politician by the same name but nothing that shed any light on her unwanted visitor's identity. She showered thoughtfully and dressed for work. She would just have to wait until Ms Williams was back from holiday.

* * *

While she was driving into work, her phone rang and she saw on her Bluetooth screen that the call was from Rob Davidson, the cameraman, in response to her message.

She didn't answer it. The signal was too up and down in the Purbecks to guarantee a good reception. It would be better to call him when she was stationary.

So, having conferred briefly with Keith, who did Sunday reception until ten, as well as nights, and learning that everything had quietened down, she phoned Rob Davidson back and discovered he was back in the country, having had a very nice break at his brother's Antigua beach house apparently. He didn't say he'd been there with Maureen at first and Clara decided not to mention it straightaway either. At least not until she had found out what she wanted to know, which was how his video had found its way on to YouTube.

'I didn't put it on YouTube,' he'd said, sounding slightly outraged at such a suggestion.

After some coercion from Clara, he'd gone on to confess that he had in fact put it on Twitter.

'But I wasn't doing anything unprofessional. There was nothing on that footage that could have identified the Bluebell Cliff. Or the climber, come to that. It was just a bit of fun.'

'Apart from his face?' Clara pointed out.

'You'd only recognise him if you knew him. And you couldn't even see the hotel. I certainly didn't put the hotel name on it.' His voice was puffed up with righteous indignation.

'Someone did and they would have needed the original video in order to edit it,' she pressed him. Mr B, who was a geek, had been pretty categorical that this was the only way it could have been done.

Rob Davidson hesitated. Eventually, he told her that he'd been approached by a bloke in The Anchor.

'He asked me if I'd send him the original video. I didn't see the harm. He bought me a drink.'

I bet he did, Clara thought. 'How did he know about it in the first place?'

'I dunno. He didn't say. Maybe he saw it on my Twitter account. I've got 681 followers.' For a few seconds, all she could hear was his breathing. He clearly wasn't going to elaborate.

'What did this bloke look like?' she pressed.

'He was tanned. Short hair. Ordinary.'

The tanned bit brought Adam Greenwood to mind, but then probably most people who drank in The Anchor in this gorgeous summer weather would be tanned. The short hair probably also ruled out Will, his had grown, but he could have tied it back.

'Was he tall or short? Fair or dark?' she tried to keep the impatience out of her voice.

'I wasn't looking that closely. Tall, I suppose.'

'So would you recognise him again?'

'I don't think so. Look, I didn't mean any harm. It was all just a bit of fun. A bit of banter.'

'Would you be able to point him out to me if I came to The Anchor with you?'

'I'm not sure. To be honest, it's all a bit hazy. I'd had a few drinks. It would probably be a waste of time. Your time, I mean. It's a pointless exercise.'

It was clear where his loyalties lay and they weren't with her. His tone of voice had become brusquer as the conversation had progressed.

Clara let the silence hang between them and, a few moments later, he said, 'I've taken it off Twitter. I've done everything I can do. And, as you said yourself, it's not on YouTube any more, so there's not really any harm been done, has there?'

If they'd been face to face, she'd have throttled him. Fortunately for him, they weren't.

'You will still recommend me on your website though, won't you?' For the first time, he came close to being obsequious.

'No, Rob, we won't be recommending you on our website any more. Arnold Fairweather wasn't just your client, he was ours too. He was heartbroken – understandably – to hear that you'd absconded with his lady friend. That was completely inappropriate. At The Bluebell Cliff Hotel, we pride ourselves on discretion and professionalism at all times.' She paused to let this sink in. 'We're going to have to terminate your agreement and we will also have to cancel any forthcoming bookings. I'll send you an email to follow. If you have any issues when you've read it, do feel free to contact your solicitor.'

8

Thank goodness for families, Clara thought for the second time in twenty-four hours as she and Foxy arrived at her parents for lunch at just before two.

She thought about phoning Will. Her parents only lived about ten minutes from his house. Perhaps she should call round afterwards and see him, rather than phone. She was loath to get in touch with him at all, but she needed to definitely rule him out of being the man behind the leaked video.

Kate had said when they'd spoken earlier that she had no idea why anyone would want to damage the hotel's reputation. Maybe that hadn't been their intention. Maybe it really was just a silly prank that had got out of hand. Kate had sounded upbeat and positive and had said again that at least the video was no longer available. She had agreed with Clara that it was too quick for YouTube to have removed it. Whoever had uploaded it must have had second thoughts and taken it down themselves. But it couldn't do any more damage, if in fact it had done any at all, and that, unless there were any further developments, it might be better to put the whole thing behind them.

Clara had agreed with her, but in her heart she wasn't so sure. Someone had had a deliberate go at the hotel, either to get at Kate or to get at her. That hadn't been accidental.

'How are you, love?' It was her father who came to the door to let her and Foxy in, not Mum, who she knew would be creating a banquet in the kitchen.

Before she could reply or even get over the threshold, Dad was stampeded out of the way by Sophie and Tom, her beloved niece and nephew, both of whom adored her and had come racing to the front door.

Clara could see her father smiling broadly just behind them.

'Hi Dad, is that a new shirt? Hi Sophie, I loved your Battenberg. Tom, you've got taller.'

'I know,' Tom said proudly. 'And my feet have grown. I've got new shoes.'

'He's always getting new shoes,' huffed Sophie. 'It's not fair. Hello Foxy? Is it OK if Foxy sits on the sofa with me, Grandad?'

'No, it's not. Sofas are for humans not for dogs. Let your Auntie Clara in for goodness' sake.'

Clara glimpsed Rosanna chatting to their mother through the connecting door between the lounge and the kitchen, where Ed was pouring drinks.

The house smelled gloriously of roast beef and garlic and herb stuffing, Mum's speciality. Even in the height of summer, Mum stuck to tradition and insisted on cooking a full roast on a Sunday lunchtime.

Clara closed her eyes and breathed it all blissfully in. Just for an hour or two, she thought, she could let go of all the trials and tribulations of the week and let the warmth of her family wrap around her.

Five minutes later, she was ensconced on the squashy red

corner sofa. So was Foxy, she noticed. The little dog had sneaked up between Sophie and Tom and Tom was stroking her head. Dad, back in his armchair, was turning a blind eye, as he so often did.

The talk was of summer camp and Sophie's violin lessons.

'She's getting on really well,' Rosanna said, coming in to tell them dinner would be ready in ten minutes and did everyone want Yorkshire pudding.

'She's not,' Tom said. 'I have to wear earplugs.'

'I had to wear earplugs when you learned the piano,' Sophie countered. 'I still do.'

'That's because it's out of tune,' Tom said.

'You're the one that's out of tune.'

'Stop it you two,' Ed said, coming in behind them. 'Hello, Clara love. How are you?'

She got up to kiss her brother-in-law on both cheeks. He had his sleeves rolled up and he smelled of aftershave and Blackthorn cider and the steamy warmth of the kitchen.

'Is that a new Radley, Auntie Clara?' Sophie asked, suddenly spotting her bag over her shoulder.

'Yes, do you like it?' Clara patted the small cream and blue multiway, which depicted a seaside scene of a deckchair and a bright yellow sun.

'It's really cool.'

Foxy let out a small whine.

'I thought I told you not to let that dog up there,' Dad said in mock exasperation from his chair.

'She's not touching the sofa, Grandad, she's only touching our laps,' Sophie defended. 'Isn't she, Tom?'

'Yep,' Tom said. Brother and sister were always a united front when anyone prodded them from the outside.

'Well, everyone can get off the sofa in a minute,' Rosanna

announced from the doorway. 'We're just about to dish up. Dad, can you come and carve please?'

'No Gran or Grandad?' Clara mouthed to Rosanna as she went through to the kitchen.

Rosanna shook her head and Clara didn't push it. No doubt she would get the full story later.

The old oak table in the kitchen, which was big enough to seat ten, had been owned by her parents for as long as Clara could remember. It was scratched and faded with age and it had hosted Christmases, birthdays and anniversary meals, children's parties and once even a wake.

She couldn't imagine life without regular meals at this table. She and Rosanna had once joked that their parents would have to stipulate in their will that it was sawn in half because they'd never be able to decide who should inherit it.

That wasn't true now, of course, Clara thought. It would go to Rosanna. What on earth was she going to do with a table for ten!

She switched off her thoughts and dragged her attention back to the room as everyone jostled to get into their seats.

For the first few moments of dinner, there was silence as everyone concentrated on the business of eating and the dishing out of home-made horseradish sauce and mint sauce, not because you had mint sauce with beef, any more than you had garlic and herb stuffing with it, but because Dad liked it with everything. Then the Sunday conversations began. The same conversations they had every time, with only minor variations.

'This is a good cut of beef, Angie.' That was from Ed.

'Where did you get these little carrots from, they're delicious.' That was from Rosanna.

'Great roasties, love.' That was from Dad.

Clara let it all wash over her. The clatter of cutlery, the buzz of conversation. It was like balm after the last few days. Sooner or later, though, she knew the conversation would turn to other subjects. They would hone in on individual members of the family.

It could be Dad's cars. Cars were his hobby – he was either selling a car or planning to buy a new one. At the moment he was planning to buy a new one. It took him months of research before he decided on make, model and year based on blogs like Honest John. Then he would scour the country via eBay for the best possible bargain.

Or they would talk about Ed's travels and the people he met. Last month, he'd told them about a 'would-be' illegal immigrant who'd tried to break into the back of his truck in the middle of the night when he was parked up in a service station just outside Calais.

'How desperate people had to be to flee their homes in search of a better life,' he'd added at the time and they'd all agreed that they had so much to be thankful for.

Or they would talk about Mum's latest Granny-isms, which was what Sophie and Tom called Angie's habit of mixing up words. They weren't spoonerisms exactly, but they were almost as funny. She regularly called iPads, eye patches and smartphones, smart gnomes, much to the glee of Sophie and Tom, who delighted in putting her right.

'You knew what I meant though, didn't you,' she would tell them, laughing and refusing to change her spin on whatever new word she had made up.

Her best one to date was when she'd told them all that she'd glimpsed the NASA International Play Station go over their house one starlit night.

No one was ever letting her forget that one, so these days she deliberately hammed it up and Clara was never sure when she was messing about or had genuinely got a name wrong.

It was only necessary to tune in occasionally, Clara thought, wondering whether to resist the last roast potato so she could fit in dessert, which was bound to be a crumble of some sort, hopefully blackberry and apple as it was a bumper year for both. But then, if she had dessert, she should probably forgo biscuits for a whole week of coffee breaks, because even walking Foxy every day couldn't offset dessert too often.

It was blackberry and apple, with a choice of custard or cream – make that two weeks of no biscuits.

'I'd really like another Lexus,' Dad was saying, 'but they only make hybrids now. I'm thinking of a SsangYong. What do you think, Ed?'

'I don't know much about them, to be honest. Are they Japanese?'

'Is it OK to take Foxy in the garden, Auntie Clara?' Tom asked.

'Yes, love.'

Then she was clearing plates from the table and turning the custard off on the hob, which had been kept hot in case anyone wanted seconds, and they were all eating home-made biscuits with the coffee – her mother rarely bought anything in a packet, even biscuits. And then finally, sometime around four, when Tom and Sophie were outside with Foxy in the rambling garden, the spotlight was turned on to Clara.

'You're looking well, love,' Dad remarked. 'You've got a real glow to your skin. Looking after that dog's obviously doing you good.'

'It's all the walking and fresh air,' she told him happily. 'I don't think I've ever been so fit.'

'How's your love life?' Mum asked. 'Have you met anyone nice lately?'

'No,' Clara said, not missing the look Mum exchanged with Rosanna. What were they up to? Please don't let it be a blind date

– they had tried that once before. They had invited this random guy round after one of the Sunday lunches who was apparently thinking of changing career from office work to catering and needed some advice. He'd been one of the most boring and earnest-looking men that Clara had ever met and it had taken her nearly an hour to get away from him.

To distract them from her non-existent love life, she told everyone about what Mr B had started calling Lighthousegate and the atmosphere became more serious.

'Do you really think Will would do something like that?' Her mother tilted her head on one side like a sparrow and looked troubled. 'I don't see what he'd have to gain.'

'I had upset him. He might have been cross with me.'

'But why have a pop at the hotel?' said Ed, who was ever rational. 'And, as you say, he'd have needed the video.'

Rosanna agreed. 'It sounds more premeditated than that, doesn't it, honey.' She looked at Clara. 'And you were ninety-nine per cent sure it wasn't him.'

'I still am.'

'Is there a chance of tracking down the photographer he sold it to?' her father asked. He's the key to all this, isn't he?'

'He wasn't keen on talking to me about that. He gave me the vaguest of descriptions. But then he clammed up and refused to say any more about it. He was fairly drunk anyway, from what I can gather. Our chef thinks the Manor House, which is our nearest competitor, has an axe to grind. There have been harsh words exchanged, but the trouble with Mr B is that he's a conspiracy theorist. He thinks everyone has an axe to grind.'

'Is he the one who won't tell anybody his name because he's so paranoid about identity theft?' Ed asked.

'The very same.'

'He may be on to something there,' Dad said. 'You can't steal something if you don't know it's there.'

'Do you know his name?' Rosanna asked.

'Yes, but if I told you, I'd have to kill you.' Everyone laughed and the mood lightened. 'My boss thinks it was a prank and that whoever did it had second thoughts when it started getting a lot of views. She may well be right.'

'The thing is,' Ed said, 'If someone does have a vendetta against the hotel, they're not going to leave it there, are they? They'll be up to other mischief, too. So you'll soon know the score.'

Clara nodded. The same thought had crossed her mind, but she was trying not to think about it.

'To coin one of Gran's expressions,' she said, 'I think it might be a case of least said, soonest mended. Where is Gran anyway? I thought you said she'd be here today.'

'Your grandmother had a date,' their mother said and her face closed down a little. 'They were going on some coach trip to a retail outlet apparently. She missed my roast dinner for that, would you believe?'

'Go Gran,' Rosanna did a double thumbs up. 'It's about time she stopped mooching about over Grandad's defection and got on with her life.' She turned towards Clara with a slightly defiant look on her face. 'Don't you think so, honey?'

Clara nodded, but she'd noticed the look that passed between her parents. Mum's voice may have been light, but there had been a flicker of pain in her eyes. Clara knew Mum did not approve of her ageing mother going on dates – however much Rosanna, who was of the opinion that what was good for the gander was good for the goose, was encouraging it.

Clara wasn't sure if Gran was quite as enamoured with the dates idea as Rosanna was either, but their grandmother wasn't the type of lady to be pressured into doing something she didn't want to do. So perhaps she was up for a diversion.

She resolved to pay Gran a visit. Since she had moved into Kate's bungalow she hadn't seen as much of her. It would be good to see her on her own. Find out how she was really – beneath the bravado.

After the mention of Gran, there had been an awkward silence. But now their mother leapt in to fill it.

'If you ask me, the pair of them need their heads banging together,' she said. 'All this nonsense at their ages.'

The back door burst open.

'Would anyone like a toffee cop up?' Mum asked, glancing at Tom, who had just come in from the garden and was stamping his feet on the mat.

'It's a *coffee top-up*,' he shouted in delight.

'Is it? What did I say?' She winked at him.

There was laughter as she got up to see to it.

When she came back to the table, she glanced at Clara. 'I've got something for you, darling.' She looked cheerful again now they'd moved off the subject of Gran. 'It's in the pantry. Your sister recommended it, but I can't get on with it. It's called George Formby.'

Clara blinked. She was pretty sure her mother didn't have a dead comedian with a ukulele hanging out in the pantry. Hopefully she was talking about a George Foreman grill.

It turned out she was. By the time Clara finally set off for home with the grill in a carrier bag, it was almost six. She forced herself to drive past Will's only to discover that his car wasn't outside and there were no signs of activity inside. He must have gone out for the evening. She breathed a sigh of relief. Interrogating Will would have to wait until another day.

9

The next week passed without any more dramas. The dog display team were model guests. Clara had never seen such well-behaved dogs. She got used to seeing one or another of the huge black and tan German shepherds padding silently about the hotel – the four canine visitors were allowed everywhere except the restaurant and the kitchen. Foxy, who was a lot smaller than they were, had been wary at first and had shot into her basket under Clara's desk the first time she'd met one, but she'd soon settled down when she'd realised they were no threat.

There were no more repercussions from Lighthousegate. There had been no cancellations because of it. In fact, they were actually up on enquiries from people who wanted to book the lighthouse, but aside from that cheeky reporter, no one else had mentioned wanting to climb up or down it.

She was doing some paperwork in the back office on Friday afternoon, relieved that another week was nearly over because this was her weekend off, when Zoe popped her head round the door.

'You have a visitor. He said he doesn't have an appointment.

He just called on spec. Adam Greenwood?' She made a face that was half grimace, half enquiry. 'What do you suppose he wants?'

'I don't know. Did he say?' Clara felt her hackles rise. She might have known the peace was too good to last.

Zoe shook her head. 'Do you want me to send him in or will you come out?'

'I'll come out.' She hesitated. Maybe that was a bad idea. She didn't want another fiery exchange with Adam in front of Zoe. 'No, second thoughts, send him in here.'

'Would you like me to bring you in some coffee?' Zoe looked hopeful. 'He's quite hot, isn't he? Not to mention charming. I thought he was the nasty one of the Brothers Grim.'

'That's not how I remember him. No, don't bring any coffee. He won't be here very long.' She hoped!

The office wasn't that small, but Adam Greenwood filled it. He had to duck his head slightly to come through the doorway. She hadn't remembered him being that tall either. Maybe it was just seeing someone out of context.

She stood up as he came in, glad she had her heels on, and he smiled. Despite her decision to dislike him, she felt warmed. She wouldn't have gone as far as to say charming, but he certainly seemed more human. Those black eyes were softer, more Cadbury's Dark Milk than Bournville, and the sculpted cheekbones less haughty.

'This is a surprise. Please take a seat.' She gestured to the swivel chair at the other desk. He'd be easier to deal with sitting down. Never had she felt more disadvantaged by her lack of height.

'Thanks.' He sat down.

She let the silence hang. Clara knew the power of silence.

He was the first to break it. He cleared his throat. She awarded herself a bonus point. Then another one when he actually spoke and said, 'I think I owe you an apology.'

That was the last thing she'd been expecting.

'Oh?'

'Yes.' He leaned forward slightly in his chair. 'When you called at the hotel last week, I was rude. I was pretty stressed. Nick, my brother, had been taken ill and we'd got a new chef covering and there was too much going on.' He gave her that disarming smile again. 'I'm not very good at multitasking.'

She relented. 'I hope your brother is feeling better now?'

'He is a little better. Thank you. He has an ongoing chronic condition. It isn't life-threatening, but it can be debilitating.'

There was another small silence.

Adam broke it again. 'I seem to remember I was very rude about your chef.'

She inclined her head. She resisted the urge to say that actually a lot of the things he'd said about Mr B were spot on. She wasn't going to let him off the hook that easily.

'That was why you came round?' he added. 'To talk about the allegations your chef had made?'

'Partly,' Clara said, deciding that as he was being so gracious then she could afford to be too. 'I also wanted to introduce myself properly. To tell you what the Bluebell Cliff does. To reassure you that there doesn't need to be any bad feeling between us. There will be times when we can't take a booking and you can – we could pass on business. It would be so much better if we could work together rather than against each other. There's an awful lot that we do here that you probably wouldn't want to do.'

'We don't have the same facilities that you do,' he agreed. 'We don't, for example, have a lighthouse that people may want to abseil down – or indeed climb up.'

So he did know about that. His face was deadpan. She

couldn't tell what he was thinking. Was he having a dig or was he being sympathetic?

'How did you know about that?'

'News travels fast.'

'But it was nothing to do with you?' The words slipped out before she could censor them, but she immediately wished she had.

His eyes had widened a little. Or had the pupils just got blacker? Was that anger? He sure as hell wasn't smiling any more. Now he was shaking his head and standing up.

'I came round here in good faith. I did NOT come round here to have more petty accusations slung in my direction.' The veneer of charm had gone. For a moment, there had been pure venom in his voice. Mind you, she couldn't really blame him. She had, to all intents and purposes, just accused him of libel – was it libel when it involved a video? – and after he'd come round cap in hand and apologised for being abrupt with her.

Shit. She stood up too. 'Mr Greenwood, I'm sorry. That came out wrong.'

It was too late. By the time she had got round to the other side of the desk, he was out of the door and walking swiftly past Zoe, who was talking to Mr B in reception.

She cursed again. Other than run after him, there was absolutely nothing she could do.

Zoe and Mr B both looked at her for an explanation.

'Was that Adam Greenwood?' Mr B asked. 'I'm glad he came to see you. Did he tell you that I'd called round and smoothed things over? I knew I'd done the wrong thing, going off on one and accusing them of having a vendetta against us. I know I can get carried away at times. I hold my hands up to that.' He held them up now. 'Mind you, he didn't look very happy. Just then – Mr Grim.'

He and Zoe both smirked.

Then their faces sobered as if they'd only just realised she wasn't joining in with their frivolity.

'Did you really go round to see him?' Clara asked.

'I did, boss. Yeah. Yesterday. I decided you were right. Things would be a lot nicer if we could all work in harmony. He agreed. He was good about it actually. I even signed another contract with One Stop Watercress, which was just as well. The other supplier was crap. What?' He broke off suddenly. 'Did I do the wrong thing? Have I pissed him off?'

'No, you didn't. You haven't. Not at all.' Clara rested her elbows on the reception desk and put her chin in her hands. 'You did exactly the right thing. But I think I may have just messed it all up again.'

She told them what had just happened.

'I should probably go after him. No, I shouldn't, should I? It would be best to let the dust settle.'

They were both nodding. Zoe wide-eyed and Mr B with more understanding. 'Might be best to let him calm down, boss.'

'He's a fiery one,' Zoe agreed and it was hard to tell whether she approved or not.

Clara didn't say anything else. It was one of the very few moments of her career when she felt not just wrong-footed, but helpless. She would have given a lot to be able to rewind the last five minutes.

* * *

An hour later, Clara and Foxy were sitting opposite her grandmother in her Church Knowle bungalow, after a brief phone conversation in the car park during which she had said, 'I think

I'm the worst manager in the world,' and Gran had said, 'Stop talking nonsense, angel, and get yourself round here, pronto.'

Now they were sipping tea from bone-china cups in her grandmother's lounge, which was all dark wood and rich reds and silver framed photos and was a lot snugger than the one at her parents – they'd downsized when they retired – but which smelled equally as much both of love and of home.

Sometimes Clara thought the family genes had skipped a generation. She had far more in common with her grandmother than she did with her mum. Certainly in appearance – they were both vertically challenged – Gran had shrunk lately as well and she was now only five foot two. She made up for this in feistiness. Nora Batty had nothing on Thelma Price.

Both Clara and her gran had tiny delicate hands and dark eyes and hair, although Gran's was white these days, and a sharp tongue if they were riled.

'I think you're being too hard on yourself, angel,' was the old lady's verdict when she had put in her hearing aid – she left it out unless she wanted to talk to people – and Clara had poured out the whole sorry story, starting with the video and ending with Adam storming out of her office. 'The man's obviously touchy. If not completely temperamental. Did you say he was a chef?'

'No, that's his brother, but yes he is temperamental.' Clara told her about the other two times they had met. 'The annoying thing is he wasn't being like that at all today. He was being pleasant. I messed it all up. Why didn't I think before I opened my big mouth and put my size four in it?'

Gran's eyes flashed. 'Because you're not perfect, my angel. You must get that from me. I've done a lot of things that aren't perfect lately.'

'Have you? Like what? Mum said you'd gone on a date on Sunday. Was that one of them?'

'Yes.' Gran gave a dry, humourless laugh. 'That was certainly one of them. I went with a chap called Sid. He could talk of nothing but his home-grown tomatoes and salad onions.'

'I thought you were interested in allotments.'

'I am. But tomatoes and salad onions for four hours solid.' She waved a hand. 'No thanks.'

'Come back, Grandad, all is forgiven?' Clara asked hopefully.

'Not quite, no, but I've certainly had my fill of Sids lately, I can tell you.'

'You mean you've met more than one?' Clara looked at her in amazement. 'How come?'

'Because in a weak moment I was foolish enough to sign up with a matchmaking agency, that's how come. So far, I've met, Sid the actor, he was a narcissist; Sid the Scrabble player, he could go for hours without saying a single word, although he was a formidable Scrabble opponent, I'll give him that.' She paused. 'And then, last Sunday, Sid the allotment owner. It must be a generational thing – you don't hear the name Sid very often these days, do you. But there are a hell of a lot of seventy-something Sids living in a forty-mile radius of Church Knowle, I can tell you that for nothing.'

Her eyes sparkled in amusement and suddenly they were both laughing.

'I have missed you, Gran,' Clara said. 'Have you heard from Grandad lately?'

'I may have done,' she said in her most deadpan voice.

'Is he all right?'

'Eric is perfectly fine. Don't you go worrying yourself about him.' She touched her hearing aid. 'One more word about him and I'm taking this out.'

Clara nodded. She knew better than to push the subject of Grandad. If she wasn't careful, Gran would clam up completely.

Stubbornness and an intense dislike of being told what to do was something else they had in common. That must also have skipped a generation because both her parents were much more laid-back.

'So, tell me some more about this matchmaking agency. Is it online?'

'Don't be silly. What do I know about computers? No, it's one of those old-fashioned ones. It's run by this very nice woman who looks more like a beautician than anything else. Done up to the nines she was when she called on me.'

'Sounds OK,' Clara said, pulling her knees up onto the settee, not surprised that Gran approved. Standards were another thing she was always banging on about.

'One must have standards,' her grandmother said on cue. 'There's not enough importance attached to them, these days. But I liked Anastasia, I have to say.'

Clara sat bolt upright in her chair. 'Did you say Anastasia? Hang on a minute.' Seconds later, she was rummaging in her bag. 'Did she have a card like this?' She must have done. There couldn't be two Anastasias surely. Mind you, there had been three Sids, so anything was possible. She pulled it out triumphantly and handed it over to her grandmother, who had to get her reading glasses on before she could see it properly.

'Yes, that's her. That's the woman. Happy Ever After. That's her company. Not that there is such a thing – er hem – as we all know.' Her old eyes clouded fleetingly. 'That's just in fairy tales.' She pursed her lips.

'I thought she was a reporter.'

'With a company name like that?'

'I didn't know that was her company name. I was hiding behind my shed at the time.'

'You're surely not talking about that shed at the bungalow. There isn't room to get a broomstick behind there.'

'I know,' said Clara, remembering when she'd first moved in and had given Gran a guided tour. 'I was hiding from her because I thought she was a reporter and I had my T-shirt on inside out. Not to mention back to front – oh, it's a long story. Anyway, never mind that now. Clearly she isn't a reporter at all. Unless she'd got a sideline.'

'I wouldn't have thought she had.'

'I was joking, Gran.'

'I know you were. And sarcasm doesn't suit you, angel.'

'The thing is though... what was the owner of a matchmaking company doing at Kate's bungalow?' Clara asked, bemused.

'Maybe she was looking for Kate.'

'She wasn't. She asked for me by name.'

'And you're quite sure you didn't invite her?'

'Of course I didn't invite her. I don't want to end up with three Sids.'

Gran chortled. 'Touché.'

There was a little pause while they both looked at each other in a silence that was only disturbed by the ticking of the old-fashioned clock above the little fireplace.

'In that case,' Gran said, taking off her glasses and polishing them thoughtfully. 'There's only one other person who could have invited her.'

'And who's that?'

She perched her glasses back on her nose and looked at Clara.

'The same person who invited her to come and see me. Your sister, Rosanna.'

10

Clara had wanted to phone Rosanna up straight away and have it out with her, but her grandmother had stopped her.

'Don't be too hard on her. You know her heart's in the right place. She just wants you to be as happy as she and Ed are. She liked that Will chappie, didn't she, although I could see why you didn't keep him on – he was too wishy-washy and clingy for you. You need someone strong. A proper partner, not a piece of climbing ivy.'

She had hugged Clara then and Clara had smelled the face powder on her cheek and felt the bony fragility of her shoulders. 'Thanks, Gran. You always put things in perspective.'

If she hadn't been so tired, she may have driven over to Rosanna's, but that would probably have been a bad idea. As Gran had also pointed out, 'Haven't you already upset someone today by saying something controversial? You're tired out, my angel. What with all the dramas you've had lately, it isn't surprising. Go and have a nice hot bath and a glass of that disgusting fizzy wine you youngsters like so much. Nothing matters half as much as you think it does.'

'How did you get so wise?'

Gran tapped her pointy nose. 'You don't get to seventy-seven without learning a thing or two.'

'You're seventy-six.'

'Only for another three weeks! Now, be off with you!'

So, for once in her life, Clara decided to do exactly what she was told. When she got home, she had a hot bath, followed by a glass of Prosecco, followed by a cuddle in her dressing gown with Foxy – dogs were always understanding – and then she went to bed.

In the morning, feeling refreshed and in a good mood, Clara decided she would spend her weekend off doing what her mother called, 'getting your ducks in a row'. Well, actually her mother called it 'getting your dogs in a show', which Clara preferred, being a fan of canines, and which worked nearly as well, as it still meant you were organising and making preparations – one of her favourite activities.

She would phone Will and, unlike yesterday's debacle with Adam, this time she would be ultra-diplomatic and tactful. Never let it be said that she didn't learn from her mistakes. She should probably phone Adam too and apologise again. See if she could get him back on an even keel. It couldn't be easy having a sick brother to worry about.

She would buy Gran a seventy-seventh birthday present.

She would buy Rosanna a thirty-ninth birthday present – it was hers a week after Gran's.

She would also phone Rosanna and practise being diplomatic and tactful some more, although she would make it obvious she was still slightly cross about Anastasia Williams.

Maybe she would phone Rosanna before she did the present shopping, as it may affect her decision on what to buy. No, that was mean. Gran was right. Her sister's heart was usually in the right place. She just had a habit of being a meddler when it came to other people's love lives.

If it wasn't for Rosanna, Gran may have got back with Grandad too and not have gone on dates with all those Sids. No, she probably wouldn't. Gran was the last person you could coerce into doing anything against her will, that was for sure.

Clara had a feeling that Gran might very well take Grandad back once she had finished proving that she could manage perfectly well without him, thank you very much. She was sure that's what the Sids had really been about. Gran wasn't the kind of woman who had ever been defined by a man. She loved the bones of Grandad, but she had never been the needy, helpless type.

Grandad had come out of all this in a lot worse position, emotionally, than Gran and he certainly still loved her. 'I've been such a fool,' he had said to Clara last time they had chatted. 'It was one of those stupid old man moments. There was this attractive woman making eyes at me. I let it go to my head. I lost sight of what was important.'

Clara had hugged him tightly and sympathised and murmured appropriate responses, which was what she knew their whole family was doing, but she also knew that neither she, nor Rosanna, nor Mum and Dad would make things any better by interfering, however tempting it was.

She decided to phone Adam first before she lost her nerve. She was half relieved and half disappointed when his voicemail kicked in. She put on her most professional voice. 'Hello, this is Clara King, manager of the Bluebell Cliff. Thank you so much for coming by yesterday. It was much appreciated. I just wanted to reiterate that I did not mean to cause offence or to in any way imply that you had anything to do with what happened at the Bluebell. I do apologise if I implied otherwise.'

That should do it. She hung up feeling a lot lighter.

Then, leaving a disappointed Foxy behind, she went into Poole to do her shopping. Swanage was closer, but there was less choice and today she was in the mood to get lost amongst crowds of anonymous shoppers. Poole had a big undercover shopping centre as well as a department store on several floors where they had perfume counters and lots of different retail outlets and quite often seventy-per-cent sales. It was worth keeping an eye on what designer bags actually cost when they were new. Not that she was thinking of buying any more at the moment.

She bought Gran some Clarins face cream and a rather beautiful half-price cashmere cardigan in the perfect shade of plum. She would love it. And who knew how many more birthdays you would have when you got to seventy-seven, even though her gran was amazing for her age. She bought Rosanna a teal scarf and then decided to splash out on some Jimmy Choo perfume too. However annoying Rosanna could be sometimes, she was still her sister and, as Gran had said, her heart was in the right place.

Feeling in good spirits and warmed by her own generosity, Clara decided to call on Will on the way home. She could phone Rosanna later. Tonight she had an appointment with a box set and a pizza. The diet could start again tomorrow and, according to her FunFit, she had walked 9,500 steps today. That was without Foxy's second walk. She had decided to overlook the fact that it wasn't entirely trustworthy.

When she got to Will's, she could see that his car wasn't in the drive again, but she parked outside anyway. That was odd. He was almost always in on a Saturday teatime. He was a creature of routine and didn't like missing meals. He usually watched an episode of *Doctor Who* with a tray on his lap.

Mind you, it was still only just five. Maybe he was on his way back. She got out her phone and called him. To her surprise, the phone didn't ring. Instead, she got a tinny voice saying, 'It has not been possible to connect your call. Please check and try again.'

Frustrated, she got out of her car and went up to the front door. She wasn't quite sure what she was looking for. He clearly wasn't there. She moved along to the bay windows on her right. The net curtains were long, but it was possible to see through if you stood close enough. With one foot in the flower beds, she leaned across the lavender, its distinctive scent in her nostrils, and peered through. Her heart thumped in surprise. The furniture was familiar, but there was nothing out of place. Not a single thing. That wasn't like Will. He was perpetually messy. It was another thing they didn't have in common.

Had he moved house and left all his furniture behind? She went back to the front door and stared through the frosted glass and then, finally, feeling slightly guilty, she bent to look through the letter box. On the mat was a pile of mail, some of it with his name on. She hoped nothing had happened to him. She may not have wanted a relationship with the guy, but she did still care about him.

As she was straightening up, a middle-aged woman came out of the house next door. 'Are you all right there, love? Who are you looking for?'

'Will Lightfoot,' Clara said, not recognising her.

'He's gone away.' The woman, who was clearly on her way out, buttoned up her jacket. 'Some round-the-world trip, lucky beggar. I'm looking after the house for him.'

'I see. Right. Thanks.' So he'd gone alone then! Blimey! 'Do you know when he's coming back?'

'No, to be honest, I don't. It was all a bit of a rush job. Poor chap had a bad break-up with his girlfriend. Heartbroken he was. I think he just wanted to get away and sort himself out. She was a real witch, from what I can gather.' She rested her elbows on the fence between the two houses and looked at Clara properly. 'Oh, 'eck, that wasn't you, was it?'

'No,' Clara lied swiftly. 'I'm just a friend. Thanks for your help though.'

She got back into her car. That was that then. There was no way on earth she was going to find out if Will had anything to do with that video now.

* * *

'I think it makes it more likely that he did have something to do with it,' Rosanna said when Clara filled her in on the phone. 'Hell hath no fury like a man scorned – it's not just women. I think men can be worse. They tend to have bigger egos, and you dumped him. Twice effectively. It was a parting shot.'

'It could have been, I suppose.'

'Why else would he change his phone number?'

'I don't know. But I guess it's immaterial now.' She hadn't thought he would be that vindictive, but he'd been upset enough to tell his neighbour she was a witch.

'On the bright side,' Rosanna continued relentlessly, 'he probably isn't going to do anything else. He'll be too busy on his world trip. Travelling changes your perspective.'

'Yes,' Clara said. 'So I hear.' She took a deep breath and settled herself more comfortably on her sofa. 'I want to talk to you about Anastasia Williams.'

'Ah,' Rosanna said. 'She called you then. She was quick off the mark. I only mentioned it a couple of weeks ago in passing.'

'She didn't phone me. She turned up at Kate's bungalow. Twice. I thought she was a flaming reporter.'

'She doesn't look anything like a reporter,' Rosanna said in amazement. 'So how did it go? You didn't mind, did you? I thought it would be a good diversion for you. What with everything that's been going on. She's ever so nice. She's one of the mums at school. She's also on the board of governors. She's one of the most organised people I've ever met. She reminded me of you actually. A proper career woman, but a supermum as well. Did you click with her?'

'No. We got off on completely the wrong foot.'

'What? But why?' There was a note of panic in Rosanna's voice now. 'You can't have done. She's lovely. You didn't upset her, did you? She said she'd fit you in as a big favour to me before she went on holiday.'

'Well, maybe you should have warned me that she was coming,' Clara said, feeling gratified at the sound of Rosanna's agitation and wondering if that made her a bad person. 'Then I would have answered the door instead of hiding behind the shed.'

'I assumed she would phone first— What do you mean you hid behind the shed?'

Clara told her what had happened. The silence got cooler, even down the phone line, especially when she got to the point about pretending to be a haughty gardener.

'Oh my God. Well, I suppose that's one saving grace. She didn't know it was you.'

'She will do though, won't she, when I phone her back and say I want to be signed up to her dating agency. She'll most likely think I'm a raving lunatic. Not to mention a compulsive liar.' Clara was starting to enjoy herself.

'You can't phone her back. No. Please don't. I'll get in touch with her. I'll cancel it.'

'But won't she think it's odd?'

'No. I'll tell her you've changed your mind. I'll tell her you've got back with your ex or left the country or something.'

'That's a shame. Now I've had a chance to consider it, I think you're right. I 'd like to join a proper dating agency. One where they interview you about your ideal mate. It's got to have a better chance of working than just meeting someone randomly. And if this Anastasia is as good as you say she is...'

Foxy had wandered across to say hello and Clara stroked her soft ears.

'I'll pay for you to join another one,' Rosanna was saying. 'There are loads. You don't have to join Anastasia's.'

Clara left it a beat. She had no intention of joining any kind of dating agency: online, offline, speed dating, singles nights, supper clubs, but she hadn't heard Rosanna so rattled for ages and maybe this would stop her interfering.

'It's OK,' she said, deciding it was time she let her off the hook. 'I don't want another man in my life. And I'm not so sure Gran does either.'

'Did she say that?'

'No, she didn't, but you know it's true. She's going to get back with Grandad when she's ready. Throwing all those Sids at her is just muddying the waters.'

'Maybe you're right.' There was another little pause. 'I've mucked up, haven't I? I'm really sorry, Sis. I know I can get carried away sometimes. I didn't mean to make things any more complicated for you. Or for Gran.'

That was something else that Clara admired about her sister. She might have bull-in-a-china-shop tendencies, but she always apologised unreservedly if she thought she was wrong.

'You're forgiven,' she said softly. 'There's no harm done.'

'No. I guess you're right. I'll stop interfering. I'll have a word with Gran. And I'll cancel Anastasia as far as you're concerned.'

'Thanks. Have a lovely, rest of the weekend.'

'I will. You too, Sis.'

As Clara put the phone down, it beeped and she realised someone had called and left a message while she'd been talking to Rosanna.

It was Adam. The signal wasn't very good and she could hear plates clattering in the background. He must be at work then, but she did make out the words, 'Thanks for ringing. Your apology is accepted.'

That was a good result. In fact, quite a lot of good had come out of today.

Will was well and truly out of the picture.

Gran wouldn't have to date any more Sids.

Rosanna wouldn't interfere with her love life again.

And now she was back in Adam's good books.

She had just got up to go and dig out a pizza from the freezer when her mobile rang again. She thought for a moment there'd been some weird telepathy afoot and Adam was ringing her back, but it was Kate's mobile number that flashed up. That was odd. It must be some unearthly hour over there. She hoped nothing was wrong as she snatched up the phone.

'Hi Clara. Is this a good time?' Her boss sounded stressed.

'Yes, it's fine. Is everything OK?'

'Yes and no.' There was a pause. 'I had an accident this afternoon. It was something really stupid. I was changing a light bulb in Mum's hall and I slipped off the stepladder. I didn't think I'd done much at first, but then my foot swelled up like a balloon and we ended up in accident and emergency. Unfortunately, it turns out I've broken it and they need to operate on my ankle to reset a couple of bones.'

'Oh my God. That sounds serious.'

'It is. Thank goodness for medical insurance. It'll be fine long term, but it does mean I can't fly back when we planned. I'm so sorry. Would you like me to get you some more help in? I can arrange a relief manager from the agency.'

'I'm fine at the moment. Phil's great, so I'm not on my own. Do they know how long it will be before you can fly?'

'They can't give me a definitive date. It depends how things go. I'll need to have stitches in for a while and get the healing process underway before they put the plaster cast on. But I will let you know as soon as I possibly can. Thanks so much, Clara.'

Poor Kate, she thought, when they had finally said their goodbyes and disconnected. She hadn't been expecting that. But her concern for her boss was threaded through with a frisson of excitement. The Bluebell, as she had reiterated to Kate, was in very safe hands. Nothing else was going to go wrong. She wouldn't flaming let it.

11

It seemed that somebody up there was on Clara's side because August progressed very smoothly. The sunshine stayed, the temperatures soared into the eighties, and the Bluebell and its lighthouse were at their most fabulous best. By day, the interior of the hotel smelled of suntan lotion and Mr B's breakfasts, and the exterior smelled of the roses that bloomed in every flowerbed. Butterflies darted around on the buddleia and crops of rapeseed turned rectangles of the surrounding countryside into fields of luminous, almost otherworldly yellow. Beyond the cliffs, the sea sparkled like a sheet of sapphires and everyone walked around in shorts and sunglasses smiling. Even Mr B and Phil Grimshaw were making a special effort to be nice to each other.

All the staff had been very concerned to hear about Kate's accident and, much to Clara's relief, they'd all reacted well to the news that she would be in charge for as long as it took for their boss to get better again.

The operation had gone well apparently, but it would be two or three weeks before they could risk putting a plaster on – they had to make sure the wound healed first.

For the second week of August, the Bluebell Cliff hosted a group who had booked in under the name of The Serious Hill Runners. And serious they certainly were.

Their leader, Malcolm Daley, told Clara that one of the reasons they had chosen the Bluebell was because of the hotel's proximity to some of the steepest bits of the coast path.

'I'm in training for a record,' he told Clara when he checked in. 'I want to break the fastest known time to run the South West Coast Path. At the moment it's held by Damien Hall. Ten days, fifteen hours and eighteen minutes.'

'Wow,' she said. 'That's going to take some beating. Isn't it six hundred miles?'

'It's six hundred and thirty,' he said proudly and beamed at her from behind thick NHS-style glasses. 'That's an average of sixty miles per day. I think I can do sixty-two over this kind of terrain.'

'Good grief, can you?' Her feet ached at the thought of it. 'I'd be lucky to do six.'

'I'm not surprised in those heels.' He peered over the reception desk.

He was one of the few men she met who she could actually look straight in the eye and this fact alone would have made her warm to him, but he was thoroughly nice too. He was wiry and angular and reminded her a little of a very friendly whippet.

'Another reason we chose you is that this is the place where dreams come true, isn't it?' He looked at the brass plaque above the reception desk. 'So we thought you might bring us luck.'

'I promise you that we will do our very, very best,' she said, making a mental note to tell Kate about this conversation. She'd be delighted. 'And you must promise to tell us if you achieve it. When will you be attempting the record?'

'Not until next May. But if I break it, I will arrange to have the biggest party ever right here in this hotel.'

'We'll throw in a magnum of champagne – on us,' Clara said and he nodded his head so enthusiastically that his glasses slid off his nose and clattered on to the reception counter.

'I wear contacts when I run,' he said, picking them up. 'These just steam up all the time.'

She didn't tell him she'd wondered how he managed. Clara loved moments like these. She loved people, particularly quirky people. It was what made her job worthwhile.

'You must do an awful lot of training. Do you have a sporty day job?' she asked.

'Oh no, I'm an accountant – freelance, which makes things easier. If my client has a shower on site, I run to work.'

'Wow, that's very impressive.'

Later, in the restaurant, when she was chatting to one of the other members of The Serious Hill Runners, she learned that Malcolm Daley had a string of titles under his belt already. He was, apparently, the fastest man ever to run The Big Beast, which was a fourteen-mile sprint up a mountain. He held the current record time for The Tester – the longest off-road race in the UK. Not to mention, having trophies for half-a-dozen endurance races involving covering hundreds of miles at a time.

She had glanced across to where he sat at a table on the other side of the restaurant, chatting animatedly to another guy, and he'd gone up another notch in her estimation. Not because he was clearly a little powerhouse of a man beneath that unlikely exterior – a regular superman, she imagined him swapping his accountant suit for Lycra – but because he hadn't even mentioned any of his previous triumphs. She had thought he might have been just another dreamer with stars in his eyes, and it wouldn't have mattered one bit if he was: dreamers were, after all, the Bluebell's lifeblood, but it appeared he was a man of substance.

The runners were a good group to host because after they'd eaten a hearty breakfast, they were off out all day. There was no supplying endless coffee and cake and tea and biscuits, like there was for groups of writers, or clearing up stage make-up spillages and helping out with emergency costume repairs, as there was for actors. And the place didn't echo with music. Clara liked music as much as the next person, but their music-based guests spent hours practising – and some of them very much needed the practice.

There was only one other woman staying in the hotel at the same time as the runners. She was an ageing artist called Milly Mills and this was her second visit since Clara had worked there. She came to paint watercolours of the surrounding countryside and to see her sister, Lillian, who lived locally.

'Her house is very small,' Milly had confided to Clara the first time they had met. 'Which is why I stay here. And also it's nice to have some space, don't you think, dear? We get on well enough, but I don't want to get under her feet. I do prefer my own company.'

Much as she liked people, Clara could relate to that. She was like her grandmother in that respect too. It was lovely to have a partner around, but she didn't need one. If she did ever end up with that smallholding she'd dreamed of buying, she would have been happy there alone.

Although an Orlando Bloom lookalike – one who wasn't subject to outbursts of totally unnecessary stroppiness, that was – would have been quite nice, she had to admit. Hell, where had that thought come from? Maybe it was because this morning Phil had told her that Adam Greenwood had phoned and asked to borrow a couple of kegs of beer. She was relieved he had got through to Phil and not her. She did not want another run-in with anyone from the Manor House. Not that she would have denied the request or been unfriendly, it's just that they seemed to get their wires crossed on every occasion they spoke, and at the moment there was an entente cordiale, which she was keen to maintain.

Anyway, Milly had been delighted when she had phoned to book this time and Clara had told her that she'd be sharing with outside enthusiasts, so during the day she'd virtually have the place to herself.

On the Friday, the penultimate day of the hill runners' stay, Clara bumped into Milly just as she came into reception carrying an easel at the end of an afternoon's painting. The white-haired old lady looked slightly stressed.

'Everything OK?' Clara enquired.

'Not entirely, dear. I've got a slight problem with my car. Nothing too major, I don't think, and I'm in the RAC so they'll come out and see to it. But I'm meeting Lillian this evening for dinner, so I don't want to call them just yet.'

'But in the meantime you need transport to get to her?' Clara guessed.

'I can call you a taxi,' Zoe said from behind reception. 'Where are you going?'

'To somewhere called The Anchor? We're meeting at six-thirty, so not right away. Lillian must already be out and about. She isn't answering the home phone and she refuses to carry a mobile. Says she doesn't need one.'

'I can drop you off at The Anchor on my way home,' Clara offered. 'No need for a taxi.'

'Could you, dear? I am grateful, thank you. Lillian will be fine to bring me back again afterwards. I will need to go and freshen up first, if that's OK?'

'Perfect timing,' Clara said and so it was that three-quarters of an hour later she opened the door of her Mini Cooper for Milly, who got in with only slightly less agility than Foxy, who'd leapt into her basket in the back just before her. Clara left the back windows open when it was hot and Foxy had a habit of resting her nose against the window jamb as they drove.

'What a pretty little car,' Milly said. 'I wouldn't mind one of these myself. Might be more reliable than my old Austin now.'

She was good company on the short drive. Today she'd been painting Durdle Door, which was a natural limestone arch of rock on the Jurassic coast near Lulworth.

'That place sure attracts the tourists,' she said. 'Not to mention the armchair artists, all of whom think they're experts and want to tell you how it's done. I had this old chap today who came over twice – once on his way down the cliff path and again on his way up – "you want a touch more charcoal in the stone, dear".' Her Dorset accent was perfect. 'I always say thank you and then ignore them.'

Clara agreed this was a good tactic as she pulled into the car park of The Anchor.

'That's odd, her car isn't here.' Milly glanced around the half-empty car park. 'She has a silver Volvo. Unless she's changed it and not told me. Oh dear. I do hope she's OK.'

'We're a few minutes early. I'll come in with you – just until she arrives. I'm sure she'll be here soon.'

'That's extremely kind of you, dear. Are you sure I'm not holding you up?'

'Positive,' Clara said. 'I'm going to have to bring Foxy with me, though. It's too hot to leave her in the car.'

She got out and went round to open the door for the old lady, glancing across at the outside patio as she did so. It was barely a month ago that she'd sat there with Will, yet it seemed like another lifetime. There was another young couple sitting there today. They were holding hands and looking intently into each other's eyes.

Inside the bar, that was shadowed and cool in comparison to the August day outside, a barman, whom she recognised as a friend of Mr B's, directed them to the table that Lillian had booked and then Milly went off to powder her nose. Clara toyed with the idea of ordering a pot of coffee. She could chat to Steve the barman for a bit if Lillian did turn up and if she didn't – and there had been some kind of mix-up – she would take Milly back to the Bluebell herself. It wasn't as if she had a packed Friday evening's entertainment.

Making a decision, she left Foxy's rope lead looped around the table leg and went up to order coffee. A couple more people had just come in, including a family, and Steve was now serving someone else. Slowly she became aware of the woman who was standing beside her. It was the scent that caught her attention first: something flowery but also exotic – and oddly familiar. Where had she smelled that before?

She turned to look at exactly the same moment the other woman did the same thing and they met each other's eyes. Oh goodness, it was Anastasia Williams.

She was beautifully made up, as she had been before, and she was carrying a gorgeous dark green Ted Baker bag – a top-of-the-range one that had just come out. Clara had seen it in the department store in Poole and coveted it briefly before spending all her spare cash on birthday presents for Gran and Rosanna. There was obviously good money in dating then!

'Hang on, don't tell me,' Anastasia said. 'I know we've met before. I never forget a face.'

'People are always mistaking me for someone else,' Clara said swiftly. 'I have one of those faces.'

'No. We've definitely met. It's my line of work, you see.'

Oh crap. How embarrassing. She could see Milly had just come out of the Ladies' on the other side of the room and was heading back to the table where Foxy was waiting patiently. She had also just heard the pub door opening behind her and she felt the swoosh of air as someone entered. Hopefully that would be Lillian and she could make a rapid exit.

'I've got it,' Anastasia said in a voice almost loud enough to rival the Chair of the WI. 'You work for Clara King. You're the gardener. You had the mildew problem behind the shed. And the very friendly dog. Do you remember? I gave you my card for Miss King.' Her face cleared. She was obviously extremely pleased with herself for recalling the events so clearly.

Clara could feel her face burning. Everyone in range was looking interested. Milly, who'd realised she wasn't at their table but up at the bar, was now waving at her from across the room. Even Steve had leaned in for a listen. Was he smirking?

'I'm Anastasia Williams, remember? I don't think I ever caught your name.'

'Um no,' Clara said. 'But I'm afraid I'm in a terrible hurry.' She glanced at her FunFit, which said, right on cue for once, Time for a sharp stroll. 'So sorry,' and she spun round towards the exit of the pub, hoping to see another little old lady, who looked a bit like Milly.

But it wasn't an old lady who had just walked in. It was Adam Greenwood. What the hell was he doing here? He was dressed casually, jeans and a pale T-shirt, and he was standing right behind her. He must have heard every word of that conversation.

He was smiling too. That made a change!

'Clara King's gardener, hey?' His voice was caramel smooth.

Don't give me away. She pleaded with her eyes

'Hi, Adam,' Anastasia said.

What? They knew each other? Yes, they clearly did because Adam was now bending to kiss Anastasia's cheek.

Clara took advantage of the distraction to make her escape and, ten seconds later, she was out in the heat of the car park again. Breathing heavily, she looked around her. She was going to have to go back in. She couldn't just abandon Milly. But then. to her intense relief, she saw a silver Volvo pull in through the entrance.

Someone up there must still be on her side, after all. She would just have to explain to Lillian that she'd had an urgent phone call or something and get her to pass this on to Milly. Taking a deep breath, she hurried across to speak to the old lady as she got out of her car.

It was only when she was about to make her escape for the second time that she remembered she'd left Foxy inside tied to the table. Shit, she was going to have to go back in and get her. Maybe she could sneak in and out without anyone noticing

Feeling like a burglar going back to the scene of the crime, Clara pushed open the heavy door of The Anchor once more and hesitated to let her eyes readjust to the dim interior of the pub. Before she'd had the chance to properly do this, there was an almighty crash that sounded like breaking glass and crockery on floor tiles, followed by a yelp. What the hell?

Oh God – it was Foxy. Clearly tired of waiting, she'd upturned the table when she'd seen her mistress reappear and now she was heading towards her, lead trailing and tail wagging frantically. She appeared to have a red serviette stuck to her front paw and her snout looked as though it had been dipped in something white – it must be sugar. It was all over her head too. Foxy loved sugar and wasn't averse to stealing it from the bowl if she thought no one was looking.

Fortunately, Milly was up at the bar with her sister and hadn't been sitting at the table, so she wasn't involved in the chaos. But so much for a subtle getaway, Clara couldn't have made more of an entrance if she'd tried. Every single person in the bar was now looking in her direction, including a family with two children who were laughing loudly as Clara bent to make a grab for the lead.

'Is that a fox, Mummy?' one of them asked.

'It's a very naughty dog, darling.'

'Why has it only got three legs?'

'I don't know. Be quiet.'

To make matters worse, Adam and Anastasia were sitting at a table close to the door and so had a ringside seat. Anastasia was open-mouthed and Adam was clearly trying not to laugh. Amused Orlando! How flaming embarrassing was this! Clara's face was on fire – she must be lighting up the room like a beacon.

'I'm terribly sorry,' she said to Steve, hauling Foxy towards her. 'I'll cover the cost of the damage obviously.'

'I wouldn't worry, Clara. It's only a couple of glasses – and – er – sugar?' He was reaching behind the bar for a dustpan and brush. 'These things happen.' His eyes were sympathetic. 'Although I may have to ban the hound,' he added, winking.

'Thank you.' She smiled at him gratefully. Hopefully Anastasia was far enough away not to have heard him call her Clara.

Then she fled for the third and what she very much hoped was the final time.

All the way home the scene played on a loop in her head. It was right up there as one of the most humiliating experiences of her life – it even topped the shed incident. But what cruel twist of fate had decreed that Adam's girlfriend – because that was surely who she was – should be present on both occasions?

It was much later when the nightmare scene was starting to fade that she remembered the little spike of feeling that had prodded her when Adam had bent to kiss Anastasia. Not jealousy surely. It was certainly nothing to her what Adam and Anastasia did.

12

'That kind of thing only happens to me,' Clara defended herself to Mr B the following Monday morning. He had popped into the office to see her about the menu for a function they were holding in a couple of weeks and he'd clearly been given a massively embellished version of Friday evening's drama at The Anchor from his friend, Steve.

Not that you needed to embellish it all that much, she supposed. It had been dramatic enough all by itself.

'And what's this about you moonlighting as a gardener?' he'd added in amusement.

She filled him in on the backstory, including the hiding behind the shed bit, due to the appearance of what she'd thought was a reporter, but not the inside out T-shirt. She would never live that one down. She was always dressed immaculately at work. As Gran pointed out on a regular basis, one must have standards.

Mr B wasn't surprised that she'd been hiding behind the shed. 'I'd have hidden if I'd thought she was a reporter. You can't trust any of them, boss. They're all total liars. Fake news is everywhere.'

'Bit of a generalisation, don't you think?' Clara said, raising her eyebrows.

'Nope.' Mr B twirled in the other chair. 'The media is in the pocket of the government. Their purpose is not to inform us but to manipulate the masses and keep us in line at all costs. Why else do you think they only ever tell us bad news?'

'Because it sells papers.'

'That's a very small part of it. They want to suppress us. Keep us cowed and in fear and remind us we live in a hopeless society where every year things get a little worse and we get a little poorer and a little more desperate. The time of the uprising is coming.'

'Sounds as though there's no hope for us at all,' Clara said in a deadpan voice and he looked at her sharply.

'OK, I may have slightly overegged the uprising bit. Not that I think I did. But they do manipulate the news. And it is all about control. So that we think what they want us to think and not what we would think otherwise. And I can tell you something else...' He broke off and, in the pause, Clara wondered how to change the subject, but then quite unexpectedly he did it for her. 'At least we've established that Adam Greenwood goes into The Anchor,' he said.

'I didn't know we were trying to establish that.' She looked at him curiously.

'Didn't you say that's where the lighthouse video got sold? To a man who drank in The Anchor?'

'Yes. That's right, I did. But I also said that lots of people drank in The Anchor.'

'Not so many that have a motive,' Mr B pointed out and did some more twirling, which made the mechanism of the chair squeak. She must get some WD-40 on that.

'I thought we'd decided The Manor House are our friends, not our enemies.'

'Maybe they're pretending to be our friends, whilst secretly still plotting against us. He was friendly enough when he borrowed the beer. I must remember to get that back off him. How did he seem on Friday night?'

'Highly amused. How long has Steve been working at The Anchor anyway? Would he have been there when our cameraman went in?'

'No. Unfortunately not. He only started in mid-July. He's doing holiday cover. The same thought had occurred to me when I realised he was working there. So I checked.'

Clara felt warmed by his loyalty and the fact that he cared enough to have done such a thing. No one else had mentioned Lighthousegate lately, which she supposed was a blessing. But it was nice to hear Mr B was still on the case.

'Kate seems to think it was a prank that got out of hand,' she said. She was still trying to forget about Will's coincidental disappearance. 'But I agree with you that it's worth keeping an ear to the ground.'

'Ear firmly on ground, boss. Always.'

'Did you say something about a menu?' Clara asked, keen to get back to the subject they were supposed to be talking about.

'Yeah I did.' His face grew businesslike and he waved a bit of paper at her. 'This is what they're proposing. It's a bit more expensive than what we had budgeted for – so I wanted to run it by you.'

'Of course.' She glanced at it. 'That's the annual dinner for the Young Farmers isn't it – that should be fine. It's the first one we've done for them. I want to impress them.'

'Apparently they usually go to the Manor House,' Mr B said,

pressing his lips into a straight line. 'Still, with a bit of luck, the Brothers Grim will never find out.'

Clara hadn't realised that. Oops.

The door opened and Zoe appeared. 'Oh sorry, I didn't know you were busy…'

'It's cool, babe, I'm just going.' Mr B untangled his legs like a stick insect and stood up. 'Laters. I'm off to plan a menu.'

Zoe was looking very pleased with herself. 'You'll never guess who has just booked rooms for the beginning of October?'

'Take That?' Mr B called over his shoulder as he swept past her.

Zoe rolled her eyes. 'Does he really think I'm that shallow?'

'Yes,' he does,' came a disembodied voice from outside the office.

'Who is it?' Clara said. 'Come on. I can't stand the suspense.'

'It's a guy who is planning to attempt to break an actual Guinness World Record.' Zoe's eyes were shining with excitement. She had a piece of paper in her hand. 'He's doing it as part of the Brancombe Oktoberfest. His mother's coming along to support him and they want to stay here for the night before and the night after. Because they think it may bring them luck. Being as we are the hotel where people can come to fulfil their dreams.'

That was the second time she'd heard that lately, Clara thought, making another mental note to tell Kate. Maybe they could find a way of incorporating it into their promotional literature: Have a record-breaking breakfast at the Bluebell Cliff.

'So what is the record?' she asked. 'It's nothing to do with lighthouses, is it?'

'Of course not. You'll love it though. It's right up your street. Go on – I'll give you three guesses.'

'Is it something to do with food?'

Zoe looked startled. 'It is. Yes. How did you know that?'

'Well, you did say it was right up my street. Is it how many ginger nuts you can eat in a minute?'

'No. But you're not a million miles away.'

'Phew. So my ginger nuts are safe. Chocolate Hobnobs then?'

'No, but chocolate is involved. My mum used to eat them back in the dark ages, long before we were born.'

'When in the dark ages?'

'The seventies.' Zoe smirked. 'Last clue. They're very chewy.'

'No idea. You're going to have to tell me.'

'Curly Wurlys – I saw an advert when I was looking for the Milk Tray one. *Outchews everything for 3p*. You must remember that.'

'I wasn't born in the seventies, you cheeky mare. Tell me about the record.'

'It's for Curly Wurly stretching. As in, the longest length you can stretch a Curly Wurly bar in three minutes. It was set in 2015 in Somerset apparently.' She referred to her piece of paper. 'The current record is 426.2 centimetres or nearly fourteen feet, if you prefer it in old measurements. That's nearly twice as high as Mr B.'

'Are you sure this isn't someone's idea of a wind-up?'

'No it isn't. The record really does exist. I checked. Our contender's called Micky Tucker. He lives in Somerset too, but the record attempt will take place at Swanage during this year's Oktoberfest. There are all sorts of chocolate challenges going on apparently. We should go.'

'If there's chocolate involved, we will definitely go,' Clara said and then caught herself. 'What I mean, of course, is that The Bluebell Cliff will be proud to be linked with something like that. And Kate will love it. If they succeed, maybe we can put their picture up in reception.'

She probably shouldn't get too carried away. It might not

happen. The record might not get broken. But it was very exciting that they had chosen her hotel.

'And talking of Curly Wurlys,' she said, glancing back at Zoe. 'It must be lunchtime. I'm just going to take Foxy for a walk and then I'm off to get some. All this talk of chocolate is making me hungry.'

Foxy pricked up her ears from her basket at the mention of chocolate and, ten minutes later, she and Clara were out on the coast path.

She was so lucky, Clara thought, as she walked with the sun in her face and the sea breeze ruffling her hair; the English Channel laid out below the cliffs with the endless blue sky curving over it. She was so lucky to have this job, so lucky to live in such a beautiful part of the world.

The last hotel Clara had managed had been in Bath, and beautiful as Bath was, the city was no match for the Purbecks. It had been expensive-going walking in Bath at lunchtimes too – all those tempting shops. She had actually managed to save quite a bit of money since she'd been living here, even before she had been living rent-free.

She was so lost in her thoughts, she didn't realise she'd reached the back of the Manor House until she was walking alongside it. She was almost in the same spot she'd been when she had mistaken Adam for a grumpy gardener. There was the gap in the hedge that Foxy had run through.

Her heart sped up, where was Foxy anyway? To her relief, the little dog was sniffing round in the grass a few metres ahead.

Then, almost as if she was walking into a flashback, she saw Adam with his secateurs on the other side of the hedge. Hopefully Foxy wouldn't spot him and hopefully he wouldn't spot Clara either. Other than ducking down and hiding from him, there was nothing she could do.

It was too late anyway. He'd seen her. Despite the fact she was in her trainers and wasn't much taller than his hedge.

'Good afternoon, Clara.'

Cheerful Orlando today. Perhaps he'd had a flashback too – of her squirming with embarrassment the last time they'd met.

'Good afternoon, Adam.' She decided dignity was the better part of valour. 'Lovely day, isn't it?'

'Superbulous. That's a cross between superb and fabulous. Just in case you were wondering.'

'You're in a good mood.' The words were out of her mouth before she'd had a chance to consider they might be a bit cheeky. Especially if he'd heard her unsaid rider. For a change.

Which he clearly had because he said mildly, 'Yes, it does happen occasionally. Contrary to popular belief.'

There was a pause.

'Good to see you've got that dog safely under control today.' His eyes sparkled with amusement.

She stroked Foxy's head protectively. 'I shouldn't have left her tied to a table. It was thoughtless.'

'I had no idea you were a gardener,' he added conversationally.

'I'm not. You didn't tell her, did you?'

'No. I didn't.'

'Thank you.' She let out a breath of relief. More for Rosanna's sake than her own, because that would have taken some explaining. 'I was hiding behind my shed,' she said, not sure why she felt the need to explain herself to him. 'And she caught me. Saying I was a gardener was the first thing that came into my head.'

To her surprise, he burst out laughing. 'I must admit I've sometimes been tempted to hide too when Anastasia comes calling.'

'If you don't want to go out with her perhaps you should just tell her?'

'It's a little more complicated than that. She's my cousin and she's very persistent. As I'm sure you're aware if she caught you hiding behind your own shed.'

His cousin huh! That was interesting. 'Ah. Well from one gardener to another, thank you for not grassing me up. Pun intended.'

'No problem at all.' He had moved a step closer.

Feeling magnanimous, partly because it was such a nice day and partly because he was being so convivial, she added, 'And sorry again about what happened when you came to see me at the Bluebell. As I told your voicemail, it was not my intention to throw your apology back in your face.'

Something flashed in his eyes. She wasn't sure what – surprise or perhaps respect. That was a plus. Maybe they could finally put the animosity between the two hotels to bed.

He cleared his throat. 'And, as I told your voicemail, your apology is accepted.' A beat. 'So how about we agree to wipe the slate clean and begin again.' He held out his hand. 'Shall we shake on it?'

'That's a very fine plan,' she said, taking his hand, which was suntanned and felt warm in hers.

'Clara, do you think it might be a good idea to arrange some kind of lunch to discuss this properly? The idea of us working co-operatively together – passing business to each other – rather than working against each other. Not that we were working against each other, exactly...' He broke off.

'You mean a business lunch meeting?'

'Um yes. Absolutely. Purely business.'

He was clearly on the same wavelength as her today. Another plus point.

'I'd be delighted,' she said, realising that she would. It was quite a shock to realise that actually she liked the man. It wouldn't be any great hardship to spend some time in his company. It would also be bloody brilliant if she could report back to Kate that the Manor House and the Bluebell had come to an amicable agreement and that from this point onwards they would be working together instead of winding each other up.

At least Mr B would have his watercress.

13

This was an important meeting, which was why she was taking so much trouble getting ready for it, Clara told herself as she tried and failed to make a decision on what to wear to meet Adam.

They had abandoned the lunchtime plan and gone for an evening meeting in the end, because Adam had said it was easier to leave Nick to cope in the evenings than at lunchtime. 'He's just started this medication which means he's better later in the day,' he'd explained.

'That's better for me too,' Clara had agreed.

A suit didn't feel quite right for an evening meal, but she didn't want to be too casual. She decided eventually on a cream vest top, rose jeggings and a casual pink jacket that she would only put on if needed. A few guests had complimented her on the jacket lately, but it was still warm in the evenings. They were having one of those beautiful summers, a few degrees hotter than the ones she remembered from childhood, that seemed to be the bittersweet side of climate change.

They were going to a gastro pub between West Lulworth and Dorchester called The Five Gold Coins that Adam had recommended. He was in living quarters at The Manor House and he had offered to pick her up. She had surprised herself by accepting.

She must, on some level, trust him. Although, of course, she realised as she let Foxy out one last time before she left her alone, if he did want to know her address, he had only to ask his cousin.

She was ready a few minutes before the time they'd agreed, which was just as well because he was early. He was wearing a pale checked shirt, open at the neck, and dark trousers and he smelled of something expensively citrus. There was a tiny fleck of dried blood to on one side of his jaw where he'd obviously nicked himself shaving.

He drove an old Jaguar with a personalised plate, AG 777.

'The number plate cost more than the car,' he quipped when she commented on it as she climbed into a seat that smelled of age and old leather. He tapped the steering wheel with affection. 'But this car is my honey. I wouldn't change her.'

Honey was an odd choice of word, Clara thought; too human for a car. She wondered if he'd ever been married. She'd asked Phil once and he'd just shrugged and said, 'I doubt it. Who'd put up with him?'

Mr B was more forthcoming about the Brothers Grim, although not about their personal lives. As far as Mr B knew, they had bought the Manor House ten years ago from a hotel chain similar to the one that had once owned the Bluebell. They had slowly rebuilt its once good reputation that the hotel chain had let slip and they had sunk shedloads of money into it, but it was debatable whether this was enough.

'Seaside hotels are in their death throes,' Mr B had told her cheerfully. 'Give it another decade and there'll be none left. They'll all have been turned into apartments owned by the Chinese.'

'The Chinese?'

'Yep, the same ones that own half of London. It's part of their world domination plan.'

For all Clara knew he may have been right. About eighty per cent of Mr B's conspiracy theories had some truth in them, and about twenty per cent of these were spot on, but it was hard to tell which were which. She wasn't sure where he got his information from, although she did know he was a self-confessed insomniac. He also had a girlfriend, although not a live-in one. He'd been seeing Kate's best friend, Meg, for the last couple of years. Meg was cool. A little eccentric, but a lot saner, on the surface at least, than Mr B. Although, apparently, Meg too had an urge to keep kunekune pigs instead of having children.

'Have you had a good day?' Adam's voice broke into her thoughts and she was suddenly aware of the passing countryside, Purbeck stone houses and pubs and the fields bathed in the golden pre-sunset light. It was still only August, but the nights were already closing in.

'Yes I have. Thank you.' She told him about a couple who had phoned to book the lighthouse for their emerald wedding anniversary in October.

'Emerald – miraculous – fifty-five years of being with the same person.'

'Yes.' She was surprised he knew.

'My parents were six months off it when my mother died,' he said.

'Wow. Gosh. I'm sorry to hear that.'

He glanced at her briefly before returning his attention to the road. 'My dad was very pleased to have had her that long.'

'That's a positive way of looking at it. But it must still have been terribly painful.'

'Sometimes life is.' He slowed for some roadwork traffic lights and while they waited for them to change, which seemed to take forever, his fingers tapped impatiently on the steering wheel.

'Have you ever been married?' she asked, because she felt as though they had passed through some invisible barrier. She glanced at him. They were close to the red traffic light and she could see the reflection of it on his face.

'I was married very briefly when I was twenty-one. You?'

'No. Not...' She'd realised just in time that she'd been about to say, yet, and substituted it for the word, '...Ever.' She didn't want him to think that she was looking for a man, because she really wasn't. 'I'm very happy with my own company,' she qualified.

'We have a lot in common then.' The atmosphere lightened in the car. She hadn't even realised it had been tense. 'As well as gardening, I mean.' He shot her a glance. Almost flirtatious. 'Do you actually like gardening?'

'As a matter of fact I do. It's one of those little-known facts about me. I'm a secret secateurs snipper and I own a pair of green wellingtons.'

Now he laughed out loud. 'I don't believe you,' he said as the lights finally turned to green and he put the Jaguar into gear and pulled smoothly away.

'Well, it's true,' Clara told him, slightly needled. 'I'm going to be self-sufficient one day and grow all my own food. I shall make my own bread from scratch too, instead of just chucking the ingredients into a bread maker.'

'That's a good dream,' he said. 'I just can't see you in green wellies.'

Bantering with Adam Greenwood. She would never have predicted that.

Then he spoilt it by saying, 'I like gardening because it means I don't have to speak to any people. I much prefer plants to people.'

'I much prefer people to plants,' she countered. 'Most people anyway.'

'Ouch. I take it I'm one of the minority.'

She decided it might be prudent not to answer that. If they fell out with each other before they even got to their destination, what hope did this business meeting have of success?

Not to mention the fact that she needed him to give her a lift home.

* * *

The Five Gold Coins was posh. It had a long straight gravel driveway, lined with laurel bushes and trees, which led up to a big tarmac car park and a classy entrance hall which smelled of lilies – there was a vase on the bar – but the place was clearly more restaurant than gastropub.

A barmaid showed them into a side room that was buzzing with low chatter and led them to one of only two remaining tables on the back wall. She lit a tall red candle, not a tea light in sight, handed them both a leather-clad menu and said she would be back to take their drinks order shortly.

'I'll have a Diet Coke please,' Clara said when she reappeared. She would definitely need her wits about her for this.

'The same for me, please. No ice.' Again he surprised her. She hadn't imagined he'd be a Diet Coke type of guy.

She studied their surroundings. It was busy, but the tables were far enough apart for it not to feel packed. It was a strange mix of old and new. Old wooden beams, strung with contemporary tungsten bulbs, a beautiful polished black tile floor and glass tables with mismatched chairs, all of which somehow worked.

She could smell red wine – someone close by must have just poured some – and the delicious scents of garlic and rosemary were in the air. This definitely wasn't a burger and chips kind of place. The atmosphere was lovely.

'Good choice,' she told Adam. 'Have you been here before?'

'Once or twice.' He didn't elaborate and she had made a decision after his comment about preferring plants to people that it would be best to keep this on a business level. Safer by far.

So, after they had ordered food – sirloin steak, cooked rare with fresh garlic butter for him and sea bream with local sea greens for her, no starters – she led the conversation around to the reason they were here. 'Thank you for agreeing to this meeting. Have you always worked in the hotel trade?'

'No. I reinvented myself about ten years ago.' He smiled.

'How long have you worked at the Bluebell?' he asked and she told him how Kate had employed her in April and how she had still been on her probationary period when Kate had needed to go to Australia.

'So you stepped into her shoes?'

'In more ways than one.' She explained how she had also ended up looking after Kate's house and Foxy and how this had meant she could let her house. 'I'm sure Kate would be pleased if we could help each other out and pass business to each other,' she added. 'As long as it's mutually beneficial.'

'I am totally up for that,' he said, looking slightly bored. 'Where did you go to school, Clara?'

'Brancombe High,' she said, slightly thrown at the twist of the conversation, but seeing no reason not to tell him. 'I was born in Swanage. So was my mum. Apparently that's unusual. There are an awful lot of incomers. Or people retiring. It's that kind of place, isn't it? Although Gran wasn't born here. She was born and brought up in Wolverhampton. They moved down for Grandad's job. He was in the rag trade, he worked for a men's outfitter. That's probably too much information,' she finished, although he didn't look bored now. He was listening and nodding, his hands steepled in front of him and his index fingers touching his chin. 'Your turn.'

'I've always lived in Dorset too, but not in the Purbecks. Nick and I were brought up on a housing estate in Poole. It was all right though. We didn't live that far from some nice walks and we could drive to the beach in about twenty minutes. My parents were both office workers. Mum always wanted a B&B, but they never had the cash for it.'

'And did you always want to buy a hotel?'

'No. Funnily enough. That was Nick's idea. I had a feeling there might be some people involved.' He shot her a glance. 'I wasn't sure I was really cut out to be a "front of house" man.' He broke off as their food arrived.

Conversation paused as they ate, returning to details such as, 'can you pass the salt please' and 'would you like a refill'. She was glad she'd ordered fillet of sea bream because it was easy to eat and still chat. It was beautifully cooked. With a butter sauce that rivalled Mr B's.

'Why did you become the "front of house" man?' She had to know. He didn't strike her as the kind of person who would be coerced into something against his will or in fact do anything without a good reason.

'Because Nick couldn't find anyone else and, of the two of us, he's by far the best cook.' He added idly, 'and because having a seaside hotel was his dream and he'd just been diagnosed with a chronic illness. For a while we thought it was MS. But it turned out to be something a lot less serious, thank God.'

There it was. She saw the flash of protectiveness in his eyes. And she thought, still waters run deep. For all of his grumpiness and 'flash in the pan anger', Adam clearly adored his brother.

'I figured we would probably be able to find someone to take over from me at some stage. I had a feeling the general public might be involved.' His smile flashed. 'I do other things too – like the gardens.' A beat. 'And general maintenance, although I have to admit that has taken a bit of a back seat lately. As you probably noticed.'

She remembered standing on the seaward side of the Manor House and looking up at the peeling paint and the damp patches on the turrets.

'Business isn't as brisk as we hoped it might be,' Adam added. 'We were probably a touch optimistic with bookings. Even hotels with a fantastic location can struggle. Neither of us actually had any experience of running a hotel. Nick was a chef in a restaurant and I—'

The waitress appeared to collect their plates and leave the dessert menu and Clara thought about how it must have felt to be running a hotel that was struggling and then to discover that less than a mile along the coast another 'all-singing, all-dancing' hotel was being opened, complete with its own high-spec lighthouse. That must have been quite a blow.

'You can't have been too pleased when The Bluebell Cliff appeared,' she said when the waitress had gone.

'Understatement,' Adam said, meeting her eyes briefly before glancing back down at the dessert menu. 'Are you tempted?'

She read the words crème brûlée and chocolate fudge brownie – two of her favourite things – twice before saying, 'Yes, but I probably shouldn't.'

'I probably shouldn't do lots of things, but I do. Wasn't it Oscar Wilde who said, "I can resist everything but temptation"? That's me.'

He appraised her face. Was that look in his eyes, admiration? It wasn't the first time she'd seen it tonight. Flirtatious Orlando? Surely not.

She struggled with herself but only briefly. 'I'm with Oscar.'

'Good.' He shut his menu. 'I can't resist chocolate fudge brownies and they do a spectacular one in here.'

'Fantabulous'. She realised she was using one of his made-up words. They must be getting on well. 'Then count me in.'

Her FunFit buzzed on her wrist:

`Time for a sharp stroll.`

She ignored it.

The chocolate fudge brownies were a melt-in-your-mouth sensation. Definitely worth giving up biscuits for another week. Even the coffee, which came with tiny home-made petits fours, was excellent.

By the time they finally paid the bill – they split it straight down the middle – Clara was feeling full of warmth and bonhomie. She wasn't sure how much of a business meeting this evening had really been, but she had enjoyed herself immensely. Adam had been at his most charming best. He'd been witty, kind, thoughtful, considerate, perceptive, a brilliant listener.

Whoa, girl – it sounds as though you might fancy the guy, warned her 'be careful of men' radar.

I don't, she told it, as they went to the main entrance and discovered it had just started to rain. A haze of fine spray was visible in the shafts of light that slanted down from the outside lighting and she could smell the scent of summer rain hitting hot tarmac.

'I'll get the car,' Adam said. 'No sense in both of us getting wet.' He headed off; his jacket pulled up over his head.

A few minutes later, he drew up beside her and she climbed into the Jaguar, feeling like a lady of the manor as they set off again down the long drive.

Raindrops sparkled like stars on the windscreen There was something very safe, very cosy about being driven through the night while the weather battered the roof of the car and rampaged across the dark fields and woodlands on both sides of the road.

They chatted some more on the way home. Clara told Adam about her stint working at the hotel in Bath.

'Not that I ever want to work out of this area again,' she said. 'Bath was lovely, but I'm a Dorset girl through and through.'

'I have an affinity with the place too,' he said. 'It's a beautiful county. Nick and I both love it.'

'Is he not married then either?'

'No. Although he is in a long-term relationship. He and Alice have never quite got round to tying the knot. They both value their independence too much and she doesn't fancy living in a hotel.'

He didn't mention being in a relationship himself and Clara decided that it was none of her business whether he was or he wasn't.

For a few minutes, they drove in an easy and companionable silence.

'So what was it that you did before you went into business with your brother?' she asked him when they were almost back at hers. 'I don't think you ever said.'

'I worked for a social media company, would you believe? Not that my job involved me being particularly social – on the contrary, I spent most of my time hunched over a desk typing code into a computer.' He grimaced at the memory. 'Great money and good hours and I didn't have to speak to anyone either, which was a bonus. But I'd had enough of it by the time I jacked it in.'

'I bet. Who did you work for?'

'YouTube.'

Clara was glad they were almost back. She didn't know why his words had given her such a jolt. Maybe the mention of YouTube would always jolt her. It certainly didn't mean anything. So what if he had worked at YouTube. So what if he went in The Anchor. So what if he and his brother had a very good reason to try and discredit the Bluebell. None of that meant they had actually had anything to do with the creation of that video. She couldn't believe he had done it. She decided, once again, to put it out of her mind. She'd end up as paranoid as Mr B if she wasn't careful.

14

The rain continued on and off for the next couple of days: a little blip in an otherwise perfect summer. Everyone agreed it was just what the gardens needed. That it would save there being a hosepipe ban and all the other clichés.

'No doubt the Young Farmers will be pleased too,' Zoe said to Clara one afternoon when they were both in reception. Clara was checking out their latest TripAdvisor reviews on her phone prior to one of their weekly team meetings. 'Crops need plenty of rain, don't they? Farmers like rain.'

'Mmm,' Clara said distractedly. 'Did you see that review that said Mr B made the best watercress soup in Dorset, if not the entire South of England?'

'He probably put it on there himself,' Zoe said. 'He's got at least four email accounts.'

'No, he did not!' Mr B appeared in reception on cue and shot Zoe an irritated look. 'I do NOT need to make up reviews about the quality of my cooking, which is first class, and I do NOT have four email accounts. I have seven.'

'Why do you need seven email accounts?' Clara asked.

'Smoke and mirrors.' He waved a vague hand. 'It keeps people on their toes. Stops them being able to find out your true identity.'

Ellie May walked past them with a tray of glasses en route to the restaurant. 'What I'd like to know,' she said, pausing, 'is why we all have to call him Mr B in the first place. What's wrong with Mr Brown?'

'My surname is NOT Brown.' He sounded rattled.

'What is it then?'

'Yes, what is it?' Zoe repeated.

'It's classified information, that's what it is.'

'Well, how about your first name then?' Ellie May persisted. 'Why can't we call you by that? Jakob says people who don't want anyone to know their names must have something to hide – something politically sensitive.'

'Jakob is misinformed,' Mr B snapped.

Zoe and Ellie May exchanged a look that Clara didn't miss. She was well aware that Phil Grimshaw had opened a sweepstake and was taking bets on what either of Mr B's names might be. She had decided to turn a blind eye for now. Maybe that had been naïve of her.

'There's a review here that mentions you, Zoe,' she said to divert them before the discussion got heated. 'It says, and I quote, "The Bluebell Cliff's receptionist is charming and helpful and nothing was too much trouble."'

'They were probably talking about Keith,' Mr B countered with a sly look at Zoe.

'No, they weren't. They said "she" not "he" further on. Anyway, good work, everyone. The last four reviews we have are all five-star ones.' Clara added it to the notes she'd made for the imminent team meeting.

'Talking of farmers,' Zoe said when Mr B and Ellie May had

disappeared again. 'Well, we were earlier...' She blushed.

'Yes...' Clara prompted. 'Is everything OK, Zoe?'

'It is, but...' A beat. '...I was just wondering what Young Farmers actually means. As in, how young are they? Are they young as in my age, say early twenties...? Or...'

'Or are they OAPs of thirty plus like me?'

'Yes, I mean no – not that you're an OAP or anything.' There was a pink tinge on her fair skin.

'Phew.' Clara reached for a biscuit. Her self-imposed ban hadn't lasted very long. 'In order to join the Young Farmers, you have to be between ten and twenty-six. You also don't need to be an actual farmer to join. You just need to have a love of the countryside and rural life. Does that help?'

Zoe was now bright red. 'How do you know all that stuff?'

'I looked on their website. There's this thing called Google.'

'Why didn't I think of that? Doh. OK, so just to get this clear, what we're saying is that on Friday night there will a whole heap of fit hotties coming in here for a meal?'

'Yes. Did you want to hang around after your shift and help Keith out? I'm not sure if that warrants paying you overtime.'

'I'd be happy to help Keith. No overtime necessary.' Zoe looked thrilled.

'Talking of Google. Do you know anything about how YouTube works?' Clara held her breath. She'd been trying to put it out of her mind, but she hadn't quite succeeded. She hadn't said anything about Adam's former job, but the key staff, which included Keith, Mr B, Zoe and Phil Grimshaw, knew she'd gone out with him to discuss a new level of co-operation between the hotels.

'In what respect?' Zoe asked.

'I was thinking about Lighthousegate, that's all. I was

wondering if anyone could put up a video. Do you need special skills?'

'No, I don't think so. You need your own channel. But anyone can set up a channel. I went out with this lad once who fancied himself as a YouTuber. He reviewed sportswear. He said he was going to make a million by the time he was twenty. He didn't, although we did get loads of free samples.'

Clara nodded. She could never make up her mind whether the internet was the most genius invention of the century, or the worst. Sometimes she thought it was on a par with splitting the atom.

'Why are you asking about YouTube? Have you found out who put up that video?' Zoe asked.

'No. I was just curious about the logistics. Thanks.' It was a relief to know anyone could edit a video. She felt bad for suspecting Adam.

Since their evening out, she had spoken to him on the phone a couple of times. Once, he'd passed on the number of a woman who'd called the Manor House about lighthouse accommodation. That had been nice of him. And the other time he'd asked which catering agency they used because the stand-in chef they called when Nick was ill was on holiday.

He'd also called in to return the kegs of beer he'd borrowed apparently, but she'd missed him because she'd been at the bank.

Clara reached absent-mindedly for another biscuit and discovered the plate was empty.

'I've got a reserve packet for the team meeting?' Zoe said. 'Shall I get those?'

'Definitely not.' Clara glanced at her FunFit. The words:

`No pain,no grain`

were scrolling across the screen. Which would have worked better if it could spell, but was quite timely! 'But you could organise the coffee if you like. I'll get the agendas.'

The team meeting was amazingly positive. They usually were. They had them once a fortnight and they rarely lasted more than forty-five minutes. Anyone, from a washer-upper to Phil Grimshaw, could suggest improvements that would add to the smooth running and/or economic efficiency of the Bluebell. If these were agreed and implemented (Clara had the final word on this) and proved to be effective, the originator would receive a share of the profits in the form of flexitime or commission.

Clara had introduced this incentive scheme and it was extremely popular. So far, the innovations had included a different supplier of the chocolates that were left in guest rooms (Janet the chambermaid), a new organic meat supplier (Mr B) and the pop-up gazebo that sold home-made lemonade in the grounds on hot days (Phil).

Clara had also opened up the sun terrace to the public for cream teas. These were popular and profitable and Mr B was working on the 'perfect Dorset Apple Cake', made from organic local flour and Bramley apples from a local orchard. The Bluebell's ethos was to provide their own produce where possible – they supplied most of the organic vegetables – and to source the finest and best-priced ingredients locally.

Every time Clara updated Kate, she seemed thrilled. The plaster still wasn't on, but she was in good spirits by the sound of it and she seemed to have accepted that rest was the key to a good recovery.

* * *

The Friday of the Young Farmers do was beautiful, as forecast, and as the day wore on and the skies remained clear and the sea gleamed a pristine blue, Clara was relieved on several levels.

The Bluebell didn't have a large bar area – it was part of the main restaurant. The place had never been designed to be a party venue. But the Young Farmers were renowned for being big drinkers and had asked for a champagne reception, which would be held on the terrace if it was a nice evening.

It was also her weekend off. Sunday was the joint birthday celebration for Rosanna and Gran. The 'party' was to be at Rosanna's and if the weather was good this would be outside in her sister's lovely garden. Everyone was chipping in with the catering so the responsibility for cooking didn't fall to any one person. Clara, who was providing two summer berry pavlovas, which everyone loved, was really looking forward to getting together with her whole family and a few extra hand-picked friends. Mum had hinted Grandad might even be there.

'I hope you've told Gran,' Clara had said.

'I wouldn't dare spring something like that on her,' Mum had replied with a touch of sadness in her voice. 'Your gran would never forgive me. But I do hope they're going to put a stop to this silly nonsense soon. Life's too short.'

Clara didn't mention that having an affair, however brief it had been and however old you were, wasn't silly nonsense and that she didn't blame Gran for reacting like she had. They had discussed it all before.

At 5.30 just as Clara was filing paperwork and closing down her laptop ready to go home, Zoe came into the office, looking anxious.

'I don't want to bother you. But no one's turned up yet for the Young Farmers do.'

'It's a bit early, isn't it?'

'Not really. I know the champagne reception doesn't start

until 7.00, but a lot of them are staying overnight. Someone should have checked in by now.'

'Yes. I see what you mean. We had confirmation though, didn't we – on Wednesday, as usual?'

'We did. I spoke to the organiser myself. A guy called Jack Halliwell. It was all systems go.'

'Maybe there's been a traffic incident somewhere.' Clara hooked out her phone to check but couldn't find any mention of traffic issues. 'There'll be an explanation. Don't worry.'

'OK,' Zoe said, unconvinced. She disappeared.

Ten minutes later, Phil Grimshaw appeared at the door, looking agitated, his eyes as black as his dark suit. 'We have a problem,' he said, standing in the doorway with his arms folded.

'Is there still no sign of anyone?'

'No. If they were coming, Clara, they'd be here.'

She knew he was right.

'Would you like me to phone?' he added.

'No, I'll do it.' She picked up the landline on the desk, feeling a prickle of coldness in her stomach. If she hadn't been so distracted with thinking about her family, not to mention Adam Greenwood who kept popping into her thoughts, she'd have picked up on this earlier. Not that she could have done anything other than what she was doing now.

Phil came right into the office as she found the number and dialled. Not far behind him was Zoe, who perched on a chair. They all waited.

The ringtone of the phone changed as it got forwarded to another number that was eventually picked up by a man.

'Could I speak to Jack Halliwell please.'

'You're speaking to him.' He sounded distracted. She could hear faint music in the background.

'This is Clara King from the Bluebell Cliff. We're expecting to host you tonight. I'm just checking that everything's OK.'

There was a sound like a strangled snort on the other end of the line. Then a clunk as if he had dropped the phone. When he picked it up again, he was breathing heavily. 'Is this some kind of a joke?'

'I'm sorry, Mr Halliwell. I'm not with you.'

'You pulled the rug on us...' When she didn't immediately respond, he went on, speaking slowly. 'Someone from your organisation telephoned yesterday morning and cancelled our evening. He said you had double-booked.'

Clara closed her eyes fleetingly. She felt as though she had just stepped into some surreal dream. Her brain kicked in, sharpening her thoughts with adrenaline. 'I am so sorry, but I don't think they telephoned from here. Could you please tell me what time...'? She realised she was talking to a dead line. He had hung up.

She told Zoe and Phil what had happened.

Zoe looked really shocked. Phil swore. 'I'll let the kitchen know.'

'Thanks. I'll need a complete list of everyone who was here yesterday morning,' she told Zoe. 'I think it's highly unlikely that anyone did phone from here. But we need to check. Just in case this is some huge miscommunication somewhere.'

''What else could it be?' Zoe asked.

Clara didn't answer. The alternative didn't bear thinking about, but however much she tried to slip back into a comfortable place of denial, it was the alternative that was the most likely explanation. Someone had sabotaged the booking. Very likely it was the same someone who had posted the video on YouTube.

At 6.45, two photographers from the local society magazine turned up. That jolted Clara too. They were far too curious about why the Young Farmers hadn't arrived. It took all of her tact, and several drinks, to persuade them there had just been an administrative balls-up and it wasn't one worthy of publishing.

By Saturday lunchtime, Clara, who'd given up taking Saturday off, had established several things. No one from the Bluebell had phoned Jack Halliwell and cancelled the booking. Or, to be more accurate, no one had owned up to it. She had no reason to disbelieve them. Sabotaging an event that was so profitable and high profile made no sense.

She had spoken again to Jack Halliwell. She had left him three messages before he'd responded, but he had finally got back to her and she'd been able to persuade him the Bluebell had not been responsible for cancelling the event. Jack had told her, in a manner a little more contrite than his previous one, that the man who'd phoned had been well-spoken and had sounded professional. He'd been profusely apologetic and had offered an alternative date, which Jack had refused. He had also offered compensation.

'What form of compensation?' Clara asked, trying to glean as much information as possible.

'Monetary. To our bank account. I haven't checked if he did it. To be honest with you, I wasn't too worried about compensation. I was just pissed off that he'd pulled the rug on us. It's a humungous amount of work – putting together an event like this.'

'Can we reschedule?'

'We've already rescheduled.' There was a pause that dragged on and on.

'But not with us,' Clara said, feeling sick. 'Do you mind if I ask who you rescheduled with?'

'We went back to our original venue. The Manor House Hotel.'

Mr B was incandescent with rage when he heard this. 'It was

probably those bastards that cancelled it in the first place. I thought you'd come to an arrangement with them. We need to speak to them again. They need to be held accountable.'

'I'll do it,' Clara said swiftly. 'But I really don't think it was them.' Correction. She didn't think it was Adam. Surely she couldn't have been so wrong about him. Could it possibly have been his brother?

Phil didn't think so. 'It's too obvious for it to be the Manor House. They must know we'd soon be looking in their direction. Particularly as they've taken back the booking.'

Mr B had reluctantly conceded that he was right. 'Someone has it in for us though,' he said. 'This is a direct attack.'

Clara's mind flicked back to something Ed, her brother-in-law, had said when they had been talking about Lighthousegate – 'If someone does have a vendetta against the hotel, they'll be up to other mischief too, so you'll soon know about it.'

This definitely qualified as 'other mischief' and it was most likely to be the same person. She could rule out Will then, which was a relief. He was probably still out of the country. He was also unlikely to know that the local branch of the Young Farmers was even having their annual do at the Bluebell.

Then again that was hardly classified information. Twenty Young Farmers knew. So did their guests. So did the society magazine. So did the suppliers. So did anyone the Bluebell staff might have spoken to in the pub.

It would be totally impossible to track down the culprit.

'I know it's a long shot, but it may be worth asking Jack Halliwell if the Young Farmers record incoming calls,' Phil suggested. 'Then maybe we could have a listen – see if anyone in the hotel recognises the guy's voice.'

'Or Jack Halliwell's mobile phone log,' Zoe offered.

'Good idea.' Clara felt a surge of optimism, mixed with anxiety. She would hate to discover Adam's voice on that recording.

But, as it turned out, there was no recording and a withheld number had been used to make the call, so this was never put to the test.

With a heavy heart, she reported the whole thing back to Kate and this time she could tell that her boss was worried.

'That doesn't sound good, Clara. On the bright side, we do have insurance that will cover the cancellation costs, in view of wasted food, vacant rooms, et cetera. I'm not sure what our excess is – it may not be worth making a claim.'

'I'll check,' said Clara, thinking about the conversation she'd had with Mr B a couple of weeks previously about the high menu costs, the staff overtime.

'I'm more worried about bad publicity than anything else,' Kate added. 'About word getting out that we're not reliable. That's much more of a problem than a few canapés.'

It was a bit more than a few canapés, but Clara agreed that she was worried about that too.

Kate gave a deep sigh. 'It is beginning to seem that somebody has an axe to grind. Can Mr B shed any light on it?'

'We've talked through some theories about a neighbouring hotel but nothing really, no.'

'He's mentioned the Manor House before,' Kate said. 'What do you think?'

'I think that we've sorted things out with them.' Clara hoped she was right. 'I had a meeting with Adam Greenwood last week.'

'Is he the one who's ill or the one with the money?' Kate asked. 'I can never remember which one's which.'

'He's not the one who's ill. I didn't know he was the financier. I thought they were partners.'

'According to my late aunt, the brother who was ill had the

dream and the other brother had the money. He got a huge redundancy package from some big I.T. company and he ploughed pretty much all of it into buying that hotel, which maybe wasn't the brightest idea because neither of them had ever run a hotel before and that place is a money pit. It needed loads doing to it.' She paused for breath. 'So did the Bluebell, but we had a bigger budget.'

'I see,' Clara said, feeling her spirits sink lower.

'What did you make of him anyway?'

'I wasn't sure at first, but after we got talking, I warmed to him.'

'I liked him too,' Kate said. 'He's got the reputation for being the grumpy one, but it struck me that was only skin-deep. I respected the fact that he loved his brother enough to risk pretty much everything he owned. He sold his house too apparently to make the sale price – and they don't employ a lot of staff in that place. Not compared to us anyway. I don't know how they do it.'

'I noticed it looked a bit run-down when I visited,' Clara said, wishing that the odds of it being Adam weren't getting higher with each passing second. She'd had no idea of just how much he'd had to lose by having another hotel set up practically next-door.

Kate must have heard her despondency because she said, 'I'm so sorry that I'm not there. Fingers crossed it won't be much longer. I've got an appointment with the consultant next Tuesday. Hopefully he'll say the plaster can go on and then I can get a date to fly back. I don't like the idea of you having to cope with this alone.'

'I'm not. I have Mr B and Phil and Keith and Zoe and a host of other brilliant staff in my corner.'

'All right. But if anything else happens – anything that looks in the slightest way as if it's some kind of sabotage – will you promise to let me know immediately?'

'I promise.'

'Also, can you please let me know if bookings are adversely affected? Or if anything gets into the papers or on social media, or if there's anything at all else that crops up.'

'I will.'

Kate finished by asking the same question she always did. 'How's my lovely girl?'

'She's absolutely fine,' Clara assured her. 'In fact, she's put on weight.' Did she dare joke that Foxy had done quite well out of the cancelled Young Farmers' dinner. As had all the staff. There had been an awful lot of food that wouldn't keep and couldn't be frozen and which she'd advised Mr B to distribute, rather than throw away.

She didn't need to say anything. Kate tuned straight into her thoughts. 'I bet she had a steak dinner last night, didn't she? Don't worry, Clara. We'll get to the bottom of this.'

As Clara hung up, she thought, not for the first time, that she must have the best boss on the planet, as well as the best job. She really could not bear to lose it.

15

The sun stayed for the Sunday afternoon birthday party. It shone out of a cloudless blue sky, picking out the light of a dozen or so sparkling glasses of Prosecco, held by people who were dotted around the garden. The King family didn't do champagne, but they did do posh glasses. Rosanna had got the best ones out and, right at this moment, they were all full in readiness for a toast, which Ed, as the host, was about to deliver. First of all, though, he was making a speech.

'I'd like to thank everyone for coming today and for helping us make another momentous birthday special.' He sounded slightly drunk. Clara wasn't surprised. Ed always knocked it back a bit at gatherings, and whereas roast dinners were good at mopping up alcohol, finger buffets weren't.

'Not that momentous,' Rosanna said under her breath. 'I'm not forty until next year. Oh My God. Forty! Can you believe it?'

Gran winked at her from her place on a patio chair on the decking. 'Wait until you're seventy-seven, angel.'

Rosanna rolled her eyes.

Their mother giggled and said, 'I think I'm a tittle lipsy.'

Dad shushed her.

Clara wished they'd get on with it. It had been a pleasant afternoon, but she'd been disappointed that Grandad hadn't turned up. Or, more to the point, as her mother had hissed to her when she'd arrived, he hadn't been allowed to turn up.

Ed cleared his throat and scratched his forehead. He'd clearly lost his thread. 'Where was I – ah yes... Birthdays are times when we all reflect on milestones and the importance of family and...' He broke off as if he'd suddenly remembered that one particularly important member of the family was missing. 'They are also a time to remember abshent friends and family.'

He was definitely drunk, Clara thought, glancing across to where he stood with one hand on the wooden rail of the decking a few feet in front of her. God bless him. Ed wasn't allowed to drink much most of the time, in view of driving artic trucks around the country. He was obviously letting his hair down. He had a grass stain on the backside of his jeans where he'd been sitting on the lawn with the kids.

'I'd like you to raise your glasses and join with me in a Happy Birthday toast to Rosanna and Thelma, without whom today would not be possible. Happy birthday, Rosanna and Thelma.'

'Happy birthday, Rosanna and Thelma,' everyone echoed.

Then, into the silence that followed the toasts, a little girl, who Clara thought might belong to a friend of Rosanna's, said in a loud voice, 'What a tittle lipsy, Mum?'

Clara smiled and took a sip of Prosecco, relishing its taste on her tongue. She hadn't drunk anything else as she was driving and she rarely drank much anyway. She was sitting on the opposite side of the wooden decking from Gran. On her left there was a lavender bush in full flower – she could smell its distinctive sweetness and she could feel the summer air on her face. In the sky, a plane had left a curving smoke trail behind it and, beneath the murmur of chatter in the large garden, she could discern birdsong.

Maybe this was the best place to be today. It was a good distraction. If she'd gone into work, she would only have been worrying. She'd have got caught up in the speculation that had been hard to stop at the Bluebell Cliff, no matter how much she'd asked them not to discuss it. Who had cancelled the Young Farmers Booking? What had they been trying to achieve? Who would possibly want to do a thing like that?

She closed her eyes for a second, but she could still see the brightness of the sun behind her lids. Then a shadow passed over them and she heard Rosanna's voice.

'Hey, Sis. We haven't had a proper chance to catch up. How's it going?' The chair beside her squeaked as Rosanna settled herself into it. 'Thanks for that beautiful scarf. It was inspired. You have exquisite taste. I've only just discovered how much I love teal.'

'You're very welcome.' Clara opened her eyes. 'Lovely party. What happened with Grandad? I thought he was coming.'

Rosanna glanced over at Gran, who appeared to be snoozing, but was in hearing range if she wasn't. 'I don't think Gran's quite finished punishing him yet. You can't blame her.'

'I'm not punishing him, girls. That is not what's happening here.' Gran's eyes snapped open and she sat up stiffly. 'I simply don't think it's appropriate that Eric comes waltzing back into a family gathering after a gap of several weeks.'

'But it's your birthday, Gran.'

'Yes,' Rosanna echoed. 'Did he send you a card?'

'He did.'

'So are you planning to meet up with him then?' Rosanna asked. 'To talk about him being integrated back into the family.'

Gran sat up straighter and adjusted her glasses on her nose

and tutted. 'Before any integration can take place – as you put it – yes, I will need to meet up with your grandfather. But the timing of that is down to me. And me alone.'

Neither of them argued. It was pointless. She had that stubborn look on her face.

Clara changed the subject. 'I keep meaning to tell you I saw your friend Anastasia in The Anchor the other day. When I was dropping off one of our guests for a meal.'

Rosanna looked worried. 'You didn't blow your cover, did you?'

'No. I don't think so. Although it was quite a close thing. She was there with someone I know. Another hotel owner.'

'Oh bugger. That must have been awkward.'

'It was.' Clara told her about Foxy's shenanigans with the upended table and Rosanna shook her head in amazement. 'Dogs and children eh – they always let you down. I'm sorry I put you in that position, honey.'

'You're forgiven. Just promise me you won't do it again.'

'I won't. And if it makes you feel any better, I may have redeemed myself by letting out your house for the next fortnight to a couple who are down here on a house-hunting mission. How's that for a good result?'

'That's fantastic, thank you.'

Rosanna looked smug and Clara sipped her drink. 'Do you know Adam or Nick Greenwood who co-own the Manor House Hotel? They're Anastasia's cousins apparently.'

She was trying to keep her voice ultra-casual. Even though saying Adam's name made her feel super aware. It was an odd mixture of emotions. Good and bad. She still hadn't totally decided whether he was friend or foe. Fortunately, Rosanna was now too distracted to pick up on Clara's mood. She was busy checking what her children were up to.

'No. I can't say I do. I don't know any of her relatives, apart from her husband, Charles – he earns shedloads of money – hedge funds.' She shielded her eyes against the afternoon sun and called across to Tom, who was feeding a delighted Foxy bits of sausage roll from the buffet. 'Don't give her too much darling. You'll make her sick.'

'He probably won't,' Clara said. 'She's got a cast-iron stomach. Perks of being a stray.'

The conversation moved on to other things, like the fact that Clara's FunFit had clocked up 400 steps when she had driven over here and only 450 when she'd taken Foxy for her morning walk. And how it misspelled many of its motivational messages. The latest one she'd noticed was, "Say no to coke." She was pretty sure it meant "cake". Clara wondered why she hadn't told Rosanna about the Young Farmers cancellation and whether she could get away with quizzing her any more about Adam without awakening Rosanna's matchmaking radar. Then Mum came across for a chat and she decided to just put everything to do with work out of her mind. She would drive herself mad if she wasn't careful.

* * *

On the Tuesday after the joint birthday party, Adam turned up in person at the Bluebell. Clara was in the restaurant talking to Phil about some holiday cover they needed when Zoe came in to give her the message.

'He's in reception and he's Mr Stroppy. I wasn't sure you'd want to speak to him, so I said I'd check if you were in.' She looked anxiously over her shoulder as if she expected him to have followed her.

'Did he say what it was about?'

'No. Just that he wanted to speak to you.'

'It's fine. Send him into the office. I'll be there in a second.'

Adam did look pissed off when she went into the office. He was standing up by the window in profile to her. Grumpy Orlando, she thought as he turned.

'Clara, hi. Apologies for turning up unannounced, but I felt it was warranted. It's about the Young Farmers.'

Her heart thumped hard. 'Go on.'

'Nick just told me what's been going on over here.'

'In what respect?' she asked carefully. She had closed the office door, but she hadn't sat down. Now she walked across and stood beside him at the window and stared out at the view across the lawns. A young couple was strolling hand in hand towards the gate that led to the cliff path. They had a group of writers in this week. They were a random collection of people, all of them escaping from the restraints and routines of home. Some more than others, by the look of it.

'Nick said they'd booked us for their annual event, last minute, because it had been cancelled by yourselves. Due to a double booking that turned out not to be a double booking.'

She glanced at him. 'You're very well informed.'

'Yes.' He didn't elaborate. But she wasn't surprised he knew. 'I'm here out of courtesy,' he went on. 'In view of our meeting.'

'Thank you,' she said. It's nice of you.'

'It felt like the right thing to do.' A beat during which she was hyperaware of him. His scent, his proximity, his tension. She could hear the worry in his voice as he went on. 'I understand that the cancellation call was made by a third party. I wanted you to know it had nothing to do with us.' Another little pause. 'That's all.'

'I didn't think it had anything to do with you.'

'Did you not? Not even for a second?' He met her eyes. 'You're more generous-spirited than I am, Clara.'

She didn't contradict him. Even though she knew she should have done. Because she had doubted him, hadn't she, and for quite a bit longer than a second. 'It was good of you to come,' she said. 'I appreciate it.'

After he had gone again, she reflected that he hadn't said a thing about the fact that the Young Farmers had traditionally always gone to the Manor House anyway.

He might be in denial about it, but he was every bit as generous-spirited as he'd credited her with being.

* * *

Clara and Phil held an extra mini emergency team meeting, where they warned the staff to be hypervigilant.

'What are we supposed to be watching out for?' Ellie May asked, smoothing down her dark skirt. 'Unattended luggage? Bombs under tables? People starting fires?'

'No. Nothing like that,' Phil said quickly. 'There is absolutely no need to turn this into a drama.'

'I thought you liked dramas,' Mr B taunted.

Phil glared at him. 'We just want you to be careful and for all of us to be aware that someone out there does seem to have a gripe with us. We clearly have an enemy.'

'Do you mean like making sure that we double confirm every booking?' Zoe asked. 'And we make sure deposits are paid. Stuff like that.'

'That's exactly what we mean,' Clara said.

'I will certainly make sure that no one sneaks into my kitchen and poisons the food,' Mr B said, with something resembling a flounce. He could be incredibly camp sometimes.

Phil glared at him again and Clara bit her lip. She wished he hadn't said that. She'd never have thought of it otherwise.

'I will patrol vigilantly the restaurant at all times,' Jakob said, swinging his arms, military-style

'And I will ensure we have no mysterious visitors in the dead of night,' Keith said. 'Although I may make an exception for attractive, twenty-something blondes. Call me the eternal optimist.'

Everyone laughed. Keith was a very stocky five foot six in his built-up heels, with thinning hair. He was definitely more Jack Nicholson than Jack Reacher. But Clara was grateful to him for lightening the mood.

'I'll keep an eye out when I'm changing beds,' Janet said. 'It's amazing what you find in people's rooms. This old couple left a pair of handcuffs under the bed last week. They were pushing seventy.'

'You're making it up,' someone said.

'I am not. They were pink and fluffy.'

'The handcuffs or the couple?'

'Did you take them home and try them out on your hubby?'

'They were locked,' Janet said, pursing her lips. 'I never found the key.'

'Give me strength,' Phil said, exchanging glances with Clara. 'Right, everybody. Back to work. Don't get paranoid.' He shot a glance at Mr B. 'But don't be too complacent either.'

'Kate will be back very soon,' Clara reminded them all. 'Her appointment with the consultant's on Friday, so I should have an update for you at our next meeting.'

There were murmurings of, 'Give her our best.'

Clara nodded an acknowledgment, but unease tugged at her. The truth was that neither she nor Phil really knew what to tell them to watch out for because they didn't know themselves. It was very difficult to be on your guard against an unknown attacker. Especially as you didn't know when or from which direction the next attack would come.

16

September began without any incidents, although they did have some false alarms.

There was chaos in the restaurant one breakfast time when a guest discovered a black beetle, which turned out to be plastic, floating in his teapot.

'How on earth did it get there?' Mr B shouted, storming around the kitchen with the offending item held between his thumb and index finger and a look of utmost distaste on his haughty, angular face. 'One of you zounderkites must know something about it?'

After about five minutes of ranting, a young waiter from the agency owned up. 'I put it there as a joke,' he admitted, holding his hands up and looking very worried. 'OK, with hindsight, I shouldn't have done it, but I knew the guy. He was the best man at my wedding. I thought he'd laugh. How was I to know his wife would find it?'

'It was in very bad taste,' Mr B scolded.

'It would have been if it had melted,' Ellie May offered.

No one dared laugh. Mr B was in too bad a mood.

Clara, who had been party to the whole thing only because she'd been in the kitchen at the time, made a tactical retreat. Everyone was still on edge. A few years ago, a prank like that would have been funny, but these days there was too much health and safety, too many rules, and too much litigation.

The second week of September began badly. Kate phoned to update Clara about what had happened with her consultant, but it was obvious as soon as she started speaking that it was not good news.

'You're not going to believe this, but I've managed to get an infection in my foot? The consultant took one look at it and started shaking his head.'

Clara could hear the despondency in her voice and she murmured sympathetically.

'It's not serious. Well, not in the big scheme of things – but it means I can't have the plaster on yet, which means, of course, that I can't fly. So I'm afraid I'm stuck out here. On the plus side, Aiden's now here with me. He flew out last week to give me moral support – so now Mum has two of us in her corner.' She sighed. 'Actually I'm really glad he's here. It's lovely not to have to do everything on my own.'

'I'll bet,' Clara said. Aiden was Kate's partner. Clara had only met him a couple of times, but she remembered him as being Mr Laid Back. He was also quite a hottie – he looked like Jude Law and managed to be ultra cool and always have a twinkle in his eyes. She was pleased he was looking after Kate.

'You don't need to worry about anything here,' she added. 'I know we never got to the bottom of the Young Farmer's cancellation, but we've had no more problems. We've warned everyone to be hypervigilant.'

'Thank you,' Kate said. 'Clara, I'm aware that I must owe you some holiday. As soon as I'm back, you must take some time off. No arguments.'

'OK,' Clara agreed.

Despite everything, there was a part of her that still didn't want Kate to come back. It would be weird no longer having total autonomy. She would miss looking after Foxy too – she'd got really fond of the little dog. And although it would be nice to be back in her own house, there were advantages to living in Kate's bungalow and having an eight-minute commute to work. She was certainly not looking forward to fighting her way through the holiday traffic every day like everyone else had to do.

To cheer herself up, she decided to invest some of her Airbnb money in another bag and she trawled through eBay for a bargain and found a Poseidon blue Mulberry with tags and a receipt for less than half the recommended retail price. There was a fierce bidding war going on and Clara felt a tingle of excitement as she joined in. The deadline was eleven a.m. on Wednesday and she was busy upping her bid at ten forty-five when Zoe came in for a tea break. She looked up guiltily.

'Are you on a bag-buying mission?' Zoe asked idly.

'Is it that obvious?'

'Only to me. Mum accuses me of having this certain look – somewhere between sparkly-eyed excitement and teeth-gritting obsession – I might be totally wrong, but I think I just saw that very same look on your face.'

'Well, you're right as it happens.' Clara beckoned her over and showed her the Mulberry and, to her alarm, Zoe looked horrified. 'What?' Clara said. 'Don't tell me we're bidding against each other again because if we are it's definitely your turn to drop out.'

'No, we're not. But I think that's a fake. Can you withdraw?'

'No way.' Clara dropped her phone as though it was hot. 'It doesn't look like a fake.'

'I know, but I think it is. There are a lot of fake Mulberries around. I was reading this blog about how to tell the difference. One of the ways is the stitching and that one's got really odd stitching. If you zoom in on the strap, you can see it. Funnily enough, I was looking at it last night.'

Zoe flipped up the blog on her phone and for a few seconds they pored over the stitching on the fake bag compared with the real thing and Clara had to concede that the younger woman was right. There were a tense few moments when she tried to retract her bid and couldn't, but then, to her huge relief, someone outbid her and the pressure was off.

'That's one way to win an auction,' Zoe said, widening her eyes. 'All's fair in love and war, isn't it, boss?'

Clara stared at her in shock. 'You wouldn't? Would you...?'

Zoe's eyes sparkled with merriment. 'Of course I wouldn't. And if I did, I'd hardly confess ten seconds later. No, I really think it is a fake.'

They both burst out laughing and for a while they found they couldn't stop.

'Oh, I needed that,' Clara said eventually, wiping her eyes.

'Me too. Things have been way too serious around here with this saboteur business.'

'How's the sweepstake going for the naming of Mr B?' Clara asked and Zoe's mouth dropped open.

'When did you find out about that?'

'The day Phil opened the book, I think. So what's the current favourite?'

'Bertram Bumppo, I think. And yes that is a real surname. Ellie May found it online. For ages, the top favourite was Bertram Bottomley with odds of two to one, but I think Bumppo's trumped that one – if you'll excuse the pun.'

'Definitely a theme going then,' Clara said, trying to keep a straight face. 'Don't let him catch you, he'll go mad.'

'He shouldn't be so secretive then, should he?' Zoe was unrepentant. 'But, no, don't worry. Phil keeps the book in the restaurant petty cash tin and he's the only one with the key.'

Clara hoped it stayed that way. She could imagine Phil and Mr B actually coming to blows if that book and its contents came to light.

* * *

During the second week of September, there was another minor incident. The fire alarm went off one afternoon, which interrupted a recording taking place in the studio. It wouldn't have mattered because the studio was soundproof, but the staff had to interrupt at a critical point, just in case there actually was a fire.

The musicians, who were sending an audition tape to a record label, were three quarters of the way through their first perfect take – of course they were – out of sixteen imperfect takes, and they were none too pleased when Clara told them they'd have to leave the building. Particularly when they later discovered that the alarm had been set off by someone who'd opened a fire door on the second-floor landing so they could sneak out for a vape.

'Why they didn't just go downstairs, like everyone else does, I'll never know,' Clara had said when she realised what had happened. But as the culprit was one of the musician's partners and not a random guest, at least she could be sure that there had been no hint of sabotage going on.

Sabotage had also been ruled out when all the hairdryers on the first floor developed faults and blew their fuses one after the other. Phil Grimshaw did some research online and discovered that they'd been part of a faulty batch that Kate had happened to buy during the Bluebell's refurbishment, and that there was actually a manufacturer's recall going on.

'My mum had a tumble dryer that got recalled once,' Ellie May had said in amazement. 'But I didn't know it happened with hairdryers. I could do with a new hairdryer.' She had gone off hopefully to check her dryer at home.

There was also the mysterious incident of the intruder on the roof. This happened when Clara wasn't on duty, but she got the complete rundown from Keith when she got in the next day.

'I've had a very exciting night,' he said, looking up from his place behind reception when she arrived.

'What kind of exciting?' Clara said, stopping abruptly by the desk and smoothing down her hair, which a brisk clifftop breeze had done a good job of mussing up on the short journey between her car and reception. 'It's windy out there today.'

'I was aware of the inclement weather.' Keith flicked over a page in front of him and cleared his throat.

Clara helped herself to one of the individually wrapped mint imperials from the bowl they kept there. She had recently stipulated that these should be sugar-free. 'Tell me more,' she said, putting it in her mouth and screwing up her face as the mint's saccharine sweetness hit her tongue. They were going to have to go back to sugar.

If Keith said it was exciting, then it would be worth hearing about. He could go on a bit, but he wasn't a drama queen.

He took a sip of the black coffee that kept him awake. He drank it by the bucketload and he didn't mind if it was hot or cold. 'At 1.00 a.m. I had a call from the young couple in room eighteen, complaining of an intruder on the roof. Unfortunately that wasn't Mr Bennett's only concern.'

Clara felt her heart sink.

'He was also under the impression that the intruder was

possibly a murderer because he and his wife had heard something that sounded like a body being dragged across the roof above their heads.'

'What the—' She just stopped herself from swearing.

'My sentiments exactly.' He chewed the end of his pen thoughtfully. 'Further questioning revealed that they'd been watching some horror film into the early hours and had become a little – what Mr B might call overwrought.'

'Thank goodness for that. So what did you do?'

Keith leaned forward. 'What I always do, Clara, in times of trouble. I made lots of soothing noises. I reassured them that no one could possibly have sneaked up onto the roof, murderer or otherwise, because I'd locked the door to the roof myself at nine p.m., having already checked that there was no one up there. Just as I always do.'

'And were they happy with that?'

'No.' He tutted. 'They were not. I even showed them the CCTV, but he wasn't having any of it. So I went the extra mile, in accordance with the Bluebell's ethos, and because we are all being particularly vigilant at the moment.' He took another slug of coffee. 'I toddled up to their room to have a listen to these mysterious nocturnal noises.'

'Thank you for doing that. Did you hear anything?'

'Oddly enough, yes I did. It was a little unnerving. Even for someone as level-headed as myself. I have to say that it did indeed sound like a body in a sack being dragged across the roof.'

Clearly it had been nothing of the sort because he was now smiling. A Jack Nicholson smile.

Trying not to screw up her face, Clara swallowed the last of the mint imperial and waited.

'So, Clara, I did what any responsible night porter would do and I hotfooted it up to the roof door. I must admit I was relieved to find it still locked.' He leaned forward, as he built up to the climax of his story. 'You'll never guess what it was?'

'Giant seagulls?' she hedged.

'Not giant seagulls, no, but nice try. You're right though. Our intruder was of a benign nature or I might not be here to tell the tale. Thank you, sir.' He broke off to take some keys from a guest going out for an after-breakfast stroll. Then he fixed his full attention back on Clara. 'Just now, you mentioned the inclement weather. I think it must have been even windier during the night because, unlikely as it seems, it was actually deckchairs that were making the noise. Two or three had been left out on the flat roof and the wind had hooked in under the seats, using them exactly like sails, if you can visualise that, and dragging them across the roof. It sounded exactly like a murderer dragging a body in a sack. A great deal more so, probably, if you'd been watching horror films.'

'Were Mr and Mrs Bennett all right after you'd explained what it was?'

'They were fine. They were feeling a little foolish, I think, but they were also very grateful that I'd taken their complaint seriously and we all had a little joke about it.' He leaned back in his chair. 'I don't get the chance to be a hero very often. It's done my ego the power of good.' He glanced up as Zoe came in through the main doors. 'Mr and Mrs Bennett haven't been down for breakfast yet, so I suspect they may be having a lie-in.' He shook his head. 'It all happens at the Bluebell.'

Clara would have preferred that it all stopped happening at the Bluebell. At least until Kate got the all-clear and finally came back, even though logic told her that it was impossible for things to run completely smoothly, no matter how much effort you put in. There were too many variables when you worked with the general public. This was one of the things she both loved and hated about her job. The unpredictability of people was fun, but the unpredictability of events unnerved her and she supposed they were inextricably entwined.

* * *

'There are three very important dates coming up in October,' she told Phil when they were going through the upcoming bookings, which they did in their mid-month handover session halfway through September.

'I saw the Curly Wurly stretching on the fourth,' he said, looking up. 'Is that genuinely a Guinness World Record?'

'It sure is.'

'Jesus. What's the world coming to! Then there's the Scargill Wedding on the tenth.'

'Yep.'

'So what's the other one?'

Clara smiled at him. 'About ten minutes before this meeting I had an email from Kate to tell me that she's booked her flight. The plaster went on this morning and she's been cleared to fly, so she and Aiden are coming back on the seventeenth.'

'And you want everything to be running like clockwork. Don't worry. It will be.' He glanced at the bookings diary that was up on the laptop. 'We've got a yoga group coming on the seventeenth for four days. Not much can go wrong with that. Although I suppose someone could put their back out. I nearly put my back out once when I was doing yoga.'

'How? I thought it was a nice, gentle exercise. Were you in an advanced group or something?'

'No, I was on stage. I was understudy for a yoga guru in this mad production and I hadn't put in quite enough work, due to the fact I was also working full-time in a restaurant. So I was too stiff to get into the pose.'

'Never a dull moment,' Clara said.

'In the theatre – or the hotel trade?' he quipped. 'To be honest, they have a lot of similarities.' He paused. 'Have you spoken to Adam Greenwood lately? I heard on the grapevine that Nick went into hospital the other day.'

'Oh really? That's not good. No I haven't.'

Adam cropped up often in her thoughts, but they hadn't spoken much recently. Their lovely evening out had been four weeks ago and Clara had to admit that for a couple of weeks she'd been disappointed there had been no suggestion of a repeat performance.

But why would there be? He'd made it perfectly clear that he didn't like people and his one brief marriage had put him off women for life. No, he hadn't said that. But it was what she'd read between the lines. And anyway, theirs had been a business meeting, nothing more, she reminded herself.

'Is Nick all right?' she asked Phil now.

'Obviously not, as he's in hospital.' Phil leaned back in the office chair and linked his hands behind his head. 'I don't think it's life-threatening. He has some chronic condition, doesn't he?'

'Yes. He has. Poor guy. I'll give Adam a call.'

'In the interests of good hotel relations,' Phil said, with a little sparkle in his eye, 'That is probably a good idea.'

Clara felt heat warming her cheeks. 'Absolutely. In the meantime, we should probably go through the details of the wedding booking.'

'There's not that much left to do. We've got detailed instructions for how they want the venue to be set up. The cake is being delivered the day before – they arranged that themselves. Likewise, the flowers. Mr B's on top of the catering. The registrar is booked and I have told him to contact me personally should he receive any phone calls instructing any change of plan. It's all in hand.'

Clara let out a breath she didn't realise she'd been holding.

'Relax,' Phil told her with one of his rare smiles. 'Nothing is going to go wrong with the Bluebell's first wedding.'

17

Clara phoned Adam on his mobile number, which he'd given her for ease of communication, on Saturday morning from home. After a few rings, his voicemail kicked in. She didn't leave a message She tried the Manor House instead.

The call was answered by a woman with a singsong Welsh accent.

'Can I speak to Adam Greenwood please?'

'I'm afraid he's not here at the moment. Can I take a message?'

'No thanks. I'll try him again later.' Clara felt frustrated. Maybe she should have pushed her pride to one side and tried to get in touch with him sooner. It must be horrible having someone you love in hospital. She wondered if he was with Nick now. If he was, then Nick must be bad. Changeover days were the times he'd be most needed at work.

Her phone rang almost as soon as she had disconnected and she snatched it up, feeling a ridiculous thrill of pleasure. He must be ringing her back. He wasn't though – not unless he was calling from an unknown number.

'Hello love.' Her grandfather's distinctive gruff voice filled her ear and she felt a flash of guilt. She had meant to ring him after the party. Poor Grandad – OK, so he might have played Russian roulette with his marriage, but he was paying a very heavy price for it.

'Hi,' she said, taking the phone out into the back garden and watching Foxy, who was doing a circuit of the perimeter. The air smelled of sunshine and jasmine. There was a trellis close to the back door. It must be blooming so late because it was in such a sheltered spot. Her feet sunk into the grass as she walked towards the back gate. 'Is everything all right?'

'No, love. Not really.' Over a background hum of voices, she could hear the sounds of his slightly laboured breathing. Grandad had COPD, brought on by years of smoking, and it was obviously troubling him today. 'Have you got time for a cuppa and a teacake, love? I want to talk to someone sensible and I think I've chewed off your mother's ear enough lately.'

'Of course I have.' She felt warmed by his call. 'Where are you? Shall I come over this afternoon?'

'Are you available sooner?' There was more laboured breathing. 'I'm at Osmington. I came down with Jim and Elsie in the car. He's taken Elsie shopping. I'm sitting in the Copper Kettle.' He ran out of breath again and the background buzz of chatter made a bit more sense.

'I'll come down now,' Clara said.

Three quarters of an hour later, she was sitting opposite him in the cinnamon- and coffee-scented friendliness of the popular cafe. The Copper Kettle was a tourist paradise and business was brisk on sunny Saturdays, even at the tail end of the season.

Her grandfather's appearance had been quite a shock. He'd lost weight since the last time she'd seen him, which couldn't have been more than a couple of months ago. He had always been on the rotund side, so the losing weight thing wasn't too much of an issue, but he also looked gaunt around the eyes and a bit shadowed. Worse than all of that, he looked sad. No, it was more than sad, Clara thought. He looked resigned and a bit beaten too. He had a teacake in front of him cut into quarters, but he'd only had one bite of one quarter before he'd pushed the plate to one side.

Clara wished fervently that they hadn't all just left him to get on with it. Even though she knew that Mum was in touch regularly. She wished they had interfered and hadn't done what they'd all agreed in the family confabs, which had been to offer support to both parties but not to offer advice. She wished they had all sat in a room and said, 'For heaven's sake, you two. This is madness. You've been happily married for your entire life. Sort it out.'

She reached across and covered his age-spotted hand with her own. His skin felt as dry as an autumn leaf and as thin. 'Can I do anything? Would it help if I spoke to Gran?'

He squeezed her fingers. Then he looked at her for a long moment and shook his head. 'I think we've gone past that, love.' With the hand she wasn't holding, he rubbed his cheek, leaving a red mark there. 'Though, if anyone could help, it would be you. Clara the diplomat. We knew you were that right from the start. Since you were about three years old, Thelma and I thought you'd end up being a politician. Or one of them diplomatic immunity types – did we ever tell you that?'

'Gran may have mentioned it once or twice, yes. Being a hotel manager probably isn't that different. It's my job to keep everyone happy.'

'But not to lie through your teeth, eh love. Not like your old Grandad.'

She felt desperately sorry for him. 'You haven't lied through your teeth. You made one silly mistake. You can't beat yourself up for ever over that.'

A waitress hovered at their table. 'Can I clear these up?' Her eyes were impatient and Clara read the subtext there: If you're not having anything else can you please bugger off. People are waiting for a table.

She ordered another pot of tea for Grandad and another cinnamon latte for her and a hunk of lemon drizzle polenta cake, which she had an idea was slightly healthier than the chocolate gateaux.

When the waitress had disappeared again, Grandad gave a wheezy sigh and then looked at her squarely. 'The thing is, love. It wasn't just the one silly mistake. There was another one.'

'Another mistake?' Now he had really shocked her. 'Do you mean there was another woman? A different one from this Mary person, I mean?'

'That's about the size of it.' He dropped his eyes now, unlinked his hand from hers and picked up his used serviette, which he smoothed out beside his plate, pushing all the crumbs into one corner. Clara felt the cool space where his hand had been round hers, in the same way you do when you've taken off a glove.

'When was this? Does Gran know?' But even as she voiced the latter question Clara knew that she must. She hadn't just been being ultra sniffy. Not that any of them had ever blamed her, because she'd had a right to be ultra sniffy. She'd had the moral high ground all along. But suddenly the three Sids made a lot more sense. She'd been hurting more than any of them realised, because this hadn't been the first time but the second. Poor Gran.

'I know...' Grandad said now as if he had read her face and knew exactly what she was thinking. 'I told you I was a silly old fool. I don't deserve a decent woman like Thelma.' He coughed quietly.

All round them, the muted conversation of the other tables merged into a single low buzz and the scents of cake and coffee and sweetness threaded through it.

The waitress arrived back with their drinks and the polenta cake and decanted them onto the table with fresh cutlery.

Clara tried to gather her thoughts, which were swirling. How could she best be the diplomat that he'd so recently told her that she was? She stirred the cinnamon into the froth of her latte. Maybe she should just listen.

He began to speak again. 'The first mistake was a long time ago – the late sixties. We'd been married for just over seven years at the time – they used to call it the seven-year itch back then. I'd got made redundant and I was having trouble finding another job – we'd been having a few financial difficulties.' He went back to smoothing the serviette. 'It doesn't matter about the details. The fact is that I got close to another woman. It didn't go anywhere. It wasn't the same as this time. In some ways, it was worse because I had strong feelings for her, but I didn't leave your gran. We had a young daughter, your mother.' He gave the tiniest of sighs. 'I didn't do anything. But I did tell Thelma about these feelings. I thought it was the right thing to do at the time. The honourable thing to do. If you can use the word honourable in such circumstances.' His eyes clouded at the ancient memory. 'She was so hurt. I didn't think we would ever get back on track.'

'When you say you didn't do anything – do you mean literally nothing,' Clara asked, torn between not wanting to pry and yet wanting to understand.

'One kiss. That was what it was, but I felt as though I'd committed adultery. As far as Thelma was concerned, I had. This woman was someone we both knew, you see. A neighbour. After it all came out, she moved away. I never saw her again.'

Clara felt a tug of compassion for him. In the big scheme of things, it didn't seem too great a crime. By today's standards, she didn't think it could even be considered adultery, yet she could see how much it could have hurt, how much damage it could have done. And how this latest transgression could have brought all the pain flooding back down the years.

She'd once had a friend, Liz, who had divorced her husband because he'd got close to another woman online. They had co-written an erotic novel, with themselves as leads, and sent it back and forth, each of them writing the next chapter. Even though they had never actually touched each other, had never even kissed, Liz had felt totally betrayed when she had found out. Sometimes emotional intimacy could be just as painful as a physical betrayal.

'But you did get back on track eventually,' Clara said now. 'And you've had a good marriage since.'

'We've had our ups and downs, but, yes, we've had a wonderful marriage. I fell in love with her, you know, from the moment we met. We were at a tea dance – she was the most beautiful girl in the room and I couldn't believe my luck when she agreed to a dance.' For a moment, his face brightened. 'I married your grandmother when I was twenty. I had this vision of everything being lovely and there being this one special person who would make you happy for the rest of your days. We were taught to believe that. It really was until death us do part. And we really did think there would only be one person. It's so different, today. It's more acceptable, isn't it – to have friends of the opposite sex.'

Not friends that you kiss, Clara wanted to say. But she didn't, because the fact that he was unburdening himself to her made her feel both privileged and humbled. She certainly didn't want to argue with him.

'What time are Jim and Elsie picking you up?'

'They're phoning me on this.' He reached into his jacket

pocket and produced the mobile he must have summoned her on and he peered at the screen. 'Ah – I think they might have done. Can you read what that says, love?'

'Three missed calls. The last one ten minutes ago. They're probably on their way here. Look, Grandad. We can stop them. I can drive you back. And we can talk some more. Maybe I could even take you round to see Gran... as we're halfway there anyway?' She broke off. His face had closed down again and she wished she hadn't mentioned Gran. 'OK, we won't see Gran. But we could talk some more.'

He shook his head. 'I appreciate it, love. But I think I'll go back now. There's nothing to be gained from talking about it any more. Don't get me wrong. That's why I asked you to come and I'm glad I did. It has made things clearer for me. The thing is, I've made a decision. Thelma doesn't want me back. She's made that very clear. I'm going to do what she wants and tell her she can have a divorce.'

'But I'm sure that's not what she wants at all.' Clara gave a gasp of horror. 'She still loves you.'

'Did she say that? Because I still love her.' His voice was suddenly full of hope.

'No. But she doesn't need to...' Why hadn't she just lied and said yes. The light that had appeared so briefly in his eyes had flickered off again.

The front door of the shop was just opening. Through its misted-up glass, Clara could see Elsie and Jim, coming in.

'Please. Grandad. Don't go over there talking about divorce. She might agree. You know how pig-headed she is. It'll make things worse.'

'It's not what I want. It truly isn't. I love your gran. But maybe it would be for the best. I've apologised until I'm blue in the face, but she still won't let me back in the house. I don't know what else to do. I miss her so much, but I can't be living in this limbo for too much longer.'

Elsie and Jim had arrived at the table. Elsie was laden with bags and smiling and Jim was his usual more taciturn self, but undoubtedly just as pleased to see her.

'Eric didn't say he was meeting you, love.'

'It was spur of the moment,' Grandad said, standing up. 'I need to pay a visit.'

He threaded his way through the tables in the direction of the door marked Toilet and Elsie put her hand on Clara's arm. 'I'm glad he called you. Has he said anything about going back to Thelma? We think they're close to a reconciliation, don't we, Jim?'

'No. In fact he just mentioned asking her for a divorce,' Clara said, watching the disappointment register on their faces.

A fine diplomat she was turning out to be.

18

As she drove back, Clara was torn between going to see Gran, phoning Rosanna, or phoning their mother to suggest they had an urgent family confab. The first option would probably be the least productive and she wasn't keen on doing the last because she had a feeling that Mum might feel betrayed that Grandad hadn't spoken to her instead. She hated being caught in the middle. But she was going to have to do something.

She took Foxy out on the cliff path to think things through. As she walked with the little dog trotting ahead in that strange, slightly crooked three-legged gait she had, she breathed in the salt air and listened to the shrieks of the gulls above and the crashing of the waves against the rocks below and wondered what to do.

The wild beauty of the coastline never failed to soothe her and the emptiness of the vast sky and the rhythms of the sea always helped to put things into perspective. Yet today, as she paused to look out at Old Harry Rocks, all she could think about was estranged families.

Old Harry Rocks were three giant chalk stacks that marked

the most eastern tip of the Jurassic coastline. They loomed up out of the sea, great white rocks that had once been part of the headland itself but thanks to the sea's erosion were now completely separate from it.

Legend had it that Old Harry was a devil that had once slept on the rocks and the smaller white chalk stack alongside him was his wife. But today all Clara could see in the small stack was Grandad, pulling away from his family, cutting himself off from three generations of love and stability. How could he do that at this late stage of his life? Surely there was some way back for him and Gran?

She couldn't bear to think of them at the end of their lives, each living alone in separate houses. It was too sad. And she was sure that deep down it wasn't what either of them wanted. Grandad was clearly depressed and Gran wasn't happy either, despite the brave face she was putting on

By the time Clara had got back to the bungalow again, her hands and legs were tingling from the sea breeze and the exercise and she'd made up her mind to call Rosanna. With a mug of coffee warming her hands and Foxy crashed out on the rug, she sat in the lounge and dialled. It was teatime. Her sister would be cooking, or maybe Ed would if he was home.

Rosanna's phone went straight to voicemail, which meant she must be in a no-signal area and then Clara remembered that they had gone away for the weekend. They had a caravan that they occasionally towed up to the New Forest and plonked in a park. It was a cheap break for them and the children. Rosanna had said something the other day about doing that. She'd forgotten.

Suddenly she was relieved that Rosanna had been in a no-signal area. Clara definitely didn't want to spoil her nice family weekend with talk of divorce. Had there ever even been a divorce in their family? Clara couldn't remember one. She knew that was pretty rare these days. Something like one in four marriages ended in divorce, but the prospect of her own grandparents doing it, after nearly sixty years, for goodness' sake, really hurt. She couldn't let it happen.

She paced back into the kitchen. She was hungry. Aside from polenta cake, she hadn't eaten today. Her mobile rang when she was in the middle of this tumult of thoughts and she ran back into the lounge to answer it. Maybe Grandad was phoning to tell her he had come to his senses. Then she wouldn't have to do anything at all.

'Hello.' She snatched it up hopefully.

'Hello,' said Adam.

'Oh. Hi.'

'You were expecting someone else. Sorry if it's bad timing. I've just found a missed call from you on my phone.'

'No. I'm sorry.' She gave a deep sigh. 'It's not bad timing. I'm just having a few family issues.' She remembered that he was too. 'How's Nick? I heard that he was in hospital.'

'He's out again now. I picked him up this morning. But thank you for asking. That's kind.' His voice had warmed up. 'How are you, Clara? Long time, no speak.'

'I'm all right. No, I'm not,' she said. 'I seem to be stuck in the middle of a family drama and I'm not quite sure what to do about it.' That had all come out of her mouth unedited and she wasn't sure why she had told him. Then he provided the answer in the next thing he said.

'Might it help to talk about it? I'm a very good listener.'

'Despite the fact that you prefer plants to people.'

'Despite that fact. Yes.' He sounded as though he was smiling. There was a beat where he neither tried to persuade her nor retracted his offer and it was this that made up her mind.

'All right,' she said. 'Thanks. Are you not busy then?'

'Sadly I am not. I have a full staff on duty and a half-full hotel of contented guests, so if you don't have pressing Saturday evening plans I can be there within the hour.'

It was a shock to realise that she was actually looking forward to seeing him – maybe because a problem shared is a problem halved, no matter who the listener.

* * *

The doorbell rang just inside the hour and Clara went to let Adam in. She had got changed out of the clothes she'd gone to see Grandad in and had freshened up and touched up her make-up. But wearing jeggings and one of her least favourite tops she wasn't dressed for a night out.

Neither was he, in old chinos and a sweatshirt which was a deep maroon. The colour suited him. They were both two shades down from dressed up, she thought, although he had recently shaved and she could smell his aftershave in the hall. It felt fleetingly odd – the owner of their nearest competitor in Kate's hall. She wondered if Kate would mind and then discounted the thought almost immediately. Once again, her instincts had told her that she could trust him. There was something very grounded about Adam.

'I wasn't sure whether you'd want to stay here – or whether you'd prefer to go out,' he said. 'To more neutral territory – or am I reading too much into this? Plants are so much simpler than people.'

'You're so right. No here is fine. Would you like some coffee? You've met Foxy before, haven't you?' She felt flustered. How could he be both things at once –relaxing to be around and yet also unnerving?

Foxy, was eyeing him warily from beneath the kitchen table. She clearly felt the same.

'She's probably wondering if you've got a pair of secateurs in your pocket,' Clara said.

'There's a joke there somewhere,' Adam quipped, before holding out his hand to the dog. 'Hello, girl. You're quite safe. I'm unarmed.'

Foxy regarded him suspiciously; she wasn't quite ready to forgive him then.

Clara made them a pot of coffee and they went into the lounge to drink it. She sat on the sofa and he sat on the armchair beside her, and as the evening wore on she knew she had made the right decision accepting his offer to listen.

It was different from their previous meeting. There had been a lot more flirting last time, it had felt more like a date, although of course it wasn't – it had simply been a casual business meeting. But she didn't see that side of him now. He was, as he had said, a good listener. He didn't interrupt when she told him about her grandparents' situation. He just nodded and listened with his whole body, not just his eyes. He leaned forward slightly in his chair, his chin on his hands. In the slowly fading light of Kate's lounge his eyes were soft.

'Our family had made a group decision not to interfere,' Clara said. 'It seemed the right thing to do. Gran is so stubborn and contrary and tends to do the opposite of what anyone else thinks she should. We thought that given enough time they'd find a way through this themselves.'

'They still might. There are years between talking about it and actually getting divorced.'

'Yes. I suppose you're right.'

'And it is their decision, isn't it? Not anyone else's.'

She knew he was right about that too.

'Before anyone else gets involved, you could try talking to your Grandad again. Ask him about his plans. Go through it all. Sometimes it takes talk of divorce and divvying things up for people to realise how much they have to lose. Not just materially – I don't mean that. But the practical reality makes the emotional reality kick in too.'

'Yeah.' She could feel the huskiness in her voice. 'I don't have any experience of this. Divorce or marriage, come to that. Everyone in my family got married young except for me. It's funny how things work out. When I was at school, I thought I'd be the same. I had other dreams too – I always knew I wanted to go to catering college – but I had this dream of maybe running my own B&B by the sea. There'd be a smallholding too with goats and chickens and home-grown veg and maybe a couple of free-range children running about.' She smiled, feeling totally disarmed. 'I don't know why I'm telling you this.'

'Like I said. I'm a good listener.' He picked idly at a loose thread on his chinos. 'It's a pity you didn't meet my brother at catering college. That was his dream too. The B&B bit anyway.'

'What about you, Adam? Did you have a dream?' The light had almost gone from the lounge now and although their eyes had adjusted it was still dark enough for an intimacy that electricity would have most likely vanquished.

'I had different dreams.' He paused briefly before going on. 'They didn't involve getting married, funnily enough. My main aim was to make a million before I was twenty-five, then retire early somewhere abroad where you can still live cheaply. Maybe Africa – there was a time when I saw myself being the owner of a tea plantation.'

'Really?' She was amazed.

'Yeah, I know. Mad! But it was a boyhood dream, inspired by photos my parents had shown us. Their holiday of a lifetime was to Africa before we were born and they'd visited a tea plantation. It was just miles and miles of green stretching off into forever, the sky was this perfect blue and the sun shone permanently. Mum described it all to us; what it was like being totally surrounded by the fragrance of tea out there in the midday sun with exotic lizards, the colour of rainbows running about And I thought, wow. Just wow!'

A note of wistfulness crept into his voice as he added, 'I'm sure the reality would have been very different and I wouldn't have made a good employer. I wouldn't have been exploitative enough, but it wouldn't have mattered because I'd have made my fortune already, you see. The tea would have just been a hobby.'

Clara had never heard him say so much at once and she had never heard him talk so passionately. 'How would you have made your fortune?'

'Oh, I had that all planned out too. I would go into I.T. You could make a real killing in those days. There weren't so many people doing it. Contractors could make a lot of money. I was very pragmatic, intensely materialistic and very focused. My whole career path was based on what made the most money.' He sighed. 'Isn't there a saying, "If you want to give God a laugh, tell him your plans."'

'I believe there is. Yes.' She held her breath, willing him to continue.

'Instead of doing all of that I got married young. I think I told you. I was twenty-one and Shona was twenty.' Another pause. 'We met at uni. She was an I.T. student, same as me. She was incredibly bright, incredibly beautiful, very career-orientated. Settling down wasn't on either of our agendas.'

He shifted in the armchair. Clara could no longer see his eyes, but she knew that he wasn't in the room any more anyway. He was looking back into some far distant point of his past.

'But we fell in love. We fell hard. We knew that we wanted to be together, have children, do the whole thing. But Shona came from a deeply religious family, so living together wasn't an option. We decided to get married straightaway. We figured out a way of how it would work. How we could still complete our degrees. Suddenly we had a whole new set of plans.'

There was such a long pause this time that Clara thought he wasn't going to say any more. But finally he did go on, in a voice that was bleaker, more detached, and as far away from the tea plantation passion as it could be.

'Clearly, God didn't think much of those plans either because exactly six weeks after we got married Shona was in a car accident. She was driving home and a woman coming the other way swerved to miss a deer and hit Shona's car. The woman was in a BMW. She got off with cuts and bruises. Shona didn't. Her car spun off the road, hit a tree and ended up on its roof. She died at the scene.'

'Oh my God, Adam, that's awful. I'm so very, very sorry,' Clara could feel tears pricking the back of her eyes, drawn there in response to his obvious pain, and suddenly she was intensely glad of the dark.

For maybe a full thirty seconds, there was silence, except for the ticking of the clock in the hall that they could hear through the half-open door. Clara could hear his light breathing and feel his sadness, like dust in the air, and she knew he must be struggling. You couldn't recount events like that, no matter how long ago, without reliving them to some extent.

Then she could bear it no longer. She slipped off the settee and went and knelt on the carpet by the armchair and she took his hand. 'I can't imagine how much that must have hurt,' she murmured.

He squeezed her fingers. 'I don't know why I told you.'

'Maybe I'm a good listener too.'

'You are.' He sounded surprised. Clara decided not to take that personally. He was the second person who'd unburdened himself to her today and she was pretty sure Grandad had been surprised too.

'I'll make us some more coffee' she said and got up without waiting for him to answer. He could have a few more moments in the dark with his thoughts or he could come out to the kitchen, but she didn't want him to be embarrassed. Or to think he had to go.

He didn't come out, but a few moments later, when she went back into the lounge, he had switched on a sidelight so there was a muted rose glow in the room. Also, to her surprise, Foxy had climbed up onto the armchair and had her head on his lap. It was funny how dogs always knew. They were such empaths.

'Is she allowed up here?' Adam looked up guiltily. 'She said she was.'

Vulnerable Orlando, Clara thought, but she responded lightly to his question. 'Oh did she now,' and she widened her eyes in mock reproof. 'Yes, I think Kate lets her. Although she doesn't often get up there.'

'She manages OK with three legs, doesn't she? How did she lose it?'

Clara hesitated, but she couldn't pussyfoot around him. 'She got hit by a car. The guy didn't stop. I was driving behind him. So I did.'

'Bastard,' Adam said, stroking Foxy's ears and causing her to open one eye in pleasure. 'So how come Kate ended up with her?'

'It turned out she was a stray. The vet couldn't trace her owner. I'd already said I'd cover the bill for whatever needed doing when I took her in. But then, of course, she needed a permanent home and I don't have a garden to speak of, so Kate came to the rescue.' She put the new cafetière of coffee on the small square table they'd been using. 'It's funny how things work out. I was driving to my interview at the Bluebell at the time. I was a bit late – being as I'd gone via the vets. I was also a bit messy. I'd got blood on my interview suit. Kate was very good about it. She loves dogs. And, as luck would have, it I've ended up looking after Foxy anyway. As well as this beautiful bungalow.' She spread her arms to encompass the oblong-shaped room. 'I'll be quite sad when I have to go back to my tiny house.'

'One day, when you get your smallholding, you can have a dozen dogs.'

'Maybe it's like your tea plantation. The fantasy is much more appealing than the reality.'

'I've got a confession to make,' he said, raising his cup in her direction. 'I much prefer coffee to tea.'

'I've got a confession too. I don't own a pair of green wellington boots. You were right.'

'I knew it.' He winked at her. 'Although I can see you tending to plants. You'd be good at it too. You're one of life's nurturers, aren't you?'

'We have that in common,' she countered, glad that they were away from car accidents. Away from divorces, even though that's what he'd come round to talk about. 'I'm assuming that much of your time is spent looking after Nick.'

He darted a glance at her. 'Some of it. But don't go telling anyone. I'll lose my street cred.'

'Your secret's safe with me.'

'Cheers.' He drained his cup and clonked it back onto the table. 'The truth is, I only do what any half-decent brother would do. Nick was there for me when I lost Shona. He was bloody brilliant. I couldn't have got through it without him. The illness is a bugger because it's progressive, but not terminal. And fortunately he has long periods of remission. Hell, have you seen the time? I should get out of your hair.'

She looked at her FunFit bracelet, which was good for telling the time if nothing else, and was amazed to see it was twenty-five to eleven. 'Blimey. No. I hadn't. Where did that go?'

'It was the same when we went out to dinner,' he said, when she finally saw him out and they were standing at the front door. 'The time just flew by.'

'For me too,' she acknowledged.

They were less than a foot apart and she didn't want him to go. Apart from that brief moment when she had held his hand, she realised they had never actually touched and yet she was totally aware of him: of the faint scent of his aftershave; of the darkness of his eyes; of the tallness of him. Tall people intimidated her usually, especially at close proximity, but he didn't. He was too gentle.

'Thanks so much for listening,' she said, aware that she was standing on the doormat, which gave her an extra inch, and looking up into his face.

'I think it was more the other way round,' he said, dipping his head, and for a hair's breadth of a moment she thought he was going to kiss her, but it was gone as swiftly as it had arrived.

Then she was closing the door, standing in the six-foot-two block of Adam-Greenwood-shaped emptiness that he'd left behind.

19

She didn't sleep well that night. She was too wired with caffeine and conversation. When she did finally drop off, she dreamed that the gap between the Old Harry Rocks had moved farther apart and that she and Adam were in a rowing boat, armed with a rope lasso, which they planned to throw over the smaller of the giant white rocks so they could tow it back into its rightful position again. The only problem was that no matter how hard they rowed, they never seemed to get any closer and then a big storm blew up and there was a tsunami that lifted the rowing boat right up onto the crest of its wave and threatened to smash it down onto the great rocks beneath.

Clara woke up, drenched in sweat with the thin summer duvet tangled up around her legs and all the pillows on the floor. It was daylight. It was just gone eight and she was safe in her bed, albeit with her heartbeat thundering. She lay there until the adrenaline of the nightmare had subsided and then reached for her mobile phone.

Curiously, she checked the sleep report on her FunFit, which said:

`Good. You indicators, this night, quite good. Yes. Healthy sleep. Fantastic.`

She threw it across the room. Then she got up and did what Adam had suggested last night and phoned Grandad.

He didn't answer the mobile phone he'd had yesterday. She wasn't surprised. It was probably still on silent. She phoned the house line and Elsie answered.

'How's Grandad today?' Clara knew her voice was artificially bright like you are when someone's ill and you fear they won't get better.

'He's still the same, I'm afraid. Still intent on getting divorced. Jim's tried to talk some sense into him. They were up late last night and they've just walked up to the paper shop.' Elsie sighed. 'What does your mother think?'

'I haven't said anything to her yet. I was hoping he'd change his mind.'

'I see. Hmmm.' There was a longish pause, during which Elsie cleared her throat. 'To be honest, love,' she said at last, 'I know this isn't what you want to hear, but maybe if that's what they both really want, it would be for the best. They can't live in limbo for ever.'

'I know.' Clara could feel tears queuing up to get into her voice. 'It can't be easy for you two either.'

'Oh, love, it's not that. Eric can stay as long as he likes. We don't mind having him at all. But it's not good for him or Thelma, is it? All these shenanigans at their age.'

'I know,' Clara said again. 'Will you tell him I called and that I'm here if he wants to chat?'

'Of course I will, love.'

'People, eh,' Clara said to Foxy once she'd put down the phone. But she couldn't deny that Elsie might be right. Adam had said exactly the same thing. Gran and Grandad were grown-ups after all.

She decided not to phone him again. Or any of the rest of her family. It wasn't a lunch Sunday, so it shouldn't be too difficult to keep things to herself for a while. She was due into work at midday anyway. When she got there, she discovered a text on her mobile from Adam. It was very brief.

Thanks again for last night. Ax

She typed back a reply straight away.

Thanks for coming over. Cx

But she didn't press send. She sat in her car staring at her phone screen.

She wanted to say so much more. She wanted to suggest they saw each other again, but this time just for the pure pleasure of it. Not because it was a business meeting to unite two hotels. Not because either of them wanted to let off steam. But just because she had felt such a connection with him on the last two occasions they had met. Just because the time flew.

He was rapidly becoming a friend, someone that she trusted, and after last night she was pretty sure he felt the same. But she couldn't say all this in a text. Maybe she should phone him.

A small whine from the back of the car jolted her into the present. She looked back at the text she'd written on her phone and in a flash of paranoia she deleted the kiss in case he thought she was being too familiar. Then she pressed send.

* * *

When the first couple of days of October passed without any more communication from Adam, Clara knew she'd been right not to phone him and suggest that they went out on a date. Good grief that could have been embarrassing.

She gave herself a good stern talking-to and resolved to put Adam Greenwood out of her mind. He was a business acquaintance and he was a friend. These were the facts.

On the plus side, she heard nothing more about a divorce, either from Grandad or from anyone else in the family.

Even when she caught up with Rosanna for a coffee the subject didn't arise. Rosanna was busy with the children and the talk was of the school's nativity play, which had just been cast, ready to begin rehearsals in November.

'Sophie's playing an angel,' Rosanna said. 'And Tom's going to be doing a piano piece in the revue they're having at his school.'

'How fantastic is that.'

'I know. Proud Mummy moment.'

Clara couldn't bring herself to mention Grandad's decision, and if no one else knew, then maybe he had decided against the nuclear option, after all. Good. She would just have to keep her fingers crossed on that one.

In the meantime, the Curly Wurly challenge was an excellent distraction. She and Zoe were getting quite excited about it. Mr B thought it was 'kind of cool'. Phil thought it was nuts, even though Clara knew he was secretly pleased to have a connection with a record-breaking attempt. Jakob said it confirmed his theory that all English people were a little crazy. Even the hard-to-impress Keith thought it was a bit of harmless fun and more sensible than that woman who grew her fingernails eighteen feet long.

'One of the things I love about working at the Bluebell is that there's always something to talk about,' Zoe said. 'Mum says I'm really lucky. She works in an old people's home and all they ever talk about is their feet, their medication and their arthritis.'

'Poor loves,' Clara said.

'It was a shame about all those hot Young Farmers though,' Zoe added wistfully. 'Do we have any more groups coming like that?'

'Well, it just so happens that I'm mid negotiation with a group of Dorset firefighters who are booking us for their Christmas party,' Clara told her. 'And there is, of course, next year's Secret Policeman's Ball. We're hoping to stage one of the events here.'

'What? Are you serious? Why didn't you tell me?' The outrage in her voice was comical.

'Because I am still in the very delicate early-stage negotiations,' Clara teased. 'Don't worry, I'll keep you in the loop once I know what's happening. And talking about keeping people in the loop, have you seen any interesting bags on eBay lately?'

'No, but if I do, you'll be the first to know,' Zoe promised.

'How's the sweepstake going?'

'William Big is currently top of the leader board. Think about it...' Zoe said.

Clara thought about it and snorted.

'Except Phil says he probably wouldn't have changed it if it were that. They get quite a lot ruder...'

'I don't think I want to know.'

'OK. Well, on the polite front, Batty's quite popular – not surprisingly. So's Buttery.'

'Buttery surely isn't a surname.'

'It actually is. It's an old Nottinghamshire name. Jakob looked it up.' Zoe paused. 'Actually, Mr B knows now. He found out. Phil accidentally left the sweepstake book out. They had a blazing row and didn't speak for a day, but in the end Mr B said he's not giving us any clues, but if anyone guesses his surname, he'll confirm that they're right. And he'll award a prize.'

'When did all this happen?'

'The day before yesterday when you were at that meeting with the tourist board.'

Clara wasn't surprised Mr B had taken control of the situation – control freak that he was. 'So what's the prize?'

'He said he'll create a new dessert for the menu to be named after the winner. So if I win it could be Zoe's Zabaglione and if Ellie May wins it could be Ellie May's Mango and Vanilla Cookies and if Phil wins it's Phil's Passion Fruit Buns.'

'I can't wait,' Clara said, shaking her head.

* * *

The world record contender, Micky Tucker, arrived with his mother, Shirley, on the afternoon before the challenge was scheduled to take place. They had booked two nights' bed, breakfast and evening meal and had sent an advance message asking if the kitchen could possibly do them a couple of Mr B's celebrated chocolate cheesecakes with spun sugar for dessert.

A message had been sent back that Mr B would be honoured to prepare his chocolate cheesecake for a potential Guinness World Records holder.

When they arrived, Zoe checked them in and then she dashed into the office to tell Clara all about them.

'Micky Tucker's got a proper Somerset accent, luuurve,' she mimicked. 'He's got bright ginger hair and he looks like he might have eaten a few Curly Wurly bars in his time, never mind stretching them!'

'I guess you'd have to do something with all the ones you

practice with,' Clara said, licking her lips. 'It would be a shame to throw them away.'

She met Micky and his mother that night at dinner and she saw that Zoe was right. Micky wasn't what she'd expected an aspiring record breaker to look like – not that she'd realised she'd had an expectation until she saw him – he was almost as wide as he was tall. In fact, mother and son both were. They were also both very nice, cheerful people and incredibly excited about the chance to break a world record.

'I've a reporter coming 'ere in the morning,' Shirley told Clara. 'He's going to interview Micky about the challenge. How 'e feels, what he's done to get ready for it – that kind of thing. It'll be a proper human-interest piece, he says. Then he'll be coming along with us to the Chocolate Challenge to take pictures and suchlike. And, with a bit of luck, we'll be back here to celebrate after we've done it.'

'Fabulous,' Clara said. 'I'll be coming along too.'

'Will you, lurve. That's kind.'

'Who's the reporter?'

Shirley consulted her notepad. 'It's a chap called Simon Tomlinson. He's from *The Purbeck Gazette*.'

Bloody hell, that name was a rather unpleasant blast from the past, Clara thought, remembering Lighthousegate and realising Shirley was still speaking.

'We'll get into the nationals too, I'm sure. If Micky breaks it.'

'I've broken it twice in rehearsals,' Micky said, looking confident. 'It's all about keeping your nerve. Keeping a steady hand. Focusing in.'

'And a good breakfast,' put in Shirley Tucker. 'Going off with a good breakfast's important.'

'Yeah. Can we have whisky with our porridge?' Micky asked. 'I've always fancied that. It's traditional, isn't it?'

'Maybe more in Dalwhinnie than in Dorset,' Clara said, 'but I'm sure it could be arranged, if that's what you would like.'

* * *

Like the mini Oktoberfest, the Chocolate Challenge was only in its second year at Swanage. Clara was amazed she hadn't heard anything about it last year. Events concerning chocolate didn't usually get past her radar.

She drove Micky and Shirley to the festival in Phil's car, as he'd tactfully said they would all have a bit more legroom in his. It was taking place on the sports field on the outskirts of town. As they got out of the car, Clara could see that there were three large marquees in situ. There was also a giant blow-up slide for the children, alongside some mini fairground rides, and a great scattering of stalls.

Brancombe, which was on the outskirts of Swanage, might not be as big as Bavaria, but it had pulled out all the stops for its mini version of Oktoberfest, Clara saw.

While the Tuckers wandered off to find the reporter from *The Purbeck Gazette*, she went into the Chocolate Challenge marquee, which wasn't hard to find – she just followed her nose – and was instantly surrounded by the divine smell of chocolate. This must be what it would smell like inside Willy Wonka's Chocolate Factory, she thought, taking a long and blissful breath. There were undertones of vanilla and salted caramel, and honeycomb – and was that toffee? Her mouth watered as she stared around her.

To her left was a chocolate fountain supervised by a woman in a pristine white coat with the words The Chocolate Foundation in swirly letters on the front. The woman was dipping marshmallows on sticks into the fountain and lining them up on a tray beside it.

Clara went further into the marquee where chocolate of every size, shape and description was on display. There were boxes, tins and bars of everything a chocolate lover could possibly desire. White chocolates, dark chocolates, milk chocolates, handmade truffles, liqueur chocolates, nut chocolate, chocolate fudge, biscuits. Oh God. There was so much temptation.

Lots of the stalls had samples. Clara clenched her fists in the pockets of her light jacket, in order to resist. Maybe this hadn't been such a good idea. If she caved in, she could easily put on four pounds by lunchtime!

At least two of the stalls were doing some kind of challenge, one was clearly running a competition: Guess the weight of the chocolate Santa. Blimey, they were early, but maybe not. There had been touches of Christmas in the shops since early September.

At the far end of the marquee, Clara spotted a banner, which said Curly Wurly Stretching. Guinness World Records. Record Breaking Attempt. Here 11.30 a.m. There was a cardboard cut-out of a giant Curly Wurly on a stand, alongside what looked like a long trestle table covered in white plastic sheeting.

So that's where it would all happen then. Clara made her way over there.

It was only just gone ten, but the marquee was beginning to fill up with people and a buzz of chatter filled the air. It might be October, but they'd been lucky with the weather. Winter still seemed a long way off.

She hooked out her mobile phone and took a photo of the whole Curly Wurly table set-up. She had to back up a little way to get it all in and she had literally just turned round again when she bumped into Adam Greenwood.

'Oh hi,' she said, feeling a thrill of pleasure. 'I didn't realise you were a chocolate fan.'

'Clara, hi.' He looked startled to see her. Or perhaps she had caught him by surprise. 'Isn't everyone?' A white plastic carrier bag swung from his left hand. 'I thought I'd do some early Christmas shopping,' he added.

'Good idea. I should do that. I was just trying to resist the temptation of the samples.'

'Why try?' he asked, opening his carrier and showing her three boxes of truffles. 'They're not all presents. I can't resist them.'

'Me neither.' They looked at each other and suddenly she felt that connection between them again and it was as though they were the only two people in the marquee – a couple, enveloped in a chocolate hug.

A little flustered that she'd put Adam in the same sentence as a hug – she dragged her mind back to reality.

'How's Nick?'

'How are things with your family?'

They spoke together and he gestured for her to go first.

'Nothing much has changed,' she told him. 'But I do know Grandad hasn't actually mentioned divorce to Gran yet and I took your advice and I haven't mentioned it to anyone either.'

'That sounds promising.' He was nodding. 'Nick's good too, thanks. He's working again and so I've sneaked out for an hour. I've been doing more than my fair share lately, and I'd heard that the chocolate fair was in town.'

'I'm here to support the Curly Wurly Stretching Guinness World Records attempt,' she told him, glancing at her FunFit. 'Although that's not for another hour and a half yet. The challenger is staying at the Bluebell with his mother,' she explained. 'At the moment, they're being interviewed by *The Purbeck Gazette*.'

'I see.' His face cleared. 'Have you time for a coffee? Or a hot chocolate even?' He gestured to a stand just behind them.

'Why not. Yes. I've plenty of time.'

A few minutes later, they were standing on the grass once more, outside the marquee and away from the heady scent of chocolate, which had been starting to become overpowering in its sweetness. Who knew!

Clara followed Adam past the beer tent and saw that Micky and Shirley Tucker were at one of the plastic tables talking to a guy with a notepad. That must be Simon Tomlinson, although he had his back to her so she couldn't be sure. All three of them had pints of cider in front of them. Its sharp distinctive scent carried on the air.

They were starting early. Micky must be in need of Dutch courage, she thought, hoping that a pint of cider wouldn't affect the steady hand he needed. No, of course it wouldn't. It was well known that Somerset men were big cider drinkers.

She and Adam sat at a table outside the beer tent, sipping the hot chocolates he'd bought them, and Clara tipped her head back, feeling the October sunshine on her face and noticing that all her senses seemed sharper than they had a few moments before. The colours were brighter. The grass seemed greener. The marquees with their taut guy ropes, looked whiter against the blue sky. The mingled scents of burger vans, coffee and cider were more pungent and the shrieks and laughter of children from the funfair shriller.

They didn't talk about anything consequential. It was very different from the intimacy of the last time they had met, but then so was the setting. They were in a very public place, with people milling about, kids squealing, the shouting of stallholders, the thrum of a diesel generator. Yet once again the time flew by and it wasn't until Clara spotted Micky Turner actually walking past her, still chatting with the reporter, that she realised it was nearly eleven.

'I'd better go,' she said to Adam, standing up. 'Will you come and watch our record-breaking attempt?'

'No, I should get back. I'll be needed for Sunday lunch. But I hope it goes well. It's been nice chatting.'

'Ditto. And thanks.' She watched him go and then hurried to catch up with Micky, who hadn't got very far. Oddly, he seemed to be weaving around. In fact, the closer she got to him, the more concerned she became that something was wrong.

Shirley was beside him and she turned as Clara caught them up.

'Is Micky all right?' Clara asked. Now she was close enough, she could see that he wasn't. His eyes were slightly glazed and his face was flushed. 'Is he drunk?' she gasped.

'No. He can't be.' Shirley was shaking her head in bemusement. 'Micky can hold his drink. Besides, he only had a pint.'

'I'm fine,' her son confirmed. 'Just got up a bit quick, thass all. No worreesh. May need a pee.'

20

As Clara waited with Shirley outside the Chocolate Challenge marquee for Micky to reappear, she could feel the anxiety rising.

This was not alleviated by the sight of him heading back towards them across the grass with the reporter she'd seen him with earlier holding on firmly to his arm.

'Good morning, Miss King,' Simon Tomlinson said. He hadn't changed much. The same ferret face and mean little eyes. He'd been the one she had promised to sue if he dared to print anything about Arnold's botched proposal. The one who'd complained about the gagging of free speech.

Oh great, that was all they needed.

Ignoring him, she looked at Micky, who, if anything, looked even worse. 'Are you feeling all right?'

'Yeah. I'm good.' He looked at his watch, tried hard to focus and gave up. 'What time is it? Are we on?'

'We're on in fifteen minutes,' Shirley told him. She had gone a bit pale, or it could have been the reflection of the white marquee behind her.

'Maybe a coffee would help?' Clara said, even though she

knew it was pointless. There wasn't time to queue up for one and, anyway, Micky looked as though he might be past the stage where caffeine could help.

To give him his due, he seemed to suddenly make a supreme effort. 'Right then – let's get cracking. Curly Wurly Curly.' He beamed around at everyone. 'Bring it on.'

'Great stuff, mate,' the reporter said. 'Let's get you to the starting line.'

A few minutes later, they were at the table. Earlier on, Shirley told Clara, they had spoken to the sponsor of the stall, a confectionary seller called Wesley from Weymouth, and they'd also spoken to the adjudicator from Guinness World Records about the rules. So they were all set.

Micky seemed to have recovered enough to speak without slurring, but Clara saw Wesley and the adjudicator exchange glances when he arrived.

'He'll be all right,' Shirley was busy reassuring them. 'He's just hamming it up. His idea of a little joke. He's only had one pint.'

They were both nodding, smiling, as though they expected nothing less from this dumpling of a man who must have had a misspent youth working out the best way to stretch chocolate-covered toffee.

'Keep it together, son,' Shirley hissed at him as he took his place at the foot of the table with her by his side.

The adjudicator announced the event to the small crowd who had gathered, heads bobbing like curious meerkats.

'The Curly Wurly has been fully inspected,' he continued, 'and I am satisfied it meets the required parameters.' He indicated with his GWR clipboard towards the chocolate bar that lay on the table. 'Give him some space,' he told the crowd, as he brandished the stopwatch.

Micky, who gave a small burp as he bent over the table said, 'Thank you,' as the countdown began.

Clara held her breath as the attempt got underway. Maybe, after all, it was going to be OK. Micky had changed from being a bumbling drunk person to having fingers that worked with speed and dexterity. Totally focused on his task, he bent over the table, pulling and stretching, working and wheedling the toffee into the thinnest of lines. It was quite incredible to watch. A couple of people egged him on. 'Go Micky.'

The reporter was videoing it. Clara sent up a silent prayer to the patron saint of chocolate: if there was such a thing. Maybe she should be praying to the patron saint of lost causes. There was definitely one of those.

Be positive, Clara.

'One minute gone,' announced the adjudicator.

Micky was still totally focused. The reporter was still videoing intently.

Someone knocked against the table and the adjudicator admonished him. 'Give him space.'

'He's smashing it,' someone shouted.

'He's smashed.' That was a woman's voice, raucous, from the back of the crowd.

'One and a half minutes.'

'Rock on, son.'

'Go for it, Micky,' Clara yelled, caught up in the excitement.

The chocolate aroma was heady, almost sickly, and it was hot in here now, amidst all these people. Micky's face was flushed and he had sweat dripping off his forehead down into his eyes. She was amazed he could see anything, but he didn't falter.

'Two minutes.'

The noise levels were rising. Clara wondered how many times Micky had done this and why he wanted to do it and she realised she had never asked him. It had seemed like such an insane idea, but was it really insane? Wanting to have your name in the record books. Even for something as crazy as this. Maybe that made it better, not worse.

'Two and a half minutes,' sang the adjudicator.

Micky was still going hell for leather. Clara glanced at the reporter's face behind the video camera and saw that he was scowling. How odd. Surely he wanted to see Micky succeed.

She looked back at Micky. They must be almost there. This had been the longest three minutes of her life. And then suddenly he faltered and he seemed to stumble. He hadn't finished. He shouldn't be stopping. But then she realised why. Micky clapped his hand over his mouth. He was trying not to retch. Carla realised this at exactly the same moment that the adjudicator began the final countdown.

'Five, four, three, two one. Stop.'

Micky had already stopped. He was close to the end of the table and then suddenly he was throwing up. People who had crowded in to see the finale were now backing away in horror. Clara was aware of their faces, screwing up with revulsion, as they tried to avoid being puked on.

She was aware of Shirley leaping to his aid, the only person in the enclosed space who was going towards him and not trying to get away.

Oh God, no. This was turning into a nightmare.

* * *

Clara hadn't thought it could get any worse, but it had. Once the initial chaos of Micky throwing up and the adjudicator declaring that the record attempt to be null and void as Micky had stopped before completion, the recriminations had begun.

At first, it had seemed the adjudicator might give Micky another chance. Apparently you were allowed to have three goes at breaking a record, but Micky was clearly too drunk to try again. Spraying vomit everywhere hadn't helped his case at all.

After a lot of staggering about and cursing from Micky, and some muttering about contestants needing to be in a fit and sober state of mind in order to participate from the adjudicator, it was decided to call it a day. The record attempt was abandoned.

Both Shirley and Micky had blamed the whole thing on him having been given a dodgy pint of cider and there had then been a furious argument between them and one of the barmen in the beer tent.

'There's nothing wrong with our cider,' the barman insisted. 'He can't take his drink. That's obviously the problem.'

'I only had one pint.' Walking about in the fresh air had clearly perked him up.

'So you say. How do I know you weren't knocking it back before you got here? You must have been glugging it from the barrel to get that flaming bladdered.'

'I most certainly was not. Your cider must be off.'

'Our cider is NOT off. You had one yourself.' The barman had glared at Shirley. 'There's nothing wrong with you.'

Neither of them had disputed this. They couldn't.

Clara had looked from one to the other of them uncertainly and then she had voiced the only other explanation she could think of. 'Could anyone possibly have spiked your drink?'

'We weren't with anyone else,' Shirley said. 'Except for that reporter. He couldn't have done it, could he?' She had nudged Micky sharply in the ribs. 'What about when I went off to the loo. Could he have done it then?'

'Could he heck! Why would he?' Micky's face screwed up fleetingly at a memory. 'Although it maybe did taste a little bit odd. Strong like – it put me in mind of Uncle Bert's scrumpy. It seemed to get stronger as I got through it.'

The reporter had vanished, Clara noticed, looking around. No doubt he'd headed back to his paper in disgust, having not got a decent headline. She nodded at Micky and addressed her next question directly to the barman. 'I know this is a long shot, but no one bought a few shots of vodka did they, from your bar this morning?'

'It'd take more than a few shots to get me that drunk,' Micky said, with a hint of pride in his voice. 'I can do vodka.'

'I don't think so,' the barman said. 'I'll check with the other lads.'

He came back shaking his head firmly.

'No one sold any vodka first thing. Not even a shot.' With one last decisive nod and a look that said he was taking no responsibility whatsoever for Micky's state of inebriation, he headed back to serve.

It was at this point that Micky had looked Clara straight in the eyes and said, 'The only other thing I've drunk today was your whisky at breakfast. How strong's that?'

'He's got a point,' Shirley chipped in, looking at Clara suspiciously. 'Whisky can be very strong.'

'I'm not used to whisky,' Micky said, nodding. 'Might be that. Or it could be food poisoning. It could be something I ate, either this morning or last night.'

Now, mother and son were standing closer together, a united front, and they were both looking at her accusingly.

'Food poisoning doesn't make you drunk,' Clara pointed out, feeling suddenly as though the ground had shifted beneath her feet.

'It makes you vomit though. I've never vomited anything like that before, have I, Mother. I feel fine now. Maybe whatever caused it has gone through me - like. Now I've vomited. Maybe that's what happened.'

'Maybe it's your fault that Micky was sick and ruined his chances of breaking a world record,' Shirley said.

Clara couldn't believe how swiftly they had turned on her and hauled her into the firing line. 'This is ridiculous,' she defended herself. 'You were clearly drunk. You were staggering around before you even went into the marquee.'

'I was light-headed.'

'He was light-headed,' Shirley affirmed. 'I could see 'e was light-headed.'

'I think it might be best if we got you both back to the hotel,' Clara said, swallowing down her anxiety. She could not afford a major dispute about the Bluebell's liability in the middle of a public place.

She managed to calm them down enough to get them to agree. For one thing, Micky needed to get a change of clothes. Although he had mostly avoided throwing up over himself, there was the odd damp splatter on his red top. He didn't smell too good either, she thought, as they got back into the hot confines of Phil's car and she opened all the windows. The one saving grace was that – as he'd said – he didn't look as though he was going to throw up again. The sickly green colour had gone. He seemed OK. Maybe she could still salvage the situation. Maybe once they had talked things through sensibly they would decide that the Bluebell had nothing to do with what had happened today.

She had virtually convinced herself of this, but then, just as they drew back into the car park, she heard Shirley say something that shot a cold chill straight into her heart.

'I should think we've got quite a good case for compensation.'

* * *

It took the rest of Sunday and Clara's offer to give the Tuckers a hefty discount on their bill to elicit a promise from them that they would not be taking it any further.

'I say, let them try,' Mr B had retorted, pacing around his kitchen last thing on Sunday evening with a murderous look in his eyes. 'How dare they suggest there is anything wrong with my food? This kitchen is as spotless as the Royal Family's operating theatre.'

At her request, he had shown Clara and Phil the size of the measure he had used for the whisky that had gone on Micky's porridge.

'That's not enough to get a gnat drunk, let alone a Somerset cider drinker who's been knocking back Scrumpy since he was thirteen.'

'The guy wasn't exactly small either,' Phil agreed. 'It is very odd. Even if someone had spiked his drink, they'd have had to go overboard. A few vodkas probably wouldn't have been enough. Besides, why would you want to nobble a Guinness World Records attempt? Not one like that anyway. One that's just a bit of fun.'

'To get at us, maybe,' Clara said quietly. 'Maybe it wasn't aimed at Micky directly but at us. Maybe like Arnold and the Young Farmers, he was just collateral damage.'

'What you're saying is that we should be checking for an upload to YouTube any time now?' Phil said, his eyes very serious.

Mr B slapped his hand against the stainless-steel dishwasher from where he'd retrieved the drinks measure. 'Surely no one would go down that route again. Not after they had an injunction slapped on them last time.'

'We don't know that they did,' Clara said, thinking she'd have to ask Kate how far the solicitor had got. 'It got taken down really quickly, I seem to remember. YouTube may have decided it was defamatory themselves.' She hesitated. 'Unfortunately, there was video footage taken of the whole thing this morning too. A reporter from *The Purbeck Gazette* interviewed Micky prior to the challenge and then he filmed it. It was the same guy who turned up after Arnold's doomed climb and asked if he could rent the lighthouse so he could propose to his girlfriend.'

'Fissilingual bastard,' Mr B said. 'Was it the small guy who looks like a ferret?'

'Yes it was. Why?'

'I know him from somewhere.'

'He's a reporter – he must be out and about all the time. You've probably seen him around.'

'No, it's not that. I know him from somewhere else. Some other context, if you know what I mean. It'll come back to me.' He tapped his nose. 'It always does.'

'At least we can't blame this one on The Manor House,' Phil said. 'We're on pretty good terms with them now, aren't we, Clara?'

He winked and she nodded, remembering Adam being in the chocolate-scented marquee this morning.

'We definitely can't blame them. But I don't think we can rule out sabotage either.' As they walked out of the hotel kitchen back towards the reception, she added, 'The only other option is that Micky Tucker's a secret alcoholic and he poured half a bottle of spirits down his own throat this morning without anyone noticing.'

'Not very secret,' Mr B said wryly. 'Besides, alcoholics can usually hold their drink better than that. That's kind of the point of being one, isn't it?'

'I'm going to have to tell Kate,' Clara murmured as they stood in reception once more and she saw Keith nod in their direction. 'In the meantime, can I ask you to please keep this to yourselves?

The one good thing about it is that no one is going to link The Bluebell with a failed Curly Wurly-stretching record-breaking attempt.'

'Of course they're not,' Phil said. 'Why would they?'

'Hmmm,' said Mr B.

Clara could hear an ocean of doubt in their voices, which was not in the least bit reassuring.

21

Clara called Kate first thing Monday and they talked the incident through, and while Kate agreed it was worrying, she also didn't see how it could possibly be their fault. Maybe it had all just been an unfortunate series of events and had nothing to do with their saboteur, which was how Clara had started to refer to their unknown enemy in her head.

Despite Kate's reassurance, and the knowledge that she would be back to take charge in less than two weeks, Clara spent all day Monday on tenterhooks. She dreaded every phone call and every email. She scanned YouTube and Twitter and all their other pages on social media. She found nothing online about the disastrous Curly Wurly record-breaking attempt. There was very little online about Brancombe's mini Oktoberfest at all.

By Tuesday morning, she was starting to relax again. But she still got into work earlier than usual. Keith was on reception. He and Zoe hadn't yet done the handover. They changed over at nine in the week.

Clara was just walking up to the main doors of the hotel when she noticed a newspaper stuck half in and half out of the hotel's letter box. This was unusual on more than one count. Firstly, Tim, the postman, usually brought the post right in, so someone else must have delivered this, and, secondly, they didn't usually get *The Purbeck Gazette*, which was what it was, until Wednesday.

Curly Wurly Shame for Shirley.

The front page headlines hit Clara in the face and her heart began to pound. Swiftly, she scanned the rest of the story.

> Heartbroken Shirley Tucker watched helplessly as son, Micky, failed in his attempt to break the Guinness World Record for Curly Wurly stretching at Oktoberfest.
>
> The chocolate challenger started well but couldn't finish due to illness.
>
> Shirley Tucker sobs, 'It's such a shame. He had his heart set on that record. He's been practising for months.'
>
> A mysterious wave of sickness stopped play at the eleventh hour. Spectators at the challenge said, 'He was so close. We thought he would do it.'
>
> Micky says, 'I'm too gutted to speak.'
>
> Supporters from the Bluebell Cliff Hotel, where the Tuckers spent the previous night, said they were devastated.
>
> Full story on Page 3.

Clara felt a cold knife of tension twist her stomach. The Bluebell was on the front page – associated with this disaster – and after everything she had done to make sure it didn't happen. A shakiness started in her legs.

Still standing outside on the front doorstep, she turned warily to page 3.

> Shirley says, 'We chose that hotel because it's the place where dreams come true, but our good-luck Bluebell Cliff breakfast didn't work. Micky was fine when he started the Curly Wurly challenge, but halfway through he had to stop due to being overcome by sickness. We don't yet know what caused the sickness. Food poisoning has not been ruled out.'

They hadn't even mentioned the cider, Clara realised as she folded up the paper and stuffed it into her bag. They'd implied that Micky had contracted food poisoning at the Bluebell. Was it possible? Oh shit, her thoughts were so jumbled, she was no longer sure.

She called out a quick hello to Keith across the vanilla-air-freshener warmth of reception before rushing through into the manager's office. Then she read the article again twice more, before putting the paper away in the top drawer. Not that there was much point hiding it. This paper had a circulation of 30,000 copies around the Purbecks. It was also online and occasionally a bigger paper picked up its stories and covered them. Especially if news was in short supply. Anyone and everyone could read it. And they were on the front page.

The brutal facts kept circling in her head. She needed to call Kate again. She needed to call another emergency staff meeting. Or perhaps she should call a mini one with key staff. What possible damage limitation could they do this time? It was too late. Why hadn't she thought about this and pre-empted it?

* * *

'You couldn't possibly have known,' Zoe said, when she came in later that morning. 'Don't we advertise with the *Gazette*?'

Clara shook her head, thinking fleetingly that Zoe had

learned a lot since she'd started at the Bluebell. 'We used to but not so much lately. I cut back on the advertising budget because we've been so busy. We're fully booked right through until spring.'

'It's still pretty damning though, isn't it? Could we sue them?'

'It is damning, but they haven't actually said that we're responsible.'

'They've managed to imply it though, haven't they?' said Mr B when he arrived and came into the office to join Clara. 'Pediculous scumbags.' He tossed the newspaper onto the desk. 'Have you spoken to Kate?'

'Yes. She's phoning her solicitor and getting back to me. But it's tricky. They haven't said anything that's not true.' Kate had sounded very serious though.

What they had done, Phil agreed with both Clara and Mr B when he arrived for the emergency staff meeting she'd called, was to leave a lot out.

'Didn't you say the guy was three sheets to the wind?'

'Yes he was. Or he certainly seemed to be.' Clara rested her elbows on the manager's desk. She was starting to doubt her own memory of what had gone on two days earlier. 'He gave every appearance of being drunk. But he was adamant he'd only had one pint of cider in the bar, aside from the whisky he'd consumed here. That's why he and his mother ended up blaming it on food poisoning.'

'Which they've managed to link with us,' Phil said. 'What I can't understand is why they would want to do that.'

'It sells papers, doesn't it?'

'*The Purbeck Gazette* isn't usually as gratuitous as this though. They're usually quite benign and gentle. The tone of this whole piece is snarly and pointed. Tabloid at its worst.'

'Someone is targeting us,' Mr B said. 'Person or persons

unknown are trying to bring us down. I know you don't think it's The Manor House, Clara, but there is someone behind all these attacks, isn't there? Someone posted the lighthouse video on YouTube. Someone cancelled the Young Farmers' event and someone sabotaged the Curly Wurly record.'

'At least we know who's responsible for this one,' Phil said.

'But we don't though, do we,' Clara said. 'We only know that *The Purbeck Gazette* reported on it. We don't know who got to Micky. Good grief, I'm beginning to sound as paranoid as you.' She glanced at Mr B.

'Just because you're paranoid, doesn't mean they're not out to get you.' He raised his dark eyebrows. 'We need to find out who's behind this or none of us are going to have a job.'

As well as being a conspiracy theorist, Mr B was very good at stating the obvious, Clara thought, noticing that she had a missed call on her mobile from Adam. There was also one from Grandad. He could certainly pick his moments. Before she could decide whose call to return first, her mobile rang again and this time it was Kate.

'I've had a word with Brian Curtis,' she began without preamble. 'He doesn't think we would have a case against the paper. They haven't directly linked us with being the cause of Micky's failure. They have just said he was taken ill. They haven't directly linked us with being responsible for any food poisoning either.' She sounded like she was quoting her solicitor word for word. She also sounded desperately sad. 'It's very clever wording, but Brian says we can't get them to retract something they haven't said. We could ask them to put in a little statement that says the Bluebell Cliff has no responsibility for Micky Tucker's illness, but if we did that it would just link us with it even more in people's minds. And anyway...' there was a deep sigh in her voice, 'we can't prove that we're not responsible for his illness.

This whole thing is really, really unfortunate, Clara, but I don't think there's anything we can do about it. Have we had any calls?'

'What kind of calls?' Clara said, although she knew what her boss was asking.

'Negative feedback? Cancellations?'

'No nothing like that.'

'Well, fingers crossed we won't. This will blow over. Today's headlines are tomorrow's fish and chip wrappers, that's what my Aunt Carrie would have said.'

When she had put down the phone, Clara relayed all this to Phil and Mr B.

'Wrapping fish and chips in newspapers went out in the eighties,' the chef remarked, screwing up his nose in distaste and getting up from his chair. 'Not a moment too soon either, if you want my opinion.'

When they had left her office, Clara phoned her grandfather back, who didn't answer, and Adam, who did.

'I heard what happened at Oktoberfest. I just wanted to say that I'm sorry. That must have been disappointing.'

'Yes, it was.' She hesitated, wondering if he'd heard it on the grapevine or whether he'd seen the newspaper headlines.

'I saw it in the *Gazette* just now,' he confirmed. 'One of our guests had a copy. I'm sorry, Clara – that must have been quite a blow.'

'Yes,' she said, her mind suddenly on overtime. 'Adam, what time does the *Gazette* usually get delivered to you? We don't normally even get it until Wednesday and yet it was here first thing when I got in.'

'We don't usually get it until Wednesday either,' he confirmed, 'but it's obviously printed before that. I'm guessing it probably depends on which delivery round you're on.'

'Yes, thanks, I'm sure you're right. And thanks for calling, Adam, I appreciate it.'

'Let me know if there's anything I can do to help.'

She hoped she hadn't cut him off too quickly, but her mind was still racing. *The Purbeck Gazette* may not have an axe to grind, but whoever had delivered that newspaper clearly did. They had gone out of their way to make sure she would see a copy early. Surely they wouldn't do that unless their motives were bad.

Finally, Clara had something positive to do. The Bluebell had a state-of-the-art security system. She could easily find out who had delivered that paper. All she had to do was to play back the front door's CCTV.

At four p.m. she was still scanning through the recordings when Zoe knocked on the door. 'Sorry to interrupt...'

'You're not. Come in.'

'We just had a booking cancelled.' Zoe came into the room slowly. Her English-rose complexion looked paler than usual.

'Who was it?'

'Do you remember the Serious Hill Runners – they were here for a week in August and they had another week booked in May?'

Clara had an image of a wiry, cheery little man with NHS-style glasses. 'I do yes. I liked them. Did they give a reason?'

'They heard about the Curly Wurly record going wrong. Someone sent them a link to the story apparently and they were worried.' She looked close to tears. 'I did tell them, Clara, that it was nothing to do with us. But the woman on the phone was adamant. She kept saying that they were doing a record too and they didn't want to put the kibosh on it. What does kibosh even mean?'

'It means bad luck,' Clara said, feeling the heaviness in her heart transfer itself to her chest. 'Oh my goodness. OK, leave it with me. I'll phone them back and see if I can reassure them.'

Zoe nodded and withdrew.

Clara made a note to call the Serious Hill Runners and glanced back at the CCTV recordings that she was still going through on the screen. There had been nothing all night. The camera only went off when it was triggered by movement and then its infrared light kicked in so you could actually see what was going on even in the dark.

The mornings got darker all through October until the end of the month when the clocks went back. She'd noticed the progression even over the last few days. Then, at just before 7.15 a.m. on the recording, she saw the camera click on and a figure appeared just beyond the front door.

She had hoped a car might pull up outside. Then she could have got a registration, but they must have parked at the back and walked round. She zoomed in. The figure was wearing jeans and a padded coat. It was probably male, but it was hard to tell because he or she had the hood up.

Clara slowed the recording down as they came to the door, bent and pushed the paper through the letter box. It looked like a man, but she couldn't see any detail because he had a scarf half covering his face.

Frustrated, she called Mr B in. Phil had gone home. He was back on shift this evening, but Mr B was still in the kitchen.

'It's that reporter,' he announced. 'One hundred per cent.'

'How can you be sure?'

'You can tell by the way he walks. He's strutting – look.' He leaned over her shoulder and fast-forwarded the file. 'Look at the way he struts away from the door.'

'Isn't that just the way the camera goes frame by frame when it's speeded up?'

'I don't think so. I'd stake my reputation on it being him, the fissilingual bastard.'

22

'Your chef may incorrectly believe the whole world is out to get him, but he does have a sharp vocabulary. Something to be commended in this day and age.'

This was the verdict of Clara's grandfather, who she had caught up with eventually on Wednesday evening. She had picked him up two hours ago and they had just eaten dinner together at Kate's.

When he'd phoned, he'd asked her to collect him, along with his overnight bag, and take him to Thelma's. Clara had ignored his request and decided to cook him dinner at the bungalow instead and see if she could have one last go at talking him out of asking Gran for a divorce.

Right now, they were both pointedly avoiding the subject in case it ended up in another argument. Their earlier discussion had been heated.

'So what does fissilingual mean anyway?' Clara asked him.

'Fork-tongued,' Grandad told her with a distinct note of smugness in his voice. He rubbed his bristly white chin with one hand and just missed putting his elbow in the gravy boat. 'Like a snake. A very helpful thing for a journalist to be.'

'You sound like you approve – it wasn't very helpful for The Bluebell. We lost a booking yesterday over this.'

'Did you?' He looked alarmed. 'You didn't tell me that.'

She had told him that. They'd been discussing it on the way here in the car, but he'd clearly forgotten. To be honest, she wasn't surprised; he didn't know whether he was coming or going. She was beginning to feel like that too.

They stared at each other across Kate's kitchen table.

'If you hadn't gone and kidnapped me, I'd have had my life sorted out by now.' He pushed his dinner plate away and coughed. His breathing was laboured again, which probably meant the COPD was getting worse. He could barely walk along the hall without having to pause for breath.

'I didn't kidnap you, Grandad. I'm just trying to stop you doing something you'll regret. I just want you to think things through.'

'I know that, love.' Suddenly his demeanour changed. 'But I have thought things through. I've done nothing but think things through, these past few months. And I'm not a fan of thinking. You know that, Clara. I'm a fan of doing things.'

She did know that. She held his gaze, over their dirty plates. The scent of herby leek sausages and mash hung in the air. Sausage and mash was his favourite meal, which she'd cooked especially, to sweeten the fact that she hadn't taken him directly to Gran's.

His shoulders sagged a bit and suddenly all she could see was an old man, who was growing increasingly frail, and for the first time she wondered if she really had done the right thing, bringing him here. Staging an intervention was a modern term, but maybe it wasn't always constructive. Maybe she hadn't acted as rationally as she'd thought. Maybe she should just accept that if a divorce was what he wanted, then he should be left alone to get on with it. It was his marriage, not hers.

'I'll take you to Gran's in the morning,' she said. 'I'll take you on the way to work. If that's truly what you want me to do.'

'It is, love.' He put the palms of his hands on the table and gave her a direct look. 'It's not that I didn't appreciate the lovely meal. I do...' He'd left two of the sausages, she saw. Foxy would be thrilled. 'But I think I'll get off for an early night. I'm feeling a bit under the weather, if I'm honest with you.' He stood up, wheezing heavily, and shot her a glance back over his shoulder. 'I suppose I should be thankful there's no stairs in this place, shouldn't I!' He headed off down the hall to the spare bedroom that Clara had made up for him.

Clara began to clear the table. She stacked the dishwasher, fed Foxy and cleared up the kitchen and then she let the little dog outside and followed her into the garden. They may be a week into October, but summer hadn't yet packed her bags and fled. Today, there had been sunshine and the skies were still clear.

Clara strolled down the path that led to the bottom of the garden and stood beside the dark oblong shape of the shed. She rested a hand against the warm wood and breathed in the evening air. The moon was almost full tonight and the stars were bright, little twinkling dots of light that stretched out into infinity. The smell of the night-time sea that swept across the cliff path on the faintest of breezes was one she knew she would never get tired of. Yet she could feel the winds of change on its breath.

Was it only a few months ago that she'd had a rock-solid family and a boyfriend, albeit a slightly misguided one, and a dream job that she could keep for the foreseeable future? These things were disappearing one by one and Clara didn't have the faintest idea how to stop them.

* * *

When she woke up the next day, she was clinging to the faint hope that Grandad might have had a change of heart in the night. But, if anything, he seemed even more determined.

'It's for the best, love,' he said, as he repacked the few bits and pieces he'd brought with him into his overnight bag. 'Once Thelma and I have had the chat, we can all move on.'

'How will you get back to Jim's?' she said when they were finally on their way. Grandad had given up his rights to the family car when he'd moved out.

'Let me worry about that. I'm sure your gran will give me a lift. It will all be very amicable, you know it will.'

When she pulled up outside his family home, Grandad seemed subdued but determined. There was a resolution in his eyes that she hadn't seen there for some time.

'Do you want me to wait for a minute in case she isn't in?'

'She's in. The car's there.'

Clara had really meant in case of any other eventuality. What if Gran wouldn't let him in? But it was too late. He was already getting out, albeit slowly, and with one last nod of thanks, he was gone, walking straight-backed to the front door to face his future.

Clara watched the door open a crack and then shut while Gran got the chain off. A few seconds later, it opened a little wider to admit him. Then it closed again and there was nothing else for her to do except leave.

All the way to work, she tried to imagine what they might be saying and couldn't. How did you even begin to unravel a marriage of so many years? She imagined all the gaps between conversation where the pain would lie in wait and that hurt so much that she had to stop and tell herself that it was nothing to do with her. She had done everything she possibly could

* * *

The next twenty-four hours passed slowly. It was now Friday morning and there had been no word from either of her grandparents or from anyone else in her family. Clara wasn't sure whether that meant no one else knew what was going on or whether her grandparents had had a change of heart.

Luckily, the hotel was so busy with preparations for the forthcoming Scargill wedding that Clara didn't have time to worry too much. She was also still dealing with fallout from *The Purbeck Gazette*'s story.

A couple of suppliers had been on, Mr B had told her, wanting to make sure they weren't going to be implicated in any possible food poisoning rumours. Clara had also received phone calls and emails from past and future guests, sympathising. To her huge relief, there had been no more cancellations.

She had tried to get the Serious Hill Runners back, but she hadn't succeeded. The most their secretary would say was that she would raise the matter again at their next meeting.

Kate had phoned every day since Oktoberfest and she'd spoken to Phil and Mr B too. This had unnerved Clara slightly, but she knew she would have done the same in her employer's shoes. A lot was at stake.

It was now lunchtime and Clara and Zoe were in the downstairs music room, which had been transformed into a fabulous wedding venue for the following day.

From the French door entrance, a wide aisle led between two rows of chairs that were five wide. At the end of each aisle were white candles in crystal holders with white ribbons trailing from them. Tall cut-crystal glass vases waited for the flowers that would fill them the following day. The entire room was draped with lace and fairy lights. The effect was stunning.

The Steinway was in its usual position, slightly off centre at the far end of the room, but the raised stage beyond it had been transformed into a pulpit, which now housed a wooden lectern and a table with two chairs.

'It looks even better than I thought it would,' Clara murmured, as Zoe looked around them, starry-eyed.

'I know. It's gorgeous. It's like something out of a fairy tale. Does it make you want to get married?'

'Marriage isn't just for one day,' Clara suddenly felt as though she were a thousand years old.

'No, I know. It's for at least a year, otherwise it's not worth all the hassle of changing your name!' Zoe winked and walked down the aisle, fingering a ribbon here and touching a seat there. 'It smells divine in here. What is that?'

'Essence of rose and amber. It's an essential oil I found in one of the catalogues. Beautiful isn't it. I wanted to preview it before tomorrow, so I burnt some in here earlier. The flowers will add their own scents once they arrive, but it's nice to have an underlay of perfume, don't you think?'

Zoe nodded and closed her eyes, tilting her face back to breathe it in.

'This is the venue for the night-time entertainment too,' Clara went on. 'They're having a brass band who will set up on stage as soon as the ceremony is over and we'll clear some of the chairs while the wedding party are having lunch. This room used to be a ballroom back in the day, did you know that?'

'Phil mentioned it once. Has it always had this floor?' Zoe rocked back and forth on her kitten heels.

'I think Kate had a new sprung floor put in. It's for dancers. This whole place is so high spec. There are lots of details like that. It must have cost a fortune to refurbish it. Mind you, apparently there was a bidding war with some developers to get the plot in the first place, so I don't think money was too much of an issue. Did you know it was her Aunt Carrie's dream to open this hotel?'

'Yes.' Zoe's face sobered. 'Her Aunt Carrie envisioned a place where people would come and live their dream and Kate did it all – even though her aunt never lived to see it come to fruition.' She met Clara's gaze and her clear blue eyes shadowed a little. 'Was there any more news on the Curly Wurly thing? Did we ever find out what happened?'

'We never got to the bottom of it, no.'

'But I thought we'd found out that the nasty reporter had also delivered the paper to us especially. That's incriminating.'

'Mr B swore that it was him, but even if it was, it doesn't mean he had anything to do with the sabotage if that's what it was. Just that he's not our friend. And I think we knew that already.' Clara looked at the sunlight spilling through the great plate-glass windows and highlighting slanted sections of the beautiful oak floor. 'It doesn't mean that he had anything to do with whatever it was that caused Micky to be sick.'

'No, I suppose not.'

'He could have had a bug. It could just have been very unfortunate timing.' Neither of them believed that, she knew, but it was possible.

She strolled a little closer to the stage, where the drama of a wedding, the beginning of someone's love story, would take place, this time tomorrow.

'And it doesn't mean that he had anything to do with the previous incidents,' she continued. 'They've all been different. There wasn't a video on YouTube this time. And he did take one. I watched him.'

Zoe nodded. She was close to the pulpit and she bent to adjust a small wooden plaque on the edge of the stage that would hold the order of service. 'Maybe there wasn't any point in putting it on there though, because it wasn't linked to us.' She straightened. 'He could point the finger at us in his paper with words, but he couldn't do it on that video. Not without being really obvious and risking getting sued.'

'I think you might have a point.' Clara joined her beside the pulpit. 'I've thought about it a lot. What I always come back to is why? Why would anyone want to drag the Bluebell's name into the mud? Why would anyone want to close down a hotel that makes people's dreams come true?'

'Mr B says we need to find out before they succeed.'

'And we will,' Clara reassured, even though she still didn't have the faintest idea of how they were going to do it. 'Kate will be back soon. She may have some ideas. Until then, all we need to focus on is this wedding. We have to make sure nothing goes wrong. It has to be superbulous,' she added, wondering why she was using one of Adam's made up words. She still hadn't managed to banish him entirely from her thoughts then!

But Zoe joined in to the spirit of things. 'It will be superbulous,' she agreed as they walked back up the aisle together. 'Absolutely fantabysuperbulous.'

* * *

On Friday evening, just after Clara had got back to the bungalow following Foxy's evening walk, Rosanna phoned.

'Something awful's happened,' she said, as soon as Clara picked up.

'Go on,' Clara said, bracing herself.

'It's Grandad. He's had a funny turn.'

'What do you mean?' Clara asked, wondering if this could possibly be a reference to him asking Gran for a divorce.

'No one's exactly sure. But he was at Gran's when it happened and she had to call an ambulance. They took him to Poole Hospital. Clara, do you know why he was at Gran's. Were they getting back together?'

Clara was saved from having to answer this because the signal disappeared, but her mind was whirring. So he'd stayed overnight. Was that good?

Her sister was obviously on her Bluetooth in a car. She phoned back instantly. 'Oh my God, Clara. I hope he's going to be all right. He's nearly eighty. I'm just on my way to the hospital now. Eddie's looking after the kids. I'm picking up Mum and Dad en route. Are you at work or at home?'

'I've just got back home. But I'll come straight away. Is he in a ward?'

'Not sure. I'll let... know... reception—' There was another burst of staccato words and then there was nothing and her phone beeped with the message:

`Call failed.`

Clara shouted for Foxy, who appeared reluctantly. Maybe even she was tired with the amount of head-clearing walking they'd been doing lately, but she couldn't leave her alone while she drove to Poole. It was only forty minutes away, but she had a feeling it might be a long night. Her stomach crunched with anxiety.

* * *

Hospitals were like airports, she thought as she went in through the main doors. It didn't matter whether it was day or night.

There was still fluorescent lighting and dry air and people milling about with tired and anxious faces.

The main reception was closed, but a sign directed her through to A&E, where she found someone in a uniform, who consulted a computer and told her that Eric Price was in a cardiac ward on floor three.

'Does that mean he's had a heart attack?'

'I can't give you any details. You'll need to ask at the nurses' station.'

When Clara got to the nurses' station, she was directed to a visitors' room, where she found the rest of her family.

Dad was hugging Mum – they were standing by the window – and Rosanna had her arm around Gran on a bench seat beside them. All of them, even Dad, looked as though they'd been crying and the recycled air in the oblong room smelled of sadness.

'How is he?' Clara asked, standing in the doorway and suddenly fearing the worst.

Mum detached herself from Dad and came over. 'He's bad, love. They're with him now. They won't tell us much.' She glanced at Gran. 'It's all been such a shock.'

Now Gran got up too and came across to where they stood. 'The bloody idiot. He's been having pains in his arm. He didn't tell me until today. He said he thought it was tennis elbow.' Her eyes flashed with pain. 'He doesn't even play tennis. Did he say anything to you?'

'He didn't say anything about pains in his arm,' Clara answered, feeling a cold dread creeping through her. 'He said he felt slightly under the weather, that's all.'

'Have you seen him then?' Rosanna looked at them from her position on the bench seat. 'When?'

'Wednesday evening. He phoned me from Jim's.'

'Your sister was kind enough to drop him over to me yesterday and then it got too late for me to drive him back, so he stayed in the spare room.' Gran shot Clara a warning look, which Clara assumed meant, 'don't say anything else'. Maybe the subject of divorce had been raised then, but it wasn't common knowledge. It certainly didn't seem to have been discussed tonight. 'So, do they think it was a heart attack,' she went on. 'Is that what's happened?'

'We think so, yes.' Dad looked at her. 'More than one. It sounds as though he's really lucky he's still here.' He gestured towards Gran. 'Your gran will tell you the full story.'

'He said he was still feeling ill when he got up this morning,' Gran said. 'So I sent him back to bed. Then he collapsed in the bathroom just before teatime. I heard him cry out and then I heard this thump and I thought he'd knocked something over and broken it. You know how cack-handed he can be.' Her voice wobbled a little and Clara reached for her hand. 'I went in to tell him off. He never locks the door luckily.' She paused to gather herself and Clara could feel her grandmother's thin arm trembling as it knocked against hers and she knew that her gran, who never let anyone get to her, who never cried, was close to breaking point.

Gran swallowed hard several times before she was ready to continue. 'I thought I'd lost him. He was on the floor and he was still breathing, but his lips were blue.'

'But we haven't lost him,' Clara said gently. 'He's still here.'

'Only just, my angel.' Gran's eyes met hers and she saw they were misted with pain and grief. 'Oh my goodness, I've been such a bloody fool.'

23

Clara was relieved there was no one else but her family in this dim little room: no one else waiting for news. She couldn't have stood to be around raw-faced strangers fidgeting and pacing and alternating between silence and trying to pretend everything was normal. It was bad enough being with the people she loved.

As the time passed, there were bursts of conversation between them when they talked about trivia, like the fact that Sophie was nearly ready to take Grade I violin, wasn't that something? Or Tom had a friend who had a cousin who had mumps – wasn't that supposed to have been eradicated? But the silences were longer.

Clara knew they were all doing the same thing. Trying to divert themselves from their fear over Grandad. Every so often, Clara thought about the bridal party arriving the following morning. The groom's party were already in situ. The Scargill wedding was the most important event that the Bluebell had ever hosted, and she needed to be on top form to make sure nothing went wrong. She thought about all the measures that she and Phil had put in place to make sure everything went with clockwork precision. How they had double-checked everything: timings; expectations; plans; hopes and dreams.

Isobel Scargill's father had paid a fortune for his 'only daughter's only wedding'. That's what he'd called it when he'd phoned up to book. Kate had passed on this information to Clara with a wry smile before she had gone off to Adelaide: '"It's my only daughter's only wedding and everything has to be perfect" – that's what he actually said. Clearly he's confident that she's found her perfect match.'

'I guess everyone is confident on the day they actually tie the knot,' Clara had said. 'Or they wouldn't do it.'

'No, they're not. I read a survey the other day. Apparently one in four people know when they're walking up the aisle that they're making a big mistake.'

'Why on earth do they go through with it then?'

'Lots of reasons. Family pressure's big apparently. Or because one or both of them think it's what's expected of them. Or because they've got caught up in the excitement of planning the wedding and are now having second thoughts but are too scared of letting everyone down to pull out.'

Clara had thought about family pressure a lot lately and how it could contribute to people doing things they didn't want to do. Like her trying to talk Grandad out of wanting a divorce and then virtually kidnapping him. And she thought about how cut off he must have felt, down in Weymouth at Jim's, while their family lunches and birthday parties went on without him. Could all of that, possibly, have contributed to what was happening now?

She knew Mum had been to see him and she and Rosanna had been too, but they hadn't seen him as much as they'd seen Gran. Because it had seemed that Gran was the injured party, which she was, of course, but they had all made judgements, hadn't they. What did anyone really know about what went on in other people's marriages?

She was terrified that they had all inadvertently contributed to the heart attacks and how Grandad might now be going to die without knowing how much Gran loved him. How much they all loved him.

These dark thoughts swirled and raced through her mind in between the little flurries of conversation that were whisked up like dust clouds of dry sand on the beach by a southwesterly wind. Everyone was trying to be positive.

'He's going to get through this. He's a tough old goat.' That was Dad.

'He is. He's too stubborn to let some little old heart attack finish him.' That was Rosanna. 'His heart's as big as a house,' she added.

'Why hasn't anyone come to speak to us?' It was Gran who voiced the question that no one else dared to ask.

'No news is good news,' Mum said, stroking her arm.

'Do you think they've forgotten us?' That was Rosanna. 'Dad, maybe you should go and ask.'

Dad coughed and put his hands in his pockets. 'I don't want to stop them doing their job – you know – stuff for him, keeping him safe. I don't want to get in the way of that...'

It was what had kept them all in this room, patiently waiting, Clara thought. No one wanted to stop the medical staff from saving his life. And it was true that no news was good news.

She wondered if Foxy was all right in the car. It wasn't hot. It was almost nine and she'd left the windows open a crack, but she decided to go and check her out anyway. It was better than waiting here in this airless room. As soon as there was news, someone would come and tell them and Rosanna could text her.

A few minutes later, she was back in the multistorey. Foxy was fine; she was curled up in her fabric basket, her nose tucked between her paws, but she didn't take much persuasion to go for a stroll around the perimeter of the car park.

A text beeped on Clara's phone, but it turned out to be Phil, letting her know that the stag night was going well. No dramas; James, the groom wasn't even getting that drunk. Before the arrival of the wedding party, they had worried about that after the Curly Wurly disaster, which they had eventually concluded was most likely down to someone spiking Micky Tucker's drink. It was the only possible explanation. He had said himself that it had tasted stronger the further down the glass he had got. 'No one will be spiking our groom's drink,' Phil had told her with a steely look in his eyes. 'I've primed all the staff. We'll be making absolutely sure he drinks only what he intends to – and not a unit more. I've got the staff on drink-watching shifts.'

'Will that work?' She had asked.

'It will for as long as he's in any of the public areas. What he does in his room is his own affair, but he won't have his drink spiked on my watch.'

Clara texted him to thank him. She didn't tell him she was at the hospital. He'd have enough on his plate, discreetly supervising the stag night.

She put Foxy in the car and went back to the family room. 'Still no news?'

Mum shook her head. 'I'd have thought they'd have told us something by now.'

Clara agreed, but what did she know? She really only knew what she had watched on television – the drama of soaps or 'reality' TV. Everything happened much quicker on television.

Until now she'd known nothing at all about the actual reality, which was: the smell of dry air, punctuated by the sanitised hand gel that she had put on her hands again when she'd come back in, an insurance policy against the terrors of superbugs; the uncomfortable chairs; the out-of-date magazines and time passing in elongated seconds and minutes and hours.

Her FunFit said it was just before ten thirty. She had been here barely two hours. But time was made longer because of the helplessness of knowing they could do nothing but wait.

'We are going to have to ask someone, aren't we?' It was Mum this time who broached the subject. 'Even if we just ask someone on the nurses' station. It's not like he's having surgery, is it? Someone must know how he's doing.'

'I'll go,' Gran said, standing up. 'I need the toilet anyway. I'll find someone. They'll tell me, won't they? I am his next of kin.'

Mum nodded. Clara was about to accompany her grand-mother to find a visitors' loo – no one seemed to think there was one on this floor – when the door suddenly opened. Everyone's heads snapped round as the young nurse became the focus of their attention. Staff Nurse Helen Jakes. In the seconds before she came fully into the room, Clara tried to work out if a staff nurse was senior enough to be the giver of bad news.

'Mr Price is stable,' she said. 'We will be monitoring him closely. But he's conscious.' She looked around and her eyes settled on Gran. 'He's asking for you, Mrs Price.'

Gran seemed to change in a moment from a defeated shadow into a flickering image of the feisty woman she usually was, like a photo on a laptop coming gradually into focus when there's a slow connection.

She looked at Mum, and then around at the rest of her family, and her shoulders straightened a little more. 'I'd better go and see what he wants then, hadn't I!'

With a quick nod at Dad, Mum went with her, and when the door closed behind them, they all let out a collective breath.

'Thank God,' Dad said.

'I thought we'd lost him.' Rosanna was wiping tears from her face. 'I know it's mad to cry now. But I can't help it.'

Clara produced an unopened mini pack of tissues and she went and sat on the bench next to her. 'It's never mad to cry.'

Rosanna sniffed and tried to get one out, but her fingers weren't working properly. 'Why do they make these things so bloody difficult to open?'

'Give it here,' Dad said, sitting down on her other side. 'You need an old person to open things.' He winked.

'You're not even remotely old,' Clara told him.

'Well, I feel bloody old today.' He ripped the cellophane off the tissues with brute force and half of them fell on the floor.

They all giggled and it was like an escape valve of tension. Laughter and tears. Clara wasn't sure which were the closest to overwhelming her as she bent to pick up the discarded tissues.

'Group hug,' Rosanna said, putting her arms around both of them and pulling them close.

Clara rested her head against her elder sister's shoulder. She was wearing what she called one of her Mummy tops because it had the softest, snuggest fleece for children to cuddle into. Clara could smell the faint scent of Jimmy Choo embedded in its fibres, mixed with the scent of product on Rosanna's hair, and she closed her eyes and thought about families and love and hope. And the black threat of divorce seemed to shrink like some banished demon and she thought surely it couldn't survive any more. Not now. Not here in the brightness and light of all this love.

24

It was almost midnight before Rosanna left the hospital with Mum and Dad. Everyone had been in to see Grandad, who was now sleeping. Gran had wanted to stay a bit longer. 'I know they say he's going to be OK, but I don't want to leave him,' she had said. 'Just in case they're wrong. You don't need to wait, angel,' she had told Clara. 'I'll get a taxi.'

Rosanna and Clara had exchanged glances, a tacit agreement passing between them. Gran shouldn't stay behind all on her own; Clara would wait with her. She was the sensible choice. Rosanna needed to get back for Sophie and Tom, and Mum and Dad looked worn out.

So Clara waited, while Gran went to see Grandad one more time before coming back to the visitors' room, where Clara finally managed to persuade her that she would be more use to Grandad when he was awake the following day. That he would need his rest and that she should get some rest too, and Gran had finally agreed to leave the hospital.

On the way back, closeted in the cool darkness of the car, she told Clara falteringly about the events that had led up to the heart attack.

'You knew what he was coming round to tell me, didn't you?' she said as Clara drove. 'You knew he'd decided that we should have a permanent separation.'

'He said something about that, yes,' Clara said, because she was too tired to pretend. She ached from head to foot with emotional exhaustion.

'I agreed with him,' Gran said. 'I was shocked as hell, but I wasn't going to disagree. I was right up there on my stubborn high horse with my nose stuck up in the air. Proud as a bloody peacock.' She huffed out a sigh. 'If that's not too many clichés for you. I wasn't going to back down. Not when he was in the wrong. Oh, Clara, I can't believe that pride and stubbornness nearly separated us permanently. But it's amazing how the realisation that there may be no going back, no second chances, puts things so sharply in perspective.'

She sniffed and Clara glanced at her and saw tears on her face. Now, she was bent forward and heaving her giant bag onto her lap and rummaging for a handkerchief. Gran didn't do tissues. There was a flash of white as she found a man-size one and blew her nose.

'I haven't told your mother,' she added quietly. 'Or your sister. The divorce part, I mean. They still think he came round for peace talks.'

Clara gripped the steering wheel. 'Peace talks, huh. So when did you decide that peace talks were the way forward?'

'I decided that as soon as I saw him lying on the bathroom floor with his lips all blue, fighting for breath. I can't imagine life without him. Not permanently. That's the truth of it.' She blew her nose again. 'I didn't tell him, though, properly that no way would we have a divorce until about an hour ago. That's why I couldn't leave. Not until I'd told him. Not until I was sure he understood.'

'And how do you know he understood?'

'He squeezed my hand and he winked. Well, he didn't wink as such, it was more that he opened one eye briefly – the opposite of a wink, I suppose – but he knew what I was talking about. I'm sure of it.' There was a little gap and she added softly, 'I did tell him I loved him when we were on the way to the hospital. I told him over and over, and he said it too. And he said he was sorry. He kept saying that.'

'I'm so pleased.' Clara felt as though a tight band of worry had been loosened, as she stopped for a red light at some roadworks and turned to look at her grandmother. 'I hated the thought of you splitting up. We all did, Gran. But none of us wanted to interfere.'

'Your sister interfered. Sending me all those Sids.' Gran sounded more amused than irritated.

'Yes, I suppose she did.'

'She probably thought it was reverse psychology, silly mare. She probably thought I'd fling up my hands in horror and say I'd never look at any man but your grandad.' She gave a little snort – somewhere between outrage and amusement.

Clara considered this. The traffic lights were taking forever.

'I've always done the opposite of what people expected me to do,' Gran added. 'It's a bad habit.' She stole a glance at Clara. 'You've got a bit of that about you, too, haven't you? We are very alike.'

'Have I? Grandad told me I was the diplomat of the family. He said you both thought I was going to be a politician when I grew up.'

'You can be a diplomatic hothead. Look at the Prime Minister.' Gran had always been a fan of Boris Johnson.

Clara felt laughter bubbling up – possibly it was borderline hysteria. 'Boris – diplomatic? If you say so, Gran!'

The lights finally changed.

Twenty minutes later, they were back at Church Knowle and Clara went into the house long enough to see that her grandmother was settled.

'Try and get some sleep. And give Grandad my love when you see him tomorrow.'

'I will.' Gran gripped her hand. 'Thank you, angel. Thank you for being you. Don't ever change.'

Clara finally arrived back at the bungalow in the early hours and woke up a disgruntled Foxy, who had been curled up snugly again in her felt basket, blissfully unaware of the night's drama.

Her body told her it was still night-time, it was certainly still dark, but her FunFit told her that in barely five hours it would be time to get up and prepare for the day, which was going to be a long one.

The Bluebell's first wedding. A prime target for their saboteur – she dreaded to think what would happen if anything went wrong with Mr Scargill's only daughter's only wedding. He was paying a fortune for the dream venue, for the beautiful lighthouse honeymoon suite for the couple's first night. He was paying a fortune for Isobel Scargill to have her perfect day.

Clara had planned to get an early night and be fresh in the morning so that she was fully up to making sure this happened, but right now she felt as though she'd been wrestled into an old-fashioned wringer and rolled back and forth a few times. Her eyes were gritty with tiredness.

She crawled into bed, set her alarm and sank into oblivion –

and her alarm woke her up again after what seemed like barely ten seconds of sleep. It tugged her out of a dream in which Gran and Grandad were dancing on a deserted beach. Gran was wearing a white satin wedding dress and Grandad was wearing a top hat and tails and behind them a tsunami was rolling in from some distant point on the horizon. As it got closer, Clara was screaming at them to run, but both of them had switched off their hearing aids and neither of them heard her. They just whirled faster and faster on the sand.

When Clara finally woke up, she was shaking. That was the second time in as many weeks she had dreamt about a tsunami. Was her life really that much out of control?

'No, it isn't,' she told Foxy, as, bleary-eyed, she got up, showered and dressed and rang the hospital, who said her grandfather had not only had a good night, he'd eaten breakfast. Thank goodness for that.

It was too early to wake Gran, and Mum was probably in bed still, but she messaged her with the good news and said she would phone her later.

Thank goodness for make-up, she thought as she did her best to camouflage her tired face. And thank goodness for dogs who listened attentively – in case there was any mention of food (in Foxy's case) and didn't answer back with smart alec remarks about being a hot-headed diplomat. No way was she as stroppy and as stubborn as her grandmother. If she'd had a lovely man like Grandad in her life, she would never have let him go. But then Grandad had strayed. He had thought the grass was greener. Gran had every right to be upset and disappointed, she decided. Grandad, although a good man, had made a mistake, but he had almost paid very dearly for it.

Clara padded around barefoot in the kitchen and made

coffee. It was only when she was at the front door ready to leave that she spotted the postcard just to the left of the mat. It must have arrived yesterday and she'd missed it somehow.

She stooped to pick it up and saw a picture of Tokyo. Turning it over in her hand, she spotted Will's familiar loopy writing. Not that he'd written much.

Having a wonderful time. Hope your job's going well!!!

That was it. There wasn't even a signature.

She wondered how he knew where she was living and then remembered he'd asked for her address the last time they'd met. It was odd that he had put so many exclamation marks after the word 'well'. He'd dotted the last one so hard, there was a small dent in the postcard. Should she be reading anything into those exclamation marks? Apart from the fact he was still angry with her for taking the job – even from halfway across the world.

She sighed and remembered what Rosanna had once said – 'hell hath no fury like a man scorned'. Will may have been responsible for Lighthousegate, but there was no way he could have done any of the other stuff. Not from afar.

She left the postcard propped up on the radiator in the hall.

'Today is going to be perfect,' she told an uninterested Foxy as she let them both out of the front door.

It was certainly perfect weather for a wedding, she thought, glancing up at the clear sky, where just a few wispy clouds were hanging lazily in the blue. That was a good omen. The weather being the one thing that she hadn't been able to arrange.

It wasn't just December that had red berries. They were abundant in October too. Maybe climate change had disrupted all the seasons because there were baby snails everywhere as well.

The baby snails climbed up the outside wall of Kate's bungalow. Every time she went out of the front door, Clara saw a couple of them on their way up. Where were they all going? She had wondered occasionally whether she should take them off very gently and put them on the grass. They would surely be better off there.

This morning, she had decided against it. Lately, she had interfered enough in things that were not her business. She felt as though God, or fate – or whatever you wanted to call it – had let her off with a warning last night. She did not want to push her luck.

* * *

It was just before eight a.m. when she reached the Bluebell. The lighthouse looked like a cream monolith rising up from the clifftop. The hotel looked dazzlingly white with the morning sunshine sparkling off its many windows. They had decorated the main door with red and gold flowers, which were the bride's autumn colour scheme, and the silver birches in the bluebell woods scattered a few more leaves every time there was a gust of wind, like so much bronze and gold confetti.

The photos were going to be amazing. Clara imagined Isobel and her new husband, James, racing up the spiral staircase of the lighthouse to the honeymoon suite, which was what they'd be doing at the end of today and she felt a little glow of pride.

They were a lovely couple. She had liked them both when she had met them at the rehearsal. That was another positive thing. At least the Bluebell's first wedding didn't have a bridezilla in the starring role. Everything was going to be perfect, she told herself once more.

She parked in a disabled bay because there was someone in her usual one. She wasn't surprised. Most of this week's guests would be gone by the time the wedding party arrived, but just to be on the safe side, yesterday they had coned off a lot of spaces for them, so parking was in short supply. Someone was in Zoe's usual space too, she noticed, as she walked across the car park.

It wasn't until she got closer to the hotel that she overheard raised voices coming from the back entrance of the kitchen.

'You cannot leave them in garden. It is not good – is not hygienic.' It sounded like Jakob's voice, Clara thought, pausing to listen.

'They're fine. They're not causing any trouble. What's it got to do with you anyway? They're not in the restaurant, are they?'

'They are not fine. NO.' Jakob was getting more agitated. 'They are beasts. Security risqué beasts.'

What on earth were they talking about? Clara headed round to the back entrance and saw that Jakob was standing outside, next to a young kitchen assistant who was carrying one of the baskets that they used to gather herbs from the garden. Jakob was arguing with Mr B, who was still inside the kitchen.

'We cannot leave this...' He stopped speaking abruptly as Clara appeared at the doorway.

'Good morning, gentlemen.' She glanced from one to the other. 'Is everything OK?'

Mr B looked heated beneath his chef's hat, although that could have been the temperature of the kitchen. Even with the door open, it was steamy.

Jakob looked red-faced and flustered. In the management hierarchy, he ranked below Mr B and actually reported to him, but he clearly had something on his mind.

They both nodded in her direction.

'Everything's under control, boss,' said Mr B.

'It doesn't sound like it is.' She frowned at him. 'What exactly is a security risqué beast?'

Mr B looked shifty.

Jakob, clearly couldn't contain his angst any more, even if it did mean dropping his boss in it. 'I show you,' he said. 'Come. This way. Please.'

'They're temporary,' Mr B shouted after them. 'Watch that pan,' he called to one of his staff, as Clara followed Jakob towards the vegetable garden, which was only a few hundred metres from the kitchen and was open to guests, if they wanted to browse, but was fenced off and accessed by a five-bar gate at the side.

When they got to the gate, Jakob didn't open it, but he paused and leaned his white shirted forearms on the top bar. 'Here...' he said, with a gesture that turned into a flourish. 'Security risqué beasts!'

For a moment, Clara wasn't sure what she was looking at. All seemed normal in the garden. Then she saw them. Two brown and black spotted creatures not much bigger than Foxy were snuffling about on the ground on the other side of the potato patch.

'What on earth are they?' she asked Jakob, as Foxy stuck her snout through the gate and sniffed interestedly.

He screwed up his face and gestured with his hands, obviously struggling for the right word. 'Porkers? Porkers crispy bacon?' He glanced over his shoulder. Both Mr B and the kitchen assistant with the basket were hurrying to catch up.

'They're not crispy bacon.' Mr B arrived first, slightly out of breath. 'They're kunekune pigs. They're not supposed to be here. I am going to move them. I just haven't had the chance.' He gave the kitchen assistant a shove. 'Go and get the parsley like I told you. Portia and Prudence won't hurt you.'

The kitchen assistant, whose name was Elliot and who was only about seventeen, didn't look convinced. He wrinkled his nose doubtfully. 'I dunno. Pigs can be aggressive.'

'Where are they supposed to be?' Clara asked Mr B. 'And who authorised them? No one told me we were starting to produce our own meat.'

'We're not. They're pets. They're my pets.' Mr B's expression hovered somewhere between mutiny and shame. They got delivered this morning. They weren't supposed to come until Monday. I've got a paddock booked for Monday, but they're using it for a dog show this weekend.'

Clara felt as though she had stepped into some surreal alternative reality. 'Well, Jakob's right, you can't keep them there. It's against regulations. They're too near the kitchen.'

Jakob stepped back from the gate and folded his arms, a look of self-righteous indignation on his face.

'Can you put them in the dog kennels?' Clara said, thinking quickly. 'That should be far enough away from the kitchens for it not to be a problem.'

'OK. I will. Thanks.' Mr B put one foot onto the rung of the five-bar gate and swung his other leg over the top.

There was a shout from the direction of the kitchen. 'Mr B. You're needed.'

'You don't have to do it now,' Clara told him. 'But don't forget.'

'I won't. Get the parsley,' he yelled at Elliot. 'Don't be such a wassock!'

Clara decided to leave them to it. But she felt rattled. It was not a good beginning to a day that was so hugely important.

She wondered if Zoe knew about the pigs. Unlikely, she thought. Mr B presided like a ruling emperor over his domain and usually it ran like clockwork. But then generally his eccentricities didn't extend further than his latest conspiracy theory.

She headed round to the front of the hotel. Zoe wasn't on reception and neither was Keith. The front desk computer had gone into sleep mode, which suggested neither of them had been there for a while.

Clara felt a stab of unease. She hadn't thought anything of it when Zoe's car hadn't been in its usual parking space. But now, suddenly, she was worried.

25

She ran back out to the car park so she could have a proper look for Zoe's car. There was definitely no sign of it. Seriously worried now, Clara tried her phone, but it went straight to voicemail, which meant it was either switched off or in an area where there wasn't a good signal.

She left a message. Zoe was as reliable as the sunrise. There was no way she wouldn't have turned up for work on the day of the wedding unless something had happened. But even then she would have told her. Clara tried to recall whether Zoe had said anything about being late – she didn't think so. Thoughts of the saboteur sprung to mind. She dismissed them. Kidnapping Zoe was a step too far. Tiredness and the shock of seeing kunekune pigs in the vegetable garden must be addling her brain.

Then, to her intense relief, Keith appeared. 'Good morning, Clara. Apologies for the temporarily unattended reception. I was obliged to make a trip – the missus cooked a curry last night.' He patted his belly and looked pained.

'It's fine. I don't need the details. Where's Zoe?'

'Ah – she's had to do an emergency dash. Let me explain.' He flicked through the notes on a pad in front of him and found the one he was looking for. 'The wedding cake, as you know, is being delivered today by Dean Curtis Caterers.'

'I thought it was coming yesterday.' She felt a twirl of panic in her stomach. 'I spoke to the caterers myself.'

'Yes, that was the original plan. But they had a vehicle mix-up at the eleventh hour apparently and so they were forced to delay delivery until this morning. They assured me that their driver would set off at 7.00 a.m. so that the cake would be here in good time. But unfortunately he broke down en route. So Zoe has gone to pick up the cake.'

Clara groaned.

'I am more than happy to cover reception until she returns.' Keith beamed at her. 'I took the precaution of factoring in some extra time today in order to cover any such unexpected eventualities.'

'Thank you. That's much appreciated,' Clara said, but actually she was thinking about the logistics of Zoe safely transporting a three-tier wedding cake in her car. She could hardly put it on the back seat. Her brain had already begun to catastrophise. What if she had to slam on her brakes? What if the cake got smashed to pieces? How was she going to explain that to the Scargills?

'It's all boxed up,' Keith added, noticing her alarm. 'They package them well to travel. It should be fine.'

'Well, I suppose it's out of our hands. But please keep me posted. Do you know her ETA?'

'Not later than nine.' He took a slug of cold black coffee from his giant mug.

'Can you please text her and tell her to let me know when she arrives. I'll send someone out to help with the transport of the cake.'

'Consider it done,' Keith said.

'Thank you.' Clara went into the office, collected her to-do list, added Zoe's jobs to it and continued with her checks.

The flowers had just arrived. She went to make sure all was in order. Fortunately the local florist was hugely efficient and already knew exactly what they were supposed to be doing and she and her team could be left to get on with it.

The registrar who was conducting the service had sent Clara a text, as instructed, to confirm his arrival at 11.45, ready for the wedding at 12.30.

So had the pianist who would play the wedding march on the Steinway. The Scargills had vetoed the idea of recorded music when they could have the real thing.

The photographer was arriving at 11.00 so he could get some candid snaps of the groom's party and be in situ for the arrival of the bride.

Clara went and checked the wedding venue – all was fine. The florist and her assistant were carrying in armfuls of red and gold flowers and were arranging them in the crystal vases.

The order of services' slips had arrived and someone had put them on a small table by the French doors where the guests and the bride would enter.

Clara bumped into Phil just coming out of the restaurant.

'All under control?' she asked.

'Of course. As soon as we've got breakfast cleared – we'll get laid up for the wedding lunch.'

'Did you know about Mr B's pigs?'

'I heard. Retrospectively.' He shook his head in disapproval. 'I think they've been taken care of. They're not in the vegetable garden anyway.' He put a hand on her arm. 'You look very tired, Clara. Are you OK?'

'My grandad had a heart attack yesterday. We were at the hospital much of the night.'

'Is he all right now? Should you be here?'

'He's going to be fine.' She was touched by the concern in his voice. 'It was just a long night.'

'I bet.'

Someone called him from inside the restaurant and he excused himself.

Clara carried on with her checks. Next stop the lighthouse. It hadn't been used since the emerald anniversary couple last week and had been prepared and checked yesterday for the newly married couple's first night. But she didn't want to leave anything to chance. This was probably ridiculous, she thought as she let herself in the front door and began to climb the spiral staircase, but it was amazing what a bit of paranoia and an unknown saboteur could do. She would have hated to be in Mr B's head – maybe this was how it had started – someone having a go at him once so that he now perceived the whole world through jaundiced eyes.

The lighthouse smelled glorious – in here she had used the same rose and amber incense she had ordered for the wedding venue. She was out of breath when she reached the honeymoon suite, but that looked amazing too. Clara ran her fingers over the crisp white Egyptian cotton pillowcases that were on the bed and adjusted the angle of the single red rose that lay on the coverlet.

Would she ever get married? Fleetingly she wondered what it was like to go from being a Miss to a Mrs. To love and to trust someone enough that you would make a vow to be with him until death do us part. She knew she hadn't felt that way about Will. Had he felt that way about her until she'd rejected him? She thought about his postcard – the anger in those exclamation marks. Maybe that's what happened when love had turned in on itself.

She remembered Rosanna's words, 'There is no knight in shining armour.' And her mother's, 'Compromise is the key.'

Then she remembered the wobble in Gran's voice in the car in the early hours of this morning. 'I can't imagine life without him. Not permanently. That's the truth of it.'

That was the kind of love that she wanted, Clara thought, as she opened the fridge to check the champagne was chilling and ran her fingers over the ice bucket to check for dust.

There was a box of luxury truffles on the dressing table. Clara imagined James and Isobel unwrapping them and popping one into each other's mouths and she caught her breath because that picture of tender coupledom had brought a sharp ache to her heart.

Adam Greenwood's face was suddenly there in her head and it wouldn't go no matter how hard she tried to dismiss it. Gorgeous Orlando! Oh God, where had that thought come from? He had crept into her mind more and more lately, without her permission, and somewhere along the way she had fallen for him.

Her heart slammed against her ribs at this thunderbolt of realisation. Oh goodness, when had that happened? When had she gone and fallen for Adam Greenwood? The most awful thing was that he wasn't even aware of it. She certainly wasn't going to tell him. They were friends, business partners, nothing more.

With a huge effort of will, she forced herself back to the present. Tiredness always made her over emotional. And she was in a wedding boudoir. Even so, she couldn't deal with this now. *Go away, Adam Greenwood.*

On her way back down the spiral staircase, she glanced out of the window and felt a rush of relief as she saw Zoe's car pulling carefully into the car park. Hopefully, the cake was still in one piece then. She watched as she got out of her car, then read the message on her phone, nodded to herself and walked towards the front entrance of the hotel. She obviously wasn't going to attempt to carry the cake without help. Good.

* * *

At 10.50, the photographer and his assistant arrived, swiftly followed by the first few wedding guests. Overseen by Phil, they milled about, some of them in the grounds as it was such a beautiful day and some in the bar area of the restaurant.

At 11.40, Mr B, looking only slightly more harassed than usual, quite some feat when he had a wedding lunch following hot on the heels of breakfast, confirmed with Clara that everything was on schedule for a 3.30 sit-down.

At 11.45, the registrar turned up, closely followed by the pianist. A couple of members of the brass band had arrived too, even though it was ages before they'd be needed.

Clara began to relax.

At 12.15, the wedding guests were herded into the venue by the ushers to wait for the arrival of the bridal party.

At 12.20, Zoe said, 'Oh my God, the cakes are still in the car. Elliot was coming to help me carry them and then Mr B called him off to do something else. Have we got time to get them in now?'

Clara glanced at her gold watch. Her FunFit which kept better time had been abandoned in favour of something a bit classier today. 'Yes, if we're quick. I'll help you.'

'Don't worry, Elliot and Jakob can give me a hand. There are only three boxes.'

Clara nodded. The bride's mother, the bridesmaids and the flower girls had just arrived in a white Bentley, which was now parked at the front of the hotel. There were four little girls, dressed in burgundy and cream, and two older ones, as well as the bride's mum. How on earth had they all fitted into that car, Clara thought as they milled about, the colour of autumn leaves on the soft green of the lawn.

Clara was glad she had waited because Zoe had only just vanished when there was a clip-clop of hooves, heralding the arrival of the horse-drawn carriage that was bringing Isobel and her father to the Bluebell Cliff. It was just coming into the main entrance.

'That's pretty spectacular,' Phil said as the carriage approached. The two white horses, controlled by two footmen who wore black suits but burgundy ties to match the plumes on the horse's heads, were pulling a Cinderella coach that glittered and shone. Inside it, Clara glimpsed the bride and her father.

'I know.' Clara breathed out a huge sigh of relief. 'Thank goodness they're here.'

'The bride not turning up definitely wouldn't have been our fault,' Phil said, giving her a quick smile. 'Although I'm pretty relieved too. Let the party begin, hey!'

The coach drew up at the main entrance and came to a halt just behind the Bentley. The horses stamped and snorted, their breath just visible in the October air, as one of the footmen jumped down to come and assist the bride.

She looked radiant, Clara thought, in a sheaf of cream silk that was surprisingly simple, compared to the lavishness of her wedding, and a delicate lace veil that covered her face, held in place by a diamanté tiara. John Scargill looked happy, albeit flushed and a little awkward as if he wasn't quite accustomed to his posh dress suit, which maybe he wasn't. He'd made his fortune in plant hire apparently.

Clara greeted them while Phil spoke to Mrs Scargill who was wearing a full-on gold silk dress and short cream jacket and an enormous beribboned hat with chocolate and cream feathers sprouting from the top – and was that more diamanté? A statement hat, Clara thought blinking.

It was a very short walk around the corner of the hotel to the entrance of the music room cum wedding venue, so they were getting into procession early – Mrs Scargill, followed by the bride and her dad, followed by the chief bridesmaid and the flower girls and the photographer snapping happily away.

Phil strode ahead to warn the ushers of the imminent arrival and they had just set off after him around the corner of the hotel when Clara heard a shriek. For a moment she thought she'd imagined it – that she must have mistaken the calls of the ever-present seagulls for a human scream, but before she had time to even process this, she saw a figure in full flight, hurtling across the lawn at the back of the hotel towards the clifftop.

It was Elliot, and he was running as though his life depended on it. He was carrying a large square pink box. How he could run so fast without dropping it was a mystery. Only then did Clara realise he was not alone. Hot on his heels were a pair of kunekune pigs.

One of the flower girls was pointing. 'What's that man doing, Granny?' Her clear voice carried across the freshness of the October midday air. 'Is he going jogging?'

'Are those pigs?' In any other circumstances, the amazement in John Scargill's voice would have made Clara smile. But at this second all she felt was a cold dart of horror.

Elliot had just reached the back fence. Any moment now he was going to have to make a decision. Would he save himself or the cake? In order to save the latter, he'd have to stop running and turn around to confront his nemesis.

Clara knew with a sickening realisation what he was going to do, just before he did it. There was a part of her that didn't blame him – she had seen the terror on his face as he'd hurtled by.

He threw the cake box at the pigs and it burst apart in a cloud of white icing and dark chunks before he dove head first over the fence. This tactic worked in the sense that it temporarily diverted the pigs. Unfortunately, it also completely diverted the bridal party, who were now all staring open-mouthed at the spectacle.

'Is that my cake?' Isobel Scargill asked, lifting her veil to see better, her eyes very wide.

'It better not be,' John Scargill snapped, staring at Clara.

'Of course it isn't,' she said. 'Your cake is safely inside the hotel. I am so sorry you had to see that.'

The chief bridesmaid giggled.

Isobel's mother, Peggy, who clearly hadn't caught all of what had just happened, adjusted her glasses on her nose and smiled at everyone. 'Are we all ready then?'

'We are if you are.' Phil took charge, even though he'd gone several shades whiter than usual, Clara noticed, and he brought the wedding party to a halt about twelve feet away from the open French doors.

Clara glanced at him gratefully. Her head was a mad jumble of emotions. If only they'd arrived thirty seconds later. If only she and Zoe had brought the cake in earlier. How the hell had those kunekune pigs escaped anyway? She was going to kill Mr B when she caught up with him. But the main thing in her head was how on earth was she going to be able to conjure up another wedding cake in just over ninety minutes?

26

After a brief, frantic confab with Phil, Clara left the wedding party and the pigs that were now happily snuffling about in the wedding cake at the end of the gardens, in his capable hands and rushed off to see what she could do about salvaging the situation.

She was striding back through the hotel towards the restaurant when she bumped into a panic-stricken Zoe.

'Oh my God, have you seen Elliott?' Zoe asked.

'Elliott's fine.' She hoped that were true. 'But the wedding cake isn't.' Clara could hear her own voice brittle with tension.

'Most of it is.' Zoe beckoned her urgently through the restaurant, which looked beautiful: serene and expectant, as it waited for its guests, silver cutlery gleaming in the sunshine streaming through the windows and autumn posies adorning every table.

At the back, on the table set up especially for the purpose and displayed on a silver stand, stood a stunning three-tier white wedding cake, complete with a cascade of exquisitely fashioned, sugar roses, in peach gold and red, artlessly trailing down one side. The roses had diamanté centres and they sparkled as they caught the light.

Clara stared at it in amazement.

'That looks fantastic, but how...? Didn't Elliot have one of the tiers?'

'There were four,' Zoe said. 'They ordered a spare. Do you remember – way back when it was ordered they had a choice to have an extra top tier – just in case? We suggested that it might be a good idea. Curtis Dean said at the time that it was amazing how often people were glad they'd gone for the extra tier and that even if they didn't want it for the wedding, it could be set aside to use as a christening cake.'

'That rings a bell. Yes.' Clara could have kissed Zoe. 'Oh thank goodness. And thanks goodness it was the spare tier Elliot was carrying.'

Zoe tapped her nose. She must have got that from Mr B. 'Not just a pretty face. I made sure he had the spare tier. I didn't want to be responsible for anyone but me dropping that cake. I figured we could always order another spare tier if we needed one.'

'You are a superstar.'

'Actually, I've learned everything I know about events management from you. You've taught me to cross every t and dot every i.' She was flushed and beaming. 'Especially in view of the fact there may be a saboteur on the loose.'

'Thank you,' Clara said. 'Thank you, thank you, thank you. But I don't think that little incident had much to do with our saboteur. Unless it was him who let the pigs out, I guess.'

In the kitchen, a stressed Mr B said that she shouldn't be too sure that it wasn't. 'They were perfectly secure in the kennels. They couldn't have escaped.'

'Well, they bloody well did. And they need to be under lock and key again before that wedding finishes.' It was the nearest she had ever come to losing her temper, Clara realised as Mr B's gaze lowered and a muscle twitched in his cheek. 'We cannot afford to muck up anything else today,' she added more softly. 'Or none of us will have a job.'

He gave the tiniest of nods. 'Message received and understood.'

Everyone else in the vicinity was pretending not to listen, but Clara was aware as she left the kitchen of how close to the surface all of their emotions were. They knew their jobs were on the line. They were a brilliant team and they worked damned hard and her management style had always been to use the carrot not the stick. But today was massively important to them and she felt as though she was right on the edge. She knew she needed to take five minutes to calm down.

She fled to the manager's office and shut the door behind her. She stood with her back to it, taking deep breaths. Her phone beeped in her bag and, a few seconds later, when she checked it, she found a message from Rosanna saying that Gran had just been in to see Grandad and he was looking a whole lot better today and they were confident that he would be able to go home either later today or tomorrow. After the word 'home' she had put the words 'his proper home' in brackets, followed by a couple of exclamation marks.

Clara let out a sigh of relief as she put her phone back. At least Grandad was OK. In all the pandemonium, she'd temporarily forgotten him. A measure of how stressed she was. She just needed to make sure there were no more hitches today. In a week, Kate would be back and the responsibility for the success of the Bluebell would no longer feel as though it rested quite so heavily on her narrow shoulders.

Three months ago, she had welcomed that responsibility. She had thought that this was her dream job. But lately she had begun to doubt that she was up to it at all.

'I'll take you out in a bit,' she told Foxy, and the little dog, who was asleep in her basket, twitched an ear and opened her eyes but didn't stir.

From her bag under her desk, Clara's phone beeped with another text. To her surprise this one was from Adam and it just said,

Hi Clara, hope all is well. Could you phone when you have a minute?

She felt a frisson of pleasure. She would have liked nothing better than to talk to Adam. To hear his warm, grounded voice. But the time certainly wasn't now.

Clara tucked her bag back under the table, locked the office door, just to be on the safe side, and headed out once more to the hotel gardens.

Neither Phil nor Mr B was in sight and neither, to her relief, were the kunekunes. There wasn't much evidence left of the cake either. That had clearly been dealt with, either by her staff or by the pigs. The only thing remaining of 'my only daughter's only wedding cake' was a stray piece of pink cardboard with tooth marks on one side.

Clara glanced at her watch. It was a quarter to one. The wedding service would be halfway through. *Please God don't let anything else go wrong.*

She crossed the lawn towards the French doors and stood a discreet distance away. She could see the backs of the heads of the guests closest to the doors, dressed in a selection of beribboned hats and extravagant feather and lace fascinators, and she could see the bride and groom at the far end of the room, facing each other at the pulpit. The bride's veil was still over her face. The registrar was speaking, although Clara couldn't quite catch his words.

She was about to take a step forward so she could properly hear when a wailing banshee screech cut through the air.

It was the fire alarm. They tested the alarms every Monday morning at eleven, but they certainly hadn't scheduled a drill for today. The voice of the registrar echoed in her head: 'It's the one thing we all dread – a fire alarm in the middle of the service. It wrecks everything. So please make sure that doesn't happen.'

Clara closed her eyes. It wasn't a drill, so it must be real. Something must have set it off inside the hotel. That something could have been smoke. Or it could have been a person. She didn't know. But what she did know was that she couldn't risk the consequences of not evacuating.

With her heart sinking faster than a leaden weight dropped into an abyss, she hurried the last few metres to the French doors. The siren sounded even louder inside than it did from the gardens. People were stirring in their seats.

'Do you think we should be moving?'

'Is it a drill?'

'It's not a drill.' Clara stood in the doorway. She had spoken as loud as she could, but no one was listening. Or possibly no one could hear her.

She picked up the nearest thing to hand, which was the white metal 'order of service' holder from the table and rapped it loudly on the wood.

'This isn't a drill,' she announced in her most authoritative voice. 'I'm afraid I'm going to have to ask you to evacuate the building now. So, without stopping to collect personal possessions, please could you follow me? Our assembly point is just out here.'

They picked up on her body language, even if they didn't hear her words. Just as she picked up on theirs: distress, excitement, anxiety, and curiosity, all of these emotions flickered across the faces of the wedding party, but Clara was most aware of the expression on John Scargill's ruddy face even from across the ten or so metres that separated them. He looked absolutely furious.

She didn't blame him. It was the worst of luck. If it even was bad luck.

As she herded them outside, she saw the registrar gathering up the big old book from the table up on the stage. He clearly wasn't leaving the precious records to burn in a fire. He clutched it tightly to his chest. Isobel had picked up her bouquet too and she and James were holding hands as they came down the aisle, rather sooner than they had expected to be doing, their progress hindered slightly by flower girls, one of whom was crying for her mum.

Clara didn't know whether the couple were married or not. It had looked as if the ceremony wasn't finished. Presumably they could finish it off, once they had sorted out the alarm situation, but she knew time was against them. The registrar needed to be away by two.

She could see a selection of waiting and kitchen staff flowing around from the back doors of the hotel next to the kitchens to the fire assembly point on the lawn. Some of them were coming round the side of the building from the front entrance too, their distinctive bluebell uniforms marking them out from the posh wedding finery of the guests.

In a moment, she would go and check the state of play with Phil, who she knew would be checking the fire panel box, as per procedure, but in the meantime Clara was doing her best to reassure people.

The bride and groom were fine. It turned out that they weren't quite married – but they had been just minutes away from exchanging their vows and were happy to finish the ceremony as soon as Clara gave them the all-clear. They were now chatting animatedly to the best man and chief bridesmaid. Isobel's tiara sparkled and flashed as she turned her head and its jewelled edging caught the sunlight. James' tuxedo was slightly awry, but they were smiling. There was even the occasional burst of laughter from their group.

'They won't be forgetting their wedding day in a hurry,' someone said.

'At least it's not boring like most of the ones you go to,' someone else interjected and there was another burst of laughter.

Peggy Scargill, who was only a short distance from the French doors, didn't look anywhere near as relaxed as her daughter. She was standing close to her husband and he was shaking his head.

That beat shaking his fist, Clara thought, feeling her heels sink into the soft lawn and wishing the rest of her could follow. John and Peggy Scargill were next on her list before she went to find Phil. Or maybe she should find him first, then at least she could establish what exactly was going on.

She was gathering her courage when she saw Zoe signalling to her from across the grass. Saved by the bell, she thought, making a decision and hurrying across.

'Someone smashed the alarm on the top floor,' Zoe panted. 'Phil said there's no evidence of a fire, but the system's already alerted the fire service. We have a monitored system, don't we, and he thought it was best to be on the safe side and let them come.'

'He's right,' Clara said. 'In view of what's been going on lately.'

'Phil thinks it might be malicious – he saw a bloke go out of the fire escape at the top, but he couldn't catch him. It's probably just as well. I think he might have killed him if he'd caught him.' She paused for breath.

'I'd willingly have helped him,' Clara said. 'This is my worst nightmare. I really don't think things could get any worse.'

'I know.' Zoe looked pained. 'Are they married?'

'Not quite.'

'At least it wasn't an actual fire,' Zoe said brightly. 'That's a good thing.'

Bless her, Clara thought nodding.

She looked over her shoulder. She had planned everything so carefully. They all had. And it was the most beautiful of days. The skies were the clearest of blues, the lawn was a perfect green. They had been watering it for weeks to keep it that way. The sea beyond the cliffs sparkled like the world's largest sapphire collection and the scent of autumn's earthy woodiness filled the air. It was such a perfect place for photos, but right now the formal-suited and floral-skirted wedding guests were mingling randomly with hotel staff and a very small flower girl in a gold dress had just shot by with a great smudge of dirt on her face. Her mother was in hot pursuit.

Then into all of this chaos walked a couple. A tall, very suntanned couple, who had just climbed out of a taxi at the front of the hotel. Clara shielded her eyes against the sun to see them more clearly and realised that one of them was on crutches.

'Oh my goodness,' she told Zoe. 'Why did I just say that things couldn't get any worse?'

'Why? Who are they?' Zoe asked, following her gaze. Then she too, cottoned on. 'Oh My God, that's our boss, isn't it? Is that her partner?'

'Yes, that's Aiden,' Clara said quietly, taking in the casually dressed, very upright, dark-haired guy beside Kate. 'They must have decided to come home a week early.'

27

Kate was looking around her with an air of faint bemusement as if she couldn't quite take in what she was seeing. Clara wasn't surprised. Clusters of chattering staff in Bluebell uniforms were now interspersed with wedding guests in posh frocks. The registrar was standing alone by the terrace, still clutching the book to his chest and frowning over his glasses.

Behind Kate, at the hotel's main entrance, the noise of a diesel engine and the hiss of air brakes alerted everyone to the arrival of a fire engine in the drop-off area.

Kate glanced over her shoulder and visibly stiffened when she saw the shiny red vehicle. Then she spotted Clara and now, armed with a sense of purpose, and with Aiden walking slowly beside her, she came hobbling across the lawn, threading her way between small groups of people.

Clara met them halfway. 'How are you?'

'I'm getting there. Thanks for asking.' Kate's eyes were curious. 'Clara, what's going on? We thought we heard an alarm going off when we pulled in. Is everything OK?'

'Um...'

Before Clara could say another word, a deep voice boomed out from behind her. 'No, everything is not bloody OK.' John Scargill had appeared and his wife was beside him, clutching onto his arm like a great gold limpet. Her oversized hat had slipped slightly and was knocking against him while the sea breeze ruffled its feathers. Both of them had faces like thunder. 'First, a pig rampages through the wedding party and writes off my wedding cake and then a bloody fire alarm goes off in the middle of the ceremony. And she…' he pointed a finger at Clara, 'has the audacity to lie to me.'

'I haven't lied,' Clara objected.

'You told me the cake wasn't ours.' He hauled something out of his pocket and held it out on the palm of his hand. It was a tiny replica of James and Isobel still half covered in icing that must have been on the spare tier.

Clara felt her face flood with embarrassment, but he wasn't finished.

'This is the only thing I have managed to salvage from my only daughter's only wedding cake.' He peered a little closer at Kate, who was wearing an orange T-shirt and light canvas jacket and mid-length shorts, possibly because it would have been hard to get trousers over the walking plaster on her lower left leg. 'You're the owner. You're Kate Rawlinson.'

'I am, yes.' She met his gaze steadily. 'I'm extremely sorry.' She glanced enquiringly at Clara.

'Isn't it John?' Aiden said, taking a step towards him and the two men sized each other up. 'Didn't you used to be Avenue Plant Hire?'

'That's right.' Some of the heat had gone out of John's voice.

To Clara's relief, Aiden's presence seemed to have diffused the situation a little. He was several inches taller than the stocky John

Scargill, but he exuded an air of calm authority and the two men clearly knew each other.

'This is supposed to be the best day of my daughter's life,' Peggy Scargill put in and Clara caught a waft of her spicy perfume as she moved and the heavy gold silk of her dress rustled.

'It's fine, Mum.' Isobel and James had arrived now too. Isobel was holding her dress up with one hand so it didn't drag too much on the grass. Her other hand was clutching her groom's. 'It's not anyone's fault that the alarms went off,' she continued, her sweet face earnest to placate. 'It's just one of those things.'

'Someone set off an alarm on the top floor, but there was no evidence of a fire,' Clara told Kate. 'Unfortunately, we were halfway through the ceremony at the time. But we'll be back on track as soon as we're cleared to go back into the building.'

'Yes, before I change my mind,' Isobel quipped.

Peggy looked at her in alarm.

'I was joking, Mummy.' Isobel gave James a lingering kiss. 'Hey, what do you suppose the chances are of us having a photo on the fire engine, Clara? Do you think they'd mind?'

'I'll ask them,' Clara said, glancing around for the photographer and anxious to try and make amends somehow for the unwelcome intermission they'd been forced to take. 'That would be a novel one for the album.'

'You should sit down,' Aiden was saying to Kate, 'and put your foot up.'

Clara nodded. She had noticed the winces of pain that her boss was doing her best to disguise. 'Everything's in hand.' She couldn't believe she was saying that. But it was true. Peggy and John seemed to have calmed down, if only because they didn't want to create a scene for their daughter. They were talking to some other guests now. Clara focused on what needed to be done.

Despite her burning eyes and overriding tiredness, adrenaline had galvanised her thoughts.

Five minutes later, she was on her way to salvaging things: she'd reassured a disgruntled registrar that as long as they were back inside in the next twenty minutes, which was absolutely doable, he would still be able to finish the ceremony and get away on time; she'd arranged an impromptu photo session for Isobel and James, which one of the firefighters was delighted to be part of, whilst his mate finished the paperwork with Phil, having confirmed there was no fire. She saw Kate talking to the band leader and shortly afterwards they had picked up the more portable of their instruments and had burst into an impromptu rendition of 'London's Burning' on the lawn, which seemed highly inappropriate but was certainly making everyone smile.

It was a pity they couldn't serve the champagne yet, Clara thought, but it didn't look as though they needed it. Even John Scargill was tapping his foot to the music.

Then someone shouted from the end of the gardens. 'Hey everyone. Look – there are dolphins out there.'

In a ripple of excitement, the whole wedding party shifted to look. Indeed there were. The shiny grey, sleek-backed outlines were clearly visible, and for the next few minutes, there was the kind of display that money couldn't buy, and that no one would ever forget as the small school of dolphins jumped and played and splashed in the sparkling sea just off the headland.

Clara felt tears fill her eyes as she watched them, along with everyone else. Against all the odds, and despite the saboteur's best efforts, it looked as though the Bluebell's first wedding might turn out to be brilliant, after all.

* * *

It was only when Isobel and James were finally married, and the last of the eco-friendly rose petal confetti had been thrown, and the registrar had sped away smiling, and the guests had been shepherded towards the restaurant, that Kate and Clara caught up again.

'Shall we have a quick chat while they're eating?' Kate said. 'Where's Foxy by the way?'

'In the office. And yes, thanks.' Clara swallowed anxiety. She might have salvaged things out of the chaos the day had nearly become, but what if Kate didn't see it that way?

En route to the office, Clara glanced into the restaurant, which smelled divine. The waiters were scurrying around serving up Mr B's exquisite creamy watercress soup with home-made, warm crusty rolls. The man himself might be as complex as a box of frogs, but his food was masterfully simple. The finest ingredients simply used by a master, was his motto. She sniffed appreciatively; she was glad they'd won the One Stop Watercress battle.

In the office, while she waited for Kate, she sat on the manager's chair and stroked Foxy and the little dog put her head on her knees and gazed up at her with liquid brown eyes.

Clara wondered if she should offer Kate her bungalow back sooner than the end of October, which was what they had recently agreed. Kate was planning to stay with Aiden until then, but a bungalow might be easier than a house with her lower leg in plaster.

Behind her, the door opened with a soft click and Clara jumped. They might have salvaged the wedding, but that didn't mean she felt any less wired. She was as tense as a battery spring.

Kate appeared, followed by Zoe, with a tray of coffee, which she put down swiftly on the desk before disappearing. This was just as well because Foxy gave her mistress an ecstatic welcome that would have sent the most robust of coffee pots flying.

'I've missed you too, little one,' she said, stroking a delighted Foxy. 'Have you been behaving yourself?'

Foxed wagged her tail and sniffed at the plaster and finally settled down again.

Clara was reminded of when she'd been interviewed here, of how lovely Kate had been, even though she'd been late and had arrived with blood on her suit. Of how warm and understanding and compassionate she was. Of how well they had clicked. Getting off a long-haul flight and stepping into a scene of wedding chaos must have been a shock, but she didn't look too pissed off, even now, just a little tired. She sat in the visitor's chair and poured them both a mug of coffee.

'First of all, I need to say a massive thank you,' she began. 'I picked the right person to leave in charge of my baby.' She glanced up at the framed portrait of Caroline Rawlinson above their heads and Clara followed her gaze. 'I wish she had lived to see this place come alive. She'd have loved it.'

'It's been my pleasure,' Clara said. 'How are things with your Mum?'

'Practically sorted. It was good having those extra few weeks, although for the last few I think I may have been more than a hindrance than a help.' She gestured to her ankle. 'I still can't believe I did so much damage falling off a flaming stepladder. Still, at least it's on the way to being mended now.' She sipped her coffee. 'We decided to try and get an earlier flight back because I was worried after that horrible piece in the paper last week. I didn't think we'd be able to change it – hence I didn't warn you – but they offered us a last-minute cancellation.'

Clara nodded. The Curly Wurly challenge felt as though it had been a lot longer ago than a week.

'You look worn out, Clara. Are you all right?'

Clara told her about Grandad and Kate's face sobered. 'Oh my goodness, is he OK? Should you even be here?'

'He's going to be fine. And I wanted to be here.'

'OK, but I am going to send you home very soon. No arguments. Remember what you promised. You should be with your family.'

'Thank you.'

'So tell me about today. Do we think our "saboteur" had anything to do with the alarm going off? Also, did I imagine it or did John Scargill say something about pigs?'

Clara filled her in. Kate knew most of what had gone on, but Clara brought her up to speed, explaining that the saboteur no longer seemed a hazy possibility any more but a concrete fact. She tried to be unemotional about it all. To just give her employer the bare facts, but she didn't leave anything out. Not even her suspicions that her ex may have had something to do with the YouTube video.

'He's away on a round-the-world trip,' she finished. 'Although I got a postcard from him yesterday with some angry exclamation marks.'

'It seems unlikely that he'd be able to cause much damage from a distance,' Kate mused and Clara nodded.

Does Mr B have any theories?' There was a glimmer of humour in Kate's eyes now. 'He usually does.'

Clara told her about the Manor House, about Mr B's altercation with Adam Greenwood, about her night out with Adam, and about her certainty that he had nothing to do with any of it.

'What about his brother? He'd have just as strong a motive as Adam and they do co own the hotel.'

Clara confessed that she had never met Nick Greenwood. 'Although I guess we can't rule him out, I do know that he's been in and out of hospital a few times lately. Then there's the reporter from *The Purbeck Gazette*,' she added. 'He seems to have it in for us. But I have no idea why.'

'Neither have I. But from everything you've said, it does sound as though it's someone close to home.' For the first time since they'd been talking, she frowned. 'Clara, I have to ask you this. Could it be someone who works here?'

Clara felt a jolt of shock. 'No I don't... We... you... have an absolutely brilliant team. They are loyal and hard-working and I think most of our staff love working here.'

'Most?' Kate queried.

'I just meant we have agency staff fairly often in the restaurant and kitchen.' She racked her brains. 'But even they tend to be regulars.'

'So how sure are you that it's not anyone who works here – in percentage terms?'

'Ninety-five per cent sure.'

'Thank you. That's such a relief. Now, I'm going to pull rank and insist that you take that leave I've been promising you. We did agree.'

'All right.' It was the gentleness in her boss's voice that got to her. Clara felt sudden tears pricking the backs of her eyes. 'Are you sure you don't need your bungalow back sooner now? With your ankle, I mean?'

'No, honey. As we said, Aiden wants to look after me at his and I've decided to let him.'

Clara reached for her bag and stood up. 'Would you like me to still look after Foxy?'

Foxy had got out of her basket and was already by her side.

'I would be really grateful, if you don't mind? She'll get more walks with you. And, besides, it looks to me as though my faithful little dog has changed her allegiance already.' She got up too, steadying herself on the desk. 'Would it be OK if I came over to the bungalow Monday or Tuesday for a proper chat about the saboteur? I'll phone first to arrange a convenient time. I want to find out what's going on.' Her voice was quietly determined. 'I want to know who is behind this and I want to know why. And I will find out. And I will stop them. The Bluebell was my Aunt Carrie's dream. Her gift to the world. And I didn't throw my heart and soul into creating it for her only to have some pediculous scumbag, as Mr B would put it, try to smash it all down again.'

'I'll do everything I can to help you,' Clara said.

28

It felt odd knowing she didn't have to go into work when she got up the next morning. Not that she went in on a Sunday that often, but even when she wasn't there, Clara was used to having the Bluebell running through her mind – who was staying – what visits were coming up – it had become part of the fabric of her life and she liked it that way. It felt odd, having handed the reins back to Kate.

On the plus side, though, it was very good timing as last night she had phoned Gran for an update and, all being well, she was picking Grandad up this morning. It was a Sunday lunch day. Plans had been changed and instead of going to Mum and Dad's they were descending on Gran. For the first time in nearly six months, the entire family would be together.

It also cheered her up considerably when she discovered there were several text messages on her phone from her colleagues.

The first was from Zoe and it was long enough for her to need to scroll through several times on her phone:

Are you OK? Phil told me about your Grandad. Is there anything I can do to help?
Ps I may have a date with a firefighter
Pps the reception was totally brilliant, Isobel said.
Ppps His surname is Baker, isn't it!

It took Clara a moment to realise she was talking about Mr B, whose surname was NOT Baker, although Zoe was close.

In the interests of fairness, she didn't reply to this part of the message.

There were also lovely messages from Phil and Mr B, offering support and telling her that the wedding had gone off brilliantly in the end. Even Janet, the chambermaid, had sent a message saying,

Hope your Grandad makes a good recovery.

Clara swallowed a lump in her throat. It warmed her to know how much everyone cared.

* * *

It was lovely to spend Sunday with her family. Mum and Rosanna took over Gran's kitchen to cook it, while Gran fussed around Grandad, who spent the time in an armchair with a blanket over his knees.

'I feel like an old person,' he grumbled to Rosanna.

'You are an old person,' she told him. 'Seventy-eight is old.'

'An old person who's just had a heart attack,' Mum joined in. 'So sit there and relax and stop complaining.'

He winked at Clara. 'See what I mean about diplomats,' he muttered. 'None of this lot would make a decent politician.'

'Isn't that a contradiction in terms,' Dad said mildly. 'After all that Brexit malarkey. You tell me a single one of them who acted decently in the last three years – or is it four?'

'Stop bullying him.' Gran bustled around with a protective expression on her face. 'I've only just got him back. I don't want him having another heart attack. I've got too much to do to look after him.'

'Selfless and self-sacrificing to the core,' Grandad sniped, but his eyes were enormously tender as he glanced at his wife.

Clara caught the look and thought, *That's love. That's the kind of love that I want. I don't want hearts and flowers and grand gestures. I want to be with someone I can spend my life with – side by side – go through all the ups and downs and come out the other side, smiling.*

Suddenly she remembered Adam's message. Oh God, he'd asked her to call him and it had completely gone out of her head. That was a measure of how stressed she had been yesterday. She hoped he was OK.

She slipped outside into the garden, where Tom and Sophie were playing ball with Foxy.

Standing by the back door, she dialled Adam's number and, to her disappointment, his phone went straight to voicemail. She left him a message saying she hoped everything was all right.

Tom spotted her and raced across the grass. 'Is dinner nearly ready? I'm starving?'

'It's not starving, Tom, it's hungry. People in poverty-stricken countries are starving,' Sophie caught up with her brother and contradicted him in a voice that was a near perfect mimic of her mother's.

'Let's go and see,' Clara said, opening the back door.

'Did Mum tell you about the latest Granny-isms, Auntie Clara?' Sophie asked as they all trooped inside.

'No,' Clara said, glancing at the granny in question. 'I don't think she did.'

'We went shopping yesterday and I said we'd been to Weird Face and Fat Fish.' Mum rolled her eyes.

'When it should have been Weird Fish and FatFace,' Sophie added gleefully.

'I still think they're very strange names to call brands of clothing,' Mum said. 'Now then, you lot, go and sit at the table so we can dish out the dinner.'

It was only a lot later in the afternoon that Clara realised she had another missed call and a voicemail from Adam. She hadn't heard the phone. He must have called when they'd all been eating and it was on silent. They had a rule that there should be no phones at the table. He'd left her another voicemail saying that it wasn't urgent and he was tied up for the evening, but he'd catch up with her soon.

* * *

On Monday morning, Clara had a visit from Phil.

'I won't stop. I just came to see if you're all right,' he said, putting his hands in his pockets as he stood on the doorstep and looking unusually self-conscious.

'Come in and I'll make you a coffee,' she said, feeling amazingly touched that he'd made the effort to come round. Phil lived on the other side of Brancombe, so he was unlikely to have been passing.

He didn't hang around long, although he did stay long enough to tell Clara that no one thought she'd been in any way to blame for the things that had gone wrong at the wedding.

'The Scargills were fine,' he said, as he drained his coffee. 'Thanks mainly to Isobel and James who were incredibly sweet –

both of them were insistent they'd much rather have had a memorable day than a perfect one. They got that all right. They loved the fire engine photos. Kate asked Isobel if we could send one to the papers and she was well up for it.'

'But perhaps not the *Gazette*,' Clara cautioned.

'Definitely not the *Gazette*, no.' A beat. 'Those dolphins were perfect too. Sometimes I think there really is a God. Also, did you hear that Aiden knew John Scargill? They're both in the building trade and they used to work together. That helped.'

'I did. And Zoe said the reception was a riot.'

'There was a lot of dancing and drunkenness. Just as a good reception should be. And James and Isobel adored the honeymoon suite in the lighthouse. She actually put a five-star review on TripAdvisor after breakfast this morning. Check this out.' He showed her on his phone.

'The little darling,' Clara said, as she read the glowing recommendation. Perhaps everything had worked out all right in the end.

* * *

On Monday afternoon, which was Mr B's day off this week, Clara had a visit from him too.

'I came to say I'm really sorry about Portia and Prudence,' he said, as soon as Clara had invited him in. 'My kunekunes,' he explained, when she looked at him blankly. 'I've told Kate that I was totally responsible for what happened. Well, I was totally responsible for taking them to the Bluebell in the first place. It was not my fault they escaped from the kennels. I am pleased to report that they are now safely in their new paddock and they're happy as pigs in...' He spread his hands and smirked. 'Fill in the blank.'

She wanted to say 'cake', but she hadn't quite reached the 'finding it funny' stage.

'How did they get out of the kennels?' she asked.

'They were let out by our saboteur.' Mr B widened his eyes dramatically. 'The same person who set off the fire alarm at the worst possible moment. At least we assume it was the same person. We don't have CCTV of that part of the top floor, but we do have CCTV of the dog kennels, which Kate has been going through. It was a man, slim build, about 5ft 8, who let them out. It was clearly deliberate – he put his toe up poor Portia's bottom, the scumbag. We think it might be the reporter again. Or someone who looks very much like him. Last time he had a scarf over his face and this time he had his head down. But that's where my money is. And, in other news...' He paused for dramatic effect. 'I've remembered where I know him from...'

'Where?' Clara asked, feeling her heart beat a little faster.

'From the Yacht Club,' Mr B finished triumphantly.

She stared at him in amazement. 'I didn't know you were even a member of the Yacht Club. I thought you hated the boating fraternity.'

'I do and I'm not a member. But Meg, my better half, goes sometimes. And I've been to a couple of their dos with her because that's the kind of supportive boyfriend I am. That ferrety reporter has been there both times with his stuck-up girlfriend, whose name I forget, but it will come to me.'

'Right,' Clara said. She still failed to see how this could help or how it was even relevant, but Mr B looked so pleased with himself that she didn't like to say anything.

'You're probably wondering what the relevance of the Yacht Club is,' he went on. 'But, believe me, that's where our problem will be rooted. It's all about money.'

'Go on.'

'They're like The Masons – secret handshakes and backhanders and lifelong allegiances. Am I allowed to say that, these days?' He looked around the room quickly as if he were expecting a Mason to pop up from behind the couch. Knowing Mr B, he probably was.

'I see,' Clara said, now totally bemused.

He steepled his hands and gave her a look which said he could see that she didn't understand a word of what he was talking about so he was now going to spell it out in words of one syllable. 'They don't like to see anyone doing well who isn't in their circle. The Bluebell is way too much of a success story. We are a victim of our own success.' He sat back in his chair.

'It's a lot of trouble to go to though, isn't it?'

'Yeah, but there'll be an endgame. There always is.' Suddenly he shot forward again. 'Veronica Cooper Clark. That's her name. The stuck-up girlfriend.' He breathed out a sigh of satisfaction. 'I knew it would come back to me. I've got a near photographic memory.' He paused. 'By the way, while we're on the subject of names, Zoe guessed my surname yesterday.' He didn't look too perturbed. 'Thanks for not telling anyone.'

'Were they surprised? It must have been a disappointment to find out it was quite ordinary, after all.'

'Oh, they've had plenty of fun with Bacon,' Mr B narrowed his eyes. 'I let them take the piss for the entire day and then I told them they've still got to call me Mr B or there will be consequences of the dire variety.'

'You're very wise.'

'I know.' He brightened. 'Fortunately, what with all the palaver about my surname and the excitement of the prize – I am currently in the design stage of Zoe's Zabaglione – they've given up on trying to guess my first name.'

'Do you think that's a permanent state of affairs?'

'Let's hope so – eh? If they ever find out my first name's Chris and my middle name starts with a P, I'll never hear the bloody end of it.'

Clara took her cue from him and she managed not to smile.

He finally left after another two coffees and several more theories about why members of the Yacht Club wouldn't want a place like the Bluebell Cliff to be doing well. These ranged from various grudge motives that were mainly rooted in the old boy's network to the fact that someone in the Yacht Club wanted the site for an upmarket marina and couldn't have it while there was a hotel there. This didn't seem that likely, considering the fact it was on top of a cliff.

Clara was quite relieved when he'd gone. He was hard work to be around when he was in full-on conspiracy-theory mode. She'd had difficulty trying to think of a single motive for someone to be attacking the Bluebell, but Mr B had difficulty in narrowing it down to just a few. He'd had way too much practice in getting to the bottom of what he called the 'real reason' people did things, as opposed to the ostensive one.

Her third visitor was Adam. He arrived early on Monday evening, not long after Mr B had left. Clara felt surprise, swiftly followed by a flash of pleasure, when she opened the front door and saw him standing there.

'Clara, apologies for just turning up like this.' His dark eyes were threaded through with concern. 'But I thought it might be easier to call in person than to carry on playing voicemail tag...'

She stepped back from the door, feeling ridiculously pleased to see him. 'Do you have time to come in?'

'Sure. If I'm not holding you up.'

'I'm off work at the moment,' she said, wondering if he knew.

It turned out that he did. 'I heard what happened on Saturday,' he said as they sat in the kitchen. His eyes were serious. 'And I heard that Kate was back.'

'News travels fast,' she said, and he inclined his head in acknowledgment, but actually it felt good that they didn't have to do small talk and beat about the bush. She liked that about him. She had liked it from the moment they met – well, possibly not on the first two or three meetings, but from then on in it had been good.

Her mind flicked back to the last time he had been here. How much they had shared then – how he'd told her about losing Shona, as they had sat in the anonymous darkness of Kate's lounge. Maybe he regretted telling her that. She had wondered if he had when they had met at Oktoberfest and neither of them had referred to it.

'Kate wasn't originally coming back until this Saturday coming,' Clara said. 'But she was worried about all the things that have been going on. The Curly Wurly disaster was the final straw. Then she managed to get a cancellation on an earlier flight.'

'It seems your chef might not have been so far out after all,' Adam said. 'With his conspiracy theories.'

'I know. I don't think he's always right. But someone certainly has been trying to discredit us. It's been happening for a few months. I wasn't sure at first. But I am now. I thought for a while it may be directed at me personally.' She told him about Will.

'I suppose it's possible, but don't you think it's just as likely, if not more so, that someone is targeting Kate? At the end of the day, it's the hotel that they're trying to discredit. Yes, you would lose your job if they succeed in putting the Bluebell out of business, but Kate would lose so much more.' He paused. 'I've been thinking about this a lot. Nick and I were discussing it the other day. It also might be easier to have a go at her hotel while she's away. Especially if whoever's behind it is someone she actually knows. Kate isn't as likely to catch on so quickly if she's not here – and then when she does realise something's amiss, she'd be inclined to look at her staff, not an outside enemy. I imagine that would suit a saboteur.'

'You have been thinking about it,' Clara said and he glanced at her.

'This is probably completely inappropriate and terrible timing, but I – I like you, Clara. The thought of someone having a go at you, either directly or indirectly, makes my blood boil... oh hell – I probably shouldn't have said that. It's a long time since I cared enough to feel protective towards a woman.' She raised her eyebrows and he rubbed his forehead, frowned and stood up, his chair legs scraping the tiles. 'I should go. I've outstayed my welcome...'

She stood up too. 'No you shouldn't. You haven't. I like the idea of you getting angry on my behalf.'

They stared at each other. But for once she didn't feel as though she was way shorter than he was, a stubby dumpling of a woman – she felt petite and protected and she also felt something she'd felt once or twice before around him. There was something about his vulnerability and his openness that made him very strong.

'I like you too,' she went on. God, that was an understatement. 'I really enjoy your company. I've wanted to ask you out for a repeat performance of our dinner at The Five Gold Coins for ages.' She shot him a glance to see how he was taking this and saw that she had his total attention.

'I'm not surprised you didn't. Nick says I built a border wall after Shona and I sometimes think he's right. It's a lot easier to add bricks to it than take it down.'

'Well, you did make it pretty clear that you preferred plants to people.'

'Yeah. I know. I was lying. It's high time I set the record straight. Would you like to go out for dinner with me, Clara King? A proper date where we don't talk about business or our past or saboteurs – unless we want to, I mean?'

'Won't we run out of things to say?' She was aware that they had taken a step closer to each other and now he put his hands on the outside of her arms, a little tentatively and she could feel the warmth of his fingers through the sleeves of her blouse and she could smell the scent of his aftershave, which was becoming familiar and something she associated very much with pleasure.

'Actually,' he said, 'I don't think we will.'

29

Adam was right. They didn't run out of things to say. They went to The Ship, which was one of the many pubs in town. But it wouldn't have mattered where they went, Clara thought later, because once they'd found a table in a little booth – The Ship was the kind of pub that had little booths – their external surroundings became muted and unimportant. She was occasionally aware of a burst of laughter from a nearby table or a waft of cinnamon and lemongrass; The Ship had a Thai menu. She was also aware that there were red carpets and curtains and a bar with friendly staff, but mostly she was aware of Adam.

It reminded her of the time they'd gone out to The Five Gold Coins in that there was a certain amount of flirting and banter, but they talked about other things too, this time. Deeper things, such as the love they both had for their families and their values and their fears and their insecurities and their mistakes.

'I didn't deliberately shut down after I lost Shona,' Adam told her. 'In fact, for the first couple of years I went a bit mad. I went on an internet-dating binge. I think I was trying to blank out the grief, overwrite all the painful memories with better ones. It didn't work. Not surprisingly. No one compared to her. It just made me depressed.'

'I'm not surprised.' Clara could feel his pain, evoked even now by the memory.

'After that, I just buried myself in work. I went back to Plan A. Making my fortune.' He shook his head. 'That didn't help much either. What about you? Did you have your heart broken? Is that why you've never got married?'

'No. My story isn't as dramatic as that.' She wiped a smear of condensation from the outside of her glass. She'd ordered a white wine as he was driving, but she hadn't drunk very much. 'It's really very boring. I just haven't met anyone I've wanted to settle down with. My family think I'm too picky. My sister says there is no knight in shining armour, but actually I know that already and I don't really want one.'

He pulled a face – mock disappointment. 'So I don't need to buy a suit of armour then? Just as well. They're blinking heavy.' A beat. 'Metaphorically too, I suspect.'

'I couldn't agree more.' They were so much on the same wavelength. 'My mum says that all relationships are a compromise,' she added. 'And I agree with that too. Of course they are, but I've never wanted to compromise to the point of losing my integrity. If I am going to settle down with someone, it has to be because I can't bear to be without them, not because I can't bear to be alone.'

'Hear hear.' He sipped his Diet Coke.

'And I think I told you before that when it comes to longevity, the bar is quite high in my family.' She suddenly remembered that she hadn't updated him about Grandad.

His expression sobered when she told him about the heart attack and then lightened again when she said that he was making a good recovery.

'It's very early days, of course. But Gran is fussing around him like there's no tomorrow. They are both so aware that there very nearly wasn't.'

'Bless them,' he said, a strange mixture of pain and relief in his eyes, and she broke off, aware that he must be remembering that sometimes there wasn't. 'It's all right,' he said, catching her look and interpreting it correctly. 'Taking things for granted is part of the human condition. We all do it nearly all of the time. It's hard not to.'

They left The Ship around ten p.m. – 'I have to get up for the breakfasts even if you don't,' Adam said. 'Not that we're full or anything even close. But you have to get up for a quarter of a restaurant just as early as you have to get up for a full one.' As he opened the passenger door of the Jaguar for her, he said, 'The other reason I came round to see you tonight – as well as to check you were OK I mean – was because I wanted to tell you something before it becomes common knowledge.' He shut her door and got into the driver's seat and put on his seat belt. 'We've just put the Manor House on the market.'

'Oh my goodness.' She stared at him in the dimness of the car. 'How come? It's not because of Nick, is it?'

'It's partly because of Nick,' he said, putting the key into the ignition but not starting the engine. He rested his hands on the steering wheel and stared out of the windscreen into the dark car park. 'His illness doesn't help. But, to be honest, it's really about the hotel. The figures don't add up. We're hardly breaking even, let alone making a profit. It's not really viable for us to continue.'

'I'm so sorry,' she said. 'That must be really disappointing.'

'It is, but we've had a long time to get used to it.' He turned to look at her. 'So it isn't surprising. With hindsight, we should probably have bought a little B&B in town, not a bloody great place on the cliffs. Bearing in mind that neither of us really knew what we were doing. Ho hum! We live and learn.'

'Well, I think it's much better to have gone full out for a dream than never to have tried at all,' she said staunchly.

'That's what Nick thinks too,' he said, starting the car and pulling out onto the main road. 'And I think I probably agree. It was actually his decision to finally throw in the towel – not mine.'

There was a sadness in the car now and Clara couldn't think of a single thing to say that would help, so she said nothing. In the end, it was Adam who broke the pause.

'I'm guessing we'll be there for a while yet. Hotels don't sell very quickly.'

* * *

Clara didn't think she would ever get to sleep that night; Adam filled her thoughts. His voice, his lovely eyes, his touch. She had a feeling they had started something important tonight. Embarked on a relationship that was going to be long term.

When he had dropped her off, he had insisted on walking her to the bungalow's front door and then he had leaned in and kissed her very gently on the lips. It had been tender and gentle and she hadn't wanted him to stop. And then, without either of them instigating it, the kiss had moved up a gear. The dozens of tiny flickers of electricity that had sparked between them all evening had morphed into several hundred volts of passion.

Bloody hell. It was a good job Kate had no neighbours near enough to overlook them, she'd thought, when they had finally pulled apart and looked at each other breathlessly. Clara could see the same slightly disbelieving look in his eyes that she knew must be in hers.

'To be continued?' he'd said.

'Oh definitely.' They'd grinned at each other like idiots.

'Shall we speak tomorrow to arrange something?' His voice was tender.

'Sounds perfect.'

As she had watched him drive away, she had felt an overwhelming rightness in her heart. A quiet certainty that this was what she had been waiting for – maybe all of her life. A relationship with someone she knew shared her values, someone who set her senses racing but who could also end up as her best friend.

Suddenly it didn't matter that absolutely everything else was up in the air.

While the saboteur was still at large, her future was uncertain. Adam's future was uncertain too. She hadn't asked what he and Nick would do when the Manor House was sold. Maybe it depended on how much money they lost. The two most likely buyers for a place that size were a hotel chain or a developer and neither of them would want to pay much. The economic climate was too uncertain. He was right about nothing being likely to happen very quickly though. Big hotels like that could take years to sell.

What with all this going on, Clara was surprised she slept at all, but she did eventually and Tuesday morning arrived. With it came Kate's promised visit.

She phoned first and arranged to call at 11.00. She arrived on time, smiling on the doorstep and leaning on crutches. 'I can manage without them, but they make me feel a bit more secure,' she explained, bending to stroke Foxy, who was a little wary of the crutches at first but capitulated when she recognised her owner.

It felt odd showing Kate into her own kitchen and making her coffee from her own percolator. Odd, but strangely comforting.

Kate didn't comment on the way the place looked. It was fairly tidy anyway; Clara didn't like mess.

Kate had a dark blue A4 folder with her – which was the only thing that reminded Clara this wasn't just a friend calling for a social visit. She put it on the table and they sat opposite each other, with Foxy lying on the rug, keeping a weather eye on both of them.

'First of all,' Kate began, 'how's your Grandad?'

Clara told her and she looked pleased. 'That's really good news. Secondly, I want to say thank you again for looking after my hotel. You inspire a hundred per cent loyalty in our staff. Not a single person I've spoken to has a bad word to say about you. Not that I was expecting anyone to say anything bad, I hasten to add.' She slurped her coffee. 'It's still impressive though.'

'That's good to hear,' Clara said, wondering what was coming next.

'I've been doing some research,' Kate continued. 'With regard to the person or persons who have been making mischief for us.' She sighed. 'If you can call it mischief. It's a bit more than that, I think.'

'I think so too.' Clara met her employer's eyes. 'They've cost the Bluebell at least some business. Not to mention Saturday's attempt to wreck the wedding. That could have been very expensive.'

'Thank goodness for dolphins,' Kate said. 'How did you arrange that anyway?'

Clara smiled. 'Thank goodness we've got such an amazing team. And thank goodness your Aiden and John Scargill were old cronies.'

'That was a bonus. Yes.' Kate opened the dark blue folder and drew out some grainy photographs. There was also a piece of paper with her handwriting on it. 'Here's what I've managed to ascertain so far,' she began, reading from it. 'It has to be someone who has something to gain. Which rules out my regular staff, you would think, because they'd lose out if the Bluebell closed down. Having said that, I do think it's likely to be someone close to home. They'd have had to know about the Young Farmers booking in order to cancel it. They'd have had to know about the Curly Wurly record too, although I'm guessing quite a few people knew about that.'

'It was well publicised,' Clara agreed.

'It has to be someone who knows their way around a computer. Mr B assures me that anyone can upload a video on YouTube, but I don't think that's quite true. Aiden says there's no way in the world he could do it.'

'I'd agree they would need to be reasonably techie,' Clara said. 'But I suppose it's possible they could have had help.'

'Yes, that's true. But you wouldn't want too many people knowing what you were up to, I wouldn't have thought.'

'No,' Clara concurred.

'It's also likely to be someone who has close links with *The Purbeck Gazette*. They were incredibly quick off the mark, weren't they? Both times. Zoe told me that Simon Tomlinson, their reporter, was the first person on the scene after the Arnold Fairweather proposal and that the only reason he didn't run the feature was because you threatened him with legal action.'

'That's right, I did.'

'Thank you for that.' Kate's eyes flashed with bulldozer-like stubbornness. She was utterly focused and Clara got a glimpse of the passion that had carried her through to the completion of the Bluebell Cliff Project. She had heard on the grapevine that Kate had come across some fairly major stumbling blocks during the refurbishment, but she'd refused to let anything swerve her from her goal.

'Simon Tomlinson was also the reporter who wrote the feature about Micky Tucker's botched record-breaking attempt, wasn't he?'

'He was.'

'I don't suppose we can prove anything, but he certainly had the opportunity to spike Micky's drink. He was with him before the event started.'

'Correct.' Phil must have told her that.

Also... And this is the big one. The mischief-maker was probably at the wedding. Either that, or they bribed someone else to let out the pigs and set off the fire alarm.'

'That makes sense. Yes.'

Kate waved another piece of paper at her. 'So, with that in mind, I've done some research. I have the full guest list here. I got it from our very obliging bride just before they left for their honeymoon. Did you know she's already given us a five-star review?'

Clara nodded.

'She was thrilled with everything. They loved the food. Mr B pulled the boat out on the lobster thermidor – we got really good feedback from everyone on that. Anyway, Isobel was more than happy to tell me who she'd invited once I'd explained why I wanted to know. I was hoping you'd help me to go through this and see if we can ascertain anything. I'm not sure how or what – but I think it's worth a try.'

'So do I. Of course I can.'

'I also have these...' She laid out the grainy photographs on the table. 'They're the stills from the CCTV. This is the person who delivered *The Purbeck Gazette* early. You've seen this already, I know, but not as a still. And this is the person who let the pigs out. I know you can't see his face clearly in either one because he's made sure of that, but I think it could be the same person. As you know, Mr B is convinced it's Simon Tomlinson.'

Clara looked at the two shots side by side. 'It does look as though he could be right. But he wasn't at the wedding.'

'He wasn't invited. That doesn't mean he didn't sneak in.' She let out a breath. 'I sound paranoid, don't I? But when someone's having a go at you and you don't know why, it makes you feel like that. Also - and this is my pièce de résistance – I have a photo of the person who we think set off the fire alarm. Phil caught a glimpse of him on the fire escape and he's pretty sure this is the guy.' This time, she produced a much clearer image of a figure running across the Bluebell car park. It was dated the same day as the wedding, but, more importantly, it was timed. It had been taken at 12.46, just after the fire alarm had gone off.

'How did you get this?' Clara asked. 'This isn't CCTV.'

'Pure luck.' Kate looked pleased. 'While the photographer was snapping the happy couple inside the venue, he asked his assistant to do some location shots outside and this man just happened to be in one. I think he might be the key to the whole thing.'

She pushed the photo towards Clara. It wasn't Simon Tomlinson, that was for sure. It was someone Clara had never seen. Someone a bit taller, maybe nearer six foot. Someone who was wearing a suit. Someone who was dressed for a wedding.

'It looks like he could have been a guest,' Kate said. 'Or someone who was masquerading as one. I don't know who he is yet. I've sent the photo to Isobel, but she's on her honeymoon, so I don't expect to hear back for a little while.'

Clara nodded. 'You said I was impressive. Right back at you.'

Kate met her gaze. 'No one takes potshots at my hotel and gets away with it. When I find out who it is, which I intend to do very soon, they are going to be very sorry.' She tilted her head on one side in a question. 'I shall need your help with the legwork. Is that OK?'

'Of course it is. I am totally at your disposal.'

'Then, from one impressive woman to another, I'd like to propose a toast.' Kate lifted her coffee mug. 'To putting an end to our mischief-maker and ensuring the Bluebell has a brilliant future.'

They clinked mugs.

Kate left the blue folder with Clara. 'I have copies of everything in it,' she had said before she went. 'I'll be looking too. I'm not exactly sure what we're looking for, but two heads are better than one.'

'If not three,' Clara said. 'Could Phil or Mr B help?'

'They're on the case. I've set up a WhatsApp group so we can stay in touch. If any of us has any kind of brainwave, we can put it on there. I wanted to check with you first, but I'll add you to the group. I think Mr B has put quite a lot of theories on there already.' Her lips had twisted in a wry smile. 'I'm slightly regretting asking him, but it's a bit late to retract it.'

Then she left, looking determined, and Clara watched her drive away. Seeing Kate had made her feel much more positive. So did having something constructive to do.' If they could track down the saboteur and stop them, then at least one thing about her future could be certain.

30

Kate had been right about Mr B having an avalanche of theories, all of which made their way on to the WhatsApp group. He tended to put them on late at night when he wasn't working. Did the man never sleep?

Over the next couple of days, Clara sifted through them, trying to decide which could be important and which definitely weren't. She also went through the wedding list with a fine-tooth comb. She wasn't exactly sure what she was looking for, but her instincts told her she might know it when she saw it.

Rather helpfully, there were a few scrawled notes from Kate on the list. She had put 'bride's side' or 'groom's side' after each one. She had also put 'friend' or 'family'.

Clara decided to focus on the friends list, which wasn't as long. It also struck her that family might not be as keen to ruin a wedding, which was basically what setting off the fire alarm and letting out the kunekunes had been supposed to do.

Interestingly, one of the names on the guest list had seemed familiar. Veronica Cooper Clark. Where had she heard that name before? It wasn't someone she knew, but it was triggering alarm bells and she couldn't think why. It had cropped up in a conversation recently she was sure and she hadn't been anywhere, apart from out with Adam.

She had spoken to him every day since their night out. Everything they'd said had cemented the strong connection that she had felt when they were together and, judging by the warmth in his voice, it had done the same thing for him.

They had made plans to go out again on Thursday lunchtime, which was the next time he thought he could get away. Clara would have loved to see him again before and he said he felt the same, but she didn't push it. He had so much on his plate. She already knew he and Nick were trying to run the Manor House on a skeleton staff and they'd be organising putting it on the market. That would be time-consuming too.

In the meantime the name Veronica Cooper Clark kept turning over in her mind and then, finally, when she was out with Foxy on the cliff path one morning, she remembered where she had heard it. It was the name Mr B had mentioned. The name of the 'stuck-up girlfriend' who was going out with Simon Tomlinson. Clara's heart began to pound and it had nothing to do with the fact that she was walking up a steep grassy part of the coast path. Or very little to do with it, she thought, pushing a strand of windswept hair behind her ear. She had got incredibly fit since she'd had Foxy to look after. That was a bonus.

She glanced at the FunFit to see how many steps she had done. The battery was flashing up empty. Bloody thing. That had happened a lot lately when it came to counting steps, although it usually had enough juice in it to send her its nonsensical weekly reports. This morning's had said:

`Speed of walking is up to optimum levels. Very good health wise. Your static activity fitness` `improvement is 85 per cent accommodation is no good target. Good news. Excellent.`

Who the hell did the translation for these things? Didn't anyone ever check? The word excellent mollified her slightly though.

Maybe she would invest in a more reliable pedometer when she got back home. Maybe Kate would still let her take Foxy out for walks. Maybe, maybe, maybe.

She called the little dog to her and clipped on her lead because they were getting to a part of the cliff that wasn't fenced and Clara was always worrying that she'd go over the edge after a rabbit. Having three legs didn't seem to have any impact on her speed, but it did occasionally interfere with her braking system.

'What do you think?' she asked Foxy, as they carried on along the path. There were red berries on the stunted bushes that survived up here and they were also covered with what was locally known as 'old man's beard', which looked like random handfuls of cotton wool.

'Do you think we're on to something? Do you think Veronica Cooper Clark and Simon Tomlinson are in league with our saboteur?'

Foxy flicked her ears to listen and then tugged on her lead; she was much more interested in the sniffs along the well-used path.

Clara contemplated the information they had already. Mr B was convinced that Simon Tomlinson was the person who'd let out the kunekunes. He certainly wasn't on the guest list. But it was odd that his girlfriend was.

When she got home, she googled the name Veronica Cooper Clark. This turned up several Facebook and LinkedIn profiles but wasn't that helpful because Clara didn't know anything about her. So she couldn't pick out which of the photos might be her.

Then she tried Veronica Cooper Clark, Brancombe Yacht Club, which was a little more successful because she was listed as a member. But there were no photos. Then she tried putting the names together: Veronica Cooper Clark and Simon Tomlinson.

Bingo! She had what she was looking for: A photograph of a couple at some press evening that was featured in the same local society magazine that had been booked to cover the Young Farmers event.

There was Simon Tomlinson, looking very sleazy and a little pissed, in a dark suit and black tie, and beside him was a bronze-haired, sharp-faced woman, who looked older than he did by maybe ten years – she must be in her late forties – but was what Phil would have called incredibly well preserved. She was smiling to reveal perfect teeth, but her beautifully made-up eyes were cold. It was a very staged pose – here was a woman who was used to being photographed.

But, most importantly, Clara was sure she had been at the wedding. It was the bronze hair. There had been a woman with that colour hair amongst the wedding guests. Clara had a snap-shot memory of them all standing outside in the sunshine after the fire alarm had gone off. There had been maybe twenty or thirty guests milling about, but she remembered that hair. She remembered thinking that it had fitted in very well with the autumn theme and wondering if she'd had it done especially. Clara had been sure it had been manufactured, not real – in an expensive salon too – it definitely wasn't out of a packet. After so many years of working with people, she was an expert on such things.

Then there was the Mulberry handbag, slung casually over her shoulder. The bag had evoked a fleeting envy. Clara had made a mental note to check out eBay for bargains. After the conversation with Zoe, she was still wary about second-hand Mulberries.

Now, Clara glanced at her laptop and came back to reality with a little thump. None of this proved anything. But she was sure it was relevant. Simon Tomlinson and Veronica Cooper Clark were the Bluebell Cliff saboteurs. She had no idea why, but every instinct she had told her she was right. She was about to add it to the growing number of theories on the WhatsApp group, but something stopped her.

Maybe it would be better to find out some more before she went blundering in. She had agreed with Kate that this time off would be part working from home and part actual holiday. But she didn't have to go back to work properly for another ten days. She had plenty of time to start packing up her things in preparation for moving back to her house.

She also had plenty of time to do some more research on Ms Veronica Cooper Clark.

* * *

On Thursday lunchtime, she called for Adam as agreed. She'd insisted it was her turn to pick him up. Also, he'd mentioned it was about time she met his brother, Nick.

Clara was really looking forward to meeting him and her stomach crunched with expectation as she walked through the automatic doors into the citrus-scented reception of the Manor House.

Adam looked pleased to see her and he went to find Nick, who he introduced to Clara as, 'The brother I would have been if I was nicer.'

As she stepped forward, Clara's first impressions were of a

man who was very similar - looking to his brother, only he was slightly thinner, maybe an inch or so shorter, and his hair had some grey in it, even though she was sure Adam had told her Nick was the younger of the two.

The other startling difference was what she could only describe as Nick's aura. He had the hugest smile and sparkling eyes and a warmth as palpable as sunshine.

'It's so lovely to meet you,' he said, gripping her hand in both of his and Clara could see immediately where the labels of Mr Nice and Mr Nasty may have originally come from. Where Adam was wary, Nick was full on. Where Adam was taciturn, Nick was gushing. 'I've heard so much about you,' he rushed on before she could speak. 'You're the lifeblood of Bluebell. Firm but fair; astute but compassionate; doesn't suffer fools gladly but has a fine sense of humour. Your reputation precedes you.'

'He hasn't heard any of that lot from me,' Adam put in, giving his brother a look that was at the same time both affectionate and exasperated.

'Blimey,' Clara said. 'I don't know what to say.'

'Sorry. I do go on.' Nick beamed some more. 'That's why they don't usually let me out of the kitchen.'

'No. That's because you're a brilliant chef,' Adam contradicted.

Privately, Clara thought he'd make a great front-of-house man too. There was something mesmerising about him. But maybe front of house would be more difficult with his illness.

'It's lovely to meet you too,' she said, finally managing to extract her hand from his.

'So, where are you taking her?' Nick asked Adam. 'Or, should I say, where's she taking you?'

'I thought we could maybe drive into Swanage and see what we fancied. We haven't booked anything.' Adam glanced at his watch. 'Although we'd better get going or lunchtime will be over.'

They picked a restaurant down by the seafront. It wasn't warm enough to sit outside, but they got a table by the window because there weren't many people about. The place smelled sweetly of rosemary and cinnamon and Adam told her they were renowned for their pastries as well as their lunches.

'I sometimes wonder if Nick and I should have bought a restaurant instead of a hotel,' he said, as they sipped their drinks. 'But the odds are so stacked against you. Something like sixty per cent of new restaurants go out of business inside the first year.' His face tightened. 'I don't think the hotel trade fares much better really. Unless maybe you have a really good USP and a shedload of backup money.'

Like Kate did, Clara thought, wondering if that was a reference to the Bluebell and feeling for him. But he wasn't looking at her now. He was looking out of the window, to where seagulls hung in the air above the sea, some of them almost motionless on the thermals. There was barely any wind today.

She didn't often come down to the seafront, which was mad when her house was less than twenty minutes away and all her family were close by. Maybe that's what happened when you were a local. You didn't go to the local places.

This place turned out to be good though. She made a mental note to recommend it to Rosanna. It was a great eatery to bring kids. As well as the menus in holders on each table, there were drawing books and crayons provided for younger visitors.

Over lunch, they chatted with the same ease they had on every previous occasion, but Clara sensed a greater sadness in him than ever before. She suspected this was because of his present circumstances. She wasn't sure whether to raise the subject of the Manor House sale or whether to avoid it altogether.

She decided in the end to leave the ball in his court and it seemed he didn't want to talk about it. So they didn't. Neither did she mention the project Kate had given her. They had talked at length about the saboteur last time they had met. She didn't really have anything new to add.

It was lovely to spend time with him, though. As she drove them the short distance back up to the Manor House, she found herself hoping this would be the first of many such lunches.

She dropped him off outside and he didn't invite her in again. 'I'm sorry. I really want to spend some more time with you, but there's so much to do at the moment.'

The brief touch of his lips on hers wasn't enough for either of them. She could see that in his eyes, but it would have been inappropriate for them to have a passionate clinch in the car park of his hotel.

'Are you free tomorrow night?' she asked.

'I think I might be.'

It was clearly as much of an effort for him to drag himself away as it was for her. But Clara was determined not to add to his burden. She started the ignition. 'Speak later.'

She was almost back at the bungalow when she realised his phone was in the footwell of her car. It must have fallen out of his pocket. She only knew it was there at all because a buzzing sound caught her attention. It was on silent, but he hadn't turned off the 'vibrate'.

She turned the car around. There may be quite a few things he could leave in her car and not miss, but his phone probably wasn't one of them.

Less than ten minutes later, she pulled up again into the Manor House gravelled car park.

A new black BMW was now parked up in the space where she had dropped him off and someone was sitting in the passenger seat with the door open. Clara didn't take much notice. She had a sense of déjà vu as she walked past the rear number plate towards the hotel and the automatic doors swished open and the citrus air freshener hit her. Adam was standing at the reception desk with his back to her. Beside him, also with her back to Clara, was a woman with bronze hair.

Clara felt her heart jolt. She was definitely getting paranoid. There must be lots of women in the Purbecks with bronze hair.

At the sound of the automatic doors, they both turned and this time she felt the numbness of shock. Not just a random woman with bronze hair – it was Veronica Cooper Clark. And just before the woman's face shifted back into neutrality, Clara caught the recognition in her eyes.

'Clara? I wasn't expecting to see you again so soon.' Adam sounded surprised. He glanced at his visitor. 'May I introduce—'

'Don't bother,' Clara snapped. 'I know who she is.'

She held out his phone, knowing her face must be suffused with colour. It was burning hot. She felt as though her brain was slowly catching up with what was going on.

Veronica Cooper Clark was holding a briefcase and her gorgeous Mulberry bag was on the reception desk in front of her. Adam clearly knew who she was, and behind reception Nick Greenwood had just appeared, wearing that same look of bonhomie with which he had so warmly greeted her only a couple of hours earlier.

Clara didn't think she could bear to see any more. Talk about getting into bed with the flaming enemy. She couldn't think of a single innocent explanation as to why Veronica would be having a cosy meeting with the Greenwoods. Thrusting the phone into Adam's hand, she turned abruptly and almost ran back into the car park.

This time she did look at the occupant of the BMW. It was

Simon Tomlinson. That was no coincidence. He must be waiting for his girlfriend. Oh God, she'd been right, they really were in this together.

As Clara charged towards her car, her FunFit buzzed on her wrist:

`Time for a sharp stroll.`

That was another really irritating habit it had, telling her to do something she was already flaming doing. She shouldn't have chosen such a cheap imitation. Oh how ironic because that's what Adam Greenwood had been too in the final reckoning.

With a little sob of pain, she ripped it off her wrist and hurled it into the neatly trimmed hedge that ran around the Manor House's car park. It caught on a branch and swung round, its screen glinting in the sunlight. Taunting her, even from afar.

She glanced over her shoulder. No one had followed her out. Why would they, she thought, when the game was so well and truly up? Suddenly she felt as though a hundred missing pieces of a jigsaw puzzle had just turned up shouting, 'Look at me. I'm here. I fit here.' Adam and Nick and Veronica and Simon. Two of them had a motive to ruin the Bluebell Cliff and the other two had been actively involved in doing it. There was no longer any doubt they were all connected.

How could she have been so stupid?

31

Clara was tempted – so incredibly tempted – to drive straight round to the Bluebell and to say to Kate, 'I know who our saboteurs are and I know why. Mr B was right all along about the Manor House. I let myself be blindsided from what was really going on by a smooth-talking bloke. I was duped. I'm so sorry.'

By some humongous effort of will, she resisted the temptation and went back to the bungalow instead. Years of self-restraint – the same self-restraint that Grandad had told her made her a diplomat – had taught her it was better never to react in anger. And boy, was she angry. She was almost as angry with herself as she was with Adam. To think she had trusted him so utterly. How had that happened? How had her judgement been so completely off the mark? How could she have thought, even for a moment, that she had found someone she could have a meaningful relationship with?

Not that she had such a brilliant track record when it came to men. Her mind flicked back to Will. It had taken her almost a year and a hugely inappropriate present to realise he wasn't right for her. She hadn't had any reason to suspect Adam was anything other than nice.

No, that wasn't true! She must still be in denial she thought, as she let herself back into Kate's bungalow. She'd actually had a dozen reasons to suspect him, a dozen pricklings of suspicion that had tingled through her on various occasions, and she had discounted every single one of them.

Adam had the motive. She had known that from the beginning.

Adam was a techie. He had once worked at YouTube, for goodness' sake!

Adam had been one of the few people who knew where the Young Farmers were having their annual get-together. And he must have been feeling pretty bitter that they'd switched allegiance.

He had also been at the chocolate festival. He had looked surprised to see her there, she remembered, although how he had spiked Micky Tucker's drink was a mystery. Maybe he hadn't. Maybe that had been down to Simon Tomlinson, as Kate had surmised. Maybe Adam's role had purely been to distract her while it was done. And he'd managed to do that admirably.

Then, at lunchtime today, he had underlined how he felt. 'I don't think the hotel trade fares much better really. Unless maybe you have a really good USP and a shedload of backup money.'

She remembered his exact words and she remembered the way his face had tightened when he'd said them. He and Nick must have been devastated when they discovered that the Bluebell Cliff was opening up practically next door. A hotel, which not only had a unique selling point, but which also had a financial backer with a huge budget, prepared to put her money where her mouth was. Kate's Aunt Carrie had been a world-famous concert pianist and rumour had it that she'd ploughed every penny of her vast fortune into creating a state-of-the-art hotel.

That must have seemed like the final nail in the coffin. No wonder they wanted it to fail. A hotel that had been created to make dreams come true would smash theirs to pieces. Clara could see the irony of that.

But hot on the heels of her anger came a searing hurt. She had really liked Adam. Now, who was in denial? It was much more than liked. She had fallen for him hard. She had let herself. And it had been against her better judgment. Adam didn't have the monopoly on border walls – she'd been a dab hand at building one around herself too and she had let him take it down, with his oh-so sincere gentleness and his pseudo empathy, brick by bloody brick.

Her mind was still whirling over the jigsaw puzzle pieces that were slotting into place when her phone rang. It was Kate.

'Clara, have you got a minute?' Her boss's voice was bright with excitement. 'Is this a good time? Only we've just discovered something very interesting.'

'Could I phone you back?' Clara heard herself saying in a voice that didn't sound much like hers. 'I'm just in the middle of something.' The lie came so easily. Or maybe it wasn't a lie. She was in the middle of a kind of grief. She couldn't bear to have it stirred up any more by other people telling her that Adam was the culprit and why hadn't she spotted it? Not until she'd had more of a chance to let that sink in herself.

'Of course. No worries. Speak later.' Kate hung up and Clara phoned Rosanna.

'I don't suppose you're in, are you? I could really use a friendly ear.'

Rosanna must have heard something in her voice. 'Hey,

honey, of course. I'm just about to pick up the kids from school, but after that my ears are all yours. Will you stop for your tea?'

'Yes please,' Clara said, feeling like a child.

By the time she and Foxy got to Rosanna's and she'd had tea and had heard about the children's plans for the coming half-term, she was feeling a bit better. But it was still a relief when a primed Ed took Sophie and Tom off to do their homework and she and Rosanna had the kitchen to themselves.

'So...' Rosanna began as they sat opposite each other. 'Is it a man?'

'Is it that obvious?'

'Not in your case and not at the moment when there's so much other stuff going on in your life, but...' she hesitated. 'Tell me to back off if you like – but I'm guessing a man.'

'Well, you're spot on. Although it is kind of work-related too.' Clara told her everything and, at the end of it, when she could feel tears dripping down her face, she said, 'I don't know why I'm so upset. It was just a kiss really—' She broke off as Rosanna pushed a box of tissues across the table and caught her hand. Foxy, who always picked up on moods, came over too.

'It wasn't just a kiss. You trusted him and you thought you had something special together and it sounds to me like he gave you every impression it was mutual. And I know I can be pretty damn cynical about knights in shining armour and all that malarkey, but that doesn't mean I don't like a happy ever after.' She shook her head. 'What a total bastard.'

Clara pulled out a handful of tissues and blew her nose.

Rosanna folded her arms. She had a look of puzzlement on her face. 'However, I do have to say, honey, that it doesn't totally add up. I mean, why would he lead you along the romance path if it wasn't mutual? Why would he take you out at all? Actually, I wasn't going to tell you this because it's a bit gossipy, but I saw

Anastasia the other day and the conversation got round to Adam and she told me he was seeing someone he really liked. That has to be you, doesn't it?'

'It could be anyone.' Clara tried to ignore the wild fluttering of hope that had just surged up through her. 'There's no reason to think he was talking about me.'

'There's every reason. He must like you if he mentioned you to his cousin. She said his first wife died tragically young and that he's never got serious about anyone since. But that it was good to see him looking happy for once.'

Happy Orlando. The treacherous thought crept into Clara's mind.

Rosanna put her head on one side. 'Playing devil's advocate for a moment, could there possibly be an alternative explanation for him being with this Veronica person?'

'Like what?'

'I don't know. Some other reason she was there. Something perfectly innocent. Could she have been a guest?'

Clara thought back to the look on Adam's face when she had walked in. He had looked surprised to see her. But he hadn't looked guilty.

'He didn't say much. But he did look shocked when I snapped at him. I suppose I didn't really give him a chance to say a lot because I walked straight back out again.'

'And you've heard nothing from him since?'

'No.' Clara checked her phone and discovered this wasn't true. Her phone, which she'd switched off when she'd driven over, burst into a flurry of activity as soon as she put it back on. There were two missed calls from Adam. There were several messages on the Bluebell WhatsApp Group from Mr B about nets closing in on saboteurs. There was also a text from Kate that said:

Don't forget to call.

'Bugger,' she said now, showing her phone to Rosanna. 'I'd better phone Kate back.'

Kate answered almost immediately. 'Hi Clara. Sorry to interrupt your evening. How's it going?'

After a brief exchange of polite chit-chat, Kate said, 'I think we've managed to track down who is targeting us and why and I really wanted to let you know.'

'Thanks,' Clara said, wondering if she should say, 'Snap!' but deciding against it. Part of her still hoped desperately that Rosanna was right, that there was, against all the odds, an alternative explanation. She didn't want Adam to be implicated. Or Nick, who had seemed so nice.

She glanced at Rosanna, who had got up to clear the table but was still listening, her face curious.

'I had an email from Isobel Jones nee Scargill,' Kate went on. 'Confirming that the man who set off the fire alarm was an invited guest. She didn't know him personally. He was someone's plus-one on the groom's side. Anyway, she did a bit of digging for me, bless her, and the upshot was that Rupert Cooper Clark – that's his name – had excused himself due to feeling ill, just before the ceremony.' She paused for breath and Clara felt her heart sink.

Kate continued, 'The name Rupert Cooper Clark probably doesn't mean anything to you, but he's connected to our reporter, Simon Tomlinson. Simon is going out with his sister, Veronica. Mr B made that connection a while ago. Rupert was Veronica's plus-one at the wedding. Are you with me so far?'

Clara confirmed she was.

'You're probably wondering what all this has got to do with our saboteur, but I'm getting to it, I promise.' She sounded bright and excited. 'Mr B was right about Simon Tomlinson's involvement, although not quite for the reasons we thought.'

Clara remembered the Yacht Club theory and she felt her heart ratchet down another couple of notches. Here it came. Adam's part in it all. Any moment now, Kate was going to tell her that Adam Greenwood and Veronica Cooper Clark had hatched a plan to close down Bluebell. She already knew why.

'Are you still there?' Kate asked.

'I'm still here.'

'It's all about money,' Kate said and for the first time her voice grew serious. 'When my Aunt Carrie bought Bluebell Cliff, there was a bidding war with someone else who wanted the site. A property developer. She talked about it a couple of times, but I didn't really pay that much attention. It was all in the past, after all. But that's what this is all about. The property developer – as I'm sure you've guessed by now – is Veronica Cooper Clark.'

'The woman with bronze hair.' Clara gasped. She hadn't seen that one coming. It certainly hadn't come up when she'd googled her.

'Yes. She was there with her brother. Lord knows how they got an invite, but Isobel said they know her dad through the Yacht Club. So we think they must have inveigled their way in. The fact that her boyfriend works at *The Purbeck Gazette* must have been a great help in terms of discrediting us. But Veronica is our chief saboteur.'

Clara's head was reeling. She was glad she was sitting down.

She was aware that Rosanna was looking at her with concern in her eyes. She became aware more slowly that Kate was still speaking.

'Apparently Veronica and Simon thought that if the Bluebell lost enough business, we'd have to close down and then she could buy up the site for a pittance.'

'But surely there are other sites she could buy...?'

'Yes, but she's always wanted that one. She was furious when Aunt Carrie outbid her in the first place. I think to be honest that's mostly what was motivating her. That sense of entitlement. From what I can gather, she has a super-rich daddy who treats her like his little princess and it was the first time in her life that she didn't get her own way. It turns out Veronica is still desperate to get a clifftop plot to build on and the only other one that's anywhere near close to suitable is the Manor House, which, she'd already been told, in no uncertain terms, by the Brothers Grim, wasn't for sale. She wants a plot of land on the cliffs to build luxury flats. Phil did a spot of digging and we've discovered she's got investors waiting.' There was a tiny pause. 'Clara. Are you still there?'

'Yes. Um...' Clara could feel her brain coming slowly back online. 'Yes, I am.' She was still trying to adjust to this new shocking but wonderful news as her brain finally processed it. 'Do they know that you've rumbled them – I mean, I know you've got photographs of them and everything, but isn't that all a bit circumstantial? How can we stop them from doing anything else?'

'I've spoken to my solicitor and he thinks we may have enough to issue an injunction, and if we haven't, then I'll keep rooting away until we have. Phil and Mr B are keen to go and issue a personal injunction of their own, but I think I've managed to talk them out of it for now.'

By the time Clara had disconnected, her ear hurt from pressing the phone against it so hard. But her heart felt a thousand times lighter.

Across a cinnamon latte with pink and white marshmallows floating in the top, she relayed everything to a fascinated Rosanna, who listened patiently and then said, 'I don't want to throw a spanner in the works, but that still doesn't explain why your man and his brother were making coffee for Cruella de Vil, does it?'

'Yes it does. You were right about there being an innocent explanation for her being there. Nick and Adam may have turned her down in the past, but they've just been forced to put the Manor House on the market.'

Rosanna nodded. 'So maybe the future doesn't look quite so bleak after all.'

'No, it doesn't. Although I think I probably owe Adam an explanation for why I was so snippy earlier.'

'Are you going to phone him?'

'No.' Clara stood up resolutely. 'I know it's late, but I'm going to go and see him.'

Rosanna clapped her hands. 'Does this mean it's possible there may still be a happy ever after?'

32

Clara was slightly regretting her impulsiveness as she drew into the car park of the Manor House. It was ten fifteen and, as Adam had pointed out yesterday, he had to get up early to do breakfast.

She switched off the ignition, but she didn't get out of her car. Maybe it would have been better if she had just rung him back. She could still do that. She was deliberating in the coolness of the night-time air when she saw a figure silhouetted briefly in the light of the hotel's front entrance. It was a tall figure wearing a dark coat that she recognised and, as she looked, she realised that it – Adam – was coming out and down the steps and heading straight towards her car.

She got out just before he reached her.

'Clara, are you OK? I've been trying to get hold of you all evening.' She realised he was jangling a bunch of keys in his hand. 'I was just going to come over and see you. You seemed so odd earlier?' He glanced at her more closely and he must have taken in her tear-stained face. 'It's not your grandad, is it?'

'No. It's not. I'm fine. Haven't you got to get up early in the morning?'

'I have... but... some things are more important.'

The way he was looking at her now, with such concern, with such tenderness, made her throat close with emotion. Thunderbolts were brilliant, but this was important too. This was what she wanted – this total care (except that sounded too much like a toothpaste brand). Someone to be in her corner – like her family always were – someone who really cared. Enough to have a late night even though they had to get up at the crack of dawn the next day to do breakfast.

She was close to crying again. Oh heck.

Adam put his arms around her. 'Come in for a minute, sweetheart, it's cold out here. Have you got time?'

A few moments later, they were walking past the night porter and through a door marked Private, into the staff quarters of the hotel and Clara had an impression of bachelor accommodation: utilitarian carpets, magnolia walls, business papers and a book called *The History of The Jaguar Car* on a low glass table. Over everything hung a slight smell of mustiness and old coffee.

Adam cleared a space on a dark red sofa by shifting a pile of magazines and she sat down.

Oddly, she thought, as she told him what had been going on, she no longer had the slightest doubt that he wasn't, and never had been, involved. She told him this too.

'I would have thought the same in your shoes,' he said, his eyes darkly serious when she got to the part about Veronica Cooper Clark. 'Particularly if I had your chef whispering in my ear. But you're correct, she was here to make us an offer, which we are considering accepting.'

'Was it a good offer?'

'No. Not really, but, as she was very quick to point out, we may not get another offer for years. If at all.' He gave her a slightly twisted smile. 'I guess she must have decided sabotage was too risky a game after her plans to wreck the wedding went awry. I can tell you one thing, though, Clara. We won't be accepting her offer now.' Anger sparked in his eyes.

'But she's probably right. You might not get another one.'

'It doesn't matter.' His face tightened. 'After what she's done.' He took her hand.

'That's really sweet of you, but business is business. Maybe you could push her up? Tell her that's the only way she'll get a quick sale. From what I've heard, her investors won't wait forever.'

'Maybe.' He frowned.

'What will you and Nick do when you sell. Do you have plans?'

'Nick's going to move in with Alice, his girlfriend. Do you remember me mentioning her before?'

'I do.'

'Well, they've had an on/off relationship for years, but this latest hospital stay of his seemed to have cemented things for them. Nick said it made them both realise that none of us is immortal and they want to spend more time with each other. Running a hotel isn't that conducive to having a social life. As we both know.'

'How about you?' she asked.

'I thought I might take a leaf out of my little brother's book and see if I could do something about redressing my work/life balance, which hasn't been that good for a while.' He shot her a sideways glance. 'I know of this hotel where people go to live out their dreams. I thought I might go and talk to their manager. Maybe see if she had any ideas.'

Clara rested her head against his shoulder. 'I think she might have,' she said.

Then, quite suddenly, but also quite naturally, she found herself in his arms again and they were kissing. And that high-voltage-electricity thing was happening again and now several explosive fireworks had also been thrown into the mix.

'It's a pity you have to get up so early,' she murmured. 'I should let you get to bed. I'd hate to be responsible for you oversleeping.'

'Maybe it would be easier not to go to bed at all. Then I wouldn't have to worry.' He shot her a questioning glance. 'Or am I overstepping the mark?'

'Not at all. But I have Foxy in the car.'

'You could always bring her in.'

'The sensible, grown-up option would be for me to go home to the bungalow and for you to go and get some sleep.'

'You're right,' Adam said. There was a huge smile in his voice. 'I'll walk you to your car.'

As they stood next to her car beneath a sky that was clear and bright and held a scattering of stars, it was Clara who looked up at the silver moon and then back once more at Adam.

'But who wants to be a sensible grown-up?' she said.

EPILOGUE

Adam and Nick Greenwood negotiated a much higher price with Veronica Cooper Clark's development company, which meant they were able to recoup all of their original investment and some extra.

With his share of the proceeds, Nick and his girlfriend, Alice, were able to buy a tearoom and a perfect little ground-floor flat in Swanage.

Kate Rawlinson tracked down the Lighthousegate cameraman and persuaded him that if he positively identified the person who'd paid him for the footage, she would put his link back on the Bluebell's website. He identified Rupert Cooper Clark, which gave Kate enough leverage to take out an injunction against him and Veronica.

Aiden told John Scargill that Veronica had tried to wreck Isobel's special day. This resulted in John, who was a patron of the Yacht Club, telling the entire membership how one of their own had been instrumental in trying to sabotage his 'only daughter's only wedding'. This, in turn, resulted in Veronica having her membership of the Yacht Club suspended. It also resulted in the severing of many of her business ties amongst the yachties and two of her investors pulled out of the luxury-flat deals. Her development company went bankrupt and the Manor House was finally bought by another hotel chain, who were keen to work in harmony with the Bluebell.

Kate visited the editor of *The Purbeck Gazette* and they investigated the Curly Wurly Challenge incident and discovered Simon Tomlinson had bragged to a colleague that he'd spiked Micky Tucker's drink. Subsequently, they ran a full retraction, saying there was no truth in the Bluebell being responsible for Micky Tucker being unable to challenge the Curly Wurly Stretching Guinness World Record and that he would be having another attempt at the record within the year. They would be sponsoring him.

Simon Tomlinson was asked to leave.

Phil Grimshaw got offered a small part in a crime drama about a conspiracy-theorist chef after a couple of screenwriters had stayed at the Bluebell Cliff for a fortnight. The screenwriters also asked Mr B if he would be interested in being a story consultant on the project.

He was delighted to be able to add the role of 'story consultant' to his CV and is also hugely relieved that, to date, no one has guessed his full name.

Zoe ended up with a hunky firefighter called Seth Bottomley!

Portia and Prudence turned out to be Portia and Percy and they had a litter of eleven piglets.

Kate offered Thelma and Eric Price, via Clara, the chance to renew their wedding vows for free at the Bluebell in a quiet family ceremony. They were delighted.

Kate's mother sent news that she was happily dating again after her divorce and had her eyes set on husband number four.

Will Lightfoot met a girl in Thailand, soon after he sent his angry postcard, and, as far as anybody knows, they are still travelling happily.

Clara and Adam were the fourth couple to get married at the Bluebell Cliff – nothing at all went wrong on their wedding day, which was attended by their extended family and closest friends, which included Foxy, and was a day full of sunshine and laugher.

They are currently looking for a smallholding and/or possible garden centre in Dorset, which is in commuting distance of the Bluebell. Adam will be running their enterprise while Clara stays on at the Bluebell as manager.

Foxy divides her time between Clara and Kate – depending on who is going on the most walks and stocking the best dog treats.

The Bluebell continues to go from strength to strength and at the end of its second full year of trading it won Best Dorset Hotel, Best Unique Wedding Venue and Best Food on The Isle of Purbeck.

Kate finishes every acceptance speech she makes with these words: 'The Bluebell Cliff Hotel was my Aunt Carrie's dream. She created it to help other people fulfil theirs. I will never let anyone stand in the way of her amazing vision and of her wonderful generosity. As our mission statement says, "We are here to help you make your dreams come true".'

ACKNOWLEDGMENTS

It takes more than one person to write a novel.

Thank you to Judith Murdoch for her unfailing encouragement. Thank you to Caroline Ridding, my excellent editor, and to the whole Boldwood team, you are amazing.

Thank you also, in no particular order, to: Adam Millward, Gordon Rawsthorne, Jan Wright, Ian Burton, Selina Hepworth, Paul Kefford, Tony Millward, Gaynor Davies and Pat, Werner and Stefan Luetolf, for your advice and patience and huge encouragement. Thank you to the Parkhurst family for the Granny-isms.

And thank you Mum and Keith for providing the inspiration for the Bluebell Cliff Hotel and one or two of the things that happened there!

MORE FROM DELLA GALTON

We hope you enjoyed reading *Sunshine Over Bluebell Cliff*. If you did, please leave a review.

If you'd like to gift a copy, this book is also available as an ebook, digital audio download and audiobook CD.

Sign up to Della Galton's mailing list for news, competitions and updates on future books:

http://bit.ly/DellaGaltonNewsletter

ABOUT THE AUTHOR

Della Galton is the author of 15 books, including *Ice and a Slice*. She writes short stories, teaches writing groups and is Agony Aunt for Writers Forum Magazine. She lives in Dorset.

Visit Della's website: www.dellagalton.co.uk

Follow Della on social media:

facebook.com/DailyDella
twitter.com/DellaGalton
instagram.com/Dellagalton
bookbub.com/authors/della-galton

ABOUT BOLDWOOD BOOKS

Boldwood Books is a fiction publishing company seeking out the best stories from around the world.

Find out more at www.boldwoodbooks.com

Sign up to the Book and Tonic newsletter for news, offers and competitions from Boldwood Books!

http://www.bit.ly/bookandtonic

We'd love to hear from you, follow us on social media:

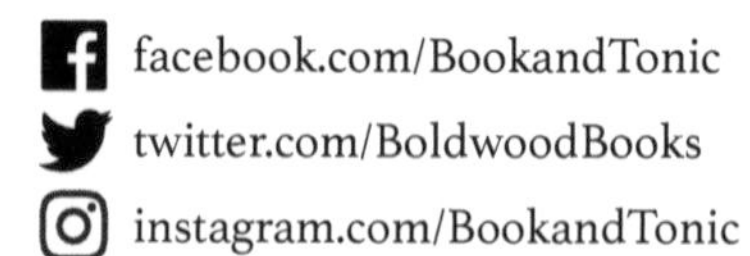